THE WEEPING GIRL

Håkan Nesser is one of Sweden's most popular
crime writers, receiving numerous awards for his novels
featuring Inspector Van Veeteren, including the European
Crime Fiction Star Award (Ripper Award) 2010/11, the
Swedish Crime Writers' Academy Prize (three times)
and Scandinavia's Glass Key Award. The Van Veeteren
series is published in over 25 countries and has sold
over 10 million copies worldwide. Håkan Nesser
lives in Gotland with his wife, and spends
part of each year in the UK.

HÅKAN NESSER

THE WEEPING GIRL

AN INSPECTOR VAN VEETEREN MYSTERY

Translated from the Swedish by
Laurie Thompson

MANTLE

First published in Great Britain 2013 by Mantle
an imprint of Pan Macmillan, a division of Macmillan Publishers Limited
Pan Macmillan, 20 New Wharf Road, London N1 9RR
Basingstoke and Oxford
Associated companies throughout the world
www.panmacmillan.com

ISBN 978-0-230-76899-4

Originally published in 2000 as *Ewa Morenos Fall*
by Albert Bonniers förlag, Stockholm.

Typeset by Ellipsis Digital Limited, Glasgow
Printed and bound by CPI Group (UK) Ltd, Croydon, CR0 4YY

Visit www.panmacmillan.com to read more about all our books
and to buy them. You will also find features, author interviews and
news of any author events, and you can sign up for e-newsletters
so that you're always first to hear about our new releases.

Thus we wreck our lives, at times and in moments
when we fail to assign to our actions their
true colour and significance

Tomas Borgmann, philosopher

ONE

1

21 July 1983

Winnie Maas died because she changed her mind.

Afterwards there were those who maintained that she died because she was beautiful and stupid – a combination acknowledged to be risky.

Or because she was gullible, and relied on the wrong people.

Or because her father was a shit who had abandoned his family long before Winnie had stopped using nappies or a baby's bottle.

And there were others who claimed that Winnie Maas used to wear skirts that were rather too short and blouses that were rather too tight, and that in fact she had only herself to blame.

None of these explanations was totally without justification; but the thing that clinched it was that she changed her mind.

The moment before she hit the ground and smashed her skull on the steel rail, she even realized that herself.

She wiped away a tiny bit of extra lipstick and contemplated her image in the mirror. Opened her eyes wide and wondered if she needed a bit more eyeliner. It was a nuisance to have to keep remembering to open her eyes wide – easier to apply a bit more liner underneath. She drew a thin line with the pencil, leaned towards the mirror and checked the result.

Pretty good, she thought, and transferred her attention to her mouth. Showed her teeth. They were even and white, and her gums were hidden behind her lips, thank goodness – not like Lisa Paaske's, who was very pretty with her green, slanting eyes and high cheekbones, but was condemned to wander around looking serious all the time, or at best to give an enigmatic smile, all because her upper gums grew down so far. Huh, Winnie thought. That must be hard to keep up.

She checked her watch. A quarter to nine. High time she was on her way. She stood up, opened the wardrobe door and checked how she looked in the full-length mirror. Tried out a few poses, thrusting out first her breasts, then her pelvis. She looked good, both high up and low down – she had just plucked out four strands of hair that had been sticking out dangerously close to her bikini line. Light-coloured, but even so . . .

Perfect, Jürgen had said. I'll be damned if your body isn't perfect, Winnie.

Smashing, Janos had suggested, she recalled that clearly. You really are smashing, Winnie – I get a hard-on every time I walk past your house.

She smiled when she thought about Janos. Of all the boys she'd been with, Janos was the best. He'd done it in just the right way. He'd somehow managed to combine sensitivity and tenderness, just as they said it should be in *Flash* and *Girl-zone*.

Janos. In a way it was a pity that it wasn't going to be Janos.

But so what? she thought, slapping her buttocks. No point in crying over spilled milk. She dug out a pair of lace panties from the dressing-table drawer, but she couldn't find a clean bra and so didn't bother. She didn't need one, after all. Her breasts were quite small, and firm enough not to sag. If there was anything about her body she would have liked to improve, it would be slightly bigger breasts. Not much bigger, just a little bit. To be sure, Dick had said that she had the prettiest titties the world had ever seen, and he'd sucked and squeezed them so thoroughly that they'd hurt for several days afterwards – but let's face it: a few extra grams wouldn't have done any harm.

But that'll come, she thought. Pulled her T-shirt over her head and wriggled her way into her tight skirt. Yes indeed, it was only a matter of time before she started putting on weight. Unless she . . .

Unless she . . .

For God's sake, she thought, lighting a cigarette. I'm only sixteen. Mum was seventeen when it happened to her, and look how she's turned out . . .

She made one last check in the dressing-table mirror, licked carefully round her lips, then set off.

Frieder's Pier, half past nine, he'd said. He came on the train that arrived at half past eight, but wanted to go home and have a shower first, if she didn't mind. Of course she didn't: she approved of men who kept themselves clean. Washed their hair and removed the dirt from under their fingernails – that showed they had a touch of class, she felt. It would be the first time they'd met for three weeks: he'd been up in Saren, staying with an uncle. A mixture of work and holiday. They'd spoken on the telephone a few times, and discussed 'the project', but she hadn't told him that she'd changed her mind. She was going to do that now, this evening. Best to do it face to face, she'd thought.

It was a warm evening. When she came down on to the

beach, she felt almost sweaty after the short walk. But it was cooler down here. There was a pleasant, gentle breeze blowing from the sea; she slipped off her canvas shoes and started walking barefoot over the sand. It was nice to feel the tiny grains rubbing against her toes. It was almost like being a child again. It didn't do her nail varnish any favours, of course, but she would put her shoes back on before she got there. Before she met Him. She liked to think about him having a capital H. He was worth that. Mind you, if he wanted to have sex with her afterwards, it struck her, he would probably want her to be barefoot. But maybe it didn't matter – in those circumstances it wasn't usually her toenails that he was most interested in.

And why would he not want to have sex with her? They hadn't seen each other for ages, after all!

She paused and lit another cigarette. Moved closer to the waterline where the sand was more tightly packed and it was easier to walk. The beach was pretty deserted at this time in the evening, but there were a few people around. An occasional jogger came running past, and she met an occasional dog-walker; she also knew that there would be quite a few young people necking on blankets in among the dunes – they always did that in the summer. She often did it herself, and maybe they would end up there this evening as well.

Maybe, maybe not.

It would depend on how he reacted. She started thinking about it. Would he be angry? Would he grab hold of her and give her a good shaking, as he'd done that time in Horsens when she'd been as high as a kite on hash, and rambled on about how she thought Matti Frege had nice muscles.

Or would he understand, and agree with her?

Perhaps he'd be able to talk her round. That wasn't entirely out of the question, of course. Perhaps his unparalleled love for her would make her think again? And the money, naturally. Was that a possibility?

No, she didn't think so. She was feeling strong and certain about the decision she'd made, goodness knows why. Maybe because she'd been on her own and able to think things over in peace and quiet for a few weeks.

But she knew that his love for her was all-consuming. He kept on telling her that, more or less every time they met. They were going to become an entity, they'd known that for a long time. There was no doubt about it. They didn't need to hurry things.

But what they certainly did need was money.

Money for food. For cigarettes and clothes and somewhere to live, perhaps. Especially in the longer term: they'd need lots of money then – after all, that's why they'd done what they'd done . . .

Thoughts had started wandering around inside her

head, and she realized now that it was difficult to keep track of everything. There was so much to take into account when you started thinking along these lines, and in the end you didn't know if you were coming or going. That's the way it nearly always turned out – it would be nice if somebody else could make the decisions, she used to think. Make decisions about difficult matters, so that she could think about what she liked to think about instead.

Perhaps that's why she was so much in love with him, of all people? *Him.* He liked to make decisions about things that were a bit complicated and major. Such as this plan they'd thought up. Yes, no doubt that was why she loved him, and wanted to be his. Yes indeed. Even if this last project had gone off the rails a bit, and she'd been forced to change her mind. As already said.

She came to the pier, and looked around in the gathering gloom. He hadn't arrived yet, she was a few minutes early. She could have continued walking along the beach – he lived out at Klimmerstoft and would be coming from the opposite direction; but she didn't bother. Sat down instead on one of the low stone walls that ran all the way along each side of the pier. Lit another cigarette, despite the fact that she didn't really want another one, and tried to think about something pleasant.

*

He turned up after another fifteen minutes or so. A bit late, but not all that much. She saw his white shirt approaching through the twilight long before he reached her, but she remained sitting there until he came up to her. Then she stood up, put her arms round his neck and pressed the whole of her body against him. Kissed him.

She could taste that he'd taken a drop of the strong stuff, but only a little.

'So you're back.'

'Yes.'

'Did you have a good time?'

'Great.'

There was a moment's silence. He was grasping her arms tightly.

'There's something I have to tell you,' she said eventually.

'Go on.'

He loosened his grip slightly.

'I've changed my mind.'

'Changed your mind?'

'Yes.'

'What the hell do you mean?' he said. 'Explain.'

She explained. She had trouble in finding the right words, but in the end he seemed to understand what she was saying. He didn't respond at first, and she couldn't see his face clearly in the darkness. He'd let go of her altogether now. Half a minute passed, perhaps a whole one, and they just stood there. Stood there, breathing in time with the sea and the waves, as it were, and there was something vaguely disturbing about it.

'Let's go for a walk,' he said, putting his arm round her shoulders. 'And have a little chat. I have an idea.'

2

Helmut had been against it all from the very start.

Looking back, she had to give him that much. 'Daft,' he'd said. 'Bloody silly.'

He'd lowered the newspaper and glowered at her for a few seconds with those pale eyes of his, slowly grinding his teeth and shaking his head.

'I can't see the point of it. It's unnecessary.'

That was all. Helmut wasn't one to waste words. As far as he was concerned, all in all, it wasn't a case of from dust thou art – stone more like.

From stone thou art, and unto stone thou shalt return. It was a thought she'd had before.

There are two sides to every coin, of course. She knew when she decided on him that she was not choosing storm and fire – not love and passion – but solid rock. Grey, primary rock on which she could stand safely, without any risk of sinking down into the mire of despair once again.

Something like that.

That's more or less what she'd thought fifteen years ago when he knocked on her door and explained that he had a bottle of Burgundy he'd bought while on holiday and wouldn't be able to drink it all himself.

And if she hadn't thought that as he stood there on the doorstep, she'd have done so shortly afterwards in any case. Once they'd started bumping into each other.

In the laundry room. In the street. In the shops.

Or when she was sitting on her balcony on warm summer evenings, trying to rock Mikaela to sleep, with him standing on his own balcony, leaning on the rail that separated them, smoking his pipe and gazing out into what remained of the sunset in the vast western sky over the polders.

Next-door neighbours. The thought came into her mind.

A godlike figure, solid and secure, holding out a hand of stone towards where she was drifting around in a floundering boat on a turbulent sea of emotions.

To her and Mikaela. Yes, that is in fact what the situation had been like: looking back, she could sometimes smile at the thought, sometimes not.

Anyway, that was fifteen years ago. Mikaela was three.

Now she was eighteen. She celebrated her eighteenth birthday this summer.

Mark my words, he had declared from behind his newspaper. As I told you, this won't make her any happier.

Why hadn't she listened to him? She asked herself that over and over again. During these days of worry and despair. When she tried to get a grip on herself and look back over the links in the chain. To think back and try to find reasons for doing what she had done . . . Or simply to let her thoughts wander freely; she didn't have much strength to speak of just now. These hellish summer days.

But she'd done the right thing, as she saw it. All I've done is what is right and proper. I haven't betrayed the decision I made all those years ago, then let it lie. In a way that's another stone – a murky boulder sunk down at the muddy bottom of the well of memory, but one that she'd promised herself she would fish up again when the time was right.

Carefully and respectfully, of course, but bring it up into the light of day even so. So that Mikaela could see it. No matter how you looked at it, that was necessary. Something that had remained in abeyance for many years, but now needed to happen to put things into perspective.

Her eighteenth birthday. Even if they hadn't discussed

it, Helmut had known about it as well. Been aware of the situation all the time, but had preferred not to confront it . . . The day would have to dawn when Mikaela was told the truth, one had no right to deny a child knowledge of its origins. One couldn't hide away her roots under mundane everyday happenings and the detritus of time. One couldn't send her out into life on false pretences.

Right? Life? Truth? Afterwards, she couldn't understand how she had been able to fit such grandiose concepts into her thoughts. Wasn't it this very pretentiousness that was hitting back and turning upon her? Wasn't that what was happening?

Who was she to go on about right and wrong? Who was she to make such hasty judgements and shake off Helmut's morose objections without giving them more than three-quarters of a second's consideration?

Until later. When it seemed to be too late. These days and nights when everything seemed to lose every ounce of significance and value, when she had become a robot and didn't so much as glance at these old thoughts which were drifting past her consciousness like tattered remnants of cloud over the blue-grey night sky of death. She simply let them sail past, on their disconsolate journey from horizon to horizon.

From oblivion to oblivion. Night to night and darkness to darkness.

From stone thou art.

From your gaping wounds your silent fury seethes up to a dead sky.

The pain of stone. Harder than anything else.

And madness, insanity itself was lying in wait round the corner.

Her eighteenth birthday. A Friday. In July, as hot as hell.

'I'll tell her when she comes back from the gym,' she had said. 'So you don't need to be present. Then we can have dinner afterwards in peace and quiet. She'll take it well, I can feel it in my bones.'

At first merely a sullen silence.

'If it's really necessary,' he'd said eventually. When she was already at the sink, washing the cups. 'It's your responsibility, not mine.'

'I have to,' she said. 'Remember that I promised her this when she was fifteen. Remember that it's a gap that needs to be filled. She's expecting it.'

'She's never said a word about it,' he said. From the side of his mouth. With his back to her.

That was true. She had to grant him that as well.

'Daft, but do whatever you like. What's the point?'

That's all. Nothing more. Then he left.

Daft?

Am I doing it for her sake, or for mine? she asked herself.

Reasons? Motives?

As blurred as the borderline between dreams and consciousness.

Unfathomable as stone itself.

Nonsense. Verbal sticking plaster. She probably knows anyway.

3

When Detective Inspector Ewa Moreno stopped outside the door of Chief Inspector Reinhart's office, it was a quarter past three in the afternoon and she was longing for a cold beer.

If she had been born into a different social class, or blessed with more imagination, she might have been longing for a glass of cold champagne instead (or why not three or four?); but today any possibility of thinking straight, any ability to think at all had been sweated away in the early hours of the morning. It was over thirty degrees, and had been about that all day. Both in town and inside the police station. A forgotten manic flat-iron seemed to be pressing down from above, overheating everyone and everything, and apart from chilled drinks, there seemed to be only two possibilities of surviving: the beach and the shade.

There was a noticeable absence of the former in the Maardam police station.

But there were Venetian blinds. And corridors where the sun was certain not to be shining. She stood there with her hand on the door handle, struggling with an impulse (that in itself was sluggish as a bluebottle high on Coca-Cola, so that the outcome could go either way) not to turn it. To retreat discreetly.

Instead of entering and finding out why he wanted to talk to her. There were good reasons for not going in. Or one, at least: in less than two hours' time she would be going on leave.

Two hours. One hundred and twenty suffocating minutes. If nothing unexpected happened, that is.

Moreno's intuition told her that he probably hadn't asked her to come in order to wish her all the best for her holiday. It hadn't sounded like that, and in any case, to do so wouldn't be Reinhart's style.

If nothing unexpected happened . . . ?

In a strange way, the unexpected didn't seem to be all that unexpected. If she'd been offered decent odds, she might well have bet on it. That's the way it was when you were in the lacklustre police business, and it wouldn't be the first time . . .

So, to beat a retreat, or not to beat a retreat: that was the question. She could always explain that something had turned up. That she hadn't had time to call in, as he'd put it.

Call in? That sounded a bit dodgy, surely?

Call in at my office some time after lunch. It won't take long . . .

Bugger bugger, she thought. It sounded as potentially deadly as a hungry cobra.

After a brief internal struggle, the drugged-up bluebottle drowned, and her Lutheran-Calvinistic copper's conscience won the day. She sighed, turned the handle and went in. Flopped down on the visitor's chair with her misgivings dancing around in her head like butterflies greeting the arrival of summer. And in her stomach.

'You wanted to see me,' she said.

Reinhart was standing by the window, smoking, and looking ominous. She noticed that he was wearing flip-flops. Light blue.

'*Salve,*' he said. 'Would you like something to drink?'

'What do you have to offer?' Moreno asked, and that cold beer floated into her mind's eye again.

'Water. With or without bubbles.'

'I think I'll pass,' said Moreno. 'If you don't mind. Well?'

Reinhart scratched at his stubble and put his pipe down on the window ledge beside the flowerpot.

'We've found Lampe-Leermann,' he said.

'Lampe-Leermann?' said Moreno.

'Yes,' said Reinhart.

'We?' said Moreno.

'Some colleagues of ours. Out at Lejnice. In Behrensee, to be precise, but they took him to Lejnice. That was the nearest station.'

'Excellent. And about time, too. Any problems?'

'Just the one,' said Reinhart.

'Really?' said Moreno.

He flopped down on his desk chair, opposite her, and gave her a look that was presumably meant to express innocence. Moreno had seen it before, and sent a prayer flying out through the window. 'Not again, please!' was its essence.

'Just the one problem,' said Reinhart again.

'Shoot,' said Moreno.

'He's not really prepared to cooperate.'

Moreno said nothing. Reinhart fiddled with the papers on his desk and seemed uncertain of how to continue.

'Or rather, he is prepared to cooperate – but only if he can talk to you.'

'What?' said Moreno.

'Only if he can talk to—'

'I heard what you said,' interrupted Moreno 'But why on earth does he want to talk to me?'

'God knows,' said Reinhart. 'But that's the way it seems to be – don't blame me. Lampe-Leermann is prepared to make a full confession, but only if he can lay it at your feet. Nobody else's. He doesn't like policemen, he says. Odd, don't you think?'

Moreno contemplated the picture hanging above Reinhart's head. It depicted a pig in a suit standing in a pulpit and throwing television sets to a congregation of ecstatic sheep. Or possibly judges wearing wigs, it was difficult to say which. She knew the chief of police had asked him several times to take it down, but it was still there. Rooth had suggested that it was symbolic of the freedom of thought and level of understanding within the police force, and Moreno had a vague suspicion that it could well be an accurate interpretation. Although she had never asked Reinhart himself. Nor the chief of police, come to that.

'My leave begins two hours from now,' she said, trying to give him a friendly smile.

'They're holding him out at Lejnice,' said Reinhart, unmoved. 'A nice spot. It would take just one day. Two at most. Hmm.'

Moreno stood up and walked over to the window.

'Mind you, if you would prefer to have him brought here, that wouldn't be a problem,' said Reinhart from behind her back.

She gazed out over the town and the ridge of high pressure. It was a few days old, but it seemed to be here to stay. That's what fru Bachman on the ground floor had said, and the meteorologists on the television as well. She decided not to respond. Not without a solicitor present, or a more detailed instruction. Ten seconds passed, and the only sound was from the bustle of the town down below, and the soft tip-tap from Reinhart's flip-fops as he shuffled about.

Flip-flops? she thought. Surely he could get himself a pair of sandals at least. A chief inspector in light-blue flip-flops?

Perhaps he'd been to the swimming baths at lunchtime and forgotten to change? Or maybe he'd been to see the chief of police and put them on as a sort of irreverent protest? It was hard to say as far as Reinhart was concerned: he liked to make a point.

He gave up in the end.

'For Christ's sake,' he said. 'Get a grip, Inspector. We've been after this bloody prat for several months now, and at last Vrommel has caught up with him . . .'

'Vrommel? Who's Vrommel?'

'The chief of police in Lejnice.'

Reluctantly, Moreno began to consider the possibility. Remained standing with her back turned to Reinhart as the image of Lampe-Leermann appeared in her mind's eye . . . Not much of a name in the underworld, quite small fry in fact: but it was true that they had been on his tail for quite a while. He was strongly suspected of being involved in a few armed robberies in March and April, but that wasn't the point. Or at least, not the main point.

The big thing is that he mixed with certain other gentlemen who were much bigger heavyweights than he was. Leading lights in so-called Organized Crime, to use a term that was heard all too often nowadays. There was no doubt about his links, and Lampe-Leermann had a reputation for grassing. A reputation for being more concerned – in certain difficult circumstances at least – about his own skin than that of others, and willing to inform the police authorities of what he knew. If doing so would serve his own ends, and could be treated with appropriate discretion.

And it could be in this case. At least, there was good reason for thinking so. Reinhart was inclined to think so, and Moreno tended to agree with him. In principle, at least. That was why they had made a bigger effort than usual when it came to tracking down Lampe-Leermann. That was why they had found him. Today of all days.

But the news that he was only prepared to unburden his mind to Inspector Moreno had come as a bit of a surprise, no question. That was something they hadn't reckoned with. Neither her nor anybody else. Just some malevolent little gremlin, no doubt . . . Damn and blast, you can never . . .

'He likes you,' said Reinhart, interrupting her train of thought. 'That's nothing to be ashamed of. I think he remembers when we were playing a game of good-cop bad-cop with him a few years ago. Anyway, that's the way it is. He wants to talk to you, and nobody else. But there's the minor matter of your leave, of course . . .'

'Exactly,' said Moreno, returning to her chair.

'It's not so far up to Lejnice,' said Reinhart. 'A hundred and twenty kilometres or thereabouts, I should think . . .'

Moreno said nothing. Closed her eyes instead and fanned herself with yesterday's *Gazett* that she had picked up from the pile of newspapers on the desk.

'Then I came to think of that house you're going to – didn't you say it was in Port Hagen?'

Oh my God! Moreno thought. He remembers. He's been doing his homework.

'Yes,' she said. 'Port Hagen, that's right.'

Reinhart tried to look innocent again. He'd be good as the wolf in *Little Red Riding Hood*, Moreno thought.

'If I'm not much mistaken it's quite close by,' he said. 'It must be only ten kilometres or so north of Lejnice. I used to go there when I was a kid. You'd be able to . . .'

Moreno threw away the newspaper with a resigned gesture.

'All right,' she said. 'Don't go on. I'll sort it out. Damn it all, you know as well as I do that Lampe-Leermann is the nastiest, creepiest piece of work that ever wore a pair of hand-sewn shoes . . . or a signet ring. Apart from anything else he always stinks of old garlic. Note that I said old garlic – I've nothing against the fresh stuff. But I'll sort it out, you don't need to strain yourself any more. Damn it all once again! When?'

Reinhart walked over to the flowerpot in order to empty his pipe.

'I told Vrommel you'd probably turn up tomorrow.'

Moreno stared at him.

'Have you fixed a time without consulting me?'

'*Probably*,' said Reinhart. 'I said you'd *probably* turn up tomorrow. What the hell's the matter with you? Aren't we playing for the same team any more, or what's going on?'

Moreno sighed.

'Okay,' she sighed. 'I'm sorry. I'd planned to set off tomorrow morning anyway, so it won't involve a lot of disruption. In fact.'

'Good,' said Reinhart. 'I'll ring Vrommel and confirm that you're coming. What time?'

She thought for a moment.

'About one. Tell him that I'll be there at around one, and that Lampe-Leermann shouldn't be given any garlic with his lunch.'

'Not even fresh?' wondered Reinhart.

She didn't answer. As she was on her way out through the door, he reminded her of how serious the situation was.

'Make sure you squeeze out of that bastard every bloody name he can give us. Both you and he will get a bonus for every arsehole we can put behind lock and key.'

'Of course,' said Moreno. 'But there's no need to swear so much. I like the colour of your shoes, though – it makes you look really young again . . .'

Before Reinhart could respond she was out in the corridor.

4

It wasn't until she was at home and in the shower that she realized it was an omen.

What else could it be? How else could one interpret it? Franz Lampe-Leermann simply turning up out of the blue and attacking her holiday two hours before it started? Surely that was highly unlikely? Or highly significant, depending on how you looked at it. He had managed to keep out of the way of the police since about the middle of April – that was when they started searching for him seriously, after a particularly clumsy bank raid in Linzhuisen on Maundy Thursday – and then the stupid idiot goes and gets himself arrested just now! In Lejnice, of all places.

Lejnice. A small, unremarkable coastal town with about twenty to twenty-five thousand inhabitants. Plus a few extra thousands in the summer. And situated, just as Reinhart had said, a mere ten kilometres away from the place she'd planned to spend the first two weeks of her holiday.

Port Hagen. An even smaller place in the sticks – but little places in the sticks were sometimes attractive places to be, and that's where Mikael Bau happened to have his holiday home.

Mikael Bau? she thought. My neighbour and occasional partner.

Occasional? she then thought. Partner? It sounded daft. But any other way of describing it sounded even dafter. Or wrong, at least.

Fiancé? Lover? Boyfriend?

Could you have boyfriends when you were thirty-two?

Perhaps just *my bloke*, she thought in the end. Closed her eyes and started to rub the jojoba shampoo into her hair. She had lived for over two years without *a bloke* since getting rid of Claus Badher, and they hadn't exactly been brilliant years – neither for herself nor for those she associated with, she was the first to admit that.

They were not years she would wish to go through again, although she supposed she had learned quite a bit. Perhaps that was how one should look at it. And she didn't want the years she'd spent with Claus back either. Good Lord no, that would have been even less desirable.

All in all, seven wasted years, she decided. Five with Claus, two on her own. Was she on the way to building up a totally wasted life? she asked herself. Was that what was really happening?

Who knows? she thought. Life is what happens when we're busy making other plans. She massaged her hair a little longer with the shampoo, then started rinsing all the suds away.

In any case, it was too soon to predict what would become of her relationship with Mikael Bau. At least, she had no desire to predict, not at the moment. It was last winter when she'd begun to see him: he'd invited her to share his evening meal the same day that his former girlfriend had dumped him – the middle of December it was, during those awful weeks when they'd been searching for Erich Van Veeteren's murderer – but it was another month before she'd invited him back. And another six weeks before she'd committed herself and gone to bed with him. Or *they* had committed themselves. The beginning of March, to be precise. The fourth – she remembered the date because it was her sister's birthday.

And they had carried on meeting, of course. Even if she was a detective inspector and he was a welfare officer, they were only human.

That's how he used to put it. Bollocks to all that, Ewa! Whatever else we are, we're only human.

She liked that. It was unassuming and sensible. Nothing like what Claus Badher would have said, and the less Mikael Bau reminded her of Claus Badher, the better. That was a simple but intuitively infallible way of judging things. Sometimes it was best to take an easy way out when it came to your emotional life, she was old enough to see that. Perhaps one ought to do that all the time, she sometimes thought. Cut out the psychology and live according to instinct instead. And it was nice to be desired, she had to admit. *Carpe diem*, perhaps?

Easily said, harder to do, she thought as she emerged from the shower. Rather like stopping thinking about something on demand. Whatever, Mikael Bau happened to own this old house in Port Hagen. Or rather, owned it together with four siblings, if she understood it rightly. It was a sort of family jewel, and this year it was his turn to have access to it in July.

Big and dilapidated, he had warned her. But charming, and very private. With running water – sometimes, at least. A hundred metres to the beach.

It sounded like everything a lousily paid police inspector could ask for, and without much pause for thought she had said yes please to the offer of a couple of weeks. Well, no pause at all, to be honest: it was a Sunday morning in May, they had made love and had breakfast in bed. In that order. Some days were easier to organize than others – hardly an earth-shattering insight.

So, two weeks in the middle of July. With her bloke, by the seaside.

And now Franz Lampe-Leermann!

A five-star bastard of an omen, and incredibly poor timing.

She wondered again what it could mean. But then, perhaps there was no point in trying to find a meaning in everything?

As *the Chief Inspector* used to point out now and again.

After the shower she packed her things, then rang Mikael Bau. Without going into too much detail she explained that she would be arriving at some point in the afternoon rather than in time for lunch, because something had turned up.

Work? he'd wondered.

Yes, work, she'd admitted.

He laughed, and said that he loved her. He'd started saying that recently, and it was remarkable how ambivalent it made her feel.

I love you.

She hadn't said that to him. It would never occur to her to say that until she felt sure of it. They'd talked about it. He'd agreed with her, of course – what else could he have done, for God's sake? Said that it didn't matter as far as he was concerned. The difference was that he *was* sure. Already.

How could he be? she'd wanted to know.

He explained that he hadn't had his fingers burnt as badly as she had, and so felt able to stick his neck out and venture into the unknown rather sooner than she could.

A likely story, Moreno thought. We all have our private relationship with language and words, especially the language of love. It doesn't necessarily have to do with bad experiences.

But she wondered – had often wondered – what the facts really were with regard to his former girlfriend, Leila. They'd been together for over three years, he'd told her, and yet the same evening that she'd dumped him he had marched up the stairs to her flat on the next floor, and rung her doorbell. Invited her to dinner – the dinner he'd prepared for Leila. Just like that. Surely that was a bit odd?

When she asked him about it, he'd blamed the food. He'd prepared a meal for two. You didn't slave away in the kitchen for an hour and a half, he claimed, and then gobble it all up yourself within ten minutes. No way.

That brought them round to the question of food.

'If you can bring a bottle of decent white wine with you, I'll see if I can find a bit of edible fish for you. There's an old bloke with a stall in the market square who has his own little boat and sells his own catch every morning. He has a wooden leg, believe it or not – the tourists take two

33

thousand pictures of him every summer . . . I'll see what he's got to offer.'

'Okay, let's do that,' said Moreno. 'I'll assume that you get something tasty. I've given you an extra three hours, after all. Incidentally . . .'

'Well?'

'No, it doesn't matter.'

'Come off it!'

'Okay. What colour are your flip-flops?'

'My flip-flops?'

'Yes.'

'Why the hell do you want to know what colour my flip-flops are? There must be at least ten pairs in the house . . . Maybe even twenty, but who owns which isn't at all clear.'

'Good,' said Moreno. 'I regard that as a good omen.'

Mikael said he hadn't a clue what she was on about, and suggested that she bought herself an efficient sun hat. She promised to think about it, and concluded the call. He didn't tell her again that he loved her, and she was grateful for that.

If somewhat ambivalent.

Reinhart rang later in the evening, and they spent half an hour discussing how to proceed with the interrogation of

Lampe-Leermann. It didn't seem to be all that complicated in principle, but then again it was important to persuade him to come out with as much information as possible. Lots of names, and especially the key figures.

And it was also important to bear in mind the incriminating evidence, so that in the long run it would be possible to put the big noises in the dock. The question of concessions granted to Lampe-Leermann in return for his evidence would also need to be taken into account: but both Reinhart and Moreno had been involved in this kind of thing before, and in the end the chief inspector announced that he was satisfied with the plans.

But if that bastard had said he was prepared to confess all to Inspector Moreno, he'd damn well better do so, Reinhart stressed.

And he'd better have something worthwhile to tell them.

'Just two things to bear in mind,' said Reinhart in conclusion. 'Everything must be recorded on tape. And we must make no specific concessions. Not at this early stage – Lampe-Leermann ought to understand that.'

'I'm with you,' said Moreno. 'I wasn't born yesterday. What's Vrommel like, by the way?'

'I've no idea,' said Reinhart. 'He sounds like a corporal on the phone, and I have the impression that he's red-haired. He could even be a different Vrommel from the old days.'

'How old?'

'Too old for you. Could be your grandfather, at least.'

'Thank you, Chief Inspector.'

Reinhart wished her good hunting, and said he was looking forward to reading her report in a couple of days' time – three at most.

'Report?' said Moreno. 'You'll get a transcript of the interrogation, and I have no intention of getting involved in that. I'm on leave, as you know.'

'Hmm,' muttered Reinhart. 'Is there no idealism left in the force nowadays? What's the world coming to?'

'We can discuss that in August,' said Moreno.

'If there's a world left by then,' said Reinhart.

5

It was a while before it dawned on her that the girl opposite her was sitting there crying.

Not sobbing. She wasn't making a fuss about it, the tears just seemed to be coming naturally. Her face seemed callow, clean-cut; her skin was pale and her reddish-brown hair combed back, held in place by a simple braid. Sixteen, seventeen years old, Moreno guessed: but she knew she was bad at judging the age of young girls. It could be a couple of years either way.

Her eyes were large and light brown, and as far as Moreno could see totally without make-up. Nor were there any dark stripes on her cheeks where the tears had been trickling down in a steady but not exactly torrential stream. Quietly and naturally. Moreno peered cautiously over the top of her book and noted that the girl was holding a crumpled handkerchief in her hands, which were loosely clasped in her lap; but she made no effort to stop the flow of tears.

No effort at all. Just cried. Let the tears flow however they liked, it seemed, as she gazed out through the window at the flat, sun-drenched countryside gliding past. The girl had her back to the engine, Inspector Moreno was facing it.

Grief, Moreno thought. She looks as if she's grieving.

She tried to remember where the weeping girl had boarded the train. Moorhuijs or Klampendikk, presumably. In any case, one or two stops after Maardam Kolstraat, which is where Moreno had got on. It was one of those local trains that stops every two or three minutes. Moreno had begun to regret not having waited for the express train instead. That would probably have gone at twice the speed, and was no doubt the reason why the old bone-shaker was almost empty. Apart from an elderly couple drinking tea from a thermos flask a few rows away, she and the girl were the only passengers in the whole carriage . . . Which made it all the more remarkable that the girl had come to sit opposite Moreno when there were so many empty seats. Very odd.

'You're crying.'

The words came without her thinking about them. Tumbled out of her mouth before she could stop them, and she wondered whether Mikael Bau had been right after all when he'd suggested she should wear an efficient sun hat. Something with a wide brim to provide protection against the sun – the high pressure was a strong as ever today.

The girl looked up at her briefly. Then blew her nose. Moreno sat up, and waited.

'Yes. I'm having a bit of a cry.'

'That's what we need to do sometimes,' said Moreno.

My God, she thought. What am I doing? I've just started to look after a teenager in crisis . . . A young girl with a broken heart running away from her boyfriend. Or from her parents. But running away in any case . . . I should start reading again and pretend I'd never spoken to her. Just ignore her until we get to Lejnice – haven't I got enough to worry about with Lampe-Leermann? Why the hell can't I hold my tongue?

'I'm crying because I'm afraid,' said the girl, looking out of the window at the sun again. 'I'm on the way to my dad.'

'Really?' said Moreno non-committally, scrapping the running-away theory.

'I've never met him.'

Moreno put her book down.

'What do you mean?'

'I've never seen him before.'

'You've never seen your dad? Why?'

'Because my mum thought that was best.'

Moreno thought that over. Took a deep drink of mineral water. Offered the bottle to the girl. The girl shook her head.

'Why would it be best for you not to meet him?'

The girl shrugged. 'I don't know.'

'What's your name?'

'Mikaela Lijphart.'

'How old are you? Sixteen, seventeen . . . ?'

I'm interrogating her, it suddenly struck Moreno. She tried to smooth things over by holding out a pack of chewing gum. Mikaela took a couple of pieces and smiled.

'Eighteen,' she said. 'I had my eighteenth birthday yesterday.'

'Many happy returns!' said Moreno. 'Of yesterday . . .'

'Please forgive me. I've interrupted your reading.'

'That doesn't matter,' said Moreno. 'I find it hard to concentrate when I'm on a train anyway. I usually read things I've read already. If you want to tell me about your dad, I'll be happy to listen.'

Mikaela sighed deeply, and looked as if she were discussing that prospect with herself. It took three seconds.

'Thank you,' she said. 'No, I've never met him. Not since I was tiny, at least. I didn't really know who he was until yesterday. His name's Arnold Maager – my mum told me that because I'm eighteen now. A nice present, don't you think? A dad.'

Moreno raised an eyebrow, but said nothing. The train started to slow down noisily as it approached the next station.

'He's in a psychiatric hospital. Something happened when I was only two years old. That's why she kept it secret from me until now, my mum.'

My God, Moreno thought. What on earth is she sitting there telling me? For an awful moment she wondered if she'd come up against a young mythomaniac – a some-what neurotic teenager who took pleasure in making herself interesting to total strangers. It was not unusual for young ladies in trouble to indulge in such escapades, she knew that from experience. The years she'd spent in the police unit with special responsibility for young people had taught her that. Two-and-a-half years, to be precise, that she hadn't exactly hated, but which she would prefer not to live through again. Like all the other years she had thrown on the scrapheap in the last few days . . .

But it was hard to believe that Mikaela Lijphart was making it all up. Really hard. She seemed more like an open book, Moreno thought – with those big, bright eyes and straightforward features. Obviously, she could be mis-taken – but she was hardly your blue-eyed innocent.

'So now you're on your way to meet him, are you?' she asked. 'Your dad. Where does he live?'

'Lejnice,' said Mikaela. 'He's in a home just outside the town. I've rung and spoken to them – they know I'm coming. So they were going to prepare him . . . Yes, that's what they said. Prepare him. Ugh, I'm scared stiff. But I know it's got to be done.'

Moreno tried in all haste to find something consoling to say to her.

'You have to do what you have to do,' she said. 'Is it really the case that you didn't know you had a dad until yesterday?'

Mikaela smiled briefly again.

'Yes. Obviously, I know that a virgin birth isn't all that common nowadays. But I've had a stepfather since I was three, and known that he wasn't my real father since I was fifteen. And then . . . Well, I had to wait for another three years until my mum told me who my real father was. Arnold Maager . . . I don't really know if I like that name or not . . .'

'But why?' Moreno couldn't help herself from asking. 'I mean, it's nothing to do with me, but . . .'

'I don't know,' said Mikaela.

'You don't know?'

'No, I don't know why she couldn't tell me. Or didn't want to tell me. She went on and on about responsibility and maturity and all that, my mum did, but . . . No, no details at all. Something happened when I was very young, that's all I know.'

Moreno looked out of the window, and saw that they had now come to Boodendijk. Not far to go to Lejnice. A couple more stops, probably. Behind the row of buildings she could already see the sand dunes. The sky seemed almost hysterically blue.

What the hell can I say to her? she wondered. The poor girl must feel completely abandoned.

'Did you consider taking somebody with you?' she said. 'If you feel worried about it. A friend . . . Or your mum . . .'

'I wanted to meet him on my own,' said Mikaela. 'My mum didn't want me to go to see him at all – but once you're eighteen years old, you do what you have to do.'

'Quite right,' said Moreno.

A few seconds passed. The train set off again.

'I don't understand why I'm sitting here, telling all this to somebody I've never seen before,' said Mikaela, trying to look a little more cocksure. 'You must think I'm a real crackpot . . . Not to mention my mum and dad. A real crackpot family. Maybe we are, but I don't usually—'

'It can be a good thing to talk to strangers now and then,' said Moreno, interrupting her. 'You can say whatever you like, without having to take other things into consideration. I often start conversations like this one.'

The girl's face was consumed by a smile, and Moreno registered that she was even more charming when the all-pervading worry dispersed momentarily.

'You're right! That's exactly what I think about my dad. About meeting him, I mean. We're strangers, after all. I don't want to have anybody else present when I speak to him for the first time. It would be . . . It wouldn't be right, somehow. Do you see what I mean? It wouldn't be right as far as he's concerned.'

Moreno nodded.

'So you're getting off at Lejnice, are you?'

'Yes. Where are you going?'

'I'm getting off at Lejnice as well. It'll all turn out okay, trust me! That business with your dad, I mean. I can feel it.'

'So can I!' said Mikaela optimistically, sitting up straighter. 'I think we're nearly there – I'd better go to the toilet and wipe away my tears. Thank you for letting me talk to you.'

Moreno suddenly felt that she needed to blink away a few tears as well. She tapped Mikaela's thigh and cleared her throat.

'Do that! I'll wait for you. Then we can go into the station together, okay?'

Mikaela stood up and headed for the toilet at the far end of the carriage. Moreno took a deep breath. Put her book back into her bag and established that you could see the sea through the window.

Checked her watch and noted that they were due to arrive in three minutes' time.

She said goodbye to Mikaela Lijphart in the forecourt outside the station building, where Mikaela boarded a yellow bus that would take her to the Sidonis Foundation, a care home about a kilometre or so north, and a similar distance inland.

Moreno took a taxi, as she wasn't at all sure where the Lejnice police station was situated.

It turned out to be in a square a couple of hundred yards from the station, and the young driver wondered if she'd like him to take her to the church and back as well, so that he could have something to register on his taximeter.

Moreno laughed and said she would be needing a cab to take her to Port Hagen in an hour or two's time, and he gave her his card with a direct telephone number she could ring.

Lejnice police station was a two-storey, rectangular building in dark pommer stone with small, square windows impossible to look in through. Evidently built shortly after the war, and flanked by a butcher's shop and a funeral parlour. Above the less than impressive entrance was a tiny balcony with iron railings and an even tinier flag, wafting in the breeze on something that could well have been a broomstick. Moreno was reminded of a decadent nineteenth-century French colony – or at least a film about such a colony – and when she caught sight of Chief Inspector Vrommel, she had the distinct impression that he preferred that century to the new one that was about to begin.

He was standing in the entrance: tall and lanky, wearing a sort of loose-fitting khaki uniform that Moreno could also only recall having seen in a film. He was about sixty, she decided, possibly closer to sixty-five. Reinhart's guess that he was red-haired might well have been correct – but that would have been ten years or more ago. Now there wasn't a lot of hair on Vrommel's head. In fact, one might say he was bald.

Round spectacles, frameless, a large reddish-brown nose and a moustache that was so thin and skin-coloured that she didn't notice it until they'd shaken hands.

'Inspector Moreno, I presume. Pleased to meet you. Did you have a good journey?'

He doesn't like female police officers, she thought.

'Excellent, thank you. A bit on the warm side, though.'

He didn't respond to the invitation to talk about the weather. Cleared his throat and stood up straight instead.

'Welcome to Lejnice. This is where the powers that be hold sway round here.' He made a gesture that might possibly – but only possibly – be interpreted as ironic. 'Shall we go in? That Lampe-bastard is waiting for you.'

He held the door open, and Moreno entered the relatively cool Lejnice police station.

The interrogation room was about six feet square, and looked like an interrogation room ought to look.

Like all interrogation rooms the world over ought to look. A table and two chairs. A ceiling light. No windows. On the table a tape recorder, a jug of water and two white plastic mugs. Bare walls and an unpainted concrete floor. Two doors, each with a peephole. Franz Lampe-Leermann was already on his chair when Moreno entered through one of the doors. He'd probably been sitting there for quite a while, she assumed: he looked fed up, and the smile he gave her seemed strained. Large damp patches of sweat had formed under the arms of his yellow shirt, and he had taken off both his shoes and his socks. He was breathing heavily. The air-conditioning system that served the rest of the building evidently didn't extend as far as this hellhole.

Or perhaps Vrommel had switched it off.

Thirty-five degrees, Moreno thought. At least. Good.

'I need a rest and a fag,' said Lampe-Leermann, wiping

his brow with the back of his hand. 'That heap of shit won't even let me smoke.'

'A rest?' said Moreno. 'We haven't even started yet. You can have one half an hour from now at the earliest. Assuming you are cooperative. Is that clear?'

Lampe-Leermann cursed again, and shrugged.

'Let's get going then,' said Moreno, pressing the start button. 'What do you have to say?'

6

Mikaela Lijphart got off at the crossroads in the village of St Inns, as she'd been instructed. Remained standing with her rucksack on the grass verge until the bus had disappeared round the long curve to Wallby and Port Hagen.

She looked around. To her left, in a westerly direction, the road ran as straight as an arrow through the dunes to the sea, only a couple of kilometres or less away. She would walk along that later – in an hour or two – in order to get to the youth hostel where she intended to spend the night. But not yet. Now she would be heading eastwards. Away from the sea, along the narrow, winding strip of asphalt that seemed to be almost roasting in the heat between high, flower-covered grassy mounds. According to what she'd been told, it was only about a kilometre to the Sidonis home, but she wished it were even shorter. Or that she'd bought a bottle of water before leaving Lejnice.

Because it was hot. Unbearably hot. It was half past

one – no doubt the ideal time for a walk in the sun. If you wanted to catch sunstroke.

That would be all she needed. On top of everything else.

She looked around again. Tried to get an overall picture of the village: it didn't seem to be more than a dozen or so houses – but something sticking out from one of them looked as if it might be an advertising placard. Perhaps it was some kind of shop . . . Maybe she'd be able to get a bottle of water at least. She heaved her rucksack up over her shoulders and set off towards the reddish-brown brick building.

She had better check that she really was on the right road for the home, she thought.

To the home and her father.

Sure enough it was a small grocery shop. She bought a litre of water, an ice cream and a packet of lemon Rijbing biscuits. The plump little lady behind the counter also gave her directions to the Sidonis Foundation: carry on along this road and turn right at the signpost on the other side of the bridge. Not far at all. The lady wondered if Mikaela had a car – if not, she could have a lift there in about half an hour: they'd be delivering a selection of goods to the home, like they did most days.

Mikaela smiled and shook her head, saying she liked walking, and it was such nice weather.

'Lovely weather,' said the lady, fanning herself with a magazine. 'Almost too much of a good thing, you might say.'

As she was walking, she started thinking about what she'd said to the woman on the train.

The truth, but not the whole truth.

Not quite the whole truth. She knew a bit more than she'd admitted, and now she had a bad conscience for keeping that extra bit to herself. A little prick, at least. The woman had been friendly and gone out of her way to help her; she could have told her a bit more, she really could.

But then she hadn't told her any lies. It really was true that her mum had said very little about the background, no more than Mikaela had told the woman on the train.

Something had happened.

Sixteen years ago.

Something involving her dad.

What? *What?* Now when she thought back to yesterday's conversation with her mother, she found it almost more difficult than ever to understand her mum's attitude. More difficult than when they'd been sitting at the breakfast table but miles apart mentally, and she'd heard the name for the first time.

Arnold Maager.

Arnold? For twelve years she'd had a dad called Helmut. For three years she'd had one without a name. But now he was suddenly called Arnold.

What happened? she had asked her mother. Tell me what happened that was so horrible. Then, sixteen years ago.

But her mother had simply shaken her head.

But you must understand that you have to say B once you've said A, Mikaela had insisted. That's what her mother always used to tell her. I have a right to know.

More head-shaking, more firmly than ever. Then that harangue.

Yes, you have a right to know who your father is, Mikaela, and I've told you that now. But it wouldn't help you at all to know exactly what happened, why I left him. Believe me, Mikaela. I wouldn't be doing this if it weren't necessary, surely you can understand that?

I'll find out anyway.

That's up to you. You're eighteen now. But I'm just thinking what's best for you.

That's as far as they'd got, even though they'd been sitting there in the kitchen for half an hour. Mikaela had begged and pleaded. Nagged and cursed and wept, but her mother wouldn't budge.

As sometimes happened. Mikaela had beaten her head against the wall before. She knew what usually happened, and what it felt like. But the distance between them never used to be as wide as this. It was quite remarkable.

Auntie Vanja was the answer: that had also happened before. Mikaela shut herself away in her room and telephoned her immediately after the conversation in the kitchen. Explained the situation with no beating about the bush, and after a lot of intensive persuasion, she succeeded. Just when she'd been on the point of giving up. Auntie Vanja had told her. Not a lot, it's true, but a little bit . . . Opened the curtain slightly, as the saying goes.

He killed somebody, your dad did. A young girl . . . Well, it was never actually proved that he did it.

Pause.

But it's obvious it was him.

Pause.

And then he couldn't cope with what he'd done. He fell to pieces – it's best not to dig around into it any more, I've said too much already.

Who?

Who had he killed? Why?

But Auntie Vanja had refused to go into that. The curtain was now closed again, it wasn't any business of hers and she'd already said too much. He was presumably still in that home near Lejnice, she thought so at least. He'd gone there more or less straight away. But it's best to forget all about it. Forget and move on.

Mikaela knew that already. That he was in that home – her mother had told her as much. I wonder why, Mikaela thought when she had thanked her aunt and hung up. Why had her mother told her that? If she didn't want her daughter to start rooting around and finding out things, surely it would have been better not to give her that piece of information?

Or to say nothing at all?

I have to, she had explained. *I'm obliged to tell you your father's name and I'm obliged to tell you where he is. But I hope . . . I hope with all my heart that you don't go and visit him.*

With all my heart? Mikaela thought. That sounded rather pathetic. And incomprehensible. Both yesterday and today. Just as incomprehensible as her mother's actions were now and then. And to be honest, she was less surprised than she ought to have been. Less surprised than other eighteen-year-olds would have been in her situation.

I'm used to living on a knife-edge, she'd thought. For better or worse. I'm prepared for almost anything.

Perhaps that was why she'd chosen to tell the woman on the train not quite everything? Because she was ashamed of her crackpot family, just as she'd said!

Killed somebody? Good God, no, that was a step too far.

She came to the bridge. Crossed over and turned right. The overgrown ditch was dried out more or less completely: only a narrow, sticky string of mud down at the very bottom betrayed the fact that this was normally where the waters of the River Muur flowed. When the climate was rather different from what it was now. A large sign on a pole imparted this information, and also that the Sidonis Foundation was a mere couple of hundred metres further on.

Two hundred metres, Mikaela thought, and took a drink of water. After eighteen years – or sixteen, to be precise – I'm a mere two hundred metres away from my father.

The buildings were pale yellow in colour and surrounded by park-like grounds inside a low stone wall and a strip of deciduous trees. Elms or maples, she wasn't sure which. Perhaps both, some seemed to be a bit different. Three buildings in fact: quite a large four-storey one, and two smaller ones two storeys high, forming two wings. A small asphalted car park with about ten vehicles. A black dog tethered outside an outbuilding, barking. No trace of any people. She followed the signs up the stairs in the main building, and stopped at an information desk. Two elderly women were deep in conversation with their backs towards her, and it was some time before she managed to attract their attention.

She explained why she was there, and was invited to take a seat.

After a few minutes a young man with a beard and wearing glasses appeared from out of a corridor, and asked if she was Mikaela Lijphart. She said that she was. He shook hands, and bade her welcome. Said his name was Erich, and that it was lovely weather. Then he beckoned her to follow him. He led her along two green corridors and up two blue staircases; she stayed a couple of paces behind him, and felt that she needed to go to the toilet. The water, of course. She had drunk the whole bottle while walking to the home.

They came to some kind of sitting room with a few sofa groups and a television set. There was still no sign of any people, and she wondered whether everybody had gone for a walk in view of the weather. For there must surely be other patients as well as her dad? Other psychiatric cases. She noticed a toilet door and asked Eric to wait for a moment.

Good Lord, she thought when she had finished and was washing away the worst of the summer heat. I want to go home. If he's gone when I come out of here, I'll do a runner.

But he was standing there, waiting.

'Arnold Maager is your father, is that right?'

She nodded, and tried to swallow.

'You've never met him before?'

'No. Unless . . . No. This will be the first time.'

He smiled, and she assumed he was trying to look benevolent. He couldn't be more than two or three years older than she was, she thought. Twenty-one, twenty-two perhaps. She took a deep breath, and realized that she was shaking slightly.

'Nervous?'

She sighed.

'It's a bit nerve-racking.'

He scratched at his beard and seemed to be thinking.

'He's not all that talkative, your dad. Not normally, at least. But you don't need to worry. Do you want to be alone with him?'

'Of course. Why? . . . Is there something . . . ?'

He shrugged.

'No, not at all. I'll take you to his room. If you want to sit there, that's no problem. Or you could go for a walk in the grounds – he likes to wander about . . . There's tea and coffee in the kitchen as well.'

'Thank you.'

He pointed the way to a new, short corridor. Let her go first.

'Here we are. Number 16. I'll be down in the office if there's anything you want.'

He knocked on the door and opened it without waiting for a response. She closed her eyes and counted to five. Then she stepped inside.

7

The man sitting in the armchair by the open window reminded her of a bird.

That was her first thought, and somehow it stayed with her.

My dad's a bird.

He was small and thin. Dressed in worn and shabby corduroy trousers far too big for him, and a blue shirt hanging loose over his hunched shoulders. The head on his skinny neck was long and narrow, his eyes dark and sunken, and his nose sharp and slightly curved. Thick hair, cut short. Mousy in colour. And stubble a few days old that was a shade darker.

He put down the book he was reading and looked at her for two seconds, then looked away.

She remained in the doorway, holding her breath. She suddenly felt convinced that she was in the wrong place. That she – or rather, the young carer – had come to the wrong room. Could this really be her father? Could this tiny creature be—

'Are you Arnold Maager?' she said, cutting short her thoughts. Felt surprised that her voice sounded so steady, despite everything.

He looked up at her again. Licked his lips with the tip of his tongue.

'Who are you?'

The words sounded as insubstantial as the creature who had uttered them. She put her rucksack on the floor and sat down in the other armchair. Waited for a few moments while continuing to look him in the eye, and decided that he didn't actually look all that old. About forty-five, she thought. Her mother was forty-three, so that could be about right.

'My name's Mikaela. You're my dad.'

He made no reply. Didn't react at all.

'I'm your daughter,' she added.

'My daughter? Mikaela?'

He seemed to shrivel up even more, and the words were so faint that she could hardly make them out. The book fell to the floor, but he made no attempt to pick it up. His hands were shaking slightly.

Don't start crying, she thought. Please, Dad, don't start crying.

★

Looking back, she found it hard to say how long they had sat there in silence, opposite each other. Perhaps it was only half a minute, perhaps it was ten. It was all so odd, every second seemed both static and gigantic, and when quite a few of them had passed she slowly began to realize something she hadn't grasped before – nor even thought about . . . Something about language and silence. And perceptions.

It wasn't at all clear, but for the first time in her life she suddenly noticed that it was possible to experience things without talking about them. Experience things together with somebody else, without putting anything into words, not even for herself. Neither while things were actually happening, nor later . . . That words, those unwieldy words, could never be one hundred per cent accurate, and that it was sometimes necessary to desist from using them. Not to let them trample all over experiences, and distort them.

Just to sit there in silence and experience things. To let everything be exactly what it was. Anyway, something along those lines is what she became aware of. Discovered during her first meeting with her dad. Her bird dad.

During half a minute. Or maybe ten.

Then he stood up, walked over to the bureau next to his bed and opened the bottom drawer.

'I've written to you,' he said. 'It's good that you've come to collect it.'

He produced a bundle of letters. It was at least six inches thick, and tied up by a length of black tape the shape of a cross on the top surface.

'It'll be best if you throw them away. But as you're here, you might as well have them.'

He put the bundle down on the table between them, and sat down again.

'I'm sorry,' he said. 'But you shouldn't have come. I think it would be best if you left now.'

He blinked a few times, and jerked his head from side to side. He was no longer looking at her, and she assumed he felt uncomfortable. That he thought it was awkward to be sitting here with his daughter who had just materialized out of nowhere.

'I want to get to know you and talk to you,' she said. 'I didn't know who you were until yesterday. I want to know why that has been the case.'

'It's all my fault,' he said. 'I did something terrible, and it's right that things have turned out as they have. There's nothing to be done about it. It's not possible.'

He jerked his head from side to side again.

'I don't understand,' said Mikaela. 'I need to know in order to understand.'

'It's not possible,' he repeated.

Then he sat there in silence, staring down at the table.

Leaned forward, clutching the arms of his chair. More time passed.

'You have another dad now. It's best the way things are. Go now.'

She could feel the sobs welling up in her throat.

Look at me, she thought. Touch me! Say that you are my dad, and that you're pleased that I've come to see you at last!

But he just sat there. The remarkable silence had gone – or was changed – and now, all of a sudden, there was merely repugnance and hopelessness. Just think that moments could disintegrate so quickly, she thought, feeling increasingly desperate. Disintegrate so totally.

'I don't even know what happened,' she whispered, trying somehow to force back the tears thumping away behind her eyes. 'My mum doesn't say anything, and you don't say anything. Can't you understand that you have to tell me? You bastards . . . You fucking bastards!'

She heaved herself up out of the armchair and stood in front of the open window instead. Turned her back on him. Leaned out and squeezed the sharp tinplate on the window ledge until her fingers caused her agony, succeeding in forcing back her despair with the aid of the pain and her fury. You bastards, she kept repeating in her thoughts. Bloody fucking bastards – yes, that's exactly what they were!

'You think you know what's best for me, but you don't at all!'

He didn't move a muscle, but she could hear him breathing in his armchair. Deeply, and with his mouth open as if he had adenoid problems. She decided to ignore him for a while. Deflate the tension, or try to at least. She looked out of the window. Summer and sunshine were making their presence felt in the grounds. The dog had stopped barking. It was lying down in the shade instead with its tongue rolled out onto the ground in front of it – you could see that from above, where she was. She had a good view over the surrounding countryside as well: she could see the road she had walked along on the way here, and the village where she'd got off the bus, St Inns. And beyond there was the sea – more of a hint than a reality, and she wondered how life here might feel so terribly enclosed by all those extensive views. All that summer, all that sunshine, all that endless sky . . .

'How old are you, Mikaela?' he asked out of the blue.

'Eighteen,' she said, without turning to look at him. 'It was my birthday yesterday.'

Then she remembered that she'd brought something for him. She went over to her rucksack and dug out the parcel. Hesitated for a moment, then put it down on the table, next to the letters.

'It's nothing special,' she said. 'But it's for you. I did it at school when I was ten years old. I want you to have it.'

He felt hesitantly at the thin packet, but made no effort to open it.

'You shouldn't—' he began.

'If I give you something will you be kind enough to accept it,' she interrupted angrily. 'I'll accept your letters, so you'll accept my story – okay?'

It was indeed a story. An illustrated story about an unfortunate bird she'd spent almost a whole term writing when she was in class four. Writing and drawing and painting. She'd thought of giving it to her mum or to Helmut as a Christmas present, but for whatever reason she hadn't done so.

She couldn't remember now if it was because they'd fallen out, or if there was some other reason. But when she'd remembered the story last night, it had felt like a symbolic gesture.

Giving her dad a story that she'd written. A sad story with a happy ending.

And about a bird as well, it now occurred to her – that fitted in with her first impression of him.

She stood by the window again and waited. Made up her mind not to say a word nor to leave the room until he had made some kind of a move. Just stand there and refuse to budge – just like her mum had done, and just as he was doing. Refuse to budge. For as long as it took. So there.

After a few minutes he cleared his throat and stood up. Paced hesitantly back and forth for a while, then stood by the door.

'I want to go out,' he said. 'I usually go out for a walk in the grounds at about this time.'

'I'll come with you,' said Mikaela. 'And I want you to tell me what happened. I've no intention of leaving here until you've done that. Is that clear?'

Her dad went out of the door without responding.

8

'So, you have to go back and continue the interrogation on Monday?' said Mikael Bau. 'Is that what you're saying?'

Moreno nodded, and took another sip of wine. She felt that she was starting to feel a bit drunk – but what the hell? she thought. It was the first evening of her four-week-long holiday after all, and she couldn't remember when she'd last allowed herself to drink away her inhibitions. It must have been years ago. What inhibitions, incidentally?

She could sleep in tomorrow. Take a towel, saunter down to the beach. Lie down and lap up the sun all day. Have a good rest and let Mikael look after her, just as he'd said he would do.

And an hour or two's work the day after tomorrow wasn't all that much of a problem, surely? In the afternoon – so it wouldn't affect her lie-in.

'That's right,' she said. 'Just a couple of hours. He wasn't as cooperative as he said he was going to be, that scumbag Lampe-Leermann.'

'Scumbag?' said Mikael with a frown. 'I take it the inspector is talking off the record.'

Off the record? she thought as she shuffled around and tried to make herself comfortable on the sagging plush sofa. I suppose so – but for God's sake, I'm on holiday after all! Mikael was lolling back at the other end of the outsize piece of furniture, and they had just about as much bodily contact as was compatible with a comfortable digestion process. He'd found a suitable fish, needless to say, just as he'd promised to do. Not just any old fish either: a sole that he'd cooked à la meunière with a divine white wine sauce and crayfish tails. It was such a luxurious delight that she'd found it quite difficult to really enjoy it. The problem was striking a balance between gorging herself and doing justice to his culinary skills. Something to do with her ability to really let herself go, presumably . . . But why should that be a problem?

When she admitted as much, he'd simply burst out laughing and shrugged.

'Just eat,' he said. 'You don't need to talk blank verse.'

She drank another slug of wine. Leaned her head back on the cushion and realized that she had a sort of idiot smile on her lips. It didn't seem willing to go away.

'Franz Lampe-Leermann is a scumbag,' she declared. 'Off or on the record, it makes no difference.'

Mikael looked mildly sceptical.

'But why does it have to be you, and nobody else? Surely anybody can interrogate a scumbag?'

'Presumably for the same reason that I'm lolling back here,' said Moreno. 'He likes me. Or rather, he likes women more than he likes men.'

'Really? And so he can dictate how he's going to be treated, can he? Is this the police force's new softly-softly approach?'

'I suppose you could say that. In any case, he prefers me to the local chief of police, and I have to say that I understand him. Vrommel isn't exactly a breath of fresh air . . .'

'Vrommel?'

'That's his name. A stiff sixty-year-old, stiff-collared, stiff-necked pain in the neck and everywhere else you can think of . . .'

She hesitated, surprised at how easily the words flowed over her lips. It must be that sauce, she thought. Summer, sun and Sauvignon blanc . . .

'I know who he is,' said Mikael.

'Who?'

'Vrommel, of course.'

'You do? How can you know who Vrommel is?'

Mikael flung out his arm and spilled a little wine.

'The house,' he explained. 'This one. Don't forget that I've lived here in the summer for the whole of my life. I know Port Hagen better than the back of my hand. Lejnice as well . . . That's the Big City in these parts.'

Moreno thought for a moment.

'I see. But the chief of police? I assume this means that you are involved in criminal activities . . . You and your family, that is.'

Mikael growled cryptically.

'Hmm,' he said, 'Not exactly. I happen to remember Vrommel because he came here once. It must have been at the beginning of the eighties, when I was about fifteen or sixteen. One of my sisters had a friend who was mixed up in something. I can't remember what . . . Or didn't know, to be more precise. Anyway, he came to interview Louise . . . Or perhaps he interrogated her? Tall and red-haired, this Vrommel, right? A bit of a rough diamond.'

'Bald as a coot nowadays,' said Moreno. 'But he's certainly a rough diamond . . . But why the hell are we lying here nattering on about bald policemen?'

'I've no idea,' said Mikael. 'It seems daft when there are hairy cops at much closer quarters.'

He took hold of her bare feet and started massaging them.

Hairy cops? Moreno thought.

Then she burst out laughing.

'I think I need a walk along the beach,' she said. 'I've drunk too much. And gobbled too much sauce.'

'Same here,' said Mikael. 'Shall we take a blanket? The moon's shining.'

'We can't possibly manage without a blanket,' said Moreno.

They got back from the beach shortly before dawn, and on Sunday she slept in until noon.

So did Mikael, and after breakfast, which consisted mainly of juice and coffee, they went out and lay back in a couple of deckchairs in the garden with more juice and mineral water within easy reach. Now that she'd had time to think about it, Moreno began to realize what a marvellous house she had come to stay in. A big and somewhat ramshackle wooden building with a veranda all the way round it and balconies on the upper floor. Creaking staircases and lopsided nooks and passages that were bound to make an indelible impression on any young child's mind. Bay windows with dried flowers, old-fashioned scratchy window panes, and furniture from four or five generations and in ten times as many styles.

How the Bau family had come to own a place like this – its name was Tschandala, for some unknown reason –

was hidden in the mists of time: nobody in the family had ever been known to have more money than was needed to buy their daily bread, Mikael insisted; but according to the most persistent theory of how the house had been acquired, it had been won by a certain Sinister Bau at a strange and notorious poker party at the beginning of the 1920s. It was also rumoured that the same evening he had lost his young fiancée to a Ukrainian gypsy king, so the family reckoned that honours were even and they had every right to own Tschandala.

Mikael Bau told her all this and more besides while they lay back naked in their deckchairs. The thicket of scraggy dwarf pine trees and Aviolis bushes was rampant and formed an effective screen so that they couldn't be overlooked. Moreno kept asking herself if he were just making it all up on the spur of the moment.

But then, perhaps the whole situation was some kind of illusion? The house and the weather and the naked man who had just stretched out his hand and placed it over her left breast – surely it couldn't all be real? It was more likely to be something she had dreamt up at home while lying in bed and waiting for the alarm clock to announce the arrival of yet another rainy Tuesday in November – that seemed to be far more likely, dammit.

She eventually decided that it didn't matter in any case. She recalled that *the Chief Inspector* – Chief Inspector Van

Veeteren, that is, who had weighed anchor and left the police station some years ago, and now spent his days in Krantze's antiquarian bookshop in Kupinskis Gränd – had once talked about that very thing. The fact that it didn't matter two hoots if everything turned out to be no more than a film or a book. Or if it was real. The conditions were the same – even if it was by no means clear what they were, they were the same anyway.

So she stretched out her hand and let it stay where it ended up.

At about four they went down to the beach for a swim. There were lots of people around, of course. Summer, sunny and Sunday; mums, dads, children and dogs; frisbees, fluttering kites, dripping ice creams and bouncing balls. For a few black seconds while they were towelling themselves down after their dip, she felt a sudden rush of envy as she watched all these family clusters. These extrovert, happy people, enjoying themselves in these simple, healthy and natural surroundings.

But it passed. She shook her head at the thought of such a naive, tuppenny-ha'penny analysis, and contemplated Mikael Bau, stretched out on his back in the sand.

If she really wanted to find herself in that kind of

company, there was nothing to stop her, she thought. Nothing to prevent her from taking that step.

Superficially nothing, that is. Only herself. He had said that he loved her, after all. Several times. She lay down close to him. Closed her eyes and began thinking about her own family.

About her mother and father, to whom she spoke once a month on the telephone. And met once a year.

Her bisexual brother in Rome.

Her lost sister.

Maud. Lost in the backyards of Europe. In the red-light districts of large cities, and in the filthy hopelessness of junkie apartments. In pimps' beds. Sliding further and further down a long, sleazy spiral. She no longer knew where Maud was.

There were no more postcards. No address, no sign of life. Perhaps her sister was no longer in the land of the living?

A family? she thought. Can you really start living in a family when you're over thirty and have never had one? Or did all families resemble her own, more or less, when you started to investigate them more closely?

Good questions, as they say. She had asked them lots of times before.

Asked and asked, but always refrained from answering.

It was so easy to blame everything on her parents as well. To polish the chip on her shoulder. Much too easy.

'What did you say his name was?'

Mikael stroked his hand over her stomach.

'Who?'

'The scumbag.'

How clever of him to drag her back into the real world.

'Lampe-Leermann. Franz Lampe-Leermann. Why do you ask?'

He began slowly filling her navel with sand. A thin trickle of warm, white sand tumbling down from his clenched fist.

'I don't really know. Jealousy, I suppose. You go to meet him every other day. Is that why he doesn't come out with everything at one go? So that he has the opportunity of spending more and more time with the most beautiful copper in Europe?'

Moreno thought that over.

'Presumably,' she said. 'But there'll only be one more meeting. I intend to explain to him that there'll be no more, no matter what happens. I'll try to be a bit nicer to him as well, in compensation. Make him a few promises . . .'

'Bloody hell!' said Mikael. 'Don't say things like that. What's he done, by the way?'

'Practically everything,' said Moreno. 'He's fifty-five years old, and has been in jail for at least twenty of them.

But he has a reputation. Child pornography. Drug barons. Weapons. Maybe even people-smuggling. It's a bit of a tangled mess, but we should be able to sort out some of it at least . . . with Lampe-Leermann's help. I have no choice but to go through with this. It's my job to open up this scumbag. But I'm only going to give up one more day to the task, I promise you that.'

Mikael blew away the grains of sand, and kissed her stomach instead.

'Do you believe in what you're doing?'

She raised her head and looked at him in surprise.

'What do you mean?'

'What I say, of course. I wonder if you think it really matters. The fact that you manage to achieve some results as a detective inspector. And that I manage to save somebody or something as a result of my welfare work. Do you think any of that matters when we're up against the bloody free market and all that bloody hypocrisy and all that bloody cynicism? Look after number one, and the devil take the hindmost. Do you believe that what you do matters?'

'I certainly do,' said Moreno. 'Of course that's what I believe. Why the hell do you ask?'

'Good,' said Mikael. 'I was just checking. That's what I believe as well. I'll carry on believing that even if it's the last thing I do.'

She wondered why he had suddenly taken up these serious matters just now, in the roasting afternoon sun on the never-ending beach.

And why they had never discussed this before.

'It's not just good that you believe,' he went on. 'It's essential. Leila didn't believe, that's why we split up. She started clinging on to all the irony and cynicism as if we simply had no choice . . . As if solidarity was no more than an outdated concept that collapsed at about the same time as the Wall, and all that was left for us to do was to look after number one.'

'I thought she was the one who dumped you?'

He thought for a moment.

'I gave her the pleasure of thinking that. But the real facts were as I've just told you, more or less. She gave up, that's all there is to it. But by now I've forgotten her sur-name and what she looked like. Who cares? All that was over two hundred years ago . . . Do you realize that you are the first woman I've ever met with whom I'd like to have a child?'

'You're out of your mind,' said Moreno. 'You'd better go to an insemination clinic.'

'I'm well known for being clever.'

'I'm thirsty.'

'Stop changing the subject.'

'What subject?'

'Children. Us. Love and all that stuff. Oh, my long-haired copper, I love you.'

She lay there in silence for a while.

'Are you hurt?' she asked. 'Because I haven't answered?'

'Mortally.'

She raised herself up on an elbow to check that he didn't look too suicidal. She noticed a little tic at one side of his mouth, but he didn't actually smile. Or cry. He's putting on an act, she thought. Why the hell can't I trust him? She stood up and started brushing off all the sand.

'If we go back to your castle and drink a drop or two of water,' she said, 'I'll tell you something. Okay? But I badly need to raise my fluid levels.'

'Hmm,' said Mikael, rising to his feet as well. 'I'm consumed with curiosity.'

'And desire,' he added when they had walked over the dunes and could see the roof of Tschandala sticking up over the dwarf pines.

'Well?' he said.

Moreno put down her glass.

'You're only showing your good sides,' she said. 'It's like going to some sort of an exhibition, dammit! It's not a foundation to build on. For as long as you keep your cupboard door shut and don't let the skeletons out, I'm not going to give you so much as a little finger of my future.'

He leaned back and thought that over.

'I like football,' he said. 'I like to go to at least two top matches per year, and to watch one a week on the telly.'

'I could put up with that,' said Moreno. 'Provided I don't have to accompany you.'

'You're *not allowed* to accompany me. And I want to be left to my own devices sometimes as well. I want to listen to Dylan and Tom Waits and Robert Wyatt without some-body coming to talk to me or turn down the volume.'

She gave him a non-committal nod.

'I often take my work home with me as well,' he said. 'There are some things I just can't let go of. It's a bloody nuisance in fact: I've considered signing up for courses in yoga and meditation in order to get over it. It's impossible to get a decent night's sleep when things are nagging at your mind.'

'We could both go to such courses,' said Moreno. 'In fact.'

'Not if we have children from the word go,' said Mikael thoughtfully. 'One of us will have to stay at home and look after them. You can't take babies with you to yoga classes. Aren't you hungry, by the way?'

'Do you mean we're going to eat today as well?'

Mikael nodded.

'There's pie and salad. And wine.'

'I hate wine,' said Moreno. 'Besides, I've got to work tomorrow.'

'Hmm,' said Mikael with a smile. 'Come to think of it, I think there's some asparagus in the pie. I read somewhere that asparagus is the only food that it's impossible to match with a suitable wine.'

'Excellent,' said Moreno. 'Long live asparagus.'

They fell asleep quite soon, having only indulged in a little sexual play, nothing serious. But after only a couple of hours she woke up, and couldn't get to sleep again. She lay there in the king-size double bed, watching the shadows fluttering around over the walls and the well-honed body lying by her side. It didn't really seem real. Not real at all, to be honest: the moon aimed a shaft of light through the open window and the thin curtains, and it felt very much as if both she and her lover (boyfriend? partner? bloke?) were floating around in some kind of surrealistic film developing tank, waiting to be developed.

Developed to make what?

I am a free woman, she thought. I belong to the first generation of free women in the history of the world. My life is in my own hands.

Nobody to be responsible for. No pressing social considerations. No obligations.

I'm a woman who can do whatever she wants.

Right now. Here. Today and tomorrow.

They had talked about this as well. This very thing. Both this evening, and earlier as well. How had he put it?

If you love your freedom too much, you'll end up hugging a cold stone for the rest of your life. Tighter and tighter, colder and colder.

She thought about that for a while.

Bullshit, she concluded. He's read that on the label of a video film, or on a carton of milk. Too many words. Tomorrow it's time for that scumbag Lampe-Leermann.

But she knew – before the sun had risen to greet a new day, and before she'd managed to fall asleep again for the second time that night – she knew that she would have to make up her mind.

Presumably she had four weeks in which to think things over. Two together with him. Two on her own. She didn't think he was prepared to give her any longer than that.

She stroked her hand gently over his handsome back, and wondered if she knew the answer already.

Then she fell asleep.

9

The youth hostel was completely full. After some desperate negotiations, however, she was allowed to share a room with two young Danish Inter-railing girls and a middle-aged nurse who had been unable to find a double room to share with her husband.

She met the nurse – thoroughly roasted after a long day on the beach – in the shower; the Danish girls were lying on their beds, writing picture postcards. They were both listening to music on their Walkman cassette players, and both nodded to her without removing their earphones.

She suppressed an urge to burst into tears. Packed her belongings into the locker, made up the rickety extra bed, and went to the canteen for something to eat. When she had eaten three sandwiches, drunk a large Coca-Cola and munched an apple, she felt a bit better. She took out her little blue notebook and read through what she had written. She thought for a while about where it would be best to begin, and having made up her mind went to reception to ask for a little help. It was only a quarter to six, and she thought that with a bit of luck she might be able to make one of her intended visits that same evening.

Things went even better than she had hoped. The two girls behind the counter spent quite a lot of time helping her, and when she got to the bus stop she found that the bus had just arrived, and was waiting for her.

She flopped down on the seat immediately behind the driver and continued to think over how best to approach the meeting. She took out her notebook, then put it away again once she had memorized the main points. The bus set off, and she started to think back over her walk through the care-home grounds instead. And the letters she had been given by her father, and read with ever-increasing surprise. The feeling of unreality took hold of her like a sudden nightmare.

Arnold Maager. Her dad.

Dad. She tasted the familiar word with its new meaning, and at the same time tried to conjure up his lean figure in her mind's eye.

His somewhat hunched figure. That heavy, oblong-shaped head on its narrow neck. His similarity to a bird. His hands thrust deep down into his trouser pockets, and his shoulders hunched as if he were feeling cold as he trundled along through the heat of summer. And the distance . . . The distance between himself and his daughter he was keen to maintain all the time, as if bodily contact were something dangerous and forbidden.

They had wandered back and forth through the grounds in this fashion for over an hour – side by side, half a metre apart. At least half a metre. Walked and walked and walked. It was quite a while before it dawned on her that she had no need to keep nagging at him.

She didn't need to question him and press him to explain things. He had already made up his mind to talk to her.

To talk to her and explain in his own good time. In his own words. With pauses and repetitions and names she didn't recognize. He had become more and more tense the further they had progressed – but of course, that wasn't so surprising.

Because the story he had to put into words for his daughter was not a pleasant one.

Not pleasant at all.

But he told her it all the same.

The bells in the low whitewashed church struck a quarter to seven just as she was getting off the bus in the square in Lejnice. Three muffled chimes that made a flock of pigeons in front of her feet take off, then land again.

She walked round the dried-out fountain, and asked

for directions at the newspaper kiosk. She had found the address in the telephone directory at the youth hostel: it turned out to be a mere stone's throw away, according to the lady behind the counter, glowing with summery sweat as she pointed down towards the harbour. Dead easy to find.

She thanked her, and set off in the direction indicated. Down Denckerstraat towards the sea – a narrow street lined with old wooden houses leaning inwards and making the street seem even narrower. Then left into Goopsweg for about fifty metres. The house before the pharmacy.

Two things happened as she walked those fifty metres.

The first was that a black cat emerged from behind a fence and strolled across the street directly in front of her.

The second was that for some unknown reason a tile fell off one of the roofs and crashed to the ground three metres behind her. It happened only a couple of seconds after the cat had disappeared behind another fence; a woman she had just passed was even closer to the spot where the tile landed, and gave a scream that frightened her even more than the tile had done. At first, at least.

She remained standing for quite a while outside number 26, wondering what to do next. She smelled a whiff of the sea drifting up on the slight breeze blowing in from the shore. And the scent of cooking oil and oregano from the pizzeria on the corner. The house – the house in question – was a small block of flats, three storeys high with only two entrance doors. Typical 1970s style with tiny built-in balconies facing the street, and perhaps also on the other side, facing the courtyard.

I'm not superstitious, she thought. Never have been, never will be. I don't believe in that sort of silly thinking that's a remnant from a less enlightened age . . . Those were words she must have borrowed from Kim Wenderbout, she realized, her gigantic social studies teacher with whom at least half the girls in her class were secretly in love. So was she.

Silly remnants? A less enlightened age? Rubbish, she thought.

But she remained standing there nevertheless. The bells in the square started to strike seven.

The cat and the tile, she thought. Perfectly natural. She counted the chimes. And made it eight.

She turned on her heel and returned the same way that she had come.

Odd, she thought when she was sitting in the bus again on the Sunday morning. Why did I do that?

A cat runs across the street and a roof tile falls down onto the road. What's so special about that?

She had slept like a log for nearly twelve hours. She'd

gone to bed the moment she had returned to the youth hostel, and only woke up when one of the Danish girls dropped a dish on the floor at half past nine.

She had a shower, then checked out and just caught the bus that left at twenty past ten. Breakfast: a pear and a pear soda. Plenty of variation there . . .

But it had been odd, her behaviour the previous evening. Very odd. Not like her at all, that was even more obvious now in the cold light of day. Not like Mikaela Lijphart, the sensible, clear-thinking Mikaela Lijphart. Quite a few of her classmates had fallen for various forms of new-age, turn-of-the-century mysticism and that kind of dodgy stuff, but not her. Not the clever, reliable Mikaela. So there really was something remarkable about it, that business with the cat and the roof tile. And her reaction to it.

What if new omens were to confront her today? How would she react now?

Don't be silly, she thought. Yesterday was yesterday. I was tired. Tired out and overwrought. Who wouldn't have been? The day had been full of tortures. Full to overflowing.

As she walked towards Goopsweg it struck her that she hadn't rung home since leaving yesterday morning.

She hadn't promised to do so, in fact, but she always used to get in touch even so. She noticed a phone box in the little lane just past the pizzeria, and remembered that she had a new telephone card in her handbag. She slowed down and began arguing with herself.

.She really ought to. Why make her mum and Helmut worry unnecessarily?

But then again, there *was* a case for doing that. There certainly was. Why shouldn't she allow herself to be a bit egoistic?

She was eighteen now, after all.

Why not let them get used to taking the rough with the smooth? she thought. Why not delay the call for an hour or two? Or even all day?

She started whistling, and passed by the phone box.

The woman who opened the door looked very like a maths teacher she'd had for a term when she was in class eight or nine. The same long, horsey face. The same pale eyes. The same straggling, washed-out, colourless hair. For a moment Mikaela was so certain it was that very same teacher she had the name on the tip of her tongue.

Then she remembered that Miss Dortwinckel had committed suicide one Christmas holiday – by eating half a dozen broken crystal glasses, if rumour was to be believed – and she realized that it was a case of similar features, no more than that. A certain charisma.

Or lack of charisma, rather. Perhaps our Good Lord had only a limited number of features to choose from – especially when it came to middle-aged women past their sell-by date.

Where do I get all these thoughts from? she wondered. And how can they come so quickly?

'Well?'

The voice was sharp and unfriendly. Not a bit like that of Miss Dortwinckel, which she could recall quite clearly.

'Forgive me. My name's Mikaela Lijphart. I hope I'm not disturbing you, but I would be very grateful if I could have a little chat with you.'

'With me? Why?'

Now the smell of strong drink hit her. Mikaela automatically stepped half a pace backwards, and had to grab the handrail in order not to fall down the steps.

Eleven o'clock on a Sunday morning? she thought. Drunk already. Why . . . ?

Then it occurred to her that it could have to do with her father. With what her father had said. Could it be that . . . ?

She lost the thread. Or dropped it on purpose. The woman was staring at her.

'Why do you want to talk to me?' she asked again. 'Why don't you say anything? Are you mentally deficient, or are you one of those bloody hallelujah loonies trying to recruit new souls? I don't have a soul.'

'No . . . Certainly not,' Mikaela assured her. 'Please forgive me, I'm just a bit confused – so much has happened in the last few days and I don't really know what to do. It's about something that happened when I was a little girl . . . Only two years old. Something I'm trying to get straight, and I think you might be able to help me. I don't live round here. May I come in for a while?'

'I haven't tidied up yet,' said the woman.

'It'll only take a couple of minutes.'

'The home help didn't come on Friday when she should have done, and as I said, I haven't tidied up yet.'

Mikaela tried to produce an indulgent smile.

'I understand. It doesn't matter – but we could go to some cafe or other if you'd prefer that. The main thing is that I can talk to you.'

The woman muttered something and hesitated. Stood in the doorway swaying back and forth as she sucked in her lips and held on to the radiator.

'What about?' she said. 'What do you want to know?'

'I'd prefer not to discuss it here on the doorstep. It's about my father.'

'About your father?'

'Yes.'

'And who's your father?'

Mikaela thought for two seconds, then said his name. The woman breathed in audibly, and let go of the radiator.

'Bloody hell!' she said. 'Yes, come on in.'

Mikaela had no doubt at all that the home help hadn't turned up last Friday – nor any other Friday for the last six months. She had never seen a filthier or more squalid flat. Couldn't even imagine a worse one. Her hostess ushered her into a cramped kitchen that smelled of tobacco smoke and old fish, and quite a lot more besides. She pushed a pile of newspapers and advertising leaflets on to the floor so that they could sit opposite one another at the table – separated by a small, sticky area just big enough for two glasses, an ashtray and a bottle.

Cherry brandy. She filled Mikaela's glass without asking. Mikaela took a sip of the bright red, lukewarm liquid and almost choked over its strength and sweetness.

The woman emptied her glass in one swig, and slammed it down on the table. Fished out a cigarette and lit it.

Why can't she at least air the place? Mikaela wondered. Why does she live cooped up in a rubbish dump in the middle of summer? Ugh.

But of course, she hadn't come to discuss hygiene and home comforts.

'So, Arnold Maager,' said the woman. 'That bloody arsehole.'

'He is . . . Arnold Maager is my father,' said Mikaela.

'So you claim. Tell me what you know.'

Mikaela could feel the tears welling up in her eyes, but she gritted her teeth and managed to hold them in check.

'Is it okay if I open the window a little bit?' she asked. 'I'm allergic to tobacco smoke.'

'No windows are ever opened in my home,' said the woman. 'You were the one who wanted to come in among all the shit.'

Mikaela swallowed.

'Let's hear it, then,' said the woman, pouring herself some more cherry brandy. 'You first. Let's do things properly.'

Mikaela cleared her throat, and began talking. She didn't really have much to say, but she had hardly started before the woman stood up and walked over to the sink, which was piled up with unwashed crockery, empty bottles and every kind of rubbish you could think of. She rummaged around in a box, with her back towards her guest, and when she turned round she was holding her right arm straight out, pointing at Mikaela with something.

It was a second before Mikaela realized that it was a pistol.

The cat, she thought. The roof tile.

10

Monday was overcast, but the high pressure was very much present in the interrogation room at Lejnice police station. Lampe-Leermann was wearing an orange shirt with a prominent collar and the top three buttons unfastened. The sweat stains under his arms were hardly visible. He smelled strongly of aftershave lotion.

Well, rather that than old garlic, Moreno thought as she sat down opposite him. Observed him closely before saying anything, and decided that on the whole he seemed to be more composed than he had been on Saturday, and she felt quite optimistic when she started the tape recorder.

It was exactly 13.15 when she did so, and when she finally switched it off after a most productive session, one hour and four minutes had passed.

So, a most productive session, and job done. At least,

that was how she assessed it. Whether or not Franz Lampe-Leermann would agree was doubtful: but as far as she could judge she had squeezed out of him most of what he had to say. Three names that were completely new to the police, half a dozen that were known already, and information that was probably sufficient for the police to start proceedings against the whole lot of them. And quite a lot more information as well, the value of which she couldn't be sure about at the moment, but which would most probably lead to more guilty verdicts. Unless the prosecuting authorities saw things differently, or other things needed to be taken into account – but there was not much point in speculating about that at this stage.

And she had not made him any significant promises regarding such things as extenuating circumstances or dropping charges against him. Needless to say she had no authority to grant such concessions anyway – but when all was said and done it was the police who eventually decided what information came into the public domain, and what didn't.

So, a satisfactory outcome: she could grant herself that much. Reinhart could look after the mopping-up: Inspector Moreno had done all that was required of her, and more besides.

'Miss Copper is looking pleased with herself,' said Lampe-Leermann, scratching his hairy chest.

'That's because I can now get out of this dump,' said Moreno.

'So you wouldn't fancy a little bit extra, then?'

The implication – or possible implication – made her see red, but she kept control of herself.

'And what might that be?'

'A titbit. A little goody to round things off. But I need a fag first.'

Moreno hesitated. Looked at the clock and wondered what the hell he had in mind.

'What do you mean?' she asked eventually.

'Exactly what I say, of course. As always. A titbit. But first a fag. There's a time and place for everything.'

'You can have five minutes,' said Moreno. 'But make sure you really do have something worthwhile to come out with, otherwise you'll lose all your bonus points.'

Lampe-Leermann stood up.

'Don't worry, young lady. I'm not in the habit of disappointing my women.'

He knocked on the door, and was let out into the smoking yard.

'It's about that hack.'

'Hack?'

'That journalist. Don't quibble about words, young lady.'

Moreno said nothing.

'I'm sitting on a fascinating little story. And I'm sitting on his name . . .'

He tapped the side of his forehead with two fingers.

'That's what these negotiations are all about.'

Moreno nodded and glanced at the tape recorder, but Lampe-Leermann made a dismissive gesture.

'I wouldn't have thought you'd need to record this. I'd have thought you'd be able to remember it without any assistance.'

'Come to the point,' said Moreno. 'A journalist who knows something?'

'Exactly. What do you think about paedophiles?'

'I love them,' said Moreno.

'I have a certain amount of sympathy for them as well,' said Lampe-Leermann, scratching himself under his chin. 'There's such a lot of cheap comments written about them . . . You might think they're being victimized. And they're everywhere, of course. Normal decent citizens like you and me . . .'

'Come to the point!'

Lampe-Leermann looked at her with an expression that was presumably meant to be fatherly understanding.

'Everywhere, as I said. It's nothing to be ashamed of – you shouldn't be ashamed of your inclinations, as my little mum always used to tell me . . . But it's such a sensitive subject nowadays, and people are up in arms about what's been happening. Anyway . . .'

He made a dramatic pause while he stroked his dyed moustache, and it struck Moreno that she'd never seen anything like this. Nor heard. Scumbag was far too complimentary a name for this creature. She clenched her teeth and kept a straight face.

'Anyway, I met that hack, and he told me he'd been given ten thousand to keep his mouth shut.'

'Keep his mouth shut?'

'Yes.'

'About what?'

'Keep his mouth shut about that name. The name of that paedophile.'

'Who?'

Lampe-Leermann shrugged.

'I don't know. *I* don't know. It's the hack who knows, but I'm the one who knows the name of the hack. Are you with me, Miss Copper?'

'Of course,' said Moreno. 'And?'

'It's his job that makes it interesting. I wouldn't call it a titbit if it weren't for the place where he works. This chappie with the inclinations. What do you think, Inspector?'

Moreno said nothing. But she noted that for the first time since they began the conversation, he had referred to her as Inspector. She wondered if that was significant.

'He lives in your little nest. How about that, eh? He's a detective officer . . . One of your crowd.'

He smiled and leaned back.

'What?' said Moreno.

Lampe-Leermann leaned forward again. Pulled a hair from out of his right nostril, then smiled once more.

'I'll say it again. There's a paedophile in the Maardam police station. One of your sleuths. He paid my informant ten thousand to keep his gob shut. It would be daft to pay up if you had nothing to hide, don't you think?'

What the . . . Moreno thought. What the hell is he saying?

The information was reluctant to register in her consciousness, but somehow it did so in the end. Seeped slowly but inexorably through the defences of her reason and emotions and experiences and crystallized as a comprehensible message.

Or rather, incomprehensible.

'Go to hell,' she said.

'Thank you,' said Lampe-Leermann. 'In due course, perhaps . . .'

'You're lying . . . Forget all the brownie points you thought you had amassed. I'll see to it that you get eight years. Ten! You bastard!'

His smile grew broader.

'I can see that you are upset. You have no sympathy,

eh, you neither? Incidentally I don't know if he took the money from his own pocket, or if it came from the public purse, as it were . . . That would depend on his rank, of course, and I don't know what that is. But the hack does.'

He fell silent. For a brief moment Moreno thought the room was shaking – just a slight swaying, as if the film they were taking part in was short of three frames instead of the full twenty-four and made a little jump . . . Or how it must feel some distance from the epicentre of an earthquake.

An earthquake?

That could hardly be a metaphor that simply cropped up without reason. She contemplated Lampe-Leermann as he lolled back on the other side of the table. In slightly less civilized circumstances – they only needed to be *slightly* less – she wouldn't have hesitated more than a mere second to kill him. If she had the chance. She really would. Like a cockroach under the heel of her shoe. The thought didn't worry her one jot.

But then she worried precisely because she hadn't been worried.

'Is that all?' she asked. She tried to make her voice sound so ice-cold that he would realize he could expect no mercy whatsoever.

'That's all,' he said. His smile shrank ever so slightly. 'I can see that you've got the message. Let me know when it's sunk in.'

Moreno stood up. Went over to the rear door and tapped on it with her bunch of keys. Before she was let out, Lampe-Leermann had time to explain one more detail.

'It was because of this titbit that I wanted to talk to a woman police officer. I hope you didn't think there was any other explanation? I couldn't risk sitting face to face with him . . . With that very policeman. Or with somebody who might possibly feel a sense of solidarity with him . . . A good word, that – solidarity. Even if it has fallen out of regular use nowadays. Hmm.'

All this was just a dream, thought Detective Inspector Ewa Moreno. But I feel a bit sick for some reason.

Five minutes later she had put both Franz Lampe-Leermann and Lejnice police station behind her.

For today.

Constable Vegesack made the sign of the cross, then knocked on the door.

It wasn't that he was religious – certainly not, and especially not in the Roman Catholic sense: but on one occasion the sign of the cross had turned out to be useful for him. He had fallen asleep in his car while keeping watch on a suspect (and as a result the said suspect, an intermediary in a cocaine-smuggling gang, had sneaked out of the building and disappeared). The following day he had been summoned to Chief Inspector Vrommel's office for a dressing-down. For want of any better line of defence, he had made the sign of the cross as he stood waiting outside the door (just as he had seen the Italian goalkeeper do before he saved a penalty in the previous week's Champion's League match on the telly), and to his amazement, it seemed to work. Vrommel had treated him almost like a human being.

Vegesack didn't bother about the fact that Vrommel's attitude was presumably due mainly to the arrest of the escapee later on in the night. From that day on, he always made the sign of the cross whenever he found himself standing outside his boss's door.

It couldn't do any harm, in any case, he thought.

Vrommel was standing between two filing cabinets, doing trunk-bending exercises. He did this for at least ten minutes every day in order to keep fit, and it wasn't something that necessarily intruded upon his work. Things got done even so, no problem.

'Sit down,' he said when Constable Vegesack had closed the door behind him.

Vegesack sat down on the visitor's chair.

'Write this down,' said Vrommel.

The chief of police was known for his parsimony in the use of words, and his bodily contortions made it all the more necessary for him to be even less loquacious than usual.

'Firstly,' he said.

'Firstly?' said Vegesack.

'That bastard Lampe-Leermann must be transported to the jail in Emsbaden either this evening or tomorrow. Ring and fix it.'

Vegesack noted this down.

'Secondly. Inspector Moreno's recorded interrogation must be typed out so that she can sign it. Do that.'

Vegesack noted it down.

'Ready by noon tomorrow. There are the cassettes.'

He nodded towards the desk. Vegesack picked up both cassettes and put them in his jacket pocket. The chief of police paused before contorting himself in the opposite direction.

'Anything else?' Vegesack asked.

'I'd have said if there was,' said Vrommel.

When Vegesack got back to his own office – which he shared with Constables Mojavic and Helme – he wondered if he ought to write down the exchange he'd just had with Vrommel in his black book. The one he'd started on six months ago, and which would eventually be his revenge, his way of getting his own back on Chief Inspector Victor Vrommel. The only thing that enabled him to cope.

The true story of the chief of police in Lejnice.

He had already written over fifty pages, and the title he was currently thinking of giving it was: *The Skunk in Uniform*.

Although he had not entirely eliminated the possibility of *The Long Arm of the Bore*, or *A Nero of Our Time*.

Constable Vegesack checked his diary, and established that there were eighteen days still to go to his leave. Then he telephoned Emsbaden and arranged transport for Franz Lampe-Leermann. That took half an hour. He looked at the clock. A quarter to four. He took out a notepad and a pen, and slotted the first cassette into the player.

With a bit of luck I'll have finished by midnight, he thought.

When she had more or less finished recounting what had happened, it occurred to her that perhaps she ought to have kept it to herself.

Not just *perhaps*, in fact. The contents of the scumbag Lampe-Leermann's rant were such that nobody ought to be exposed to them. Or to be bothered by them.

Especially if it was all a bluff.

And it was a bluff, of course. There was no plausible alternative.

So why had she recounted it all for Mikael Bau the moment they'd sat down on the veranda of the harbour cafe? Why?

She couldn't think of a satisfactory answer, hesitated for a moment, then bit her tongue.

'Well, well,' he said. 'For Gawd's sake! What do you make of it?'

She shook her head.

'It's all made up, of course. What I don't understand is what he thinks he's going to get out of it.'

Mikael said nothing, just looked at her as he slowly adjusted his posture.

'What if it isn't?'

'Isn't what?'

'Made up.'

'It *is* made up.'

'By whom?'

'What do you mean?'

'Who's made it up, of course. I wonder if it's that Lampe-Leermann himself, or if it's that journalist?'

Moreno thought for a moment.

'Or somebody else again,' she said. 'I mean, we don't even know if the journalist really exists.'

'Not until Scumbag comes up with a name, you mean?'

'Exactly,' said Moreno. 'And he won't do that for free.'

They sat for a while without speaking. Mikael continued to look at her, his eyebrows slightly raised. Moreno pretended not to notice.

'Hypothetically . . .' he said.

She didn't respond. He hesitated for a few more seconds.

'Hypothetically. Let's assume that he isn't bluffing in fact. Then what do we do?'

Moreno glared at him, and clenched her fists. Took a deep breath.

'Well, then . . . Then we find ourselves in a situation where one of my closest colleagues is a bloody childfucker.'

'Don't speak so loudly,' said Mikael, looking around furtively. Nobody at any of the neighbouring tables seemed to have noticed anything amiss. Moreno leaned forward and continued in a somewhat lower voice.

'We find ourselves in a situation that's so damned awful that I won't be able to sleep a wink at night. That's obvious, isn't it?'

Mikael nodded.

'I think so,' he said. 'How many are there to choose from? Possible candidates? . . . We're still being hypothetical, of course.'

Moreno thought that over. Forced herself to think it over.

'It depends,' she said. 'It depends on how many you

count as CID officers – several constables double up with different sections, and there are a few borderline cases. Eight to ten, I'd say . . . Twelve at most.'

'A dozen?'

'At most, yes.'

Mikael emptied his cup of cappuccino and wiped the foam away from his mouth.

'What are you going to do about it?' he asked.

Moreno didn't answer.

There wasn't any appropriate answer.

11

By the time they got back to Port Hagen and Tschandala it was five o'clock, and a red-haired woman was sitting on the veranda, waiting for them.

'Oh my God,' muttered Mikael. 'I'd forgotten about her.'

The woman turned out to be called Gabriella de Haan, a former girlfriend of Mikael's, and had come in connection with a cat. This was apparently called Montezuma, and was a lazy-looking ginger-coloured female aged about ten. It seemed to Moreno that there were several striking similarities between the two ladies. Quite a few, she decided after a cursory inspection.

'Don't you like cats?' Mikael wondered when fröken de Haan left after less than five minutes.

'Oh yes, I certainly do,' said Moreno. 'I used to have one a few years ago, but it disappeared in mysterious circumstances. But this one . . . ?'

She nodded in the direction of Montezuma, who was stretched out on her side in the old, faded garden hammock and seemed to have made herself at home.

'This one, well . . .' said Mikael, looking appropriately guilty for a brief moment. 'I thought I'd mentioned her. She's going to live here for a few weeks while Gabriella's in Spain. I couldn't very well say no – we got her when we were living together, and Gabriella took her when we split up. She could do with a bit of sea air, poor old Monty. She normally spends all her time cooped up in a flat . . . Anyway, she's unlikely to disturb us. She's as good as gold, even if she does occasionally give the impression of being a bit prickly.'

He bent down and started stroking the cat's stomach, which seemed to transport her into feline heaven.

Moreno couldn't help smiling. She closed her eyes and tried to look into the future. In ten years' time or so . . . How things might be if she made certain decisions and stuck to them.

Her and Mikael Bau. A couple of children. A big house. A few cats.

The image was no more specific than that, but it somehow appeared quite naturally, and on the whole she found it quite acceptable. To say the least.

I'm falling, she thought. I must build up a bit of

strength and some defence mechanisms, otherwise I shall just drift along with the current.

That evening they walked to Wincklers, the restaurant furthest out on the promontory at the northern end of the beach with a reputation for good food. They began with fish soup and mineral water, then lemon sorbet with fresh raspberries, and all the time managed to avoid talking about Franz Lampe-Leermann.

Until they were on the way back home and stopped in front of a pile of jellyfish that somebody had fished out of the sea and placed in a hollow in the sand.

'Scumbag,' said Mikael. 'Is this what he looks like?'

Moreno looked down into the hollow with revulsion.

'Ugh,' she said. 'Yes, more or less. But who cares what he looks like. I just wish he hadn't come out with that last accusation.'

'Hmm. I thought the detective inspector had something nasty at the back of her mind while we were eating the dessert.'

Moreno sighed.

'Thanks,' she said. 'But let's face it, how could I avoid thinking about it? Tell me how if you can. No matter how you look at it, it's an accusation . . . an absolutely horrific accusation about one of my colleagues. Somebody I've been working with and respected and thought I knew and could rely on. If it should turn out that . . . No, for Christ's sake, it's just a bluff of course – but the thought is still there, nagging away. Ugh! Can you understand that?'

Mikael said he could. They turned their backs on the nasty heap and started walking again. In silence to start with, but then he took the opportunity of telling her about the day nursery in Leufshejm called The Happy Panda. A rumour started to circulate to the effect that there was a paedophile among the staff . . . There was a comprehensive investigation which concluded with a hundred-and-ten per cent certainty that the rumour was false and all the staff were as clean as the driven snow: but nevertheless The Happy Panda was forced to close down after a few months because no parent was prepared to send their child there.

And because all the nine female staff stood shoulder to shoulder with their three male colleagues. That was another way of putting it.

One of the three men was an old childhood friend of Mikael's. The nursery had been closed for four years now, but his friend's wife had left him and he was retraining as an engine driver.

'Nice,' said Moreno.

'Very nice,' agreed Mikael. 'At least he's moved on after

his suicidal phase. But I think we're getting away from the point.'

Moreno said nothing for a while.

'Are you suggesting that it's sufficient for Lampe-Leermann to have sown the seed of doubt in my mind? That I won't be able to forget it, no matter what?'

'Something like that,' said Mikael. 'It's basic psychology. It's so damned easy to cause irreparable damage . . . When even you can't fend off an accusation like this, how do you think the general public would react if they got to know about it? No smoke without fire and all that. Bloody hell!'

Moreno didn't respond.

'Although I wonder what you think, deep down,' he said after a little pause. 'Seriously. It would be easier to talk about it if you didn't feel you needed to protect your colleagues. Could there be any truth in it? Is there any possibility – any possibility at all – that it's any more than a malicious lie?'

Moreno continued walking, and gazed out to sea in the rapidly descending darkness. It was no longer possible to make out the horizon, but a series of lights from the fishing boats that had just gone out for the night seemed to indicate where it was.

'I can't believe it,' she said. 'I simply can't. I'd prefer to approach it from a different angle. Try to understand the motive . . . Lampe-Leermann's motive, that is. How could he benefit from it?'

'Do you think he's lying?'

'Very probably. I want to believe that. Although it could also be that journalist who lied to Lampe-Leermann.'

'Why would he do that?'

Moreno shrugged. 'I've no idea. I don't see the point of saying something like that to somebody like Lampe-Leermann. Unless it happened in a fit of drunkenness . . . Which is a distinct possibility, of course. One shouldn't overestimate the logic and the ability to follow a plan that's characteristic of those circles. That's something I'm beginning to realize.'

'Coincidence?' said Mikael. 'An unguarded word?'

'Could be,' said Moreno. 'There's a sort of grey zone. The chief inspector – the one I was telling you about, *the Chief Inspector* – he always used to say that everything that happens is an unholy brew made up of the expected and the unexpected. The hard part is deciding the proportion in a given case: sometimes it's 8:2, sometimes 1:9 . . . That might sound a bit speculative, but it makes a hell of a difference.'

'Order or chaos,' said Mikael, picking up an empty scrunched-up Coca-Cola can somebody had dropped a couple of metres away from one of the green-painted rubbish bins the local council had provided at regular intervals all the way along the beach. 'And the relationship between them . . . Yes, it sounds very plausible. We've talked about this before. But in any case, the accusation itself from Lampe-Leermann sounds carefully planned, doesn't it?'

'Without a doubt,' said Moreno with a sigh. 'Without a doubt. He's expecting a concrete offer in exchange for the name of his bloody hack. The more I think about it, the more I feel sure that there must be an informant, and that there must be some truth in it. Unfortunately.'

'Why do you think that?'

'Because that's the way negotiations work. Even a nasty creep like Lampe-Leermann must realize that. If we were to give him some assurances, we'd only need to cancel them if he turned out to be bluffing. He simply can't dictate whatever terms he likes.'

Mikael thought that over as they walked across the dunes and the spiky roof of Tschandala came into view.

'But what if he wants ready cash? He'd be able to get you to cough up a suitable sum – and wouldn't it be difficult to get that back if it was already in a bank account somewhere? Or hidden away in a mattress?'

'True,' said Moreno. 'At least, I assume so. In any case, it's not my problem. I must make sure I pass the buck. I'm supposed to be on holiday, after all. Enjoying peace and quiet by the seaside with my talented young lover.'

'Dead right,' Mikael grunted as he hugged her tightly.

'Give them a bell the moment we cross over the doorstep and hand the case over to whoever is on duty.'

'Hmm,' said Moreno. 'I think I'll wait until tomorrow.'

'Tomorrow?' said Mikael. 'Why?'

'I have to work out who I'm going to talk to.'

He thought about that for three seconds.

'Aha,' he said. 'Yes, I see your point. A bit tricky?'

'Yes,' said Moreno. 'A bit tricky.'

She woke up at half past two. Spent twenty minutes trying to go back to sleep, then slipped quietly out of bed and sat down at the large circular kitchen table with a sheet of paper and a pencil.

She wrote down the names one by one, as they occurred to her.

Intendent Münster

Chief Inspector Reinhart

Inspector Rooth

Inspector Jung

Intendent deBries

Constable Krause

Those were her closest colleagues. The ones she worked with more or less every day.

The ones she'd known inside out for the last six or seven years.

Inside out? Was it possible that one of them . . . ?

She could feel that question sticking in her throat, in a physical way. When she tried to swallow, she couldn't.

She abandoned the thought and continued with her list, wondering why she had bothered to give them all their ranks. Would rank be relevant in a case like this?

Intendent le Houde

Sergeant Bollmert

And then the others, not actually members of the CID, but she'd better name them even so.

Joensuu

Kellermann

Paretsky

Klempje

She leaned back and contemplated the list. Twelve names in all. She couldn't think of any more. Heinemann had retired. Van Veeteren had quit.

Who? she thought. Who could possibly . . . ?

That question floated around in her consciousness for several minutes. Then she tried another angle.

Who? Who shall I ring?

Which of these men do I trust most?

While she tried to sort out the answer to that problem, the clock indicated a quarter past three, then half past, and she just felt more and more sick.

12

13 July 1999

'He's busy,' said Constable Vegesack for the third time. 'Can't you understand what I'm saying? Either you sit down and wait, or tell me what it's all about.'

The woman shook her head in irritation and flung her hands out wide. Steadied herself in order to demand once again to talk to the chief of police – that's what it looked like, at least – but changed her mind. Breathed out audibly through gritted teeth instead.

Forty, perhaps slightly more, Vegesack decided. Well built without being fat. Looks pretty healthy, in fact . . . Short, dark red hair, certainly dyed.

Jittery.

Devilish jittery. It was impossible to persuade her to sit down. She strode back and forth around the room like a dachshund in need of a pee. Constable Vegesack had grown up with a dachshund, so he knew exactly what that meant.

'Could you perhaps give me some indication of what it is you want?' he said. 'Maybe we could start with your name.'

She paused. Held her arms by her sides, fists clenched, and eyed him up and down. His left hand shot up automatically and adjusted the knot of his tie.

'Sigrid Lijphart,' she said. 'My name's Sigrid Lijphart, and I'm looking for my daughter Mikaela. She's been missing since Saturday.'

Vegesack noted the information down.

'Do you live here in Lejnice? I don't think I've—'

'No,' she said, interrupting him. 'I don't live here. But I did do sixteen years ago. The chief of police knows all about why I had to move away. That's why I want to talk to him, instead of having to go through a mass of stuff that I can barely cope with even thinking about. Damn it all . . . !'

She flopped down on a chair, and he saw that she had tears in her eyes.

'I see,' he said. 'But I'm afraid that Chief of Police Vrommel isn't even in the station . . .' He glanced at his watch. 'He's at the Cafe Vronskij with an inspector who's come here from Maardam. He should be back any minute now, so the best plan is simply for you to wait. If you don't want to tell me all about it, that is. Would you like something to drink?'

Fru Lijphart shook her head. Took a handkerchief out of her handbag and blew her nose.

'How old?' Vegesack asked. 'Your daughter, I mean.'

The woman seemed to be debating with herself whether or not to answer. Then she shrugged and sighed deeply.

'Eighteen. She celebrated her eighteenth birthday on Friday. She came here to meet her father, but she hasn't come back. We live in Moorhuijs . . . Something must have happened to her.'

Vegesack made more notes: *Father? Moorhuijs? Something happened?*

'Why do you think something's happened to her? Have you been in touch with her father? I assume you're divorced?'

Mikaela. 18, he added.

'We most certainly are,' said fru Lijphart after another long exhalation through gritted teeth. 'No, I haven't been in contact with him. He's in the Sidonis Foundation care home, if you know where that is.'

'Oh dear,' said Constable Vegesack before he could stop himself. 'I understand.'

'Do you?'

'Yes. Well . . . no, not really.'

This isn't going very well, he thought, adjusting the

knot of his tie again. Wrote down *Sidonis* in his notebook and avoided looking her in the eye.

'She hasn't rung,' said the woman. 'Mikaela would never leave it this long without ringing, I know that for a fact. Something's happened to her, and it's your bloody lot's responsibility to find her and make sure she comes back home.'

'Could you perhaps say a bit more about . . . about the background? While we're waiting for Vrommel. Instead of just sitting around.'

'Vrommel,' snorted fru Lijphart, standing up again. She started pacing aimlessly back and forth in front of Vegesack's desk, reminding him of a mentally deranged polar bear he'd once seen at Aarlach zoo.

As an alternative to the dachshund.

'You mustn't think I've got much time for your boss,' said fru Lijphart, standing still for a change. 'But it's still the police we turn to when we suspect a crime has been committed, isn't it?'

'A crime?' said Vegesack. 'What sort of crime?'

'Bloody hell!' groaned fru Lijphart, dropping her hands down by her sides again. 'Is this what we pay our taxes for, for Christ's sake? I think I'm going out of my mind.'

Vegesack swallowed and tried desperately to think of something to say that would calm things down, but was spared the trouble. The glass door slammed shut, and a few seconds later in came the chief of police with the woman from Maardam, the detective inspector. Moreno. She was pretty good-looking, that's for sure. Sigrid Lijphart opened her handbag, then shut it again. The constable stood up.

'Ah,' he said. 'May I introduce Chief of Police Vrommel, Inspector Moreno . . . fru Lijphart. But you've met already, of course. You two, I mean . . .'

He blushed, and gestured towards Vrommel and fru Lijphart.

'Good morning,' said Vrommel. 'What's this all about, then?'

'Fru Lijphart has a little problem,' explained Vegesack. 'She says her daughter has gone missing.'

'I expect you remember me,' said Sigrid Lijphart, glaring at Vrommel.

'What did you say your name was?' asked Moreno. 'Lijphart?'

Later – during the weeks that followed and during the autumn when everything had been explained and put on the shelf – Moreno would keep asking herself what made her remain so passive during that first brief meeting between Vrommel, Sigrid Lijphart and herself.

What vague intuition dictated that she should simply sit on a chair and listen?

Just sit there and observe and take note – instead of immediately coming clean and admitting that she had both met and conversed with Mikaela Lijphart while on the train to Lejnice last Saturday.

Surely that would have been the most natural thing to do? To tell the worried mother that she had actually spoken to her missing daughter – albeit a few days ago.

But she said nothing. Simply sat on a chair diagonally behind Sigrid Lijphart and let Vrommel take charge. Let him run the show – it was his baby after all, nobody else's. Full stop.

To begin with he wiped his bald head with a paper tissue.

'I expect you remember me?' said fru Lijphart again.

Vrommel checked in the mirror next to the door that his bald patch was sufficiently lustrous, chucked the tissue into the waste-paper basket and sat down at his desk. Five seconds passed.

'Of course I remember you. It wasn't exactly a pleasant story.'

'I hoped I would never have to come back here again.'

'I can understand that.'

Fru Lijphart took two deep breaths, and tried to lower her shoulders. She's not in love with Vrommel either, Moreno thought, but she's trying to give the impression that she respects him.

'Let's hear it from the beginning,' said Vrommel.

Fru Lijphart took another deep breath.

'We live in Moorhuijs now. We've lived there since . . . well, since then. I've married again.'

Vrommel picked up a ballpoint pen from the black stand.

'Mikaela, my daughter, had her eighteenth birthday last Friday. As we'd planned, we told her then who her real father was. Children have a right to know . . . Once they're old enough. No matter what the circumstances.'

Vrommel clicked his pen and wrote something on the notepad in front of him.

'No matter what the circumstances,' said fru Lijphart again. 'Mikaela said immediately that she was going to go and visit him, and the very next day – last Saturday – she came here. She took the early morning train, it was her decision and I respected it. But since then she's been missing.'

'Missing?' said Vrommel.

'Missing,' said fru Lijphart. 'I've phoned the Sidonis home, and they say she was there between about two and half past four. On Saturday afternoon. But she's not been seen since then.'

Vrommel stroked his moustache with his index finger.

'Hmm,' he said. 'Girls of her age can easily—'

'Rubbish,' said fru Lijphart. 'I know my daughter. She

doesn't conform at all to prejudices of that sort. She had planned to be away for one night, no more. Something's happened to her. I know there's something funny going on. I demand that you do something! For Christ's sake, do something for a change! My girl's disappeared, make sure you find her, or else . . . or else . . .'

The desperation in her voice surged up out of an abyss, it seemed to Moreno. Barely camouflaged panic that originated of course in the most horrific of all horrific scenarios.

A mother who can't find her child. Never mind that the child is now eighteen. Never mind that only a few days have passed. Moreno was about to say something at last, but she was prevented by the chief of police who clicked his pen again and cleared his throat.

'Of course, fru Lijphart. Of course. We shall look into this without further ado. There's no need to get too upset. Let's see now, did you speak to him when you phoned Sidonis? To her father, that is. Perhaps she told him what her plans were.'

'To Arnold? Did I speak to Arnold?'

'Yes. We're talking about Arnold Maager, aren't we?'

Fru Lijphart looked down at the floor for a while. Then:

'Yes,' she said. 'We're talking about Arnold, of course. But I didn't speak to him. I spoke to a carer.'

'Do you have any contact?'

'No.'

'None at all?'

'No.'

'I see,' said Vrommel. 'Where can we get in touch with you?'

It was obvious that fru Lijphart hadn't thought about this aspect of the problem. She sucked her lips and raised her eyebrows.

'Kongershuus – is that still going?'

Vrommel nodded.

'I'll take a room there. For one night at least.'

'Good. I don't suppose you know where your daughter intended to spend the night? Assuming she was intending to spend the night here.'

Fru Lijphart shook her head again. Vrommel stood up to indicate that the conversation was at an end.

'Excellent. We'll be in touch the moment we know anything.'

'This evening?'

'This evening or tomorrow morning.'

Fru Lijphart hesitated for a moment. Then she nodded grimly and left the Lejnice police station.

This has nothing to do with me, thought Detective Inspector Ewa Moreno. Absolutely nothing at all.

TWO

13

21 July 1983

'What is this idea of yours?' she wondered.

He didn't answer. Just put his arm round her, and squeezed her gently. Then they started walking.

In towards the town centre at first, but when they came to the water tower he turned off into Brüggerstraat instead of continuing straight ahead. He was leading, she followed. As usual, she thought. Perhaps she had hoped they would go to one of the cafes in Polderplejn or Grote Marckt, but that was not to be. In recent weeks – for the last two months, in fact, ever since she told him how things stood with her – he had avoided places like that. She had noticed the change before, and had even raised the matter with him; he'd said he preferred to have her to himself.

She both liked and disliked that response. She liked to lie around in the summery darkness with him of course, cuddling and kissing. And being caressed. She enjoyed caressing him as well, and riding on him with her hands on his chest and his hard cock deep inside her. But it was pleasant sitting around in cafes as well. Sitting and smoking and drinking coffee and chatting with people. Just sitting there, looking good and letting them look at her. Maybe that was why, she thought. Maybe it was because he knew she liked being looked at that he'd turned off towards Saar and the football pitches instead of towards the town centre.

'Where are we going?' she asked.

'We need to talk a bit,' he said.

They came to the park behind the fire station, she couldn't remember what it was called. Fire Station Park, perhaps? He was holding his right hand quite a long way down her hip, and she suspected he was beginning to feel randy. It was quite a long time since that had last happened. He led her into the park, and they sat down on a bench well hidden behind some bushes. She couldn't see any other people, but knew that there were usually a few couples cuddling close to the playground at the other end of the park. She'd been there herself quite a few times, but never with him. She couldn't help smiling at the thought.

'Would you like a drop of this?'

He handed her a bottle he'd taken out of his shoulder bag. She took a sip. Some kind of schnapps. It was strong, and made her throat burn. But it was also sweet, warmed her up nicely and tasted of blackcurrants or something similar. She took another bigger sip, and placed her hand between his legs. Just as she'd thought, he already had an erection.

When they had finished they emptied the rest of the bottle and smoked a few cigarettes. They didn't say much – he didn't usually like to chat afterwards. She began to feel quite drunk, but she had a strange feeling of seriousness deep down inside, and guessed that it had to do with Arnold Maager.

And with the baby.

'What was this idea of yours?' she asked again.

He stubbed out his cigarette and spat twice into the gravel. She realized that he was probably just about as drunk as she was. He'd been drinking quite a lot earlier as well. But he could take more, of course: men always could.

'Maager,' he said. 'You said you'd changed your mind. What the hell do you mean?'

She thought for a moment.

'I don't want to go through with it,' she said. 'I don't want to deceive him like that. You and me . . . It's you and me . . . No, I don't want to.'

She was having difficulty in finding the right words.

'We need the money,' he said. 'That's why we did it, can't you see that? We have to put pressure on him.'

'Yes,' she said. 'But I don't want to even so. I intend to tell him the truth.'

'Tell him the truth? Are you out of your mind?'

Then he muttered something that sounded like 'bloody bitch', but of course, she must have misheard him. In any case, he sounded really angry with her: this was the first time it had happened, and she could feel her stomach churning.

'I don't want to,' she said again. 'I can't. It's so wrong . . . Such a bloody lousy thing to do.'

He didn't respond. Just sat there, kicking at the gravel without looking at her. They had lost contact with each other now. There was a vast chasm between them, despite the fact that they had just made love and were still sitting on the same bench in the same bloody park. It felt odd, but she wondered if it would have felt like that if she hadn't been drunk.

'For Christ's sake, it's our baby,' she said. 'I don't want to pretend that anybody else is involved with our baby.'

'Money,' he said simply. He sounded both tired and angry. And drunk as well.

'I know,' she said

She suddenly felt extremely sad. As if everything was

going to pot at a very high speed. Half a minute passed. He was still kicking at the gravel.

'We worked out a plan,' he said eventually. 'For Christ's sake, you were with me all the way . . . You can't just let the old bastard exploit you and then change your mind. He must cough up – or would you rather have the randy old goat instead of me? He's a bloody teacher, for God's sake!'

She suddenly felt sick. Don't throw up now, she told herself. Gritted her teeth and clutched her knees tightly. Breathed deeply and carefully, felt the waves coming and going. When they slowly began to ebb away, she burst out crying instead.

At first he just sat there and let her sob away, but gradually he moved closer to her and put his arm around her shoulder.

It felt good, and she let the tears keep on coming for quite a while.

When you cry, you don't need to speak or think, her mother had once told her, and there was some truth in it. Sometimes her hopeless mother could come out with something sensible, but not very often.

The bells in Waldeskirke, where she had been confirmed two years ago, chimed three times: a quarter to one. He lit two cigarettes, and handed her one. Then he produced a can of beer from his shoulder bag, and opened it.

131

He took several large swigs himself before passing it to her. She drank, and thought that the schnapps had tasted much better. Beer simply couldn't make you feel warm inside. Strong spirits and wine were much better, she'd always thought that. And they didn't make you want to pee so much either.

They sat there in silence for a few more minutes, then he said:

'I have an idea.'

She reminded herself yet again that this was exactly what he had said a few hours ago. Down on the beach. She thought it was strange that he'd been carrying this idea around for such a long time without telling her what it was.

Mind you, this might be another one now.

'What is it?' she asked.

'Let's talk to him,' he said.

She didn't understand what he meant.

'Right now,' he said. 'You can give him a call and we can have a chat with him. And then we'll see.'

He emptied the can of beer and opened a new one.

'How many have you got?' she asked.

'Just one more. Well?'

She thought for a moment. She badly needed a pee. Really badly.

'How?' she said.

'There's a phone box over there.'
He pointed in the direction of the fire station.
'Well?'
She nodded.
'Okay. I must just have a pee first.'

The viaduct? she thought as she stood in the cramped phone box and dialled the number. Why do we have to meet him up there at the railway viaduct?

She got no further with that train of thought as she could hear the telephone ringing at the other end of the line, then somebody picked up the receiver. She took a deep breath, and tried to make her voice steady.

I hope it's not his wife who's answered, she thought.

It was his wife.

14

Sigrid Lijphart managed to get a room at Kongershuus, thanks to a cancellation – the phone call came while she was still in reception, wondering what to do. It was the holiday season, and vacancies in Lejnice and district were just as hard to come by as usual. In a brief moment of weakness she had played with the idea of turning to somebody she had known back in those days – in her former life, sixteen years ago and more – but she rapidly decided that doing so would be about as pleasant as a foul-tasting belch.

Mind you, there were quite a lot of possibilities for her to choose from. Quite a lot of people who would no doubt have received her with open arms. In order to demonstrate how much they sympathized with the problems she'd had, and to find out a bit more about the details, if for no other reason.

But that was all in the past. She had left those people and those relationships – every single one of them – without a moment's hesitation, and she had never missed them at all. The very thought must have been no more than a piece of jetsam floating around in the back of her mind, that was obvious. The idea of making contact with somebody from the past. It would never occur to her to make use of any of those ancient contacts that no longer existed in her consciousness, not in normal circumstances and not now either. It would have felt like . . . well, like opening a box and being hit by a foul stench from something that had spent the last sixteen years rotting away. Ugh, no!

I'd rather sleep on the beach, she thought as she stepped into the lift. Thank goodness I got a room.

It was on the fourth floor with a balcony and a splendid view to the west and south-west over the dunes and the long, gently curving coastline as far as the lighthouse at Gordon's Point.

It was rather expensive, but she only intended to stay the one night, so it was worth it.

She phoned Vrommel and told him where he could contact her, then took a shower. Ordered a pot of coffee from room service, and went out to sit on the balcony.

It was two o'clock. The sun came and went – or the

clouds, to be more precise; but it soon became so warm that she could easily have sat there naked if she'd wanted to. Nobody could see her, apart from helicopter passengers and seagulls. Nevertheless, she kept her bra and pants on. And her wide-brimmed hat and sunglasses. As if there had been somebody watching after all.

Now what? she thought. What the hell am I going to do now?

And panic came creeping up on her like a fever in the night.

Guilt?

Why should I feel guilty? she asked herself. She'd only done what she had to do. Then and now.

She had done what she knew was inevitable. Sooner or later. A child must know the truth about its parents. One side of it, at least. A child had a right to that, an incontrovertible right, and there was no way round that fact.

Sooner or later. And her eighteenth birthday had been decided on long ago.

She thought about Helmut, and his grumbling the previous night.

About Mikaela and her immediate reaction, which had been just about what she had expected.

Or had it really been? Had she really thought that her

daughter would take her mother's advice and let the whole matter rest? Leave everything just as it was, untouched, like something dumb and withered away and forgotten? Not even try to open the lid on it?

Is that really how it was? Had she really believed that her daughter wouldn't try to find her real father?

Of course not. Mikaela was Mikaela, and her mother's daughter. Mikaela has reacted exactly as she had expected. Just as she would have done herself.

Had she blamed her?

Had Mikaela blamed her mother for not telling her sooner? Or for telling her now?

No, and no.

Perhaps to some extent because she hadn't been told the full story – but when she discovered all the facts she would no doubt understand. Definitely. And she had to leave something for Arnold to tell her. Or at least, give him a chance to do so.

But what about Helmut's grumbling?

Not worth bothering about. As usual.

So why this suffocating feeling of guilt?

She'd bought a packet of cigarettes to help her out if an emergency arose. She went to fetch them from her handbag. Went back out onto the balcony, lit one and leaned back on her chair.

The first drag made her feel dizzy.

Arnold? she thought.

Is there something I owe Arnold?

A preposterous thought. She took another drag.

And started thinking about him.

Not a single telephone call.

Not a letter, not even a line, not a word.

Not from him to her, nor from her to him.

It suddenly struck her that if he were dead now, she wouldn't have known. Or was there some kind of duty to inform? On the part of the Sidonis Foundation? Had she signed any documents to that effect? Did they have her name and address? She couldn't remember.

If he'd moved out of the home, perhaps Mikaela would never find him?

But he was still there. She'd rung yesterday to check. Oh yes, Mikaela had been there, and he was still there. Those were the facts.

Presumably he'd been sitting there in his own silent hell for all those years. Sixteen of them. Waiting. Perhaps he'd been waiting for her? Waiting for Mikaela to come? Or maybe for her, his lost wife, to visit him?

But probably not. Most likely he had no memory of anything. He hadn't been well when she took their daughter and abandoned him. There had never been any question of sending him to prison. Not as far as she was aware, at least.

Mad. Completely out of his mind. He'd even wet himself in the middle of the legal proceedings – for some reason that was the detail she had remembered down to the tiniest detail. How he'd just sat there in the middle of the courtroom and let it come gushing forth without moving a muscle . . . No, Arnold had crossed the border into insanity sixteen years ago, and there was no way back.

No way, and no bridges. Just oblivion and a new inner landscape. The more barren and desolate the better, presumably.

She stubbed out her cigarette. Too many words, she thought. There are too many words whizzing around inside me, they're preventing me from thinking clearly.

Arnold? Mikaela?

But underneath the swirling mass of words was only panic, she knew that – and suddenly she wished she had taken Helmut with her.

Helmut the solid rock, the primary rock.

He had offered to come, insisted in a way, but she had kept him at bay.

This had nothing to do with him. Helmut had no part to play in this situation. It was a transaction to be sorted out between Mikaela and her father. And possibly also her mother.

A transaction? she thought. What on earth am I saying? What do I mean?

And what has happened?

It was not until she'd smoked half of her second cigarette and realized that she'd soaked it through and through with her tears that she went inside and made a phone call.

He wasn't at home, but eventually she remembered the number of his mobile and got through to him.

She explained that she had spoken to the police, and that they would no doubt have sorted it all out by the evening – but that she'd taken a room for the night, for safety's sake. And because it would have been a bit too strenuous to drive all the way back home that same day.

Helmut didn't have much to say in reply. They hung up. She went back out on to the balcony. Sat down on the chair and prayed to God for the first time in fifteen years.

She didn't think He was listening.

15

In the end she picked on Münster.

The reason was simple, and she was glad that she didn't need to explain it to anybody. Not to Mikael Bau, nor anybody else.

The facts were straightforward. Detective Inspector Moreno had been in love with Detective Intendent Münster, and they had very nearly had an affair.

Well, no: not in love, she decided. That word was too strong. Something else similar, but . . . but not quite as significant. Much less, in fact. In any case, the thought that she might have been able – if circumstances had been somewhat different – to start a relationship with a man of paedophile tendencies was so absurd, so utterly out of the question, a definite non-starter. Even the mere thought. She swept it to one side with her big biology broom. It was

141

impossible to think of Münster in that role. Absolutely unthinkable.

It was true, needless to say, that it was extremely difficult to imagine any of her colleagues as a child molester, but she hadn't been in love with them (not even in the least significant sense of the phrase). So there wasn't really any contradiction per se. As she seemed to recall having read in her philosophy textbook at grammar school.

So, Münster it was. A rock-solid card to play.

Luckily, he didn't ask her why she had turned to him rather than anybody else. But he did ask several other questions.

Was she out of her mind? for example.

What the hell did she mean?

How could she put any trust in anything said by an arsehole like Franz Lampe-Leermann?

Moreno explained in measured tones that she didn't believe Lampe-Leermann any more than she would believe a horoscope in a girl's magazine, but that she wanted to pass on the allegation as a pure formality since she was now on holiday.

Münster accepted this, but continued commenting for quite some time and she could hear that he was beginning to retreat from his original stance of outraged rejection.

Just as she had done herself. Just as that bastard Lampe-Leermann had no doubt assumed they would do.

'He must have something up his sleeve, don't you think?'

'I don't know,' said Moreno.

'But he must surely have good cause to come out with an allegation like this.'

'You'd have thought so, yes.'

'What conclusion have you drawn yourself?'

'I haven't drawn any conclusion at all,' said Moreno. 'But I haven't been sleeping very well.'

'I can well believe that,' said Münster. 'What the hell is one supposed to do in a case like this?'

'Don't go to Hiller with it, whatever else you do.'

'Thanks for the tip,' said Münster. 'Do you have any more?'

'I suppose there's only one possibility.'

'What's that?'

'Go and talk to Scumbag.'

'I beg your pardon?'

'I'm sorry. Talk to Franz Lampe-Leermann.'

'Hmm,' said Münster. 'Where is he now?'

'In Emsbaden,' said Moreno. 'He's sitting there, waiting for you. I suggest you take care of this yourself, and be extremely discreet.'

Münster said nothing for a few seconds.

'I'll be in touch,' he said eventually. 'Thank you for

ringing. Have lots of enjoyable, lazy days, so that you're a good cop again when you come back to work in August.'

'I'll do my best,' said Inspector Moreno.

That afternoon they took the ferry out to the islands. They spent an hour at low tide strolling along the beaches on Werkeney, then took a smaller boat to Doczum, the site of a bird sanctuary, where they had dinner at an inn in the square surrounded by pot-bellied and well-coiffured tourists of a certain age, showing off their tans.

Mikael explained to Moreno, who was eyeing their fellow-diners with some scepticism, that it was the custom for him and his family to tour the islands every summer. They had done that every year for as long as he could remember, with the exception of 1988 when he had spent a year as an exchange student in Boston.

'You mean you've spent every single summer in Lejnice – or Port Hagen – for the whole of your life?' Moreno asked.

'Yes, apart from that one. As I said. Why do you ask?'

Moreno didn't answer.

No, she thought. I've already decided that it's none of my business.

Nothing to do with me and certainly not with Mikael.

★

It was not until they were on the evening ferry back to Lejnice that the topic cropped up. And it was not her fault.

'You haven't said a single word about Scumbag all day,' said Mikael.

'True,' said Moreno. 'Case closed.'

Mikael raised an eyebrow.

'Really? How did you manage that?'

'I've delegated it. I'm on holiday.'

His eyebrow remained high up on his forehead. It suddenly struck her that he looked like an actor – a third-rate actor in a turkey of a B-film. Was the veil about to fall off at last? she wondered.

'What's the matter with you?' she asked. 'You look odd.'

'There's nothing the matter with me,' he said, and his face began to take on a sort of pedagogical expression. 'It's you there's something the matter with. If the Lampe-Leermann business is over and done with now, I'd like to know what the hell you're brooding over instead.'

'Brooding? Me? What the devil do you mean?'

She felt what must be a mixture of resignation and irritation beginning to rise up inside her. And perhaps anger. At his would-be-wise posture – who did he think he was talking to?

He seemed to register her reactions and remained silent for a while. Stared out to sea while tapping his knee with his index and middle fingers. It was a bad habit of his; she'd noticed it long ago, but it was only now that she had recognized it for what it was: a bad habit.

'Brooding,' he said again. 'Don't be silly. Either you're beginning to grow tired of me, or there's something else the matter. I prefer to think it's the latter. I'm not an idiot.'

Her immediate reaction was to agree with him. Mikael Bau was not an idiot. Claus Badher, who she had dumped five years ago, had been an idiot, so she had some experience of the type. She could make comparisons, and knew what was involved.

One needed to know when one had completed the first chapter of a relationship and was on the way into chapter two – she had read that somewhere, and committed it to memory. Oh, bugger, she thought. Is it never possible to leave your job behind? Does it always have to be there in the background, imposing itself on everything else?

She immediately received an answer from another voice inside her.

It's not a question of your job, it said. It's a question of being considerate and sympathetic towards other human beings. A missing girl and a desperate mother.

Mikael continued drumming his fingers. The evening sun broke through a cloud: she closed her eyes to shut out the almost horizontal beams and thought for a while.

'Something odd happened at the police station,' she said in the end.

He stopped drumming with his fingers. Then burst out laughing.

'*King of the Royal Mounted*,' he said.

'What the hell has *King of the Royal Mounted* to do with this?'

He flung out his arms.

'Never rests. Never sleeps. Why do women so seldom have a real literary education?'

It took her five minutes to tell the story.

That's all there was to it. A girl crying on a train. An unknown father in a home. A worried mother in a police station.

Something that had happened rather a long time ago.

When she had finished, the ferry had just begun to dock and she noticed that Mikael had acquired a vertical furrow on his forehead that wasn't usually there. It suited him, in a way; but she didn't know what it signified.

He had no comment to make before they had gone ashore; and once they had left behind all the pot-bellied and well-coiffured, most of his concentration needed to be directed at remembering where they had parked the car. It had been bright and sunny in the morning, but now the car park was enveloped by a damp mist that seemed to distort the perspective and change the circumstances in some strange way.

'Over there,' said Moreno, pointing. 'I recognize that seagull on the shed roof.'

Mikael nodded, and twirled the car keys round his index finger. Then it all began to come back to him. Slowly, like a patient suffering from dementia on a rainy Monday.

'It must be . . .' he said. 'Yes, as far as I can remember, that must be it. What else could it be?'

Moreno waited.

'What the hell was she called? Take it easy now, it'll come . . . Winnie something? Yes, Winnie Maas, that was her name. It must be . . . er, what did you say? How long ago?'

'Sixteen years,' said Moreno. 'Are you saying you know about it?'

'Hmm,' said Mikael. 'I think so. I've lived out here every summer, as I said . . . 1983, then? Yes, that must be it.'

'She was two years old when her father vanished,' said Moreno. 'And she was eighteen last Friday. Or so she said,'

'Winnie Maas,' said Mikael again, nodding. 'Yes, it was a pretty distasteful story. I was about the same age as she was. But I didn't know her, we never really made close contact with the natives – that's what we used to call them. With the occasional exception, of course. There were half a dozen of us cousins, quite enough company to keep us going, and more besides. If you wanted some time to yourself you had to lock yourself into the outside loo, or dig yourself down into the dunes.'

'But who was Winnie Maas?' asked Moreno impatiently. 'I'm sorry, but I couldn't care less about your cousins.'

They found Mikael's old Trabant between a glistening silver-coloured Mercedes and a glistening red BMW. Like an old jackdaw between two eagles, Moreno thought. But not quite dead yet. They clambered into the jackdaw. Mikael started the engine, producing a considerable cloud of smoke, and they started manoeuvring their way out of the car park. It seemed that he was trying to create some kind of dramatic pause before he answered.

'Winnie Maas was a girl who was murdered that summer,' he explained eventually as he switched on the headlights. 'She was found dead on the railway line under the viaduct. We shall be passing over it in two minutes from now, so you can get an idea of what it's like, Inspector.'

He laughed, but seemed to notice that it sounded hollow.

'Sorry about that. Anyway, she was lying dead down

there on the railway line, and the murderer was sitting beside her. At least, that's the official version.'

'The official version? Do you mean there are other versions?'

He shrugged. 'Who knows? I recall that there was a lot of chatter about this, that and the other, but I suppose that's only to be expected. I think it was the only murder there's been out here for the last thirty or forty years . . . I seem to remember that there was a blacksmith who killed his wife with a crowbar at the end of the fifties. So it's no wonder that there was a lot of speculation. And there was something else as well . . . Something scandalous. The whole town was going on about it . . . You know what it's like.'

Moreno nodded. 'And who was the murderer?'

'I can't remember his name. But it could well have been Maager. In any case, he was a teacher at the local school, which didn't make things any better of course. He'd had the girl as a pupil of his and . . . Well, it seems they had an affair as well.'

'Really?' said Moreno, watching the paedophile cloud welling up so quickly and strangely in her mind's eye. But sixteen years of age? It must have been just inside the limits of the law, thought the police officer inside her. At that time.

But not the laws of morality, objected the woman and

the human being Ewa Moreno. At any time. Teacher and pupil, that was outrageous, even if it wasn't exactly anything new.

'I think she was pregnant as well. Oh, it was a pretty juicy story, when you come to think about it. And this is where it happened.'

They followed a long bend and came up to the viaduct that ran over the railway line. A good twenty metres above it, Moreno reckoned. Unusually high, but no doubt there must be a reason for that. Mikael slowed down and pointed.

'Down there, if I remember rightly. They say he pushed her over the edge from up here – the railing wasn't as high then as it is now. I think they built this new railing as a direct consequence of what happened then, in fact.'

He pulled up close to the railing, and came to a halt.

'Mind you, she could have jumped over the railing of her own accord,' he added.

Moreno wound down the window and looked out. Tried to make a sober and factual analysis. The way it looked today it wouldn't have been easy to heave a body over the railing and down on to the track below. Not, at least, if the body had been more or less alive and able to resist. The railing was now almost two metres high.

'There's no memorial plaque at least,' said Mikael. 'Thank God for that.'

He released the clutch pedal and they started moving forward again. Moreno wound up the window, and noticed that she had goose pimples on her forearms.

'I don't remember what happened next – the outcome of the trial and so on. It must have been held in the autumn, after we'd moved back to Groenhejm.'

'But he was the one who did it, was he?' Moreno wondered. 'That teacher. Did he confess?'

Mikael drummed on the wheel with his fingers before answering.

'Yes, it must have been him. What happened sent him round the bend. He was sitting beside the body when they found it, as I said. Didn't try to run away. But they couldn't get much sense out of him. But what does this business of the girl and her mother have to do with all this? Can you enlighten me? You're not suggesting that there's a link, are you?'

Moreno didn't answer immediately. She tried to run through everything inside her head one more time first, but it was difficult to draw any conclusion different from the one she'd drawn already.

'I don't know,' she said. 'But in a way I think it probably is. Mikaela Lijphart was going to visit her father, who for some reason she hadn't seen since she was two. Something had happened then, that's how she put it: *something had happened*. Her father was evidently in a care home just outside Lejnice. Everything seems to suggest it has to do with this Winnie Maas business. Do you know if he had any children, this teacher? A little daughter, for instance . . . Aged about two or thereabouts.'

'I've no idea,' said Mikael. 'How the hell could I know? But I do recall reading something about the court case later on . . . While it was taking place. Apparently it wasn't possible to cross-examine him. Either he would break down, sobbing, or he'd just sit there as silent as the grave. I probably remember that because it was the exact phrase the reporter used: "as silent as the grave".'

'So he must have been a psychiatric case, irrespective of the verdict – is that what you're saying?'

'Presumably. Sidonis, did you say?'

Moreno nodded. 'Do you know it?'

'Only by name,' said Mikael. 'All children know the name of the nearest loony bin, don't they?'

'I'm sure they do,' said Moreno. 'So that explains that, then. What an uplifting story . . .'

They drove in silence for a couple of minutes.

'Ergo,' said Mikael eventually. 'Correct me if I'm wrong. The girl comes here to visit her father, the murderer, whom she hasn't seen since she was two years old. She meets him, talks to him for a few hours, then disappears. Is that what you've been brooding over all day?'

'Not quite,' said Moreno. 'It was you who told me her

father could call himself a murderer – only a few minutes ago. How's your short-term memory?'

Mikael didn't respond. Merely changed the rhythm of his drumming, and sat there in silence again.

'What are we going to do?' he asked just as a sign saying *Port Hagen 6* flashed past Moreno's window.

Moreno thought for a few seconds. Then:

'Turn back,' she said.

'Eh?'

'Turn back. We must go and speak to Vrommel.'

'Now?' said Mikael. 'It's nearly half past nine. Can't we leave it until tomorrow? I suspect he hasn't read *King of the Royal Mounted* either.'

Moreno bit her lower lip and pondered for a moment.

'All right,' she said. 'Tomorrow it is.'

16

Vrommel was doing heel-raising exercises.

'Achilles tendons and calves,' he explained. 'You've got to keep your body in trim as well. On a day like this I thought you'd be lying on a towel on the beach.'

'This afternoon,' said Moreno. 'I just thought I'd ask if the Lijphart girl had turned up.'

'Unfortunately.'

'Unfortunately not?'

'Unfortunately not.'

'Could we sit down for a bit?' suggested Moreno. 'I actually met the girl on the train, and so perhaps—'

'A routine matter,' interrupted Vrommel. 'Nothing you need worry about. If she doesn't get in touch today we'll send out a Wanted notice tomorrow.'

He continued stubbornly raising himself up and down on his toes. After every raise he emitted a brief guttural grunt, and the colour of his face confirmed that he wasn't cheating, but putting his heart and soul into it.

He's not compos mentis, Moreno thought, leaning on the edge of the desk. Another one of 'em. Ah well . . .

'What do you think has happened?' she asked.

Vrommel sank down on his heels, and stayed there. Took two deep breaths and started head-turnings. From right to left. Left to right. Slowly and methodically.

'Nothing,' he said.

'Nothing?' said Moreno. 'But the girl's disappeared.'

'Girls do disappear,' said Vrommel. 'Always have done. They come back a little redder in the cheek.'

What the hell . . . ? Moreno thought, but managed to twist her lips into something she hoped might be interpreted as a smile. Albeit a stiff one. And a brief one.

'So you don't think it has anything to do with that other business from a few years ago?'

'Oh, you know about that, do you?'

'A bit. It was pretty sensational, I gather . . .'

Vrommel said nothing.

'I'd have thought there might be some sort of link . . . Somehow or other.'

'I don't think so.'

'No? But wouldn't it be an idea to talk to the staff at the Sidonis home even so? Ask how the meeting between father and daughter went . . . Where she went afterwards, that kind of thing.'

'Already taken care of.'

'Really?'

Silence. Right, left. Breathing out, breathing in.

'Vegesack went out there last night. Why are you poking around in this business, Inspector? Do you think I don't know how to do my job?'

'Forgive me,' said Moreno. 'Of course not. It's just that I was a bit taken by the girl. I met her quite by chance on the train when I was on my way here. You were the one in charge of the investigation sixteen years ago, is that right?'

'Who else?' said Vrommel. 'What do you do in the way of physical training?'

Talk about changing the subject, Moreno thought, and smiled genuinely.

'Oh, I go jogging, and to the gym,' she said.

'Gym!' snorted Vrommel. 'A bloody silly newfangled racket.'

Moreno decided not to take the bait.

'What did Vegesack have to say?' she asked instead.

'Nothing at all,' said Vrommel, twisting his head so far to the right that Moreno could hear his cervical vertebrae creaking.

'Nothing at all?'

'He hasn't delivered his report yet,' said Vrommel. 'He takes the morning off on Thursdays. Looking after his ancient mum, or something of the sort. Another bloody silly newfangled racket.'

Moreno wasn't sure if the chief of police was attacking motherhood itself, or the fact that there were still people who accepted a certain amount of responsibility for their parents. She also began to feel that it was becoming more and more difficult to remain in the same room as Vrommel without giving him a kick between the legs or suggesting he should go and take a running jump . . . So she cleared her throat and stood up instead. Thanked him for being so cooperative. So extremely cooperative.

'No problem,' said Vrommel. 'Code of honour. Go and lie down in the sun now. We'll do all that's required of us, in accordance with the rulebook.'

Kiss my arse, thought Moreno when she had emerged into the sunlight. Code of honour! In accordance with the rulebook! Oh yes! She didn't doubt for one second that Chief of Police Vrommel knew precisely what to do in a situation like this.

How to handle girls who disappeared then turned up again a little redder in the cheek.

She crossed over the square and sat down at a table in

the pavement area of Cafe Darm. Ordered a cappuccino and freshly pressed orange juice and continued to wonder what to do next – Vegesack wasn't due back at the police station until one o'clock, she had already established that after a chat with fröken Glossmann in reception. Then she suddenly caught sight of Sigrid Lijphart sitting only a couple of tables away.

She hesitated for a moment, then took her cup and glass and asked if she might join fru Lijphart.

Of course. Fru Lijphart didn't look as if she had slept very well that night – hardly surprising, after all. She seemed to have been crying, Moreno thought, repressing an impulse to place her hand on fru Lijphart's arm.

She wasn't quite sure why she had repressed that impulse, but it seemed obvious that the explanation had to do with her profession as a police officer rather than her being a woman. It wasn't always easy to reconcile these two natures side by side within her. She had thought about that before. Many a time.

'How are you feeling?' she asked cautiously.

Fru Lijphart took out a handkerchief and blew her nose.

'Not so good,' she said.

'I understand,' said Moreno.

'Do you?' said fru Lijphart. 'Do you have children of your own?'

Moreno shook her head. 'Not yet.'

Yet? She gave a start and wondered why that phrase had just popped out of her mouth. Noted that whatever else it might be, it wasn't a police expression – rather some sort of Freudian slip: so the balance between her natures seemed to have been restored.

'I'm so worried,' said fru Lijphart, scraping her coffee cup against the saucer. 'So really, really worried. Something . . . Something must have happened to her. Mikaela would never . . . No, so many days have passed now.'

Her voice broke. Her body shuddered violently – like the after-effects of an attack of sobbing, Moreno thought – then she straightened her back and tried to collect herself.

'I'm sorry. It's just that it's so hard.'

'I understand,' said Moreno again. 'If I can do anything to help, just say the word.'

Fru Lijphart looked at her in surprise.

'You are . . . Are you a police officer here in Lejnice?'

Moreno smiled.

'No, Maardam. I'm here on holiday. It's just that I had to see the chief of police about a certain matter.'

'I see.'

There followed a moment's silence, and Moreno had time to ask herself what that *I see* might mean. If her interpretation was right, it seemed to indicate a certain degree of relief that Moreno wasn't a member of Vrommel's normal staff.

Very understandable, in that case.

'Have you tried to do anything off your own bat?' she asked.

Fru Lijphart shook her head.

'No. I'll meet Vrommel and that constable of his at one o'clock . . . No, I don't feel that I can go round talking to people in this town. Not after what happened. I've sort of turned my back on it all . . . Left it behind me. I simply wouldn't be able to look it in the face again now.'

'I don't suppose you know where Mikaela intended to spend the night, do you?'

Fru Lijphart looked unsure.

'I've no idea,' she said. 'She just upped and left. Natur-ally . . . naturally it was a sort of punishment on her part – that's how I interpret it, at least. Punishing me for not having told her sooner. And punishing Helmut as well, perhaps. He's my husband, Mikaela's stepfather. A sort of demonstration, I reckon. She simply said she was going to come here and meet him, then she left. But I know that she wouldn't keep out of touch like this. I don't suppose everybody knows their own children inside out, but I do.'

'So you don't think that this is part of the demonstra-tion? Leaving you to stew for a while?'

'No.' Fru Lijphart shook her head emphatically.

'Absolutely not. Obviously I was prepared for her to stay away for a day and maybe a night as well, but not as long as this. It's now . . . it's now nearly a week. Good Lord, why doesn't he do something, that damned chief of police?'

Moreno thought it best not to respond to that, so she said nothing for a while and tried to look benignly neutral.

'And you don't want to go and talk to your ex-husband?' she asked in due course.

Fru Lijphart gave a start as if she had just burnt her fingers.

'To Arnold? Talk to Arnold? No, I can't see what good that would do.'

'You could find out what they talked about, for instance,' said Moreno. 'Mikaela and him.'

Fru Lijphart didn't answer at first, looked as if she were contemplating the difference between the plague and cholera.

'No,' she said eventually. 'I don't think that whatever has happened had anything to do with that. Besides, that police constable has been to talk to him, so there's no point in anybody else doing so.'

'What actually happened?'

'What do you mean?'

'Sixteen years ago. What happened?'

Fru Lijphart looked genuinely surprised.

'You must know, surely.'

'Only what was said at the police station,' she lied.

'You're not from here?'

'Maardam, as I said.'

Fru Lijphart fished a cigarette out of her handbag. Put it into her mouth and lit it in so clumsy a fashion that Moreno realized that she was not a regular smoker.

'He had sex with a sixteen-year-old,' she said after the first puff. 'A pupil of his.'

Moreno waited.

'He made her pregnant, then he killed her. My husband. I'm talking about the person I was married to, the father of Mikaela. Note that.'

'That's terrible,' said Moreno. 'It must have been horribly traumatic for you.'

Fru Lijphart eyed her for several seconds, apparently assessing her.

'There was only one thing to do,' she said. 'Close the door and start all over again. That's what I did. I knew that I had to create a new life for myself, for me and my daughter. If we were going to keep our heads above water. There are some things you can't do anything about. You just have to turn your back on them. I hope you understand what I'm saying.'

Moreno nodded vaguely. Wondered if she really did. Understand, that is. If she agreed with this sorely tried woman that there were certain things that couldn't – shouldn't – be faced up to. Understood or forgiven. They should simply be forgotten.

Perhaps, she thought. But perhaps not. No doubt you ought to be fully aware of all the circumstances before you made up your mind, in any case. All the circumstances.

'Why did you tell your daughter about it?' she asked.

'Because I had to,' answered fru Lijphart without hesitation. 'I've always known that despite everything, I would have to tell her. Always known. It wasn't something I could get round, so I made up my mind that that was the right moment. Her eighteenth birthday. It's easier if you pin a time on to difficulties like that – I don't know if you've found that as well.'

Moreno wasn't convinced she could see the logic in that, but it seemed obvious that fru Lijphart believed what she said.

'What about that girl?' wondered Moreno. 'The one that—'

'A little whore,' interrupted fru Lijphart just as unequivocally. 'There are types who are born to become whores – I'm not being prejudiced, just realistic. Arnold wasn't the first man she went to bed with, not by any means. No, I don't want to talk about this, I'm sorry.'

'What was her name?' asked Moreno.

'Winnie,' said fru Lijphart, curling her lips in disgust.

'Winnie Maas. He went out of his mind as a result, my husband – I take it you knew about that in any case? Went mad, just like that.'

'I gathered that when you spoke to Vrommel,' said Moreno, glancing at the clock. 'Oh dear, I think I'm going to be late. Forgive me for intruding, but if there's anything you think I could help you with, don't hesitate to get in touch. You can ring me on my mobile. I'm really sorry for your sake, and I hope Mikaela turns up again soon.'

She handed over her card, and fru Lijphart looked at it before putting it away in her handbag.

'Thank you,' she said. 'I'm going home tomorrow no matter what happens. I'm not spending more than two nights in this town, I couldn't cope with that. I'm very grateful for your concern, it's been good talking to you.'

'No problem,' said Moreno, getting to her feet. 'Now, I must dash. My fiancé will be sitting waiting for me.'

Her fiancé (lover? boyfriend? bloke?) wasn't sitting in Donners Park waiting for her, as arranged. He was lying on his back under a chestnut tree instead, his head resting on a root, trying to eat an ice cream without spilling it all over his face.

'You're late,' he pointed out as she flopped down beside

him. 'But it doesn't matter. That's a woman's privilege after all, and I desire you just as much anyway.'

'Good,' said Moreno. 'I suspect you're also a little bit desirable in some people's eyes. A pity you ended up with somebody as hard-boiled as I am. But don't give up. How did it go?'

Mikael raised himself into a half-sitting position, leaning against the trunk of the tree. As a gentlemanly gesture he gave her the remaining twelfth or so of the ice cream and wiped his hands on the grass.

'Not too badly,' he said. 'If you bear in mind that I'm an amateur at this sort of thing, at least. I've dug up fru Maas's address – she still lives here in Lejnice. In a flat in Goopsweg. More or less in the very centre of town. And the mystery of where she spent the night is also solved.'

'Where she spent the night?' said Moreno. 'You mean that Mikaela Lijphart spent the night in Lejnice, despite everything?'

'Yes. In the youth hostel, as we thought. Out at Missenraade. But only the Saturday night, unfortunately. She took her rucksack and caught the bus into town at about ten on Sunday morning, and that's where the trail peters out, I'm afraid. I talked to one of the girls in reception at the youth hostel. She claimed she remembered her very well, but she had no idea about where Mikaela was intending to go to. They are always more or less full up out there in the summer, but nevertheless she was pretty sure that Mikaela had taken the bus into Lejnice on Saturday evening as well. And come back again, of course. So there you have it – but goodness knows where that leads us to. Nowhere, I assume.'

'You never know,' said Moreno with a sigh. 'That's the problem with what we do. And the charm, of course. A pretty grim sort of charm, but that's what it usually looks like. Lots of straggling strands leading out higgledy-piggledy into the darkness – I'm afraid that's yet another quotation from *the Chief Inspector* – and then all of a sudden one thing leads to another and it's all sorted before you know where you are. Hmm, why am I sitting here babbling on like this? It must be the heat.'

Mikael observed her with interest.

'You like it,' he said. 'It has nothing to do with the heat. You don't need to be ashamed of liking the job you do.'

'There's like and like,' said Moreno. 'You have to try to look at things from an angle that makes them bearable, don't you think? I don't suppose what you do in the social services is idyllic all round the clock.'

Mikael scratched at the stubble on his chin that must be about three or four days old now.

'You mean you have to be an optimist even though you're really a pessimist?' he said. 'Yes, that's not a bad principle, I suppose. Do you know who the funniest humorists are, by the way? Gravediggers. Gravediggers and pathologists. There must be a reason for that. Anyway, do you want to carry on playing the private detective for the whole of your holiday, or shall we go and lie on the beach for a while?'

'The beach,' said Moreno. 'Several hours, at least. I want to exchange a few words with Vegesack before I pack it in, but there's no rush. Perhaps he was right after all, Vrommel. Perhaps she's just run off for a bit of fun. We'll see what happens when they slam a Wanted notice on her tomorrow. It's not as easy to turn one's back on things as a lot of people seem to think.'

On the way down to the sea another question cropped up inside her head.

In connection with that business of having children. And very definitely in connection with the business of optimism versus pessimism.

Wouldn't it be better never to have any – children, that is – than to have to cope with their disappearance one fine day?

Or their being found dead on a railway line under a viaduct?

Another question without an answer, but she didn't take it up with Mikael.

17

'Coffee?' said Vrommel.

'No thank you,' said Sigrid Lijphart. 'I've just had some.'

Constable Vegesack was about to say that he wouldn't mind a cup, but held himself in check.

'Well?' said Vrommel, sitting down at his desk. 'Arnold Maager. What have you got to report?'

Vegesack cleared his throat and leafed quickly through his notebook.

'There's not a lot to say, really,' he said. 'He's a pretty uncommunicative type, this herr Maager.'

'Uncommunicative?' said Vrommel.

'Introverted if you prefer,' said Vegesack 'Still, he's ill, of course. It wasn't easy to squeeze anything out of him.'

'Did you tell him that Mikaela had gone missing?' asked fru Lijphart.

Her voice is reminiscent of a violin string, Vegesack thought.

'Of course,' he said. 'More or less straight away. Maybe I should have kept that back for a while. He was sort of struck dumb when I told him that.'

'Struck dumb?' said Vrommel.

'Well, he was dead quiet in any case,' said Vegesack. 'I tried to find out what they'd talked about when she visited him on Saturday, but he just sat there shaking his head. In the end he started crying.'

'Crying?' said Vrommel.

Does that idiot have to sit there repeating a word out of every sentence I say? Vegesack wondered. But he managed to restrain himself. Looked at the woman sitting by his side instead. Fru Lijphart was sitting with her back as straight as a poker, her hands on her knees, and she seemed somehow distant. Almost as if she'd been drugged.

What a strange collection of people I find myself surrounded by, Vegesack thought. Arnold Maager. Chief of Police Vrommel. Sigrid Lijphart. They all seem to be a sort of caricature. Comic-strip characters.

Or was everybody like this, if you got to know them a little better? That could be a topic worth thinking about in connection with the book, perhaps. Psychological realism, as it was called. He turned over a page in his notebook.

'I spoke to one of the carers and a doctor as well,' he said. 'They said it was quite typical behaviour on Maager's part. Confrontation avoidance, they called it. That means that you avoid all uncomfortable situations and retreat into yourself instead of confronting things or people—'

'Thank you,' said Vrommel. 'We understand what it means. Did you meet anybody who had talked to the girl while she was there?'

'One person,' said Vegesack. 'A carer by the name of Proszka. He was simply the one who received her when she arrived, and took her to where she wanted to go. He didn't see her leaving Sidonis, unfortunately. Anyway, I'm afraid all this isn't going to help us very much – with regard to Mikaela's disappearance, that is.'

Fru Lijphart sighed deeply and seemed to shrink somewhat.

'Something has happened,' she said. 'I just know that something has happened to her. You must . . . You *must* do something.'

Vrommel leaned back on his chair and tried to frown.

'All right,' he said. 'We'll issue a Wanted notice. I'm not as sure as you are that she isn't just staying away of her own free will, but never mind. Radio, television, the press, all the usual outlets. Vegesack, look after that.'

'Shouldn't we check up with her acquaintances?' Vegesack wondered.

'Acquaintances?' repeated Vrommel.

'Yes, her friends . . . Or boyfriends. I mean, it's possible that she's just lying low somewhere and has been in touch with somebody she knows. Somebody apart from her mother, that is.'

'I don't think so,' said fru Lijphart.

Vegesack closed his notebook.

'Maybe not, but surely we should check up even so?'

'Of course,' said Vrommel. 'Fru Lijphart, you can sit down with Constable Vegesack and go through all the possible names. No stone must be left unturned from now on. One hundred per cent effort.'

Good God, Vegesack thought.

'Okay,' he said.

'When you have a complete list, phone all those who seem most likely. Any objections, fru Lijphart?'

He stroked his tiny moustache and glared at Sigrid Lijphart. She avoided his gaze. Looked down at her hands, which were still clasped in her lap. It was several seconds before she replied.

'No,' she said. 'No objections at all. Why should I have any objections?'

As Moreno was walking the short distance from Grote Marckt, where she had been dropped off by Mikael, to Goopsweg, she asked herself why on earth she didn't just walk away from all this.

Why she refused to drop the disappearance of Mikaela Lijphart.

Or assumed disappearance. After all, the probability that the girl had simply taken the opportunity of lying low for a few days (now that she had celebrated her eighteenth birthday) and as a result arousing guilt feelings in her parents (in Arnold Maager as well?) . . . well, despite everything it was surely quite strong?

Or wasn't it?

Had something happened to Mikaela Lijphart? To use her mother's euphemism, *had something happened to her*?

If so, what?

And what about this old story? Her father – the teacher Arnold Maager – who had an affair with one of his pupils. Made her pregnant. Killed her. Went mad as a result.

Was that really what had happened? Was it so straightforward?

It was a horrendous story, of course, but somehow or other Moreno thought it sounded too clinical. Clinical and neatly tied up. Shove the man into the loony bin, get rid of the girl. Put the lid on it for sixteen years, and then . . . ? Yes, what then?

But she was well aware that it wasn't merely curiosity that drove her. There was something fascinating about the story, Moreno was the first to acknowledge that: but there were other motives too.

Other reasons why she didn't want to drop the whole thing. Why she couldn't simply turn her back on it all.

Ethical? Yes, in fact. It's only when you're on leave that you have time to be moral – somebody had said that, she couldn't remember who. Reinhart or Van Veeteren, presumably – no, hardly *the Chief Inspector*: if there was anybody who never ignored the moral aspect of things, he was the one. Not even in the most trivial of circumstances. Was that why he'd retired early? she asked herself. Was that why he'd had enough?

Anyway, there was something in the thought. The one about morals and being on leave. When we're pedalling away on the usual treadmill, Moreno thought, we slip hastily past goodness knows how many blind beggars (or terrified children or women beaten black and blue). But if we come across one of them while we're strolling along a beach – well, that's a totally different situation.

Morals need time.

And now she had time. Time to remember the weeping girl on the train. Time to think about her and her background and her worried mother.

And Maager, the teacher.

Time to make a diversion and take an extra hour on a sunny morning like this one – while Mikael had gone off to make arrangements with some workmen about something that needed doing on Tschandala: the gutters, if she remembered rightly.

She turned into Goopsweg and started looking for the right number. Twenty-six. There it was. A block of flats, three storeys high. Boring seventies design in grey brick and concrete speckled with damp patches. But such buildings no doubt had to exist even in a comfortable if slightly tarnished little idyll like this.

I'm a journalist, she reminded herself. I must remember to behave like a journalist. Be friendly and courteous, and make lots of notes. She hadn't managed to think of a better cover to enable her to talk to a woman about her murdered daughter.

She certainly didn't want some kind of accreditation from Chief of Police Vrommel. Not yet, anyway.

She crossed over the street, entered the courtyard and found the right entrance door without any difficulty. She walked up the stairs to the top floor. Stood for half a minute outside the door, composing herself, then rang the bell.

No reaction.

She waited for a while, then rang again. Pressed her ear cautiously against the door and listened.

Not a sound. As quiet as the grave.

Ah well, thought Detective Inspector Moreno. At least I've made an honest attempt.

But when she came out into the sunshine again, it felt as if she still had some way to go before she'd fulfilled her moral obligations. As if she didn't have the right to wash her hands of the Lijphart girl. Not really the right, and certainly not yet.

If all citizens had the same sense of responsibility as I have, she thought as she very nearly stumbled over a black cat that came scuttling out of a hole in a fence, what a marvellous world we'd live in!

Then she burst out laughing, making the cat turn round and scamper back to where it had come from.

Sigrid Lijphart just managed to catch a train that left the station in Lejnice at 17.03. It set off as she was sitting down on a window seat in the half-empty coach, and she was almost immediately overcome by a feeling of having abandoned her daughter.

She lit a cigarette in an attempt to counteract the attack of conscience. And looked around meticulously before drinking the last drops in the hip flask she kept in her handbag.

It didn't help much. Neither the nicotine nor the spirits. By the time the train had reached full speed, it was obvious to her that it had been a mistake to leave. To return home like this without Mikaela.

How could she leave her fate – and her daughter's fate – in Chief of Police Vrommel's hands? she asked herself. Was there anything at all to suggest that he would be able to solve the problem? Vrommel! She recalled how even sixteen years ago she had regarded him as an utterly useless berk, and there was nothing to suggest that he had improved since then. Nothing that she had noticed during the days she had spent in Lejnice, at least.

And now he was the one who was going to find out what had happened to Mikaela. Chief Inspector Vrommel! How could she – as a mother and a thinking woman – allow that to happen? How could she hand over responsibility to such an arch-cretin?

She stubbed out her cigarette and looked out of the window at the sun-drenched polder-landscape. Canals. Black-and-white cattle grazing. A cluster of low stone-built houses with a church steeple sticking up like an antenna or a tentative attempt to make contact with the endless sky.

What am I going on about? she suddenly thought. What am I sitting here gawping at? It doesn't really matter if it's Vrommel or somebody else. It's all about Mikaela. Where on earth is she? What's happened? Arnold . . . Just think that Arnold might actually know something about it!

And once again this inexplicable feeling of guilt dug its claws into her. As inexplicable and irritating as a sore on her soul. Why? Why should she – Sigrid Lijphart, formerly Sigrid Maager – have anything to reproach herself for? In fact she had done more than anybody could have demanded of her . . . Much more. She had told Mikaela about Arnold, despite the fact that it would have been much easier to say nothing. She could just as well have remained silent about the whole affair. Now and for ever. That was the line Helmut would have preferred to take – he hadn't said that in so many words, of course: but then, Helmut was not one for saying anything in so many words.

Keep quiet and let the past be buried. That's what she could have done. Nobody could have asked more of her than that, and nobody had done so either.

So why? Why hadn't she taken the easy way out for once? Why always this unreasonable and inflexible demand for honesty?

But hardly had she formulated these questions than his voice rang out from the past.

Motives, it said. *You are falsifying your motives.*

She couldn't remember the context in which he'd said it, but that was irrelevant. She didn't understand what he'd meant even so.

Not then, and not now, perhaps twenty years later. Odd that she should remember that. Odd that it occurred to her now. Motives?

She sighed and lit another cigarette. Scrunched the

packet up and chucked it into the litter bin, despite the fact that there were four or five cigarettes left in it.

Enough of that now, she thought. I don't want to come back home to Helmut stinking of tobacco. I must observe the proprieties.

But nothing seemed to go right. That question that she didn't even dare to formulate in silence, not even deep, deep down at the bottom of her consciousness – it continued to float around inside her without being expressed, forcing all other thoughts to flee.

That question.

18

'Do you think she's dead?'

Moreno didn't reply straight away. Got out of the car. Walked round to his side and thought of giving him a kiss on the cheek, but for some reason found that inappropriate and desisted. Put her hand on his arm instead.

'I don't know,' she said. 'Let's hope to God that she isn't, but I really have no idea. I have to keep following this up for a bit longer, though. I'm sorry, but I need to know a few more answers before I can let go of it.'

Mikael nodded.

'Take it easy with the headmaster,' he urged her. 'Don't forget that he's over eighty. Shall we say an hour?'

'Plus or minus a half,' said Moreno. 'Find yourself a table in the harbour cafe, so that you don't get irritated unnecessarily.'

She waited until he'd driven off before opening the

white-painted gate and walking along the stone-paved path to the house. It looked large and well cared-for. A substantial two-storey house in yellowish-white pommer stone; balconies on the upper floor and terraces on the ground floor, and generous picture windows facing the sea. It must be worth a million, Moreno thought. Especially when you think of the position and the garden. The large lawn was newly mown, the flower beds, bushes and fruit trees well tended, and the large array of garden furniture under an orange parasol looked as if it could have been delivered by the carpenter only a couple of hours ago.

Former headmaster Salnecki was lounging back in one of the comfortable armchairs, and seemed to be about as old as Adam.

White trousers, white shirt, white cotton cardigan. A sporty-looking yellow cap and blue leisure shoes. But none of that helped. He looked older than the gnarled apple trees. He can't have much longer left, Moreno thought. This is probably his last summer. I hope he's clear in the head.

He was.

Unusually clear, that was obvious after only a few seconds. And a couple of comments. A rather younger, light-haired and suntanned woman came out carrying a tray with a carafe and glasses. And a dish of bread sticks.

'A mixture of red and white,' explained herr Salnecki, filling her glass. 'Life and death, in the form of blackcurrants and Riesling. I don't suppose I need to point out that white is the colour of death in quite a lot of cultures. Welcome, and your very good health.'

'Cheers,' said Moreno. 'Thank you for agreeing to see me.'

'My niece's daughter . . .' He nodded in the direction of the woman who had just disappeared round the corner. 'She looks after me. She's writing a dissertation on the Klimke group, and is making use of my library. Sylvia. A nice girl, as good as gold. My wife passed away a few years ago, I need somebody to look after me . . . But I think there was something you wanted to see me about?'

Moreno put her glass down on the table and leaned back in her chair.

'Maager,' she said. 'Arnold Maager. You were still the headmaster at Voellerskolan when it happened, weren't you?'

'I suspected as much,' said Salnecki.

'Suspected? What do you mean?'

'That that was what you wanted to talk about. You see, I've worked in schools all my life, and I've no doubt there have been a few irregularities during that time – but if a detective inspector on holiday comes and asks to talk to me, there's only one conclusion I can draw. It's not a pretty tale, that Maager business.'

'So I've gathered,' said Moreno.

'Why do you want to drag it up again? Isn't it better to let things lie in peace?'

'Perhaps,' said Moreno. 'But now there are certain circumstances that have come to light.'

Salnecki burst out laughing.

'Come to light? I like it! You're speaking more like a lawyer, Inspector, if I might be allowed to say so. But in any case, I understand that discretion can be a virtue, and my natural curiosity has waned as the years have gone by . . . I'm not sure if one should be pleased about that, or sorry . . . But what's not in doubt is that I talk too much. What do you want to know?'

Moreno held back a smile.

'What happened,' she said. 'What you thought about Maager, and so on.'

'You don't know the details already?'

'Very few,' said Moreno.

Salnecki emptied his glass and put it down firmly on the table.

'A tragedy,' he said. 'There's no other word for it. And yet at the same time such a banal business. Maager was a good teacher. Liked by both his pupils and his colleagues. Young and ambitious . . . And then he goes and jumps into bed with that young chit of a girl. Beyond belief. You have to be able to handle young teenaged girls with hormones, that's among the first things a male teacher has to get to grips with.'

'He didn't just jump into bed with her,' said Moreno, 'if I've understood the situation rightly.'

Salnecki shook his head and suddenly looked sombre.

'No. But that's what started everything off. A cautionary tale, in a way. There's always a price to pay.'

Moreno raised her eyebrows.

'Are you saying it was Maager who paid the price? Surely you could say that the girl also paid a price . . .'

'Of course,' said Salnecki, quick to correct that impression. 'Of course. That's what makes it so tragic. Everybody has to pay for a moment of thoughtlessness. Some with their life, others with their sanity. You get the impression that the gods sometimes overdo the retribution thing.'

Moreno thought for a moment. Her host took off his cap, fished a comb out of his back pocket and drew it a few times through his thin, white hair.

'How did people react?' asked Moreno. 'They must have been rather shocked.'

'Hysterical,' said Salnecki with a sigh, replacing his cap. 'People went mad, there were those who wanted to lynch him – I kept getting phone calls in the middle of the night.

In a way it was lucky that it happened during the summer holidays, we'd have had to shut down the school otherwise. It was my final year, incidentally. I finished in December. I wish I'd gone in June instead . . . But there again, it wouldn't have been much fun for a new headmaster to start his career with a scandal like that.'

'What about their relationship?' Moreno wondered. 'Maager and the girl, I mean. Had it been going on for long? Did the other pupils know about it, for instance?'

'Relationship!' snorted Salnecki. 'It wasn't a relationship. The girl offered herself to him on a plate on one single occasion, and they ended up in the same bed. I would guess they were both drunk. I mean, Maager had a family – a wife and a little daughter.'

'I know about that,' said Moreno. 'How did it go for Maager afterwards? Have you had any contact with him?'

Salnecki looked sombre again. A bit of a guilty conscience, presumably, Moreno thought. Wondering if he could have intervened and prevented the disaster in some way. He leaned forward and refilled his glass from the jug.

'No,' he said. 'None at all. He went mad. He's in a home not far away from here. A few colleagues used to go and visit him during the first few years, but they could never get a single word out of him . . . No, it finished him off for the rest of his life.'

'What happened when they . . . met, Maager and young Maas? It happened only once, you said.'

Salnecki shrugged.

'As far as I know. It was after a disco at the school for the pupils. Maager and a few other teachers had acted as stewards. Afterwards the teachers went to a colleague's house, a handicraft teacher – a bachelor – and had a few drinks and sat and talked. There was only a week of term left. Anyway, a gang of pupils turned up in the small hours. It should never have happened, of course, but they were invited in and things just went on from there. Maager jumped into bed with Winnie Maas, and—'

'– she got pregnant and he killed her,' said Moreno. 'Six or seven weeks later, was it?'

'More or less, yes,' said Salnecki. 'Not a pretty tale, as I said before. Anyway, your good health!'

They drank. Moreno decided to try another line.

'This girl, Winnie Maas – she seems to have been a bit, er, precocious. Is that right?'

Salnecki cleared his throat and tried to find the appropriate words.

'*De mortuis nihil nisi bonum,*' he said. 'Let's say she was precocious.'

'Why did he kill her?'

Salnecki pulled at an ear lobe and looked thoughtful.

'He lost control, I would guess. It really was as simple as that. The girl presumably wasn't prepared to have an abortion. She wanted to have the child – and might well have demanded lots of money in return for her silence. Or alternatively force him to admit that he was the father . . . I don't know, but I guess those were the conditions. She phoned him the night when it happened. They met on the railway viaduct, and he took leave of his senses. And went mad as well, as I've said before. If he went mad before or after he'd thrown her down is a matter for discussion – and it certainly was discussed. That became a crucial point in his trial – how far he was responsible for his own actions and compos mentis: if he knew what he was doing or not when it actually happened. Ah well, it's a pretty vulnerable contraption, this thing that drives us . . .'

He smiled and tapped his right temple with two fingers. Moreno smiled.

'Mind you, this one has kept going for eighty-one years,' he added, with a modest smile.

'What about the girl's family?' Moreno asked.

'Ah well, yes,' muttered Salnecki. 'Single mother. No siblings. The mother took it very badly. She was one of the lynch mob, you might say. Calmed down a bit afterwards. But she still lives here in Lejnice, I bump into her occasionally . . . Poor woman, she doesn't seem to have any strength left. But now it's my turn to ask if there's any justice left in the world. What are you after? There must be a reason for your interest in these unpleasant goings-on.'

Moreno hesitated. She had expected the question, of course. And she had several more or less plausible responses already worked out: but somehow or other it didn't seem right to come out with half-truths and evasive answers when faced with this outspoken and foxy old schoolmaster. Not tempting and certainly not right. Especially bearing in mind her thoughts about ethics.

She thought for a few seconds while taking a sip of the mixture of red and white. Of life and death. Then she told him the absolute truth.

'In the name of all that's holy!' exclaimed Salnecki. 'What the hell's going on?'

'That's what I'm trying to find out,' said Moreno.

While Moreno was talking to Salnecki, Mikael had been buying groceries in the market, which had been held in Grote Marckt every Saturday within living memory. That morning both of them – especially Moreno – had been sceptical about swimming and sunbathing, and when a cold front began to move in from the south-west that afternoon, it came as a relief. Instead of conforming with convention and lying stretched out under the unforgiving sun, they could devote themselves with a clear conscience to a ratatouille with curry, Indian cumin and thick cream, a dish they duly enjoyed in the conservatory while the rain pattered against the windowpanes and the tin roof.

And an Italian red to wash it down. Malevoli cheese with slices of pear for afters. And a glass of old port wine from a dust-covered bottle without a label – Mikael claimed that it was from a cellar that came into the family with the house in the twenties. Moreno didn't know whether to believe him or not. But it was very good in any case. Like a sweet, deep-frozen fire.

They eventually ended up in rocking chairs on either side of the open fire, and Montezuma indicated that Moreno had begun to be accepted by coming to lie in her lap. As she sat there digesting the food and stroking the lazy cat between its ears, Mikael took the opportunity of taking twenty-four photos of them.

'Very pretty,' he announced. 'So very damned pretty. The fire, the woman and the cat.'

She felt too full to protest.

'You think of her as your own child, don't you?' he said when he'd put the camera away.

'Who? Montezuma?'

'Mikaela Lijphart. You're assuming a mother's responsibility for her . . . Because you don't have any children of your own.'

'Tuppeny-ha'penny psychology,' said Moreno.

Is he right? she wondered. Why the hell is he raising this now?

'Tuppence-ha'penny is worth something. Or used to be,' Mikael said. 'What are you trying to convince yourself? That there's something fishy about this old scandal?'

'What do you think yourself?' Moreno asked, aware of the tone of irritation in her voice. 'Don't you agree that it's a bit odd for this girl to go missing at a moment like this? Just after she's visited her loony father for the first time? Just after she's finally discovered why she's had to grow up without him?'

'Yes, I agree,' said Mikael after a moment's silence. 'It's just that I thought you'd had enough of stuff like this nagging you when you're supposed to be on leave, that's all.'

'Are you suggesting that I should just let it all drop?'

He suddenly looked quite angry. Teeth clenched and grinding – for the first time, she thought.

'Rubbish,' he said. 'I think you're doing the right thing. Absolutely. You don't need to defend yourself, but it gets more complicated if you keep changing your mind all the time.'

What the hell is he on about? Moreno thought, giving

Montezuma a pat which sent her jumping down to the floor.

'Now listen here,' she said. 'I'm not very receptive to all that psychobabble about my motives just now. My period's due tomorrow or the day after, so we can blame it on that. But in any case, I can't just stop thinking about that poor girl. And if I'm thinking thoughts, I might as well do something about them as well. If you can't take that, just say so. But none of these half-baked comments, if you don't mind.'

That's blown it, she thought. I might as well pack my things and book into a hotel for tonight.

But he just looked sorry.

'For pity's sake,' he said. 'What are you talking about? Do you have to empty your brain before your period starts? I'm saying I think you're doing the right thing. If you're not sure about that, stop projecting your doubts on to me . . . Because that's exactly what you're doing. Now, where were we? What did Mikaela Lijphart do after she'd visited her father at the Sidonis home?'

'Booked herself into the youth hostel,' said Moreno.

Thank goodness I don't have to pack my things, she thought.

'And then?'

'She took the bus into Lejnice and back. On Saturday evening.'

'Why?'

'I don't know. Then she took the bus again on Sunday. Into town. And since then there's been no sign of her.'

Mikael nodded.

'Any response to the Wanted notice?'

'It only went out this morning,' said Moreno. 'If anybody's seen her, the police ought to know by now. But Vegesack did say he'd ring . . .'

Mikael looked at the clock.

'Why don't you ring and ask?'

'I don't know,' said Moreno. 'I've eaten too much.'

It took quite a while to get through to Chief of Police Vrommel, since he was in the shower after an 8-kilometre jog.

These details were in the recorded message on his answering machine, and twenty minutes later he responded. Newly scrubbed, fresh and fragrant, one could assume. And well stretched. Moreno came straight to the point and asked if the Wanted notice regarding Mikaela Lijphart had produced any results.

'Negative,' said Vrommel.

'Do you mean nothing?' Moreno wondered.

'As I said,' said Vrommel. 'Negative.'

'So didn't anybody see her on Sunday?'

'Nobody who has contacted us,' said the chief of police. 'Where I am it's Saturday evening. Don't you have anything better to do while you're on leave, Inspector?'

'Lots,' said Moreno, and hung up.

Forty-five minutes and one-and-a-half glasses of port later she telephoned Constable Vegesack.

'I apologize for ringing so late,' she began.

'No problem,' said Vegesack. 'My girlfriend's on a flight due into Emsbaden at half past two tomorrow morning. I'm going to collect her and have to keep awake until then.'

'Glad to hear it,' said Moreno. 'We've just come home, my . . . boyfriend and I. I'd be very interested to hear what came of the Wanted notice. For Mikaela Lijphart, that is.'

'I'm with you,' said Vegesack. 'No, nobody's taken the bait. Not today, at least.'

'Nothing at all?'

'Well,' said Vegesack, 'there was a woman who turned up at the station this afternoon. She said she was respond-ing to the Wanted notice, but it turned out that she had nothing of any value to contribute.'

Moreno thought for a moment.

'Nothing else?'

'No,' said Vegesack. 'But tomorrow is another day.'

'I hope so,' said Moreno. 'I wonder if I could ask a favour of you.'

'You don't say,' said Vegesack. 'What exactly?'

'Well,' said Moreno, 'I'd like to take a look at the interrogation records of the Maager case. I assume you still have them?'

'I assume so,' said Vegesack. 'There are loads of shelves full of files – I take it that what you are after is in one of them. Just call in and take a look.'

Moreno waited for three seconds.

'Another thing.'

'Yes?'

'Could we do this without involving the chief of police? He doesn't seem too pleased at the thought of my poking my nose into this case.'

'Of course,' said Vegesack, and she could hear from his tone of voice that if there was anything in this world that didn't worry him in the slightest, it was going behind his boss's back. She couldn't help but sympathize with him.

In any case, as it was a matter of Sunday morning (Vegesack pointed out) the chances of the chief of police turning up in the station were less than a thousand to one.

So there was no problem at all if Inspector Moreno wanted to call in. Some time between eleven and twelve, Vegesack suggested, when he would be there anyway, sorting out various matters.

'So early?' Moreno wondered. 'Will you really manage to get enough sleep if you're going to collect your girl-friend at half past two tomorrow morning?'

'We aren't actually intending to sleep,' said Vegesack.

Moreno smiled. Thanked him and hung up.

So that's that, she thought. A shot in the dark. But a shot even so.

That was another quotation, she was aware of that. She asked herself what the point was of all these set phrases that seemed to be imposing themselves on her thoughts.

No point at all, she concluded.

19

'I must,' said Sigrid Lijphart.

Helmut folded up the newspaper.

'I've no alternative to doing what I'm going to do, and I can't give you any more details. You must trust me.'

He took off his glasses, and made quite a play of putting them into the case.

'I'll explain everything for you afterwards. If anybody rings, tell them I'm just visiting a friend. And that I'll get back to them.'

'Who?'

'What do you mean?'

'Which of your lady friends will be honoured by your fake visit?'

The ill-humoured irony in his voice was unmistakable. She noticed that his neck was red and blotchy, which is how it looked when his favourite football team was losing an important match. Or when Soerensen in the butcher's had made some unusually preposterous remark.

No wonder, she thought. No wonder that he was angry. She had excluded him from this whole business: perhaps that had been a mistake from the start, but it was too late to do anything about it now. Much too late.

And without doubt the wrong time to stand here feeling sorry for him. They would have to put right whatever was still capable of being put right when the time came. Afterwards. If he really was a rock, now was the time for him to live up to it.

'I'm sorry,' she said. 'I'm treating you unfairly, but I have no choice. Try to understand, if you can. Trust me.'

He looked at her with eyes of stone. Hard, but not malicious. Unswervingly rock-like. But also vacant, in some strange way, so that one might be justified in wondering if they expressed anything at all . . .

'Trust me,' she said again. 'I'm off now. I'll phone.'

He didn't answer, but she hesitated for another moment.

'Is there anything you want to say?'

He put the newspaper down. Put his elbows on the table and rested his head on his hands. His eyes were still rock-like.

'Find her,' he said. 'What I want is for you to bring her home.'

She stroked his cheek, and left him.

★

The first hour in the car was almost like a nightmare. Dusk was falling and it was raining, the traffic was dense and spasmodic. She was a poor driver in normal circumstances, she was the first to admit that, but on an evening like this everything was seven times as bad.

I mustn't have a crash, she thought, gripping the steering wheel so tightly that her knuckles turned white. That would be too much. Nothing must happen, I really must bring this off.

Then everything fell to pieces. Tears came welling up as if from a hot geyser, and she was forced to drive onto the verge and stop. That was a risky manoeuvre, of course, but it would have been even more risky to continue. She switched on the hazard warning lights, and started sobbing. Might as well let it all come out, she thought.

It took a long time, and when she set off again she wasn't at all sure that she felt any better than she had done to start with.

For the second time in just a few days, she prayed to God, and for the second time she doubted very much if there was anybody listening. When she finally joined the motorway at Loewingen, she made a deal instead.

If we come out of this unscathed, I'll thank You on my bare knees.

Did you hear that, God? It's a promise.

★

He was standing waiting at the crossroads, as agreed. When she caught sight of him in the combined light of the streetlamp and her headlights, she felt dizzy for a moment.

What's happening? she thought.

Am I dreaming?

Why does it feel as if I'm falling down through space?

Then she gritted her teeth, slowed down and signalled to him with her headlights.

For the first half-hour he didn't say a word.

Neither did she. They sat next to each other in the front seats like two strangers who know from the start that they have nothing to say to one another. Not even a common language in which they can exchange politeness phrases.

Perhaps it was just as well. She hadn't thought about whether they would have anything to talk about, but now that she began to think about it, it soon felt like an impossibility. After all those years there was nothing to add.

Time passed had made no difference. That's the way it was, full stop.

Just as it had been that night in July sixteen years ago. Immovable and fixed, once and for all.

We hardly ever made love after our daughter was born, she suddenly thought. I didn't want to. I don't think I ever wanted him. Strange.

But then, life was strange. Sometimes like a wind blowing through a birch wood in the spring, sometimes like a hurricane. Sometimes like a sick, emaciated animal that wanted nothing more than to hide away and die in peace . . . Strange thoughts, she didn't recognize them. As if they were somehow being generated by him, by the man who was sitting beside her again, the man she had excluded from her life so long ago, and who had no possibility of finding a way back again.

No way. And when she glanced at the thin, shrunken figure on the passenger seat beside her she regretted not having told him to sit in the back instead. It struck her that his wretchedness had become a part of him. Oozed out from inside him, and now it was obvious to everybody what kind of a man he was. She wished it had been as obvious as this many years ago.

In that case perhaps things wouldn't have developed as they had done.

But then, if she had realized from the start what kind of a man he was, she would never have become involved with him. And if she hadn't become involved with him, Mikaela would never have been born. That was a fact of life she could do nothing about, she was well aware of that. Mikaela had his blood inside her, and when all was said and done, that was something she had to acknowledge. Without him her daughter wouldn't have existed and the image of the wind and the sick animal came into her mind once again . . . Only to be replaced by something he had said once.

I like the silence between us.

Those were his exact words. *The silence between them?* It had been good, he maintained. She was the first girl he had ever been able to be silent with.

Good Lord, she thought. Surely he isn't sitting here imagining that there is something good about this bloody failure to communicate?

But she didn't ask. Just increased her speed somewhat: the rain had eased off and would soon stop.

Shortly after Saaren she pulled into a petrol station to fill up, and just as she was getting behind the wheel again and fastening her seat belt, he spoke for the first time.

'Where are we going?' he asked.

His voice was reminiscent of an autumn leaf falling to the ground. She didn't answer.

20

Interrogation of Paula Ruth Emmerich, 19.7.1983.

Location: Lejnice police station.

Interrogator: Inspector Walevski.

Also present: Chief Inspector Vrommel, Chief of Police; Soc. Asst. Bluume.

Interrogation transcript: Inspector Walevski.

Walevski: Your name is Paula Emmerich?

Emmerich: Yes.

W Born on 22 May 1967, here in Lejnice?

E Yes.

W Until 17 June you attended Voellerskolan here in Lejnice?

E Yes.

W You were in the same class as a girl by the name of Winnie Ludmilla Maas for six years. Is that correct?

E Yes.

W Would you say that you knew Winnie Maas well?

E Yes. Although we weren't such close friends as we used to be.

W But you socialized now and again?

E Yes.

W You know what happened to Winnie, and why we want to talk to you?

E Yes.

W To what extent are you acquainted with Arnold Maager?

E He was our teacher in Social Studies and History.

W At Voellerskolan?

E Yes.

W How long did you have him as your teacher?

E Two years. In class eight and nine.

W How did you rate him as a teacher?

E Not bad. Quite good, I think.

W Can you describe him in a bit more detail?

E /No answer/

W Was he liked by the other pupils in your class?

E Yes. He was good. Handsome.

W Handsome?

E For a teacher.

W I see. Do you know if Winnie Maas thought the same about him as you did? That Arnold Maager was a good teacher. And handsome?

E Yes, she did.

W Are you sure? I'm talking about the time before the disco.

E She liked him.

W Did you talk about that?

E Maybe. I can't remember.

W But she never said that she was in love with him, for instance?

E No. Not to me, at any rate.

W Were there any other pupils in your class who knew Winnie better than you did?

E I don't think so. No.

W So if Winnie had wanted to confide in anybody, she would have chosen you?

E Yes. Although she was a bit more private recently.

W What do you mean?

E She didn't talk so much, sort of.

W I see. Do you know if she had a boyfriend?

E Not now. Not then, in May-June, I mean. I don't think so at least.

W But she had had boyfriends previously?

E Of course.

W Lots of them?

E Quite a few, but not at the end of class nine.

W Can you tell us what happened at the disco on 10 June?

E What do you want to know?

W What it was like. Who you were with. If you know what Winnie was up to.

E It was the same as usual.

W The same as usual?

E We had a few drinks on the beach first.

W Who's 'we'?

E A few pupils from our class. And other classes.

W How many?

E Fifteen or so.

W Was Winnie Maas there?

E Yes.

W And then?

E We went on to the disco at about half past nine or thereabouts.

W And then?

E We danced and chatted and so on.

W Were you aware of what Winnie Maas was doing during the evening?

E Yes.

W Let's hear it.

E She was a bit drunk. She danced quite a lot, like she usually did. She danced cheek-to-cheek with Maager.

W Are you telling me that Winnie Maas danced cheek-to-cheek with Arnold Maager, her teacher in Social Studies and History?

E Yes. I thought it was a bit of a joke. Some of the other girls danced with other teachers as well.

W How many dances?

E Winnie or the others?

W Winnie.

E I don't know. Quite a lot.

W With other teachers as well?

E I don't know. I think it was just with him.

W Did you talk about it? You and your friends?

E I don't really remember. Yes, probably.

W Didn't you all think it was odd that Winnie danced such a lot with just one teacher?

E I don't remember.

W Why don't you remember?

E I don't know. I suppose I was a bit drunk. It was a bit of a blur.

W Let's move on to what happened later on in the evening. Can you tell us a bit about that?

E We went down to the beach again, after the disco was over.

W We?

E A group of us. Eight or ten.

W Was Winnie Maas with you?

E Yes.

W What did you do?

E Nothing special.

W Nothing special?

E No.

W But you must have done something?

E I suppose so.

W What, for instance.

E What the hell do you want me to say? That we drank, smoked, did some necking?

W Is that what you did in fact?

E I suppose so. Chatted as well. One of the lads did some skinny-dipping.

W Really? Did you talk to Winnie at all?

E I don't think so. Not especially. For Christ's sake, we were all together.

W You didn't talk about her dancing so much with Arnold Maager?

E I suppose we did.

W Do you recall anything she said?

E Yes, one thing.

W What?

E She said Maager really turned her on.

W Maager really turned her on? You're sure about that? That Winnie Maas said that?

E Yes.

W Did you believe her?

E Why shouldn't I? Why shouldn't she get turned on by whoever she wanted?

W All right. What did you do after you'd been on the beach?

E We went back up to town again.

W Winnie Maas as well?

E Of course. For God's sake . . .

W Go on.

E Somebody had heard that they were all at Gollum's house, having a party.

W Who's Gollum?

E Our handicrafts teacher. His real name is Gollumsen.

W Who exactly were partying at his house?

E All the ones who'd been supervising the disco.

W The teachers.

E Yes.

W Including Maager?

E Yes, including Maager.

W And you knew that those teachers were going to be at Gollumsen's house?

E Yes.

W How?

E I don't know. Somebody had heard about it.

W Somebody?

E I don't know who, for God's sake.

W Was it Winnie Maas who knew?

E Could have been.

W But it could have been somebody else?

E /No answer/

W Okay, tell us what happened when you got to Gollumsen's place.

E They were sitting around and singing. They were all pretty drunk. Songs from the sixties. We rang the doorbell and they let us in.

W How many teachers were they?

E Four.

W Four?

E Yes. Gollum and Maager, and two others.

W Which two others?

E One is called Nielsen. And the other was Cruickshank.

W And how many pupils were you?

E Seven. But two left quite soon.

W But you and Winnie stayed on?

E Yes.

W Who were the other three?

E Tim Van Rippe and Christopher Duijkert and Vera Sauger.

W So, five pupils and four teachers. What time was it when you got there, roughly?

E Two o'clock, half past, somewhere around then.

W And what did you do at Gollumsen's house?

E We had a few drinks, and sang songs – Nielsen played the guitar.

W Go on. What happened between Arnold Maager and Winnie Maas?

E They sat necking for a while. Then they disappeared into the bedroom.

W And what did the rest of you do?

E The rest of us?

W Yes. What did the rest of you do after Winnie Maas and Arnold Maager had disappeared into the bedroom?

E We sat around and sang and chatted.

W For how long?

E I don't know. An hour, maybe.

W And then you left the flat?

E Yes.

W Were Winnie Maas and Arnold Maager still in the bedroom when you left?

E Yes. Unless they'd jumped out through the window – but I don't think so.

W Why don't you think so?

E Because it's on the second floor.

W I see. Anyway, did you discover what they were doing in the bedroom?

E Yes.

W How? And when?

E We could hear what they were doing.

W Really?

E   They were screwing so frantically that the whole
    house was shaking.

Moreno put the papers on one side. Checked the clock. A quarter to one. This was the third interrogation transcript she'd read, and the picture was becoming clear.

Depressingly clear, she thought.

. . . *the whole house was shaking!*

What a creep, she thought. No wonder he went and hid himself away in a loony bin. No wonder he went mad.

A wife and a two-year-old daughter.

Was this what Mikaela discovered when she visited the Sidonis home?

Was this what his wife suspected had happened?

No, it wasn't difficult to understand why he had gone out of his mind. Most certainly not. Screwing a sixteen-year-old girl in front of five witnesses, more or less. And the whole house was shaking . . . For Christ's sake!

And then killing her when she had the nerve to get pregnant.

Detective Inspector Moreno leaned her head on her hands and gazed out at the Sunday-deserted square. The cold front was still persisting, but the rain had stopped as yesterday turned into today.

Basic instincts? she thought.

Sex backed up by a certain amount of heart. The brain adrift in a dinghy with no oars. And drunk, to be on the safe side.

The parallel between the Maager incident and her own deflowering had been nagging at her for several days, and now she could see the incident in her mind's eye more clearly than for many years.

That cramped hotel room in the Piazza di Popolo in Rome. The eternal city. Eternal love.

Moreno. A seventeen-year-old schoolgirl. Only one year older than Winnie Maas – and only a year later chronologically, it now struck her, to her horror. 1984. A school trip for those studying languages. Early summer. Good to be alive.

Him. A thirty-six-year-old Latin teacher.

Strong. Learned. Sophisticated.

A man of the world with a hairy chest and warm hands. They hadn't made love so frantically that the whole hotel shook, but they'd had quite a lot of sex even so, and had managed it without being observed. He promised to leave his wife for her sake, and she believed him.

So much so that she eventually telephoned his wife to discuss the situation with her.

Afterwards: his cowardice. His monumentally pitiful performance.

It was the first time she had come across anything so humiliatingly weak-kneed, and when she met his wife several years later they had a very fruitful woman-to-woman conversation. She had left her Latin teacher, and as far as she knew he was still busy seducing schoolgirls in charmingly cramped rooms in Rome.

With warm hands, a hairy chest and a ready wit.

But he wasn't the prat at the centre of the current emergency. Nor was Ewa Moreno one of the players.

It was all about a dead girl by the name of Winnie Maas. And a girl they hoped was still alive, Mikaela Lijphart.

And the latter's father, Arnold Maager.

He had had sixteen years in which to prepare his story before he met his daughter. Sixteen years alone with his thoughts and his remorse, presumably.

Sixteen hundred wouldn't have been enough, Moreno thought. Time heals many wounds, but not those caused by shame. She recalled a line of poetry, she couldn't remember the context:

For the roses of shame glow throughout eternity

She put the files back on the shelf. Glanced at the door to Constable Vegesack's room and established that he was still asleep in his desk chair. His head leaning back and his mouth open.

She had intended to have a word with him about his conversation with Maager at the Sidonis home, but decided to let it pass.

On purely humanitarian grounds. In case he and his girlfriend didn't intend to sleep tonight either.

Instead she left the Lejnice police station, and crossed over the square to Vlammerick's sweetshop to buy a peace-offering for her boyfriend (fiancé? bloke? lover?).

And to some extent also to balance out her own pre-menstrual blood sugar deficiency.

21

19 July 1999

The call came just after she had parked in the shade of an elm tree, and she thought twice before answering.

'I just thought you'd like to know,' said Münster.

For a confused second she had no idea what he was on about.

'Know?'

'Lampe-Leermann. That paedophile business.'

'Ah, yes,' said Moreno.

'I've found the journalist.'

How is that possible? Moreno thought. I've almost managed to forget all about the Scumbag after only a couple of days . . .

'So there really was a journalist, after all?'

'It seems so,' said Münster, and sounded more sombre than she could ever remember him being.

'Go on,' she said.

Münster cleared his throat.

'I'm in a bit of a jam,' he said. 'It's a bit of a bugger, this business – as they say.'

'Why are you in a jam?'

'Well, maybe not in a jam – but the whole business is very dodgy. Lampe-Leermann wasn't a problem: he told us the name in exchange for a guarantee that he would be sent to the Saalsbach prison. I think he has enemies in a few of the other establishments, and felt threatened. Anyway, he gave me the name of that reporter, no beating about the bush.'

'Why are you not telling me his name?'

'I don't know,' said Münster.

'Do you mean you don't know what he's called, or that you don't know why you don't want to tell me his name?'

'I know what he's called,' said Münster.

'Have you spoken to him?'

'Yes.'

'And?'

She suddenly felt that hand squeezing her throat again. *Paedophile? One of her colleagues . . . ?* She started chanting their names to herself . . . *Rooth, Jung, deBries . . .* Like some kind of mantra, or whatever . . . *Krause, Bollmert . . .*

'He admits that he's spilled the beans to Lampe-Leermann,' said Münster. 'While drunk, of course. He claims that he has the name of one of our officers. He has pictures to prove it, and has been given ten thousand to hush it up – exactly what Lampe-Leermann told us, in other words.'

'God help us,' said Moreno.

'Exactly,' said Münster. 'And there's another little snag.'

'What?'

'He wants another ten thousand before he'll tell us the name.'

'What? What the . . . ?'

'That's what I thought as well,' said Münster. 'At first. But there's a sort of black logic behind it. If he's been given ten thousand to keep quiet about it, wouldn't it be immoral to talk about it for nothing? Unethical, as he put it.'

'But if we pay him another ten thousand . . . ?'

'Then the situation is quite different. Have you gathered how things stand?'

Moreno thought for a moment.

'Yes,' she said. 'I suppose I have. What a prat.'

'Amen to that,' said Münster. 'What do you think I should do now? Go in to Hiller and ask for ten thousand in cash?'

Moreno didn't reply.

'How's the weather where you are on the coast?' Münster asked.

'Changeable. It's sunny again today. Do you have a plan?'

'Not yet,' said Münster. 'But I suppose I'd better make one. I just thought I ought to inform you first.'

'Thank you,' said Moreno.

A few moments of silence ensued.

'It can't be . . . You don't think he was bluffing,' she asked, 'that damned hack of a journalist?'

'Of course,' said Münster. 'I'm sure he is.'

'There's nothing worse than false accusations.'

'Nothing,' said Münster. 'Apart from genuine ones. I'll be in touch.'

'Do,' said Moreno.

A black dog was on a lead attached to a kennel, barking at her as she made her way to the office. Deep, muffled, echoing barks as if they were coming from out of a well – an almost surrealistic contrast with the well-tended grounds and the pale yellow buildings, Moreno thought.

But quite a good image for her own black thoughts. Could it be Cerberus? A reminder of the abyss, and the path we shall all tread sooner or later? She wondered why they didn't get rid of the dog, or at least let it run around loose: it could hardly be an especially encouraging companion to the poor battered and lost souls who lived here, in any case.

She found her way to reception, and introduced herself

to a red-haired woman in a white coat behind a glass counter. She explained why she was there.

'Arnold Maager, er . . . yes . . .' said the woman, smiling nervously. 'I think you'd better have a word with fru Walker.'

'Fru Walker?'

'She's in charge of the clinic. Just a moment.'

She pressed four buttons on the internal telephone.

'Why do I need to talk to the boss? I just want to pay a visit to herr Maager.'

The red-haired woman blushed.

'Just a moment.'

She took three steps away from the counter and turned her back on Moreno. She spoke softly into the receiver, then returned to Moreno blushing slightly less obviously.

'Fru Walker will be pleased to see you straight away. The third door on the right over there.'

She pointed in the direction of a short corridor.

'Thank you,' said Moreno, and set off as directed.

Fru Walker was a dark-haired little woman in her sixties. She was sitting at a gigantic desk. Moreno thought she looked out of place. A bit like a pigeon on the long side of a football pitch. She stood up, walked round half the pitch and shook hands when Moreno had closed the door behind her. There seemed to be something wrong with one of her legs – she walked with the aid of a brown walking stick. Perhaps this slight handicap was why she had gone to the trouble of getting up to greet Moreno. To make a point.

She was noticeably worried. She seemed to have made an excessive effort to be welcoming, obviously so, and Moreno wondered why. She had telephoned in advance and informed them of her visit, but she had only spoken to an answering machine. She had mentioned that she was a detective inspector, but it seemed unlikely that this fact would have put the wind up the care-home staff as much as this woman seemed to be signalling.

But the explanation soon emerged.

'Please take a seat,' said fru Walker. 'I think we have a little problem.'

'Really?' said Moreno without sitting down. 'I just want to meet Arnold Maager for a short conversation. What's the problem?'

'He's not here,' said fru Walker.

'I beg your pardon?'

'Arnold Maager isn't here in the care home. He's gone away.'

Gone away? Moreno thought. Arnold Maager? Is she out of her mind?

'What do you mean?' she asked. 'Where has he gone?'

'We don't know. He's been missing since last Saturday afternoon. I'm really sorry that you've come here for nothing, but as you didn't give us a number we couldn't ring you back.'

'How exactly did he go missing?' Moreno asked.

Fru Walker moved back to sit down at her desk.

'We don't know exactly when, or how. But it was during the afternoon in any case. He usually goes for a walk round the grounds in the afternoon, but he didn't turn up for dinner. On Saturday, as I said.'

'And he said nothing about where he was going?'

'No.'

'Has herr Maager gone missing like this before?'

'No,' said fru Walker wearily. 'Some patients do go away sometimes – they usually go home. But Maager has never left this place during all the years he's been here.'

'Sixteen years?' said Moreno.

'More or less, yes,' said fru Walker. 'We're very upset, and we had a meeting this morning to discuss what we ought to do next.'

'Have you reported him as missing?'

'Yes, of course,' said fru Walker.

'When?'

The head of the care home contemplated her clasped hands.

'Two hours ago.'

Brilliant, thought Moreno, gritting her teeth so as not

to say anything over-hastily. Absolutely brilliant! A depressive mentally ill patient goes missing for two whole days, and then they arrange a meeting and decide to contact the authorities. Perhaps it's time to take a look at routine procedures, as those in authority generally say in circumstances like these.

'Another police officer was here last week and spoke to Maager. Do you know about that?'

Fru Walker nodded.

'Yes, I know. Last Wednesday. And he'd been visited by his daughter a few days prior to that. Might there be some connection, do you think? He doesn't usually have so many visitors.'

Moreno ignored the speculation.

'You say that Maager went missing on Saturday afternoon, is that right?'

'Yes. He had lunch as usual at about half past twelve – so it must have been some time after that.'

'Have you spoken to all the staff?'

'Yes, and the patients as well. Nobody saw him after two o'clock.'

'Did anybody see him leave?'

'No.'

Moreno thought for a moment.

'What did he take with him?'

'I beg your pardon?'

'Clothes? Suitcase? Or didn't he have anything with him?'

Fru Walker had obviously not thought about this aspect before, but she did so now and hurried round her desk once more.

'We'll look into that immediately. We have lists of all the things the patients have in their rooms. Most of them, at least. Follow me.'

'All right,' sighed Moreno.

Half an hour later most things had become clear. By all appearances Arnold Maager had not rushed away on the spur of the moment. When all the carers and assistants pooled their observations, it became clear that missing from his room were a small shopping bag and several changes of clothes from his wardrobe. Shirts, underpants and socks, in any case.

There were no other indications, either in Maager's room or anywhere else, so Moreno thanked everybody for their help and went back to her car.

I must talk to Vegesack without delay, she thought. I need to find out exactly what Maager came out with when Vegesack spoke to him.

Vegesack had made it abundantly clear that Maager

hadn't said very much at all. Moreno assumed that meant there was all the more danger that the constable might have let slip too much. Regarding Mikaela Lijphart, for instance. That she seemed to have disappeared, for instance.

She flopped down behind the wheel. Wound down the side window and turned the ignition key.

Dead.

Not a sound from the starter.

She tried again. And again.

Not so much as a sigh.

I don't believe it, she thought. I simply can't believe it. Not just now.

How the hell? she went on to think. How the hell can anybody choose to drive around in an old East German car ten years after the fall of the Wall? A tin-pot old banger that ought to be in a museum!

My dear Mikael, she hissed as she fished for her mobile in her handbag. You're in a right old mess now. A right old bloody mess!

It was 19 July, and the sun was scorching down from a cloudless sky. Detective Inspector Ewa Moreno's holiday had just entered its second week. She was in a car park outside a remotely situated mental hospital two kilometres away from the sea, her period had just started, and Mikael Bau's damned Trabant refused to start.

The first liberated woman in the history of the world? Is that how she had defined her position in life's system of coordinates just a few days ago?

Huh.

22

'The world is round,' said Henning Keeswarden, six years and five months old.

'As round as a ball,' said Fingal Wielki, a mere four years and nine months old, but a keen promoter of everything that seemed to be new and modern. Especially if the one who announced it was his adorable cousin.

'There are people on the other side,' said young Keeswarden. 'Do you understand that?'

Fingal nodded enthusiastically. Of course he understood.

'If we dig a deep, deep hole down into the ground, we'll eventually come out on the other side.'

'On the other side,' agreed Fingal.

'But we have to dig really, really deep. Then all we need to do is to climb down and come out of the hole on the other side. In China, where the Chinese live.'

'China, Chinese' said Fingal. He wasn't quite sure where that was, nor who the Chinese were, but didn't want to admit it. 'We'll have to dig deep, deep down!' he said instead.

'Let's get going,' said Henning. 'We've got all day. I once dug a hole that very nearly came out on the other side of the world. I was nearly there – but then I had to go in and eat. I could hear them talking down there.'

'Talking?'

Fingal couldn't suppress his surprise.

'The Chinese. I was that close. I placed my ear against the bottom of the hole, and I could hear them talking quite clearly. I couldn't understand what they said, of course – they speak a different language, the Chinese do. Shall we dig a hole now that goes all the way through?'

'Of course,' said Fingal.

The cousins dug away. Fingal's spade was red and much newer than Henning's, which was blue and a bit worse for wear. Perhaps it had been used during the previous China excavation, so it was understandable. But a red spade always digs faster than a blue one.

It was still only morning. They had just come down to the beach with their mothers, who were sisters and currently busy lying down on their backs and tanning their titties – it was that kind of beach.

It was quite easy to dig. At first, at least. But soon the

sand they'd dug out started to run back down into the hole. Henning said that they'd have to make the hole a bit wider at the top.

It was rather boring to have to make the hole wider when what they really wanted to do was to dig straight down and come to the Chinese as quickly as possible. But if they wanted to get through, they would have to put up with a few annoying little problems. And keep at it even so.

And so Henning got stuck in, and Fingal followed his example.

'Shut up now, I'm listening and trying to hear something!' said Henning when the hole was so deep that only his head and shoulders stuck out when he stood upright on the bottom. That was certainly true of Fingal, at any rate, who was some ten centimetres shorter than his cousin.

'Sh!' said Fingal to himself, holding his index finger over his lips when Henning pressed his ear down on the wet sand.

'Could you hear anything?' he asked when Henning stood up again and brushed the sand out of his ear.

'Only something very faint,' said Henning. 'We have quite a bit to go yet. Shall we play at slaves?'

'Slaves? Yes, of course!' said Fingal, who couldn't re-member just now what a slave was.

Henning clambered up out of the hole.

'Let's start with you as the slave and me as the slave driver. You have to do everything I say, otherwise I'll kill you and eat you up.'

'Okay,' said Fingal.

'Get digging!' yelled Henning, threateningly. 'Dig away, you idle slave!'

Fingal started digging again. Down and down, with sand being sprayed around left, right and centre: it was wet and quite hard going, halfway down to China.

'Dig!' yelled Henning again. 'You have to say: Yes, Mister!'

'Yesmister!' said Fingal, digging away.

We ought to be making contact with those Chinese soon, he thought; but he daren't break off to lie down and listen. If he did, his cousin might kill him and eat him up. That didn't sound very pleasant. Instead he started digging slightly to one side, where it seemed to be easier. Maybe that was the right way to China. He had the feeling it must be the case.

'Get digging, you idle slave!' screeched Henning.

His arms were really beginning to ache now, especially the right one that he'd broken when he was out skiing and fell on the ice six months ago. But he didn't give up. He dug away with the spade and stuck it into the sand wall at the side of the hole with all his strength.

A large chunk of sand fell down as he did so, but that was okay. He realized that he had got there. At last. A foot was sticking out of the sand.

A foot with all five toes and a sole with sand stuck to it. A real Chinese foot!

'We're there!' he shouted. 'Look!'

The slave driver jumped down into the hole to check. Good God! They really had dug so far down that they'd come to a Chinaman's feet.

'Well dug!' he said.

The only questionable thing – which seemed to challenge the theory that the earth was round – was that the foot hadn't appeared at the bottom of the hole. It was sticking out from the side instead; and the leg to which the foot was attached also seemed to be sticking out sideways instead of from the bottom up.

But that was a bagatelle.

'Let's dig the sand away and take a look at the rest of it,' said Henning, who had now given up his job as slave driver and was prepared to dig out that leg – and indeed all the rest of the body, which didn't seem to be a Chinaman after all, but the corpse of an ordinary mortal.

Which didn't necessarily make matters any worse – although he would never admit to his cousin that he had never seen a corpse before.

But just as he dug in his blue spade and made another

chunk of sand fall down into the hole, his auntie Doris appeared at the top of the hole, glowering down at them.

His auntie, Fingal's mum.

At first she glowered.

Then she screamed.

Then his own mum appeared and she screamed as well. Both he and Fingal were lifted out of the Chinese hole and people came swarming up from all directions – bare-breasted women and women with their breasts hidden away, men with and without sunglasses, some of them with big, flashy swimming trunks, others with tiny ones that more or less disappeared up their backsides . . . But all of them pointing and singing from the same hymn sheet:

'Don't touch anything! Don't touch anything!' shouted a large, fat bloke, louder than anybody else, 'There's a body buried down there in the sand! Don't touch anything until the police get here!'

Henning's mum lifted her son up, and Fingal's did the same with hers: but there was a red and a blue spade left lying in the hole, and nobody seemed to have the slightest interest in them.

But those feet – they'd exposed another one when Henning made his final thrust with his spade: everybody seemed to be extremely interested in them.

So, Fingal thought: it really was one of those Chinese we dug up.

'The earth is round!' he shouted, waving to everybody while his mum did her best to whisk him away to where their picnic hampers were waiting, filled with apples and buns and sandwiches and juice that was both red and yellow. Oh yes, the earth is round!

THREE

23

She didn't register what the girl said at first. The red digits on the clock radio said 01.09; her irritation that somebody had had the cheek to ring at that time of night was mixed with worry that something must have happened. An accident? Her parents? Her brother? Arnold or Mikaela – no, that wasn't possible, they were both asleep in the same room as she was.

'I'm sorry – what did you say?'

'I want to speak to my teacher, magister Maager.'

A pupil. She stopped worrying. A fifteen- or sixteen-year-old chit of a girl telephoning at ten past one in the morning . . . *Magister Maager?* Arnold rolled over in his bed, and the first unmistakable coughs came from Mikaela's cot: she was awake, and would start howling at any moment. No doubt about it. If that didn't happen every night, it happened every other, at least.

Some nights more than once. And without any help from the telephone. Her anger burst forth in full bloom.

'How dare you telephone us in the middle of the night? We have a little child, and we've got better things to do than . . .'

She lost the thread. No response. For a moment she thought the girl must have hung up, but then she heard the sound of slightly asthmatic breathing at the other end of the line. Arnold switched the light on and sat up. She gestured to him, telling him to see to Mikaela, and he got out of bed.

'What do you want?' she asked sternly.

'I want to speak to Maager.'

'What about?'

No reply. Mikaela started howling, and Arnold picked her up. Why the hell did he have to pick her up? she wondered. It would have been enough to stick the dummy in her mouth. Now she wouldn't go back to sleep for at least half an hour.

'What's your name?' she asked. 'Surely you realize that you simply can't just ring people up at this time of night?'

'I need to speak to him. Can you tell him to be at the viaduct a quarter of an hour from now?'

'At the viaduct? Are you out of your mind? What are you on about, you little . . . You little . . .'

She couldn't think of a suitable name to call her. Not

without swearing, and she didn't want to lose control altogether. Mikaela's first shrill shriek echoed through the room. Hell's bells! she thought. What's all this about?

'Can I speak to him?'

'No.'

'It's . . . It's important.'

'What's it about?'

Silence again. Both from the receiver and from Mikaela, who was evidently tired and didn't have the strength to run through her whole repertoire. She seemed to be happy enough to hang over her father's shoulder and whimper, thank goodness.

'Tell him to come to the viaduct.'

'Certainly not! Tell me who you are, and explain why you're ringing in the middle of the night.'

Arnold came to sit on the edge of the bed, and looked enquiringly. She met his gaze, and as she did so the girl at the other end of the line decided to lay her cards on the table.

'My name's Winnie, I've had sex with him and I'm pregnant.'

It was strange that Arnold and Mikaela should be so close to her just as these words drilled their way into her consciousness. That thought struck her now, and recurred later. The fact that they were all sitting next to each other in her half of the double bed at that very moment. The inseparable family. Extremely damned strange, in view of the fact that the chasm that had suddenly opened up between them was so deep and so wide that she knew immediately they would never be able to bridge it. That they would never even try. No chance. She knew that immediately.

What was also strange was that she was able to think such thoughts in a mere fraction of a second. She handed him the receiver and relieved him of his daughter.

'It's for you.'

But she didn't remain calm for long. Once Arnold had replaced the receiver and collapsed in a pathetic heap on the floor beside the bed, she lay Mikaela down between the pillows and began hitting him. As hard as she could, with clenched fists. On his head and shoulders.

He didn't react. Made no attempt to defend himself, just bowed his head slightly; and soon her arms began to ache. Mikaela woke up again but didn't start crying. She sat up and watched instead. With eyes open wide, and her dummy in her mouth.

Sigrid ran out of the bedroom, into the bathroom, and locked herself in. Bathed her face in cold water and tried to take control of all the frantic thoughts bombarding her brain.

Stared, first at her own face in the mirror, and then at all the familiar, trivial items beside the washbasin and on all the shelves: all the tubes and jars and tablets of soap and scissors and toothbrushes and packets of plasters – all the things that were the most mundane features of her mundane life, but which now suddenly seemed alien and tainted with threatening and horrible overtones that she couldn't grasp. I'm going mad, she thought. I'm going out of my mind in this damned bathroom at this very damned moment . . . There are only seconds to go.

She dried her face with a hand towel and opened the door.

'The viaduct, a quarter of an hour from now – is that right?'

He didn't answer. Not a sound, neither from him nor Mikaela. Nothing but silence from the bedroom. She fished out a jumper and a pair of jeans. Her blue deck shoes. She was dressed and ready to go within half a minute.

Goodbye.

She thought that, but didn't say it

'Wait.'

She didn't wait. She opened the outside door and went out. Closed it behind her and hurried out into the street. The night air was cool and pleasant.

She could breathe.

★

When he left Mikaela he wasn't sure if she was asleep. But she was in her cot with her dummy in her mouth, breathing audibly and regularly, as usual. All being well she would be okay for an hour or so on her own.

He closed the outside door as quietly as he could. Thought about taking his bike, but decided not to. He wouldn't be first there in any case.

It would take eight to ten minutes to walk up to the viaduct, and perhaps he needed to make the most of those minutes. Did he even want to get there first? Didn't he need these minutes in order to work out some kind of decision? To make up his mind what he was going to do?

Or was everything already cut and dried?

Wasn't everything decided as soon as he'd overstepped the mark, a month ago? Decided irrevocably? Six weeks ago, to be precise. Hadn't everything since then been no more than a slowly ticking time bomb?

Had he ever expected anything else? That he would get away with it? That he wouldn't have to pay for such a catastrophe?

He registered that he was almost running along the dimly lit Sammersgraacht. No sign of another soul, not even a cat.

He turned off right along Dorffsallé, and continued along Gimsweg and Hagenstraat. Past the school.

The school? he thought. Would he ever . . . ?

He didn't follow that thought through. Passed by the north-west corner of the playing fields and increased his speed further. Only a couple of hundred metres left.

What's going to happen now? he thought. What will happen when I get up there?

He suddenly stopped dead. As if the thought had only just struck him.

Why don't I go home and look after my daughter instead? he asked himself. Why not?

He hesitated for five seconds. Then made up his mind.

24

Interrogation of Ludwig Georg Heller, 2.8.1983.

Interrogator: Chief Inspector Vrommel, Chief of Police.

Also present: Inspector Walevski.

Location: Lejnice police station.

Interrogation transcript: Inspector Walevski.

Vrommel: Your name and address, please.

Heller: Ludwig Heller. Walders steeg 4.

V Here in Lejnice?

H Yes.

V What is your relationship with Arnold Maager?

H We are colleagues. And good friends.

V How long have you known him?

H Since we were sixteen years old. We were at school together.

V Have you been in close communication ever since then?

H No. We studied at different universities, and lived in

different places. But we resumed our friendship when we ended up as teachers in the same school. About three years ago.

V Would you claim to know Maager well?

H Yes, I think one could say that.

V Think?

H I know him well.

V His wife as well?

H No. We have only met once or twice.

V Once or twice?

H Three times, I think. We acknowledge each other if we meet in town.

V Do you have a family?

H Not yet. I have a girlfriend.

V I see. You know what has happened, I take it?

H Yes.

V You know that Maager had a relationship with a schoolgirl, and that the girl is dead?

H Winnie Maas, yes.

V Did you teach her as well?

H Yes.

V In what subjects?

H Maths and physics.

V What marks did you give her?

H Marks? I don't see what relevance that has.

V You don't? Please answer my question even so.

H I gave her a six in physics and a four in maths.

V Not especially high marks, then.

H No. I still don't see the relevance.

V Was she pretty?

H I beg your pardon?

V I asked you if Winnie Maas was pretty.

H That's not something I have an opinion about.

V Did Arnold Maager think Winnie Maas was pretty?

H /No answer/

V I suggest you make an effort to answer that question. In all probability you'll be asked it again during the trial, so you might as well get used to it.

H I don't know if Maager thought that Winnie Maas was pretty.

V But you know that he had an affair with her?

H I'd hardly call it an affair.

V You wouldn't? What would you call it, then?

H She offered herself up to him on a plate. He made a mistake. It only happened once.

V So you think his behaviour is defensible, do you?

H Of course I don't. All I'm saying is that you could hardly call it an affair.

V Were you present in the flat when Maager and Winnie Maas had intercourse?

H No.

V But you know about it?

H Yes.

V Did you know about it before the girl's death as well?

H Yes.

V How and when did you hear about it?

H Some colleagues talked about it.

V Who?

H Cruickshank and Nielsen.

V Two of those who were present at the party after the disco on the tenth of June?

H Yes.

V And they said that Maager had sexual intercourse with Winnie Maas?

H Yes.

V When was that?

H A few days afterwards. The last week of term. Maager said so himself not long afterwards.

V In what connection?

H We'd gone out for a beer. At the very beginning of the summer holiday – round about the twentieth.

V Where?

H Lippmann's. And a few other bars.

V And that was when he told you that he'd had intercourse with a pupil?

H He told me a bit about how it had happened – I already knew about the basic facts.

V What did he say?

245

H That he'd been as pissed as a newt, and regretted what had happened. And he hoped there wouldn't be any repercussions.

V Repercussions? What did he mean by that?

H That neither he nor the girl would get into trouble as a result, of course.

V I see. But the other pupils must have known what had happened?

H I assume so. Although I didn't hear anything about it from pupils. But then it was just before the summer holidays, of course.

V So perhaps the main thing was that none of the parents got to hear about it?

H That's one way of looking at it, yes.

V Anyway, let's go on. This wasn't the only time you discussed the Winnie Maas business with Maager, was it?

H No.

V Let's hear details.

H We met in the middle of July as well.

V When and where?

H We made a trip out to the islands. One Saturday afternoon. It must have been the fifteenth or sixteenth, I think. Arnold rang me and said he'd like to have a chat. I had nothing else on at the time.

V So what was it all about this time?

H Winnie Maas. She was pregnant. Maager had just heard.

V What sort of state did he seem to be in?

H He was worried, of course. More than just worried, in fact. Winnie evidently wanted to have the baby.

V And what about Maager?

H You'd have to ask him about that.

V We already have done. Now we want to hear what you have to say, herr Heller. No doubt Maager made his own views clear during your trip to the islands.

H He wasn't his normal self.

V I didn't ask you if he was his normal self. I want to know what he said in connection with the fact that the girl was pregnant.

H He wanted her to have an abortion, of course. That's understandable, surely. She was too young to be a mother, and he was worried about how his wife would react.

V Really? So he hadn't told her about his, er, indiscretion?

H No, he hadn't.

V Was he afraid that Winnie Maas might do so?

H That's possible. I don't understand the point of all this. Why are we sitting here, discussing whether—

V It doesn't matter whether you understand or not. The police have to do their duty, no matter what. Do you think there was anything else that Arnold Maager was afraid of?

H Such as what?

V Think about it. What did you talk about, in fact?

H Everything under the sun.

V How many islands did you visit?

H Doczum and Billsmaar. We just sailed round them. We didn't go ashore at all.

V Did you come up with a solution to Maager's problems?

H Solution? What kind of a solution?

V If you spent several hours on the ferry, you must surely have discussed this and that? Toyed with various thoughts?

H I don't understand what you're talking about.

V I'm talking about escape routes. Possible escape routes to enable Arnold Maager to wriggle out of the awkward situation he found himself in. I hope you're not pretending to be more stupid than you really are – I thought you had a university degree.

H /No reply/

V Surely that's why he wanted to meet you? To get some help.

H He didn't only want to talk. He was desperate, for God's sake.

V Desperate? Are you saying that Arnold Maager was

desperate when the pair of you made that trip round the islands on Saturday, the sixteenth of July?

/Pause while a new tape is fitted into the recorder/

Vrommel: Did you have any further contact with Arnold Maager during the weeks before Winnie Maas's death? After July the sixteenth, that is.

Heller: He phoned me a few times. Before it happened, I mean.

V A few telephone conversations. What did you talk about?

H All kinds of things.

V About Winnie Maas as well?

H Yes.

V And what did Maager have to say?

H He was worried.

V Explain.

H What do you mean, explain?

V Did he say anything about what he intended to do? How did you assess his state of mind?

H He said he was having trouble sleeping. He didn't know whether or not he should tell his wife.

V Did you give him any advice?

H No. What could I say?

V Did you think he was unbalanced during these telephone calls?

H Not really unbalanced. Worried and tense, more like.

V Do you know if he had much contact with the girl?

H They'd talked things over. He'd tried to persuade her to have an abortion. He'd offered to help her out financially.

V And what did she say to that?

H She stuck to her guns, it seemed. She wanted to have the baby.

V And what about the financial side?

H I don't know.

V You don't know?

H No.

V All right. When you heard what had happened, that the girl had been found dead on the railway line, how did you react then?

H I was shocked, naturally.

V Yes, naturally. We were all shocked. Were you surprised as well?

H Of course I was surprised. It was horrendous.

V So you hadn't expected that development?

H No, of course I hadn't. He must have taken leave of his senses. It's horrendous.

V Do you think it's surprising that he took leave of his senses?

H /No reply/

V I'll ask you again. Bearing in mind all the

circumstances, do you think it's surprising that Arnold Maager took leave of his senses?

H I don't know. Perhaps not.

V Thank you, herr Heller. That will be all for now.

25

For a brief moment – just a fraction of a second – she thought he was going to hit her.

But nothing happened. Not even a gesture. But the very fact that such an image appeared in her mind's eye must mean something, of course. Not necessarily that he was that type of man – somebody who would start using his fists when he'd run out of words: but something nevertheless. A suspicion? A warning?

Or was it just a distorted figment of the imagination? A projection of her own dodgy emotional life?

In any case, it stayed there. And would continue to stay there, she knew that even before the moment had passed.

'You did what?' he snarled through gritted teeth.

'I left it up there and took a taxi instead,' she said.

'You left my car up there in the forest? Without arranging for anybody to see to it?'

She shrugged. He's got a point, she thought. I wouldn't be exactly pleased in those circumstances either.

'A Trabant,' she said. 'I didn't think it was worth bothering about.'

He ignored that comment. Drummed with his fingers on the table, and stared above her shoulder. The skin over his cheeks became taut.

'So now what?' he said.

'I'll sort it out,' she said with a sigh. 'If it's so damned important for you to have a car at your disposal, maybe you could hire one for the time being. I'll pay. Unfortunately a lot of other things have happened, and I haven't time to worry about such trivia at the moment.'

He allowed a few seconds to pass before he asked.

'What exactly has happened?'

'Maager has gone missing. Things were hectic, and I didn't have an opportunity of looking for a garage just then.'

'Gone missing? Why?'

'I've no idea. He hasn't been seen at the home since Saturday.'

'So both the father and the daughter are missing now?'

'So it seems.'

'Do the police know about it?'

Moreno took a sip of juice and made to stand up.

'If they do, they haven't got round to doing anything about it yet,' she said. 'Those layabouts up at Sidonis reported it a few hours ago. Despite the fact that he's been gone for two days. No, I really must talk to Vrommel and Vegesack about this – it's high time for them to wake up now.'

Mikael leaned back and looked at her with a trace of a smile on his lips. She wasn't sure how to interpret it.

It was rather easier to interpret what he said.

'So, Inspector Moreno is back on duty now, is she?'

Moreno leaned back and thought for two seconds.

'I'm moving out this evening,' she said. 'Thank you for the last few days here.'

His smile seemed to freeze, but before he had a chance to say anything she had stood up and left the table.

'I'll sort your car out as well,' she said over her shoulder. 'Hire a car and spend time on the beach until you get it back!'

Why don't I even feel sorry for him? she thought when she had turned the corner. Is it because I'm becoming a bitch?

'Yes, I'd heard about that,' said Constable Vegesack, looking sombre. 'It's a damned nuisance that they've left it for so long before reporting it. Not that I know what we can do about it, but things are not made any easier when you're two days behind even before you've started.'

'The most important thing is not what we can do about it,' said Moreno, 'but what has happened.'

Vegesack frowned and felt for the knot of his tie which, for once, wasn't there. He was wearing a marine blue tennis shirt and thin cotton trousers in a slightly lighter shade – absolutely right for the weather and the time of year, and Moreno wondered in passing if the return of his girlfriend had anything to do with his outfit. She hoped so – and hoped that the bags under his eyes were also connected with her presence. In the way he had indicated a few days previously.

'Okay,' he said. 'What do you think's happened, then?'

Moreno cast a glance at the half-open door before replying.

'Where's the chief of police?'

'He's on the beach,' said Vegesack. 'Something has happened. We'll come to that later.'

Moreno nodded.

'I hope you don't mind my poking my nose into this business?'

'Why should I do that? Everybody has a right to decide how to spend their own holidays.'

She decided not to investigate how large a dose of irony there was in that remark. Not just now, at least.

'Either Maager has run away,' she said, 'or something has happened to him. What do you reckon is most likely?'

Vegesack rubbed both his temples with the tips of his fingers and seemed to be thinking for all he was worth.

'I've no idea,' he said eventually. 'How the hell should I know? But what I understand least of all is why anybody should want him out of the way – I assume that's what you're fishing for?'

Moreno shrugged.

'Why should he do a runner? Is that any more likely?'

Vegesack sighed.

'Would you like a drop of mineral water?'

'Yes please,' said Moreno.

He went into the kitchenette and returned with a plastic bottle and two glasses.

'Dehydration,' he said. 'I suffer from it. And lack of sleep.'

But not lack of love, Moreno thought as he was filling her glass. Nor would I if I weren't so damned snooty.

'Anyway,' she said. 'If we assume – hypothetically – that he's run off of his own free will, where does that get us?'

'He must have some reason or other,' said Vegesack.

'Precisely. Give me a reason.'

'He hasn't left the care home for all of sixteen years.'

'That's true.'

'So it must . . . It must be connected with his daughter's visit.'

'Really? What makes you think that?'

'Surely it's pretty obvious . . . But just how it's linked, God only knows.'

'She visited him a week last Saturday. Why wait for a whole week?'

Vegesack started rubbing his temples again. Moreno wondered if he'd been on some kind of yoga course and learned to stimulate the flow of blood to his brain by doing that. In any case it looked more intentional than absent-minded; but she didn't ask about that either.

'Maybe it doesn't have so much to do with her visit,' he said in the end, 'but more with her disappearance.'

'That's what I think as well,' said Moreno. 'And how come that Maager knows about Mikaela's disappearance?'

Vegesack stopped massaging his temples.

'Oh hell,' he said. 'Through me, of course. I told him when I was there and tried to talk to him.'

'When was that?'

Vegesack worked it out in his head without any further assistance.

'Last Wednesday, I think. Yes, Wednesday.'

'That fits. It would be useful if you could recall exactly what you said to him,' said Moreno. 'And how he reacted.'

Vegesack flung out his hands and almost overturned the bottle of water.

'He didn't react at all. Not to anything. He said hello when I arrived, and goodbye when I left. But that's about all . . . But he did listen to what I said, yes, he did that. I told him how things stood, and that it looked as if Mikaela Lijphart had disappeared. That we knew she was his daughter, and that she'd been to see him, and that her mother had come to Lejnice in order to look for her. Naturally, I tried to find out what he'd said to her, about that business sixteen years ago and so on. If she'd been upset, or how she'd reacted. They'd evidently spent a few hours in the grounds, talking.'

'But he didn't give you any answers?'

'No.'

'Did you get any impressions? Did he seem worried about her disappearance?'

Vegesack gazed out of the window for a while.

'Yes, I think so,' he said. 'I think that news might even have prevented him from saying anything. He might have said something if I hadn't told him about Mikaela right away. But then again . . . For God's sake, I don't know. I was only with him for twenty minutes. Are you suggesting that he might have gone looking for her? Is that the conclusion you've reached?'

Moreno took a sip of water.

'I haven't come to any conclusions at all,' she said. 'It could just as well be that something has happened to him. You spoke to him last Wednesday, but he didn't disappear from the care home until Saturday. Why did he wait? Something else might have happened – on Thursday or Friday – to influence events. I ought to have asked more questions when I was out there, but that didn't occur to me until I was on the way back.'

'It's Monday today,' said Vegesack. 'That means he's already been missing for several days. He's not used to being out there. Mixing with people. Isn't it a bit odd that nobody seems to have noticed him?'

Moreno shrugged.

'How do you know that nobody's noticed him?'

Vegesack didn't answer.

'There's so much about this business that seems a bit odd,' said Moreno. 'That's why I just can't go off and enjoy my holiday. I've dreamt about that girl two nights running. I've just told my boyfriend to go to hell because of this business . . . I don't know if that can be classified as occupational injury – what do you think?'

Why am I telling this to Vegesack? she asked herself, when she noted his blush and raised eyebrows, and realized that this was intimate information that he didn't know how to handle.

'Oh dear,' he said diplomatically.

'You can say that again,' said Moreno. 'I've been poking my nose much too far into this business, but at least I've now received confirmation of a few things. I now know I haven't been imagining things that are too wide of the mark. I take it you didn't notice any indications that Maager was intending to run away when you were together with him?'

Vegesack shook his head.

'And heaven only knows how he took the news about his daughter's disappearance, you reckon?'

'I wonder if even the heavens know,' said Vegesack. 'But it's all so damned awful – for Maager, I mean. Even if you take into account that he's a murderer and all the rest of it. First she turns up out of the blue after sixteen years, and then she's more missing than she's ever been. It must be hard for him, whichever way you look at it.'

'Hard indeed,' agreed Moreno. 'Could you please help me with one other thing?'

'Of course,' said Vegesack, suddenly looking wide awake and raring to go. 'What?'

'Find out if Maager had any other visits or telephone calls between Wednesday and Saturday last week.'

'Okay,' said Vegesack. 'I'll give them a ring. How shall we get in touch – will you be calling in?'

'I'll be in touch in any case,' said Moreno with a sigh.

'Have there been any more responses to the Wanted notice regarding Mikaela?'

Vegesack rooted around in the pile of papers on his desk.

'Two,' he said. 'We can forget about one of them – a certain herr Podager who always gives advice to the police on occasions like this. He's over eighty-five and sees all kinds of things, despite the fact that he's been almost blind for the last twenty years.'

'I see,' said Moreno. 'What about the other one?'

'A woman up in Frigge,' said Vegesack, reading from a piece of paper. 'Fru Gossenmühle. It seems she phoned the local police last night and claimed she had seen a girl looking like the photograph of Mikaela Lijphart. At the railway station. They were going to talk to her this morning, and then they'll no doubt be in touch with us.'

Moreno thought for a while.

'How far is it to Frigge?' she asked

'About a hundred and fifty kilometres.'

Moreno nodded.

'So we just need to wait, then. By the way, to change the subject, can you recommend a decent garage in Lejnice?'

'Garage?'

'Yes. A repair workshop. Not too expensive. It's about mending a Trabant.'

'A Trabant? Surely you don't drive around in a Trabant?'

'Did,' said Moreno. 'Well?'

'Er . . . Let's see . . . Yes, Kluiverts, they are reliable.'

She made a note of the number, and another one of a guest house that Vegesack thought charged reasonable rates. He pointed out that he had never actually stayed in a B&B establishment in Lejnice, and that of course it was the summer season now.

Naturally, Moreno could have used the police station telephone to make the two calls, but something told her that it was high time she started restoring that old dividing line between work and her private life.

Start sketching it in at least, she thought with grim self-irony as she shook Vegesack's hand and thanked him for his help.

'Oh, I nearly forgot,' she said as she stood in the door-way. 'What had happened down on the beach? You said that Vrommel had been called out.'

Vegesack frowned again.

'I don't really know,' he said. 'But they've evidently found a body.'

'A body?'

'Yes. Some little kids were playing around in the sand and dug it up, I think.'

'And?'

'That's all I know,' said Vegesack apologetically, looking

at the clock. 'We heard about it just over an hour ago. Vrommel took charge of it. Apparently there are officers there from Wallburg as well – scene-of-crime boys and technicians: we don't have resources like that, and . . .'

He fell silent. Stood there with his hands half raised, as if he had been going to start massaging his temples again, but didn't need to as a thought had struck him.

'Good Lord! Surely you don't think . . . ?'

'I don't think anything at all,' said Moreno. 'Man or woman?'

'No idea. He just said a body, that's all the Skunk said. A dead body.'

The Skunk? Moreno thought and hesitated for a moment with her hand on the door handle.

'I'll be in touch,' she said eventually, and went out into the sunshine.

26

She came to Florian's Taverna – a somewhat shabby-looking establishment that according to Mikael had looked exactly the same ever since the fifties, and presumably made a point of maintaining that profile – at five minutes past two, and suddenly realized that she had eaten nothing at all since that morning's wretched cheese sandwich. She had drunk quite a lot, of course – juice and water and coffee and more water – but her stomach was rumbling and it dawned on her that it was time she started using her teeth for something other than grinding and gritting. Especially as she had thirty-two of them. Or was it only twenty-eight?

She didn't get round to counting them, but sat down at a table on the terrace under a parasol instead. She ordered some garlic bread, a shellfish salad and a telephone directory. The latter was to enable her check that all the local garages were not shut due to holidays and the local guest houses were not full up, thanks to the lovely weather.

They were not, thank goodness. Neither type of establishment. A gruff-voiced woman at Dombrowski's guest house promised to hold a room for her until nine o'clock – for three nights: they didn't let rooms for a shorter time than that during the holiday season. No balcony and not much of a view, but the price was not unreasonable. By no means. So there was no reason not to thank the woman and confirm the booking.

She thanked the woman and confirmed the booking. Monday night, Tuesday night, Wednesday night, she thought. I'll go back home on Thursday. That suited her down to the ground: by then no doubt things would have become sufficiently clear for Vrommel (the Skunk?) and Vegesack to handle everything without assistance.

Egon Kluivert, of Kluivert, Kluivert and Sons, claimed he was up to his ears in work; but after a bit of bargaining (despite the fact that he couldn't understand for the life of him why a sweet girl like Moreno – yes, you could tell that from her voice if you had ears to hear and were a man of the world – why such a sweet girl should be driving around in a bloody sardine tin like a Trabant) he promised both to fix the ignition and arrange for the sardine tin to be transported to Tschandala in Port Hagen. No problem, he knew where the house was situated. If not this evening, then tomorrow morning at the latest – where should he send the bill to?

She explained that she would call in and pay it before Wednesday.

He wondered if she needed a new car. It so happened that he had a few peaches standing in his forecourt. Ridiculously cheap prices, and just nicely run in.

No, she didn't need a new car at the moment, she told him. But she promised to be in touch as soon as she did.

The food arrived, and she ate with the vague feeling that things were going to turn out okay, despite the fact that she had no right to believe that they would. Never mind to demand that they should.

She ordered a small calvados with her coffee, to remind herself that she was still on holiday, and then she made another call. This time to her old friend and confidante Clara Mietens.

She got through to an answering machine. In thirty-five seconds Moreno gave her a summary of the situation, explained that she would probably be returning to Maardam towards the end of the week, and asked if the planned project of a several-day bicycle tour around the Sorbinowo region was still on the cards. Next week, perhaps?

She left her mobile number, and urged Clara to respond as soon as she had checked her messages and thought it over.

I need to get some exercise, Moreno thought. My head will coagulate if I don't.

Then she paid her bill and headed for the sea.

The beach was just as full as it had been during the hot days of the previous week, but she saw the red-and-white police tape the moment she passed over the brow of the hill and started walking down towards the sands.

A bit to the north and quite a long way up from the waterline (it was almost low tide, and the shiny ridges of the sandbanks were becoming visible) an area about half the size of a football pitch had been cordoned off. The tape formed a rectangle all the way round, and was fluttering peacefully in the gentle sea breeze. It occurred to Moreno that it was a long time since she had seen anything so surrealistically bizarre.

To both the north and the south – more or less as far as the eye could see – people were romping around merrily, swimming, sunbathing, playing beach tennis and football, and throwing frisbees: free and easy in both mood and dress. But things were different inside the grim rectangle of death. There uniformed scene-of-crime officers were crawling around sweatily in their hunt for clues, and three dog-handlers patrolled the cordoned-off area to make sure curious spectators kept their distance while fine-grained sand slowly but surely filled their regulation low black shoes.

The spot where the body had been found, roughly in the middle of the half football pitch, was marked by another square of police tape, but this area had obviously been searched already. The scene-of-crime crawlers – she counted five of them plus a senior officer standing upright – were currently in a concentric circle a good ten metres away from the hole.

It was indeed a hole. And she knew the score: the team started in the middle and worked outwards, of course. Picked up everything they could find in the sand that seemed to have come from a human hand, and put each item into a plastic bag which was then sealed. Cigarette butts. Bits of paper. Chewing gum. Capsules. Condoms and spent matches.

All with the aim of finding a clue. Preferably a murder weapon. Even before she started walking down towards the warm, powdery sand, she knew that this was a murder investigation. Everything pointed to murder. And of course it was this insight that gave rise to the feeling of surrealism. Of bizarre reality.

Inspector Moreno had been there before, and knew the significance of what her eyes were telling her.

*

One of the three armed dog-handlers had blue eyes, and she chose him.

His name was Struntze, it turned out. She allowed him to take his time over studying her ID, then explained that she had just been allocated to the case, and had come to get a clear picture of what was happening. Where was Chief Inspector Vrommel? She had expected to find him here.

Strunze said that he had left only a quarter of an hour ago, but would be coming back.

Moreno said it didn't matter as she would meet him later in any case. Meanwhile, could Struntze please explain what had happened.

Constable Struntze was more than willing to put her in the picture, and did so in a series of well-judged stage whispers.

Murder. Everything pointed to murder.

The body was that of a man between thirty and forty, according to the doctor's preliminary conclusions. It had been lying there, buried in the sand, for about a week – give or take a day or two, it was difficult to be precise at this early stage.

He had been killed by a stab from a sharp instrument straight into his eye. His left eye. He must have died on the spot. Or within a few seconds, at least. Presumably quite close to the place where he had been buried. And where he had been found. By a couple of small boys – wasn't that awful?

Moreno agreed that it certainly was.

Struntze thought it would leave them marked for life.

Moreno pointed out that they would see a hundred and twenty murders every week on the telly. And time heals the occasional wound. But who was he? The dead man.

They didn't know yet, Struntze explained. He'd been dressed in jeans and a short-sleeved cotton shirt, but he had no identification papers on him. No money or anything else in his pockets. About a hundred and seventy-five centimetres tall. Dark brown hair. Quite sturdily built. Thirty-five, plus or minus five, as he'd said already.

What about the weapon, Moreno wondered.

No idea. Something pointed. It had passed right through his eye and into the brain. They hadn't found it, of course. Somebody had suggested that it might have been a tent peg. Or a pair of scissors.

A tent peg? Moreno wondered. In that case it hardly seemed like a premeditated murder.

'Do you know if they've found anything?' she asked by way of conclusion, pointing at the crawling scene-of-crime officers.

Struntze stroked his dog and permitted himself a grim smile.

'Sand,' he said. 'A hell of a lot of sand.'

*

It was a few minutes past four when Moreno left Constable Strunze and his King in peace. After a few moments' thought she decided to go back to Port Hagen on foot along the beach. It was at least a seven- or eight-kilometre walk and would take a couple of hours, but as she had already established, she needed some exercise. She might as well take this opportunity.

She also needed to think. To work out exactly where she stood with regard to Mikael Bau, and all the other things. Her voluntary involvement in the Lijphart–Maager problem, for instance. Always assuming it was a problem . . . In any case, few things were more appropriate when it came to disentangling a mish-mash of thoughts than a long walk by the sea.

That's what Van Veeteren always used to say.

If you don't have a car in which to drive around and think, you can always try the sea. If it happens to be handy.

Perhaps it was a bit on the warm side for such a walk today, but never mind. She walked out to the waterline, put her sandals into her rucksack and started walking barefoot on the firm, wet sand that felt pleasantly smooth and cool. Less than an hour ago it had been the bottom of the sea. If she wanted to cool down the rest of her body as well, she only needed to walk a bit further out – a little salt water on her thin, faded cotton dress she'd been wearing for ten years or more was nothing to complain about. Nothing at all.

And a sandy beach all the way. Never-changing sea, never-changing sand dunes up to the edge of the shoreline. Sky, sea and land. Why haven't I been for a walk here before? she wondered. I ought to have done.

Then she switched on her thoughts. Started with the problem that entered her mind first: Mikael Bau.

Why had it turned out like this? she asked herself, determined to be broad-minded about it. It had started so well. He had claimed that he loved her, and she had almost been prepared to move in with him only a few days ago. So why?

There was no satisfactory answer, she soon realized. No clear and unambiguous answer, in any case; but if she was going to walk along at the water's edge for the next two hours, she might as well spend a little time thinking about it.

Had she grown tired of him? Could it be that simple? When it came down to the nitty gritty, was the answer as mundane as that?

Was she ready to share her life with somebody else in any circumstances, no matter who he might be? she asked herself, in the best girl's magazine fashion. Or woman's magazine fashion come to that – it was a long time since she'd read either.

Well, was she? Nothing crucial had happened between her and Mikael Bau, for God's sake. Nothing at all to justify a hasty break-up like the one that had happened. He hadn't hit her, even if she thought he might do for one brief, dizzying moment.

He hadn't played the male chauvinist pig. Hadn't done anything stupid. Hadn't displayed any hitherto hidden obnoxious sides to his character.

No skeletons in the cupboard. No sudden yawning gaps in his character. Just an old Trabant.

Had she simply grown tired of him? Would that be enough?

There hadn't been anything wrong with their relationship, nothing disturbing had happened in their daily existence together – nothing she could put her finger on, at least: but perhaps that was the best that could be said about it. That there was nothing wrong.

There's nothing wrong with my old refrigerator either, she thought, but I wouldn't want to have a child with it.

Perhaps something more was needed. Not simply the absence of negatives.

It was a stroke of luck that I had to leave that wretched old banger at Sidonis, she thought. So that things were brought to a head at last.

The Trabant syndrome?

She found it hard not to burst out laughing at that

273

thought. Bitch? she then asked herself. Am I really becoming a bitch? For several years Clara Mietens had claimed to be one with regard to the opposite sex, but Moreno hadn't bothered to try to understand or to analyse that relationship. And she didn't need to do so now, she decided. She found it hard to imagine a whole life without a man; but as for the rest of her holiday – there were less than three weeks to go – well, that was another matter.

Nothing to worry about. Being together with Mikael had been no problem at all in that respect – and there was no need to analyse it, she decided. Why should women always feel obliged to hum and haw about their putative emotional lives? To put everything into words? (An example of a permanently bad conscience, perhaps?) Surely it was enough simply to feel things. In a way women were much more guilty of intellectualizing emotions than men were – of making them tangible, as Clara used to say – it wasn't the first time this had occurred to her. Men just kept quiet, and made the most of the feelings instead.

Well, the former at least.

In any case, she hadn't given him any promises or commitments. None at all. So what?

No matter how you look at it, I'm a free woman. The first one in the history of the world. Ah well, hallelujah.

I hope he's not sitting there waiting for me when I go back, she thought in horror. With a bottle of wine and some new delicacy or other. I couldn't cope with any emotional outbursts and dramatic farewells today.

The sun went behind a cloud. She pushed her sunglasses up on top of her head, and her thoughts about Mikael to one side.

She noticed that she slowed down the moment she stopped thinking about him. As if she had shaken off an irritation that had increased her speed unnecessarily.

As if item number two – Mikaela Lijphart and her broken family – somehow needed more copious and more thorough attention. Perhaps that wasn't all that odd.

The weeping girl on the train. The worried mother. The father who had been hidden away and forgotten for so long. And the disgusting business of him and the schoolgirl Winnie Maas.

An epilogue sixteen years later? she thought. Was that possible?

But on the other hand, what other explanation could there be?

How else was it possible to explain that Mikaela Lijphart and her father went up in smoke within only a few days? After having met for the first time in sixteen years. Having met for the first time ever in a way, since Mikaela was only two years old when Arnold Maager was shut up in an institution. She could hardly have any memories of him at all.

So the question was: could these two disappearances be totally unconnected?

Not on your life, Moreno decided. Even a seven-year-old could grasp that they must be connected.

But how?

She changed direction by thirty degrees and found herself knee-deep in the water. Cool and pleasant, but it didn't help. The question was still unanswered. *How* were they connected? *What* was the slender thread between 1983 and 1999?

And what ought she to do in order to disentangle it?

The more she thought about it, the more obvious at least one thing seemed to be. Maager must have said something crucial while they were walking through the grounds at Sidonis last Saturday. Absolutely crucial.

Something to do with the Winnie Maas business.

Something new?

Question mark, question mark. But Mikaela Lijphart had never heard the old version of what had happened when she met her father, so for her ears everything – every single painful admission and every single degrading disclosure – must have been completely new and fresh, irrespective of how far it fitted in with the old established picture of what had happened.

276

And so it wasn't possible to be sure about anything, Moreno concluded. It wasn't possible to speculate about whether Maager had come up with some clarification or other. That couldn't be helped.

And where had the girl gone to on the Sunday morning, when she took the bus from the youth hostel to Lejnice? Had she been to visit somebody? If so, who?

Questions breed worse than rabbits, Moreno thought, and washed her face in cooling water. Are there no hypotheses I can come up with? Any assumptions? Any wild guesses? What's going on here?

But unfortunately she was bereft of ideas. Although a new thought occurred to her from a different direction.

The dead body that had been buried in the sand.

A thirty-five-year-old man. Lying there for a week, if what Struntze said was correct. That meant it must have happened last Sunday, surely.

Connection? Moreno thought again.

What bloody connection? she thought soon afterwards. I'm thirsty.

She made her way through the warm, dry sand and bought a Coke in a little kiosk that seemed to be strategically placed to repair dodgy fluid balances in walkers between Lejnice and Port Hagen.

She returned to the waterline, drained the can and

dumped it in a rubbish bin evidently placed there in accordance with the same strategy.

She checked her watch. It was ten minutes to five, and in the distance, in the quivering afternoon light, she thought she could make out the pier and the boats off Port Hagen.

About an hour left, she thought. Unless it's a mirage. I'm not getting anywhere with all these thoughts. And I don't want to start thinking about Franz Lampe-Leermann. Anything but that.

What was it that Constable Vegesack had said, incidentally? That there hadn't been a murder out here for thirty years?

Now they had two missing persons and an unidentified body in the space of a single week. Surely that was a set of circumstances worth investigating rather more closely?

But instead of considering any more unanswered rhetorical questions, Inspector Moreno began to think about what measures she could possibly take in the next few days. If she was going to have to stay here until Thursday.

And she was.

If for no other reason than to pay for the repairs to the car of her former boyfriend (fiancé? bloke? lover?).

★

He wasn't sitting there waiting for her when she finally arrived at Tschandala – more tired and dehydrated than she could ever have imagined when she set off.

It was five minutes past six. The military green Trabant was parked outside the gate with an envelope tucked under a windscreen wiper and Montezuma asleep on the roof.

But no Mikael Bau: he would have been sitting out on the terrace if he'd been at home, she knew that. She took the invoice, left Montezuma to sleep in peace and went inside to pack her things.

No letter, no message, nothing to indicate that he had returned from Lejnice at all, when she came to think about it.

So be it, thought Moreno when she had finished packing. She remained standing in the kitchen while wondering whether to write anything herself, but in the end decided not to.

I can't raise enough inspiration, she thought.

But I've plenty of perspiration. And I'm tired and dirty – I hope the shower in my luxurious guest room works.

She took her suitcase and her rucksack, and started walking to the bus stop. It was a quarter to seven, a bus was due at five minutes to, if she had read the timetable rightly.

It must be the same bus that passes the youth hostel, it suddenly struck her. She wondered how many drivers there were.

27

Constable Vegesack's girlfriend was called Marlene Urdis, and the previous evening they had made a solemn promise not to make love that night. Two nights in succession and another session in the afternoon would have to suffice.

According to plan, they had gone to bed and fallen asleep before eleven o'clock – but a few hours later she rolled over and came a bit too close, and off they went again. But what else could one expect? They had been apart for three weeks (Marlene had been in Sicily with a girlfriend of hers, a combined working trip and holiday paid for partly by a glossy monthly magazine specializing in travel and interior decor and such-like), and the separation had left a sort of void, an erotic vacuum that needed to be filled and balanced out retroactively. They needed to make up for every missed opportunity, the sooner and more thorough, the better.

You only live once, after all – if that.

But it feels a bit odd even so, Vegesack thought as he drained his second cup of black coffee at about half past seven the next morning. And tiring. If they carried on like this much longer, he would have to take sick leave. Marlene was on summer vacation from her architecture studies, and could stay in bed all morning; but it was his duty to turn up at his office in the police station, and try to stay awake with the aid of every means of assistance available.

In other words, coffee. *The heartblood of tired men*, as the Great Man Chandler had put it.

And a murder, he reminded himself.

And perhaps also that attractive detective inspector. She had got her teeth into that old Maager business, God only knows why. Ah well, it's good that there are things to occupy oneself with, he thought optimistically as he took his bicycle out of its stall. There might be enough to keep him awake today as well.

Always assuming he didn't fall off his bike on the way to the police station, and he didn't usually do so.

Chief of Police Vrommel hadn't turned up for work yet today, but fröken Glossmann in the office, and one of the probationers – Helme – were present and correct as usual.

Plus a blonde well into her thirties who seemed to have

spent at least a hundred hours lying in the sun this last week. She was sitting opposite Helme at his desk, chewing at her cerise lower lip while Helme wrote something down in his notebook.

'Ah,' he said when he saw Vegesack appear in the doorway. 'This is Damita Fuchsbein. She's been waiting for a quarter of an hour, but I thought it was best if you or Vrommel took care of her.'

Vegesack shook her hand and introduced himself.

'What's it all about, then?' he asked.

'That dead body on the beach,' said Helme in a stage whisper before Damita Fuchsbein had stopped chewing her lower lip.

'I see,' said Vegesack.

He looked at the clock. A few minutes to eight. Vrommel rarely put in an appearance before nine. Perhaps he might turn up a bit earlier today, in view of the situation and the circumstances . . . There was supposed to be a summary session with colleagues from Wallburg as well. But why wait?

Why indeed. He nodded, and invited the woman to move over to his desk. Asked her if she'd like a cup of coffee, but she shook her head. There was a rustling sound from her dry locks of hair.

'Well,' he said, clicking his ballpoint pen. 'What do you have to say for yourself?'

'I think I know who it is.'

'The man on the beach?'

'Yes. I heard about it last night, they said you hadn't identified him yet.'

'That's right,' said Vegesack, wondering quickly if he knew her. He didn't think so, but he was far from certain. Both her hair and her skin could well be very different in colour, depending on the time of year. In any case, Damita Fuchsbein seemed to have a hobby that was very much in tune with the times, and one she made no attempt to hide. Her body.

'Who is it?' he asked.

She cleared her throat and blinked a few times.

'Tim Van Rippe,' she said. 'Do you know who that is?'

Vegesack wrote the name down in his notebook. Thought for a moment, and said that he didn't think he knew who that was.

'He lives out at Klimmerstoft. Works at Klingsmann's. How should I put it – we haven't exactly been having a relationship, but we see each other now and again. And we'd agreed to go to Wimsbaden last Monday . . . To the music festival. But he never turned up. I've been ringing and trying to get hold of him all week, but he hasn't answered.'

Her voice was shaky, and Vegesack realized that she was on the point of crying underneath her elastic exterior.

'Tim Van Rippe? Have you any special reason for thinking that it's him? Anything more besides the fact that he's been difficult to get in touch with?'

Damita Fuchsbein sighed deeply and adjusted her hair.

'I've spoken to quite a few others who've been trying to contact him. Nobody seems to have seen him since Sunday – last Sunday, that is.'

'Does he have a family?'

'No.'

'Any relatives that you know of?'

'He has a brother in Aarlach, I know that. His father's dead, but I think his mother's still alive. But she doesn't live here either. I think she married again, and lives in Karpatz now.'

Vegesack noted it all down.

'Okay,' he said. 'We'd better go and take a look. Do you think you're up to it? It might be a bit unpleasant.'

Talk about understatement, he thought.

'Where is . . . Where's the body?'

'Wallburg. The forensic medicine centre. I can take you there – we'll be back here in an hour and a half.'

Damita Fuchsbein seemed to be at a loss for a second or two, then pulled herself together and clasped her hands in her lap.

'Okay. I suppose I don't have any choice.'

★

It was Tim Van Rippe.

If one could believe what Damita Fuchsbein said, that is: and of course there was no reason to doubt her tear-soaked identification. Together with the pathologist himself, an incredibly overweight Dr Goormann, and a police nurse, Vegesack spent some considerable time consoling the devastated woman, and he began to wonder if she was in fact on rather more intimate terms with the dead man than she had admitted so far.

Perhaps, perhaps not, Vegesack thought. No doubt that would become clearer in due course. While they were sitting in Goormann's poky little office, supplying a steady stream of paper handkerchiefs to Fuchsbein, Detective Intendent Kohler turned up: he was one of the two Wallburg officers who had been loaned to Vrommel as a result of the discovery of the dead body on the beach. He was a reserved, thin-haired man in his fifties, and immediately made a positive impression on Vegesack. He undertook to track down and make contact with Van Rippe's relatives – his brother in Aarlach and his mother in Karpatz, if one could believe the information Fuchsbein had provided while she was still able to talk.

Although there was no reason to doubt that either.

Vegesack took care of fröken Fuchsbein. Escorted her gently out of death's visiting room and treated her to a cup of coffee and a glass of calvados in one of the cafes in the square before they got into the car and set off to return to Lejnice.

He drove her to her home in Gloopsweg, and promised to telephone her later that evening to see how she was.

Don't go and lie down in the sun again, he thought, but he didn't say so.

By the time he returned to the police station it was ten past eleven, and Chief of Police Vrommel had just started a small press conference in connection with yesterday's macabre discovery on the beach. Vegesack sat down on a vacant chair behind a dozen journalists, and listened in.

Yes, the police were working all out.

Yes, they had every reason to believe that a crime had been committed. It was difficult to die a natural death in that way, and then dig oneself down into the sand.

Yes, they were following several lines of investigation, but there was no principal line. Extra resources had been moved in from Wallburg.

Yes, the leader of the investigative team was the chief of police himself; but there was no suspect, and they were still awaiting the results of certain technical tests.

No, the dead man had not yet been identified.

I ought to have rung him from Wallburg, Vegesack thought.

★

Moreno was woken up at a quarter to seven by the sun shining into her face. She had pulled down the old-fashioned dark-blue roller blind before going to bed, but at some point during the night it must have felt tired and rolled itself up again. Very discreetly, it seemed, as she hadn't been woken up by any noise.

She sat up in bed and thought for a while. Then dug a pair of shorts, a vest and a pair of trainers out of her rucksack, and set off.

To the beach, of course. But southwards this time, in order to avoid any intrusive memories of bodies in the sand and abandoned lovers. (Blokes? Boyfriends? Fiancés?)

It was a lovely morning, she felt that immediately. The beach was deserted, the sea mirror-like, and after only a couple of hundred metres she had to ask herself seriously why she didn't begin every day of her life in this way. Was there any possible argument against it?

Well, perhaps a windy morning in January had a different sort of charm. And of course there was a distinct shortage of seaside in central Maardam.

She turned back after twenty minutes, and was back in Dombrowski's at a quarter to eight. Took a shower and had breakfast in the company of a couple of morning newspapers in the shady garden. There were reports on the discovery of the body in both of them – especially in *Westerblatt* of course, which was the local paper – and as she read, drank coffee and chewed sandwiches made with thick slices of home-baked bread, cheese and paprika rings, she tried to sort out her programme for the day.

It wasn't straightforward. Above all she would presumably have to be discreet in the way in which she worked together with the Lejnice police. There were special circumstances, of course, but it was perfectly obvious that Vrommel was not interested in any kind of cooperation. Not at all. One might well ask why, but that could wait until another time. It would be better to stick to Vegesack – and probably best to leave it until the afternoon, she decided. If for no other reason than giving herself the chance of doing something off her own bat. And to be honest, Vegesack could do with a bit of time in order to get down to work, even if he had so far displayed no great desire to get stuck into the investigation.

But perhaps one couldn't expect him to have done so, Moreno thought. Bearing in mind the recent return of his girlfriend. But at least he had promised to investigate whether anybody had been to visit Maager at Sidonis. Or telephoned him. It had to be of crucial importance to get that sorted out as quickly as possible.

As she was thinking that, her mobile rang.

It was Mikael. They had spoken for a quarter of an hour the previous evening. Nothing very profound, but at least they had found an appropriate pitch at which to communicate with each other, which had to be good news.

And he hadn't said a word about being in love with her.

Now he was ringing just to say that he intended to pay Kluivert, Kluivert and Sons' bill himself: he had thought the matter over and concluded that he had been unfair. After a short discussion, she let him have his way.

When they had hung up, she remained seated for a while, thinking. She realized that she was having difficulty in suppressing a grim smile, but then took out her note-book and wrote down three questions.

What the hell has happened to Mikaela Lijphart?

What the hell has happened to Arnold Maager?

What the hell am I poking my nose into this business for, instead of enjoying my holiday like any normal person?

She stared at the questions and drank up the rest of her coffee. Then she wrote down a fourth question.

What the hell can I do today in order to find an answer to any of these questions?

She thought for a while longer, until she had decided on Plan A. It was five minutes to nine. Not a bad start to a day.

The woman who opened the door reminded her of a fish.

Perhaps it was something to do with her looks, or

perhaps it was the smell. Probably an unholy alliance of both, with each sensual reaction reinforcing the other.

'Fru Maas?'

'Yes.'

Moreno introduced herself and asked if she might come in for a chat.

No, she may not.

She asked if she could treat her to a cup of coffee and a glass of something somewhere. Maybe in Strandterrassen?

Yes, she could.

But not in Strandterrassen. There were too many capitalists and other schmucks there, explained fru Maas, and instead led the way to Darms cafe in the bus square. Honest people could sit here at a pavement table and watch the crowds in the square. If you got tired of that, you could always watch the pigeons.

It was congenial, in other words. What the hell did she want?

Moreno waited until the coffee and cognac had been served, then explained that she was a private detective looking for an eighteen-year-old girl. And that it was linked in a way with the tragic happening concerning fru Maas's daughter Winnie. Sixteen years ago, she thought it was.

'Private filth?' said Sigrid Maas, downing the cognac in one gulp. 'Go to hell!'

Bitch? Moreno thought. I have a lot to learn.

'I'll make it easier for you,' she said, cupping a protective hand round her own glass of cognac. 'If you answer my questions truthfully, and cut out the nonsense and insults, you'll earn yourself fifty smackers.'

Fru Maas glared at her, her mouth a mere narrow strip. She didn't answer, but it was obvious that she was weighing up the offer.

'You can have my cognac as well,' said Moreno, removing her hand from the glass.

'If you diddle me, I swear blind I'll kill you,' said fru Maas.

'I shan't diddle you,' said Moreno, checking in her purse to see if she really had that amount of cash with her. 'How could I?'

Fru Maas didn't answer, but lit a cigarette and moved the glass of cognac closer to her.

'Fire away!'

'Mikaela Lijphart,' said Moreno. 'She's the daughter of Arnold Maager, who murdered your daughter. A girl aged eighteen, as I said – she was only two when it happened. My first question is whether she's been here to see you during the last few weeks.'

Fru Mass inhaled deeply and sniffed at the cognac.

'Yes, she's been,' she said. 'Last Sunday, I think it was. 'God only knows why she came, God only knows why I allowed her in – the daughter of that bloody swine who ruined my life. I suppose I'm too kind-hearted, that's the problem.'

For a moment Moreno suspected the woman sitting opposite her was lying through her teeth. In order to keep Moreno happy and not lose out on the promised payment, perhaps. But it was easy to check.

'What did she look like?'

Fru Maas glared at her for a second, then leaned back on her chair and launched into a rather colourful description of Mikaela Lijphart: it was obvious to Moreno that this was the right girl. No doubt about it. Mikaela Lijphart really had come to visit fru Maas when she took the bus from the youth hostel that Sunday morning. What an unexpected bull's eye!

She suddenly felt that little nervous twinge – that sudden stimulus that could almost send her shooting off on a high and which might well have been the main reason why she decided to become a detective officer in the first place. If she were to be honest with herself.

Or which kept her in her job, at least. Something clicked. A suspicion was confirmed, and loose assumptions suddenly became reality. She felt totally and thrillingly alive – there was something sensual about it.

She had never spoken to anybody about this, not even Münster. Perhaps because she was afraid of not being taken seriously – or of being laughed at – but also because she didn't need to. She had no need to discuss this special pleasure with anybody else – or to attempt to put it into words. The fact that it was there was quite sufficient. It is, therefore it is, she had concluded on a previous occasion.

And now here she was, sitting at this cafe table with this ravaged, drunken woman, and experiencing this same vibrating excitement once again. Mikaela Lijphart had been to see her. That Sunday. Exactly as she'd thought.

Exactly as she would have done if she had been Mikaela Lijphart – gone to see the mother of the poor girl her father had killed. Sought her out so that . . . Hmm, why?

Hard to say. Certain moves were so obvious that you didn't really need to ask yourself why you had made them: reflex reactions in a way, but nearly always correct in the context. Just as instinctively straightforward as that nervous twinge.

'Why the hell are you looking for this young lass?' asked fru Maas, interrupting her train of thought.

'She's gone missing,' said Moreno again.

'Gone missing?'

'Yes. Nobody has seen her since that Sunday when she came to see you. Nine days ago.'

'Hmm. I expect she's run off with a bloke. That's what they do at that age.'

She took a swig of coffee, then poured the contents of

the glass of cognac into the cup. Sniffed at the resultant brew with the expression of a connoisseur. Moreno didn't doubt for a second that fru Maas used to run off with blokes when she was at that age, but she doubted whether Mikaela Lijphart had done that.

'What did you talk about?' she asked.

'Not much. She wanted to talk about her bloody father, that bastard, but I didn't want to. Why should I have to sit there remembering that shit-heap who killed my daughter? Eh? Can you tell me that?'

Moreno was unable to do so.

'Do you know that he's in the Sidonis care home, Arnold Maager?' she asked instead.

Fru Maas snorted.

'Of course I bloody well know. He can be where the hell he likes, as long as I don't have to think about him. Or listen to people talking about him.'

'And so you spoke about something else instead, then?' asked Moreno. 'With Mikaela Lijphart, that is.'

Fru Maas shrugged.

'I don't remember. We didn't talk about much at all. She was quite a cheeky young lady, that Mikaela girl, yes indeed.'

'Cheeky? What do you mean?'

'She suggested that it wasn't him.'

'Not him? What do you mean?'

'She started going on about how she might have jumped down from the viaduct of her own accord, and a load of crap like that. My Winnie? What? I was furious of course, and told her to hold her tongue.'

'Did she say why?'

'Eh?'

'If she suggested that her dad might be innocent, she must have had some reason for saying that.'

Fru Maas stubbed out her cigarette and immediately started fumbling in the pack for another one.

'God only knows. A lot of crap in any case – although she had been out at the loony bin and spoken to him. He evidently hadn't the courage to admit to his own daughter what he'd done, the cowardly bastard! Of course he did it. Screwing a schoolgirl! A sixteen-year-old! My Winnie! Can you imagine it, such a shit-heap?'

Moreno thought for a moment.

'What did she do next?'

'Eh?'

'Do you know where Mikaela went after she'd been speaking to you?'

Fru Maas lit her cigarette and seemed to be thinking things over.

'I don't know,' she said eventually.

Moreno said nothing, and waited.

'I suppose she wanted to speak to a few others,' said

fru Maas after a while, reluctantly. 'Friends of Winnie – though God only knows what good that would do.'

She took a deep swig from her cup, and closed her eyes as she swallowed it.

'Who exactly? Did you give her any names?'

Fru Maas inhaled and tried to look nonchalant. As if she didn't want to say any more.

'You haven't exactly earned your reward,' said Moreno.

'A few,' said fru Maas. 'A few names, I seem to remember . . . Since she was so bloody stubborn and wouldn't shut up. I couldn't get rid of her. So in the end I told her to go to Vera Sauger and leave me in peace.'

'Vera Sauger?'

'Yes, a hell of a nice girl. Best friends with Winnie since infants' school. And she's kept in touch as well, while all the others have just ignored me, and looked God in the arse when I've bumped into them in town.'

Looked God in the arse? Moreno thought. Reinhart would love that.

'So you suggested that Mikaela should go and see Vera Sauger, did you?'

Fru Maas nodded as she emptied her cup. Pulled a face.

'Do you know if she did visit her?'

'How the hell should I know? I just gave her a telephone number. No, come on, it's time for you to cough up. I've got better things to do than sitting around here being pestered.'

Moreno realized that she'd had enough as well. She handed over the money, and thanked fru Maas for her help. Maas grabbed the note and marched off without a word.

Vera Sauger? Moreno thought. The name sounds familiar.

28

'Van Rippe?' said Intendent Kohler. 'And what do we know about him?'

Vrommel brushed aside a fly that seemed to have taken an incomprehensible liking (as far as Constable Vegesack was concerned, at least) to his sweaty bald pate. (Presumably it thought it was just another dung heap, Vegesack thought, and made a mental note to enter this analysis into his black book.)

'We know what we know,' asserted the chief of police, and began reading from the sheet of paper he was holding in his hand. 'Thirty-four years old. Lived out at Klimmerstoft. Born and bred there, in fact. Bachelor. Worked at Klingsmann's, the furniture manufacturer, had done so for the last four years. There's not a lot to say about him. Lived with a woman for a few years, but they split up. No children. Played football for a few years, but stopped after a knee injury. No criminal record, never involved in anything dodgy . . . No enemies as far as we know.'

'Churchgoer, Friends of the Earth and the Red Cross?'
wondered the other detective officer from Wallburg.
His name was Baasteuwel, and was a small, somewhat
unkempt detective inspector in his forties. With a reputation for being shrewd, if Vegesack had understood the
situation rightly. In any case, he was the direct opposite of
Vrommel, and it was a pleasure to observe their mutual
antipathy. To crown it all, Baasteuwel smoked evil-smelling
cigarettes more or less all the time, totally oblivious to the
chief of police's objections, stated and unstated. This place
wasn't a day nursery, for Christ's sake.

'Not as far as we know,' muttered Vrommel. 'Not yet,
at least. We only identified him this morning, and so far
we've only talked to a few of his friends. He has a brother
and a mother still living: we've made contact with the
brother and he's on his way here. His mother is on a
motoring holiday in France, but will probably be back
home tomorrow. The day after at the latest.'

'Mobile phone?' asked Kohler.

'Negative,' said Vrommel. 'We'll know more about Van
Rippe when we've talked to a few more people. He seems
to have been missing since last Sunday in any case. Can we
move on to the technical details?'

'Why not?' said Baasteuwel. He stubbed out his cigarette and lit a new one.

Vrommel gathered together his papers, then nodded to

Constable Vegesack who took a sip of mineral water and began speaking.

It took almost ten minutes. Tim Van Rippe had died at some point on Sunday or Monday last week. The murder weapon was a pointed but not necessarily sharp instrument, as yet unidentified and unspecified, probably made of metal, which penetrated his left eye, continued into the cerebrum and wiped out so many vital functions that Van Rippe was probably clinically dead within three to six seconds after the penetration. It was not impossible that he might have delivered the fatal blow himself, but in that case some other person, as yet unidentified and unspecified, must have taken away the weapon and buried Van Rippe on the beach.

He had been lying there buried in the place where he was found by Henning Keeswarden and Fingal Wielki, aged six and four respectively, for about a week. It was not possible to establish how long had passed between the moment of death and the burial, according to the pathologist, Dr Goormann, but there was no reason to suspect that it would have been very long.

So much for the medical science. As for the results of the efforts of the scene-of-crime officers, most of them were not yet available. Roughly sixty more or less sandy objects had been sent to the Forensic Laboratory in Maardam for analysis. All that could be said for certain at this point in time was that no possible murder weapon had been found – nor anything that could throw light on what it might have looked like.

Nor who had been holding it.

The fact that the victim had been wearing a blue short-sleeved cotton shirt, jeans and underpants, but was without shoes or socks, was not a matter that the technicians needed to comment upon, as it was obvious to everybody who had been at the scene of the crime.

Vegesack – who hadn't been present at the scene of the crime – completed his run-through, and looked around the table.

'Drunk?' asked Baasteuwel.

'No,' said Vegesack. 'We'll get details of his stomach contents tomorrow.'

'Who was the last person to see him alive?'

'He was out fishing with a friend on Sunday morning. It could have been him.'

'Has he been interrogated?'

'On the telephone,' said Vrommel. 'I shall talk to him this evening.'

Baasteuwel didn't seem too satisfied, but desisted from asking any more questions.

'It must have happened during the night, I assume,' said Kohler after a few seconds of silence. 'The beach is presumably anything but deserted during the day, or . . .'

'Anything but,' said Vegesack. 'No, nobody's going to go there and murder somebody in broad daylight.'

'So, there we have it,' said Vrommel, brushing aside the fly again. 'I think that's enough. Have our friends from Wallburg any ideas to bestow upon us? If not, I'll declare the meeting closed for today. We have a few minor interviews to see to, as I said earlier, but Vegesack and I can deal with those without any need for assistance.'

Intendent Kohler closed his notebook and put it away in his brown briefcase which looked as if it had survived at least two world wars. Baasteuwel knocked the ash off his cigarette into his coffee cup, and scratched at his blue-grey stubble.

'All right,' he said. 'We'll be here at nine o'clock tomorrow morning. But make sure you've got somewhere by then. This is a murder investigation, not a bloody children's party.'

Vegesack could hear the grating of the chief of police's teeth, but no words managed to force their way out – which was probably just as well. Nobody else had anything to add, so after some thirty seconds, he and Vrommel were alone in the room.

'Clear up in here,' said Vrommel. 'And for God's sake make sure that the room is properly aired. Don't leave until it's done.'

Vegesack glanced furtively at the clock. Twenty minutes to five.

'What about the interrogations?' he asked. 'What shall we do about them?'

'I'll see to that,' said Vrommel, standing up. 'Your job is to clear up and lock up. I'll see you tomorrow morning. Good evening, Constable. And remember, don't say a word to any damned reporters.'

'Good evening, sir,' said Vegesack.

Moreno was sitting waiting with a half-empty glass of beer when he came to Strandterrassen.

'I'm sorry I'm late. It lasted longer than expected.'

'Murder investigations generally take time.'

Vegesack didn't bother to explain that it had more to do with his clearing-up duties. He gestured to a waiter and ordered another beer instead, and sat down.

'Did you have a restful day off?'

Moreno shrugged.

'You could say that. I met the girl's mother.'

'Whose mother?'

'Winnie Maas's.'

'I see. A nice lady.'

'Do you know her?'

'Most people do.'

'I get you. Anyway, she was visited by Mikaela Lijphart last Sunday.'

Vegesack raised an eyebrow.

'Good God! Well, what did fru Maas have to tell you?'

'Not a lot. She says she spoke to the girl, and then passed her on to somebody else. Vera Sauger – is that a name that means anything to you?'

Vegesack thought about that as the waiter came with his beer.

'I don't think so. Who's she when she's at home?'

'A friend of Winnie's. Or so her mother claimed. If Mikaela wanted to know anything about Winnie, Vera was the person she should go and talk to, she reckoned. So maybe that's what she did.'

Vegesack took a deep swig, and closed his eyes with satisfaction.

'Tastes good,' he said. 'But I knew that already. Well, I take it you've tracked her down by now?'

Moreno sighed.

'Yes, of course. But unfortunately I only got as far as a neighbour who's looking after her canary and potted plants. She's touring the archipelago, and is due back home tomorrow evening. I think it's called a holiday.'

'Not many people are at home at this time of year,' said Vegesack.

'Too true,' said Moreno. 'How about you? Have you got anywhere? The Wanted notice, for instance?'

Vegesack shook his head.

'Nix, I'm afraid. She came to see us, that woman from Frigge, but she was so unsure about the person she'd seen that she didn't dare to say anything for certain. It might have been Mikaela she saw at the railway station, but it might just as well have been somebody else.'

'And nobody else has reported anything?'

'Not a living soul,' said Vegesack. 'But I spent some time at Sidonis, in fact. If anything useful came out of it is questionable, but I promised to have a go, and so I did.'

He paused, and massaged his temples for a while before continuing. Moreno waited.

'I spoke to a few people up there. Nobody can remember Maager having received any telephone calls before he went missing. They reckon that it's out of the question that anybody could have visited him without their being aware of it – although if anybody wanted to take him away from the care home, for whatever reason, there are apparently other ways of doing it.'

'Such as?' asked Moreno.

'The park,' said Vegesack. 'The grounds surrounding the buildings – you've been there, you know what it's like. Maager used to wander around there for a few hours every day. It wouldn't be all that difficult to hide away among the

trees and wait for him to come along at a distance sufficiently far away from the home itself. There's no boundary
wall nor anything similar – nothing that runs all the way
round in any case. We'll send a few officers out to search
the area around the home: he could be lying somewhere in
the woods.'

Moreno didn't respond. She sat in silence for half a
minute, gazing out over the same beach and the same sea
as Constable Vegesack.

The same people, the same dogs running after sticks,
the same clusters of holidaymakers. But nevertheless, it
somehow seemed that the passage of time, albeit only a
few days, had cast a sort of membrane over it all. As if it
didn't concern her any more, that kind of life.

'But why would anybody want to attack Arnold
Maager?' she asked.

Vegesack shrugged.

'Don't ask me. But he's gone missing, and there must
be something behind it.'

'What about his wife?' Moreno asked. 'Sigrid Lijphart.
What do we know about her?'

'She rings every day, wondering why we haven't done
anything.'

'How did she react to the fact that Maager had also
disappeared?'

'It's hard to say,' said Vegesack, frowning. 'It's the

daughter she's interested in. To be honest, I don't think she cares all that much if her ex-husband is dead or alive. But nevertheless, we'll be issuing new Wanted notices tomorrow. In newspapers, magazines and so on.'

Moreno thought that over for a while. Tried to conjure up an image of Arnold Maager the man, but the only images of him she had were from a few old photographs, and it was hard to produce a clear picture. The story attached to him became all the more vivid – what he had been guilty of doing sixteen years ago. It seemed as if actions could somehow overshadow the people who had carried them out, make them incomprehensible, irresponsible: it wasn't an implausible way of looking at things, and perhaps there were resonances with that membrane she seemed to have sensed, covering the beach. He must be an absolute wreck of a human being, she thought. Must have been even then.

'What a fascinating story,' she said in the end. 'The girl's missing and her father's missing. Can you tell me what the hell is going on?'

'Hmm,' said Vegesack. 'I haven't really got round to thinking about it all that much. I've been too busy trying to sort out that business of the bloke buried in the sand. Tim Van Rippe.'

'Yes, of course,' said Moreno. 'Where have you got to with him?'

'The only thing we're sure about is that we aren't sure about anything,' said Vegesack, draining his glass of beer.

'Hmm,' muttered Moreno. 'As far as I remember, that is the basis of all knowledge.'

29

Aaron Wicker, editor of the Lejnice local newspaper *Westerblatt*, was not exactly enamoured of the town's chief of police.

He probably wouldn't have been, no matter what the circumstances; but as things stood, he thought he had unusually good reasons. Ever since Vrommel had succeeded in raiding the newspaper offices on false pretences at the beginning of the nineties, Wicker felt such a deep and genuine hatred for the main local upholder of law and order that he never bothered to try to hide it. Or to analyse it.

Shit is shit, he used to think. And you don't always reap what you sow.

The ostensible reason for searching the premises was that the police had received an anonymous bomb threat aimed at the newspaper. No bomb was found, but Wicker had known from the start that there had been no threat either. The real reason for the raid was an attempt to find the names of some of Wicker's informants for an article about financial irregularities in the town council. So that was that, and ever since, relations between two of the town's powerful institutions had been irreparable. As long as the chief of police was called Vrommel, at least.

No names had been found during the operation, since Wicker had had time to erase them; but the mere thought that the forces of law and order could ignore such fundamental matters as freedom of the press in this way was enough to send shivers of impotent fury down Wicker's spine. Still.

And now he was expected to submit once again.

'We know who the victim is, of course,' said the chief of police.

'Bravo,' said Wicker.

'But unfortunately I can't give you his name.'

'Why not?'

'Because we haven't been in touch with his next of kin yet.'

'The mass media can be pretty effective in getting through to people,' said Wicker. 'If your telephones are out of order, for instance. And we are pretty good judges.'

'That may be,' said Vrommel. 'But there is nothing wrong with our means of communication. I'm speaking on the telephone just now, for instance, even though I ought to be devoting myself to more important things. But that aside, you're not going to get the victim's name.'

'I shall find out what it is even so.'

'If you do, I forbid you to publish it.'

'Forbid? Since when have we had official censorship in this town? Not that it would surprise me if we did, but it must have escaped my notice.'

'It's not the only thing that escapes your notice,' said the chief of police. 'The way things are nowadays we don't need to keep an eye simply on compliance with the law. As the press can't be trusted to obey its own ethical rules, we have to ensure that they do. I'm rather busy at the moment – is there anything else you'd like to raise?'

I would quite like to raise my right fist and give you a punch on the nose, Wicker thought, but he made do with slamming down the receiver and decided to put Selma Perhovens on the case.

Selma Perhovens was Wicker's only colleague on the newspaper: only part-time, it's true, but if there were two people in Lejnice – or in the whole of Europe come to that – who knew the identity of the dead man on the beach, Selma was just the person to discover his name in no more than a few hours. Unless he misjudged her.

The first murder here in sixteen years, and the local newspaper didn't know the name of the victim? Bloody hell!

He took two tablets to lower his blood pressure, and started looking for her mobile number.

Moreno had dinner at a restaurant called Chez Vladimir, and promised herself that this would be not only the first time, but also the last. She assumed the same would apply to the evening's other three diners. The minced meat pie with salad she had ordered – and was served after a long wait, and tried to eat – was not something that inspired a desire to set foot inside the place again.

Nor did the wine, despite the fact that it matched rather accurately the roughness and sourness of the waitress. Moreno thanked her lucky stars that she had only ordered one glass.

Whether or not the following day would be her last one in Lejnice was a more open question.

Or perhaps it wasn't so open after all. Go home now? she thought as she forced down the last of the gall. With two people missing and an unsolved murder on the beach? Is it really Detective Inspector Moreno asking herself that question? The first liberated woman in the history of the world?

She couldn't help but smile at the implausibility.

I'll make up my mind tomorrow, she thought. A pot of hot coffee in my room tonight, then I'll massage my temples until either I make a hole or reach a conclusion. It would be quite nice to settle down in my own bed one of these nights.

She started off by writing down the names of those involved on a blank page in her notebook.

Winnie Maas

Arnold Maager

Mikaela Lijphart

It looked neat. She thought for a while before adding another name.

Tim Van Rippe

Not because he seemed to have anything to do with it, but he had been murdered after all. And then two more.

Sigrid Maas

Vera Sauger

She gave free rein to her thoughts for a few minutes while she wrote question marks after Mikaela Lijphart and Arnold Maager, and a cross after Tim Van Rippe. But she wrote nothing after the last two names.

Brilliant, my dear Holmes, she thought, and then tried to regain control of her thoughts. Took a sip of the coffee her hostess had prepared for her, reluctantly and extremely expensively. Press on!

What do I know? Are these names connected at all? All of them? Some of them? How?

Vera Sauger clearly didn't have so much to do with the others – those dead or missing persons – she was just a link. A presumed supplier of information, not a mystery. She would have to be handled especially carefully.

She suddenly realized why she thought the name had sounded familiar. Surely it had been mentioned in one of the interrogation records she had been provided with by Constable Vegesack.

Yes, no doubt about it. She couldn't remember in what connection, but Vera Sauger had been there, she was convinced of that, despite the fact that her temples had barely been massaged at all.

It wasn't all that remarkable, in fact. Sigrid Maas had told Mikaela Lijphart to contact Vera Sauger, and if the latter girl had been interrogated in connection with the events of 1983, it merely confirmed the fact that she was someone who was closely linked with Winnie in one way or another.

And that Sigrid Maas was telling the truth – in this respect, at least.

She went back to the first trio. One dead, two missing.

What had happened to Mikaela Lijphart was just as incomprehensible as ever. Before beginning to think about her and speculating, she turned her attention to her father.

What were the possible scenarios as far as he was concerned?

There were only two, as far as she could see.

Either Maager had run away from the Sidonis home of his own free will – the little of that he might still possess. Or there were other motives behind his disappearance. Somebody wanted him out of the way.

Why? Why on earth should anybody feel threatened by the existence of Arnold Maager?

There was only one answer, of course. It had to do with that business in the past. Maager might have information about what had really happened sixteen years ago, and such information could be dangerous for somebody who . . . well, somebody who – what?

Somebody who had a finger in the pie, and more than that, most likely.

Stop, Moreno thought. I'm going too quickly. It's pure speculation. Wasn't the most likely scenario by far – let's face it – that Maager had run away under his own steam? He'd packed a bag, for instance. The reason why he would want to run away was just as obscure as all the rest of it, but it seemed obvious that it must have to do with his daughter. There were no other stimuli in his life that could set things moving in this way.

Rubbish, she then thought. What do I know about

Arnold Maager's inner landscape? And other people's motives? Nothing at all.

But then again? She had the feeling that it could be the explanation. That he had simply run away, perhaps in a state of pure desperation to look for his daughter . . . Like an aged and crazy King Lear looking for Cordelia. Surely that must be a possibility? She drank half a cup of coffee and rubbed her temples. It made the roots of her hair hurt, but of course didn't do them any harm.

When no more sensible thoughts occurred to her, she turned over the page in her notebook instead and began writing down her conclusions in order. It took quite a while, and perhaps it was over the top to call them conclusions. It was more like therapy. Brain gymnastics for a mentally retarded detective inspector, she thought. While she was doing this she heard the first heavy raindrops hitting against the window, and in the next-door room the young couple started making love.

She sat there listening for a while, to both the rain and the lovemaking. There's a time for everything, she thought with a sigh. She switched on the radio to distract herself and poured some more coffee. When she had finished she read through what she had written, and established that the problems remained.

What had happened to Mikaela Lijphart? What had happened to her father?

HÅKAN NESSER

And the dead man on the beach? Had he anything to do with this other business?

I'll talk to Vera Sauger tomorrow evening, Moreno thought. That should help me to make progress.

But what if Mikaela never actually visited her? she thought. What would that indicate? What do I do then?

And what should she spend tomorrow doing? Sunbathing and swimming?

In the rain? It was coming down quite heavily now. In any case, it was obvious that she couldn't carry on pestering poor Vegesack any more than she had already done. Especially as she hadn't been able to make a single contribution to the case herself, despite all her efforts. There were limits, after all . . . Mind you, one might also ask oneself what on earth the police did in these parts.

So, what should she do? Perhaps dig a bit into the past instead? Go back to 1983 again?

But where, in that case? Dig where? Who should she interrogate this time?

She suddenly felt exhaustion threatening to overwhelm her, but gulped down another half cup of coffee and kept it at arm's length. Well? she thought. Who? Who should she turn to? Needless to say, everybody who was around when it all happened sixteen years ago would be able to supply a certain amount of information, some more than others; but it would be helpful to acquire a better overall view.

It didn't take her long to hit upon an alternative that seemed promising.

The press, of course. The local daily newspaper. *Westerblatt*: she knew what it was called and where its office was, since she had passed it several times on her way down to the beach.

Satisfied with this decision, she poured the rest of the coffee down the sink and went to bed. It was a quarter past midnight, and it occurred to her that Mikael Bau hadn't tried to contact her one single time during the evening.

Good, she thought as she switched off the light. But she realized that it was not a wholly satisfactory conclusion.

30

The *Westerblatt* editorial offices in Lejnice comprised two cramped rooms, one in front of the other, in Zeestraat. The inner room was the place where most of the work was done, and two-thirds of the floor space was occupied by two large desks, pushed up against each other and laden with computers, printers, fax machines, telephones, coffee machines and a higgledy-piggledy mass of papers, pens, notebooks and various other things that journalists claim to need. Sagging bookshelves with files, books and old newspapers covered all the walls from floor to ceiling, and hanging above everything was an American ceiling fan that had ceased to work in the summer of 1997.

The front room looked out on the street and had a counter where Joe Public could submit the copy for adverts and notices, pay subscriptions or complain about things that had appeared in the paper.

Or that hadn't appeared in the paper.

When Moreno stepped in out of the light drizzle in Zeestraat it was twenty minutes past ten in the morning. A dark-haired woman of about her own age and with an energetic appearance was standing behind the counter, telling somebody off on the telephone, gripping the receiver between her cheek and shoulder while making notes on a pad and leafing through a newspaper.

That's what I call multi-tasking, Moreno thought. The woman nodded to her, and she sat down on one of the two plastic chairs and waited for the call to come to an end.

Which it did after about half a minute, and judging from the unconstrained wording with which she closed down the call, Moreno gathered that the woman was not unduly worried by having been overheard.

'Bloody idiot!' she said as she replaced the receiver. 'Pardon my French. How can I help you?'

Moreno hadn't managed to make up her mind what tactics to use, but something in the woman's bright eyes and sharp tongue told her that it was probably best to put all her cards on the table. Besides, it was difficult to lie to somebody of the same sex and age as oneself: that was a phenomenon she had thought about before. This woman did not seem to be somebody who would believe any old thing you told her, and if you put a foot wrong at the beginning it would probably be difficult to repair the damage.

'Ewa Moreno, detective inspector,' she said. 'My errand's a bit special. I'd like to speak to somebody on the newspaper who knows about the Winnie Maas business from 1983 . . . and who has a few minutes to spare.'

The woman raised an eyebrow and sucked in her cheeks, suggesting she was rapidly thinking things over.

'You've come to the right person,' she said. 'Selma Perhovens. Pleased to meet you.'

She stretched her hand out over the counter, and Moreno shook it.

'Police officer, you said?'

'On holiday,' said Moreno. 'Not on duty.'

'Cryptic,' said Perhovens. 'Actually, I could do with a bit of police information myself, in fact. If you can supply me with it, maybe we could call it a fair exchange?'

'Why not?' said Moreno. 'What do you want to know?'

'Well, my boss has instructed me to find out the name of a body that was found buried on the beach last Monday. Do you know the answer?'

'Yes, of course,' said Moreno.

Perhovens dropped her jaw for a moment, but picked it up again.

'Well I'll be . . .'

'I know his name,' said Moreno. 'I'm here in Lejnice incognito, but I know a bit about this and that.'

'Well I never!' said Perhovens, hurrying out from behind the counter. 'I think we'd better close the office for a while.'

She pulled down the curtain over the milk-coloured glass door, and locked it. Took hold of Moreno's arm and steered her into the back room.

'Please take a seat.'

Moreno removed a pile of newspapers, an empty Coca-Cola can and a half-full bag of sweets from the chair indicated, and sat down. Perhovens sat down opposite her and rested her chin on her knuckles.

'How do I know you're not just a loony pretending to be a police officer?'

Moreno produced her ID.

'All right. Please forgive my scepticism directed at fellow human beings. It goes with my job. I ought to place more trust in my intuitive judgements.'

She smiled. Moreno smiled back.

'Gullibility is not a virtue these days,' she said. 'If I can explain what I'm after first, I can give you the name afterwards. Okay?'

'Fair deal,' said Perhovens. 'Coffee?'

'Yes please,' said Moreno.

She started from the beginning. From as far back as the

train journey and her meeting with the weeping Mikaela Lijphart until the previous night's somewhat dodgy attempts to analyse the situation in her guest-house room. But she omitted Franz Lampe-Lehmann and Mikael Bau, since they didn't really have any connection with the matter – and even less connection with each other – and the whole recapitulation took barely more than a quarter of an hour. Perhovens didn't interrupt once, but managed to drink two-and-a-half cups of coffee, and fill four pages in her notebook.

'That's a real bugger,' she said when Moreno had finished. 'Anyway, I think you've come to the right person, as I said. I was just finishing my apprenticeship year when the Maager trial was taking place – I was only nineteen, but I attended it all week and followed what happened closely. I wasn't allowed to write the newspaper reports, of course: Wicker wrote those himself, but he made me produce basic texts every day, the slave-driver. So I remember it quite well. A nasty business.'

'So I've gathered,' said Moreno.

'Besides . . .' said Perhovens, and seemed to be unsure of what to say next. 'Besides, I had my doubts about the whole proceedings, I suppose you could say; but everything went like clockwork, and I was much more of a wide-eyed innocent in those days.'

Moreno felt something click inside her.

'Doubts? What kind of doubts?'

'Nothing precise, I'm afraid, but the whole trial seemed to be prearranged. Theatre. A sort of play set in a court-room that was written long before it actually started. The girl was dead, the murderer was found with her dead body on his knee. He was branded a loony from the start, and in people's eyes he was as guilty as anybody could be. A teacher gives a pupil a bun in the oven and kills her! We had no problem selling the paper that summer.'

'What was his defence? What line did his lawyer take?'

'Mentally deranged.'

'Mentally deranged?'

'Yes. Not responsible for his actions. There was no other possible strategy. The lawyer's name was Korring. Maager pleaded guilty through him – he hardly uttered a single word from start to finish of the trial.'

Moreno thought for a while.

'But what was it that made you think it might not be as simple and straightforward as it seemed? I gather that's what you thought, is that right?'

Perhovens shrugged.

'I don't know. Perhaps just my juvenile instinct to rebel. I didn't like the consensus – still don't, come to that. I prefer fruitful differences of opinion. But never mind that, what does all this that you've just told me about mean? What the hell has happened to that poor girl?'

'That's what I would like help in sorting out,' said Moreno with a sigh. 'I've been brooding over it for quite a few days now, and the only possible thing I can come up with is that there must be a link with the past. Something fishy about that whole business, not everything can have been satisfactorily explained . . . Mikaela Lijphart talks to her dad for the first time in sixteen years. The Murderer with a capital M. Then she starts visiting several other people – I think there are several of them at least – here in Lejnice. Then she goes missing.'

'And then her father goes missing as well. Why the hell haven't we written about this? I know we've asked for information about the girl, but we haven't written anything about this background.'

'Do you have a good relationship with the local police?' Moreno asked tentatively.

Perhovens burst out laughing.

'A good relationship? We've been conducting trench warfare that makes the Western Front seem like a kiddies' playground.'

'I see,' said Moreno. 'Vrommel?'

'Yes, Vrommel,' said Perhovens, and her eyes suggested a regrettable degree of impotence.

They could hear a cautious tapping on the glass door in the outer room, but she ignored it with a snort. Moreno took the opportunity of changing tack.

'Did Maager have any sort of support during that time?' she asked. 'From any quarter? Were there any other suspects, for instance?'

Perhovens sucked her pen and thought hard.

'No,' she said. 'Not as far as I can remember. He seemed to have every bloody inhabitant of the whole town against him. And I mean every single one of 'em.'

Moreno nodded.

'In some societies the poor bastard would have been lynched.'

'I understand.'

It was not the first time Moreno had come across a comment similar to Perhovens' last, and she wondered briefly how she would have reacted herself. Given what the circumstances must have been. Perhaps it was better not to follow up that question too assiduously. It was better, of course, to believe that she would never have entertained the possibility of joining a lynch mob, that no matter what the circumstances she would be able to retain her own sense of justice and integrity.

'What exactly is it you're thinking?' asked Perhovens after a short pause. 'That it was somebody else who did it? Forget it, if so. It's impossible. The bastard was sitting there weeping with the corpse on his knee.'

Moreno sighed.

'Isn't it possible that she jumped?'

'Why would he confess in that case?'

Good question, Moreno thought. But not a new one.

'Who was the doctor?' she asked, without really understanding why. 'The one who carried out the post-mortem, that is.'

'DeHaavelaar,' said Perhovens. 'Old deHaavelaar, he used to do everything in those days. Births, illnesses and post-mortems. I think he even dabbled in veterinary matters as well. Anyway, it was his word that counted. As infallible as amen in church. Although he didn't appear in court, that wasn't necessary.'

'Wasn't necessary?' said Moreno in surprise. 'Why ever not?'

Perhovens flung her arms out wide.

'I don't know. But they just read out his verdict. The clerk of the court, if my memory serves me correctly. I suppose he had other matters to see to, deHaavelaar.'

The shadow of a suspicion flashed past inside Moreno's head. From left to right, it seemed, and that very fact – that she noticed the direction – made the actual content disappear. At least, that's what it felt like. Just a symbol from an alphabet she had never learned. Remarkable.

And immediately afterwards came just as fleeting an image of Chief Inspector Van Veeteren, sitting at a desk and looking at her. Or rather, boring his gaze into her.

Very odd, she thought. Surely I'm a bit on the young side for brain haemorrhages?

'I see,' she said, taking a deep breath. 'Is he still living in Lejnice, this doctor?'

'DeHaavelaar? Yes on both counts. Still living and still in Lejnice. He must be getting on for eighty, I would think, but he struts around town scattering cynicisms left, right and centre. Why do you ask?'

'I don't know,' said Moreno. 'It was just a thought that flashed past.'

Perhovens looked hard at her for a few seconds, apparently somewhat confused. Then she slammed the palm of her hand down on her notebook.

'I'm going to write about this – do you have any objections?'

Moreno shook her head.

'By the way,' said Perhovens. 'I think we had an agreement. That bloke on the beach, what's his name?'

'Ah yes, of course,' said Moreno. 'Van Rippe. His name's Tim Van Rippe.'

Perhovens frowned again.

'Van Rippe? Sounds familiar. But no, I don't know who that is. Are you sure about it?'

'Do you think I'd sit here giving the wrong name of a murder victim to a journalist?' said Moreno.

'Sorry,' said Perhovens. 'I forgot that I wasn't talking to the local police mafia. To change the subject, what do you say to lunch? Maybe we can reach some definite conclusions if we get some protein inside us.'

Moreno looked at the clock and nodded.

'No harm in trying,' she said.

Former Town Medical Officer Emil deHaavelaar lived in Riipvej, it turned out, in a large patrician mansion among the dunes. But he declined to meet her there – if it was just about a bagatelle, as she maintained. He might possibly be able to exchange a few words with her at Cafe Thurm later in the afternoon, after a visit to his dental hygienist to have some tartar removed.

At about four o'clock, if that was all right with her. Moreno accepted, hung up and returned to Selma Perhovens at the table where they were eating lunch.

'A grumpy old curmudgeon?' she asked.

'An aristocrat,' said Perhovens. 'The last one, if you believe what he says. I interviewed him when his book came out a few years ago. About his forty years as Aesculapius here in Lejnice – you know, the ancient Greek god of medicine and healing. That's what he called his book, believe it or not: *Through Aesculapius's Magnifying Glass*. An incredible load of crap, but I was forced to read it. On the very edge of racial biology. Anyway, he lives alone, with a housekeeper and two greyhounds. Twelve rooms and a tennis court – no, he's not my type, full stop. How long are you staying, by the way?'

Moreno shrugged.

'I was intending to go home tomorrow,' she said. 'But I want to talk to that Vera Sauger first – I have a meeting with her this evening. Assuming she turns up. I don't know why I'm poking my nose into all this stuff, to be honest. I can't afford to stay in a guest house for ever. My police wage doesn't allow much in the way of extravagance, I'm afraid. Not even at Dombrowski's.'

Perhovens gave her what could only be described as a grim clown-smile.

'How very odd,' she said. 'I have to say that money is my biggest unrequited love as well, come to think of it. It always lets me down, is never there when I need it. If you decide to stay on for a few more days you're welcome to stay at my place. I've got a little girl aged eleven, but no man to get in your way, and you can have your own room. I mean it.'

'Thank you,' said Moreno, and felt a sudden rush of sympathy for this energetic journalist. 'Let's see what things look like tomorrow morning.'

Perhovens gave Moreno her card, and checked her watch.

'Oh hell! I'm missing the stallion prize-giving ceremony at the horse show in Moogensball. I must dash!'

After she'd left Moreno stayed behind at the table for a while, wondering whether or not to ring Vegesack. Just to catch up on the latest situation.

But after mature deliberation she decided to postpone that until the evening.

Dr deHaavelaar ordered a cognac and a glass of milk. Moreno restricted herself to a cappuccino.

'It's for balance,' explained the doctor when the waiter came with the tray. 'Bodily balance is all you need to worry about if you want to live to be a hundred.'

She didn't doubt for a moment that Emil deHaavelaar would live to be a hundred. He had another twenty years or so to go, to be sure, but he looked like a well-dressed grizzly bear. Tall and broad-shouldered, and with the charisma of a spoilt film star. His white hair was thick and combed back, his moustache as dense as it was trim, and the colour of his skin suggested that he had spent enough hours in the sun out among the sand dunes to last him through any winter, no matter how long it turned out to be. She remembered that Selma Perhovens had used the word 'strut', and wondered why.

'Always assuming one might want to hang on that long

in this mish-mash of a world,' he added, swirling his glass of cognac.

'Yes,' said Moreno, 'one might well wonder about that.'

'What do you want?' asked deHaavelaar.

Moreno hesitated for a moment.

'Winnie Maas,' she said.

DeHaavelaar slammed his glass down onto the table with a bang. I've put my foot in it, Moreno thought. Dammit!

'Who are you?' said deHaavelaar.

'Ewa Moreno. As I said on the telephone. Detective inspector.'

'Can I see your ID?'

Moreno dug it out and handed it over. He put on a pair of glasses with very thin and presumably extremely expensive frames, and examined it carefully. Handed it back and took off his glasses.

'Does the chief of police know you're meeting me?'

She thought for a moment again.

'No.'

He emptied his glass of cognac in one gulp. Washed it down with half a glass of milk. Moreno sipped her coffee and waited.

'Why the hell do you want to come here and root around in something that happened twenty years ago?'

'Sixteen,' said Moreno. 'I only wanted to ask a few simple questions. Why are you so agitated?'

'I'm not agitated,' he snarled. 'I'm furious. You're not even from Lejnice, you don't know a bloody thing and I'm not going to answer a single question. But what I *am* going to do is report this to the chief of police.'

He stood up, stroked his thumb and index finger rapidly over his moustache and marched out of the premises.

For Christ's sake, Moreno thought. What did Selma Perhovens call him? An aristocrat?

31

During the late afternoon and early evening dejection began to dig its claws into her.

Perhaps it had to do with the rain showers that came sailing in from the south-west in a never-ending stream. She lay down on the lumpy bed and tried to read, but it was impossible to concentrate on anything unconnected with Mikaela Lijphart and the major issues associated with her.

Or with herself.

What am I doing here? she wondered. What am I playing around at? A police inspector on holiday! Would a bicycle repair specialist spend his hard-earned leisure repairing bicycles for nothing? I must be mad.

She phoned Clara Mietens, but her solid rock was still not at home. She rang the police station, but Constable Vegesack was out on official business. She rang the automatic weather forecast number, and was informed that several more belts of rain were queueing up over the Atlantic, waiting to move in.

Great, Moreno thought as she started reading the same page for the fourth time.

At seven o'clock she tried Vera Sauger's number for the first time. No reply. She tried again half an hour later, and continued at half-hourly intervals for the rest of the evening.

After her half-past-seven attempt she considered going out for a meal, but decided not to. Yesterday's dodgy minced-meat pie didn't exactly encourage her to risk a repeat performance. She did two hundred sit-ups and forty arms-raises instead, and two hours later she installed herself in the shower and tried to work out what on earth could have made Dr deHaavelaar so extremely upset.

She failed to do so. Not especially surprising, seeing as she told herself it was an impossible task. There was no point in trying to draw conclusions when the grounds for doing so were so inadequate. It was like trying to find footprints in a swamp. Hopeless. Even a confused police inspector ought to understand that.

And eighty-year-olds were not always logical, even if they looked like well-dressed grizzly bears and didn't strut at all.

One more try, she thought as she dialled Vera Sauger's number at a few minutes past eleven. If she doesn't answer now, I'll give up.

The answer came after three rings.

'Vera Sauger.'

Thank goodness for that, Moreno thought. Please let me exchange a few words with you as well. Despite the late hour.

And preferably have something constructive to tell me.

She was yet another single woman of about Moreno's own age.

Will there be any children at all in Europe ten years from now? she thought, as she was ushered into the flat in Lindenstraat. Or will all women have renounced the option of contributing to the proliferation of the human race? What was it Mikael had said? *Embrace the cold stone of freedom?*

She shrugged off the uninvited questions and sat down at the kitchen table, where her hostess had served up tea and small reddish-brown biscuits that looked like nipples. Coming to visit her hadn't been a problem, despite the fact that it was almost midnight and that Sauger seemed to be badly in need of some sleep after five days and nights in the archipelago. When Moreno had mentioned the name Mikaela Lijphart on the telephone, Sauger had interrupted her immediately and invited her over.

It's better to look the person you're talking to in the

eye, Sauger had explained. Moreno had been of the same opinion.

'So she's still missing, is she?' Sauger asked after pouring tea into the yellow cups with large blue hearts on their sides. From some Swedish interior design outlet, Moreno guessed.

'So you know about it?'

Sauger looked at her in surprise.

'Of course I do. Why do you ask? Who are you, in fact?'

Moreno produced her ID and wondered how many times she'd already needed to do that this seemingly never-ending day. This was the third, she thought.

'Are you new here in town?' Sauger wondered. 'I don't recognize you. Not that I have much to do with the police, but still . . .'

'I'm from Maardam,' said Moreno. 'I'm here on holiday. But I met the girl before she went missing.'

Sauger nodded vaguely.

'So you don't have any contact with the police station here?'

'Only occasionally,' said Moreno. 'Why do you ask?'

Sauger stirred her tea slowly and looked even more bewildered.

'Because you asked if I knew about it,' she said.

'Well?'

'Of course I damned well know about it. I was at the police station to say my piece before I set off for Werkeney.'

Two awkward seconds passed, then Moreno remembered that Vegesack had said something amounting to what Sauger had said several days ago. That a woman had turned up in connection with the first Wanted notice, but that it hadn't led anywhere. Wasn't that the case?

Yes, as far as she could recall. There'd been one woman from Lejnice and another from Frigge. And the one from Lejnice must have been this Vera Sauger who was now sitting opposite her, popping a nipple-biscuit into her mouth.

It suddenly felt as if a rather large-scale short circuit had taken place inside Inspector Moreno's head. The only thing that seemed anything like certain was that something must be wrong.

And outside her head as well.

'I'm afraid . . . I'm afraid I must have missed that,' she said with an attempt at an apologetic smile. 'What exactly did you have to report?'

'That she came to see me, of course. I think it's odd that you don't know about it.'

'You reported that Mikaela Lijphart had come here to see you?' said Moreno. 'Is that what you're saying?'

'Yes, of course,' said Sauger.

'That you spoke to her that Sunday, ten days ago?'

'Yes.'

Moreno said nothing while the next question slowly took shape in her mind. It took a while.

'And who did you report this to?'

'Who to? To the chief of police, of course. Vrommel.'

'I see,' said Moreno.

That wasn't really true, but it didn't matter. It was more important to take matters further now.

'And when Mikaela came to see you, what did she want to talk about?' she asked.

'About her father, obviously,' said Sauger. 'About what happened sixteen years ago. She'd only just heard about it.'

'Yes, I know about that,' said Moreno. 'And what did she want to hear from you?'

Sauger hesitated again.

'I'm not really sure,' she said. 'She was a bit vague, and we didn't talk for very long. Winnie's mum had given her my name. It seemed . . . Well, it seemed as if she'd got it into her head that her dad was innocent. She didn't say so straight out, but that's the impression I had. She'd been to talk to him the day before. On the Saturday. It can't have been easy . . . Not for either of them.'

'Could Arnold Maager have told his daughter that he didn't kill Winnie Maas?'

'I'm not sure,' said Sauger. 'She just gave that impression. Mind you, it wouldn't be all that surprising if he'd told her something of that sort . . . To portray himself in a rather better light. That occurred to me afterwards.'

Moreno thought about that for a while.

'I was at that bloody party at Gollumsen's place,' said Sauger. 'And I was a friend of Winnie's. But not as close a friend as her mother seems to think. When we were a bit younger, perhaps, but not when it happened. We'd sort of drifted apart.'

'That happens,' said Moreno. 'But was there anything more specific that Mikaela wanted to know about? Something more than what you might call the general picture?'

Sauger thought about that and took another nipple.

'Boyfriends,' she said. 'She asked about which boys Winnie had been together with before that business with Maager.'

'Why did she want to know that?'

'I've no idea. We only talked for about fifteen or twenty minutes. I was in a bit of a hurry.'

'But you were able to help her with that question about boyfriends?'

'Yes, I gave her a few names.'

'Which names?'

Sauger thought for a moment again.

'Claus Bitowski,' she said. 'And Tim Van Rippe.'

FOUR

32

Interrogation of Markus Baarentz, 22.7.1983.

Location: Lejnice police station.

Interrogator: Chief of Police Vrommel.

Also present: Inspector Walevski, Prosecuting Secretary
Mattloch.

Interrogation transcript: Inspector Walevski.

Authorized by: Secretary Mattloch, Chief of Police
Vrommel.

Vrommel: Name, age and occupation please.

Baarentz: Markus Baarentz. I'm 49 and work as an
accountant.

V   Here in Lejnice?

B   No, in Emsbaden. But I live in Lejnice. Alexanderlaan
4.

V   Can you tell us what happened last night?

B   Yes, of course. I'm a bridge player. I and my partner,
Otto Golnik, took part in a two-day tournament in

Frigge. Doubles. It went on and on and didn't finish until about eleven p.m. We came third, and had to stay on for the prize-giving as well. Anyway, then we drove home. We were in my car – we usually take it in turns. I dropped Otto off first, he lives out at Missenraade, and then I continued home. I took the usual route, of course, and as I drove along Molnerstraat alongside the railway, I saw them.

V   What time was that, roughly?

B   Two o'clock. A few minutes past. It was shortly after the viaduct, there's a street lamp just there, so it was impossible not to notice him, to notice them.

V   So what exactly did you see?

B   Maager. Arnold Maager, who was sitting right next to the railway lines with a girl in his lap.

V   How did you know it was Maager?

B   I recognized him. I have a boy who goes to the Voeller School. I've seen him at a few parents' meetings. I saw straight away that it was him.

V   I see. What did you do?

B   I stopped. I could see immediately that there was something wrong. There was no reason to be sitting there, almost on the rails themselves. Even if there aren't any trains at night, now that they've stopped the goods traffic. There was something odd about the girl as well. She was lying stretched out, and he was holding her head on his knee. I think I realized there must have been an accident the moment I saw them.

V Did you see anybody else around?

B Not even a cat. It was the middle of the night, after all.

V So you stopped and got out of the car, did you?

B Yes. Although I first wound down the window and shouted. Asked if there was anything wrong, but he didn't answer. Then I got out of the car. I shouted again, but he didn't react. Now I knew that there must be something seriously wrong. I climbed over the fence and went up to them. He didn't even look up, although he must have heard me. He just sat there, stroking the girl's hair. He seemed to be in another world, as it were. As if he'd had a shock. For a moment I thought he was drunk, and maybe the girl as well, but I soon gathered that wasn't the case. It was much worse than that. She was dead.

V How could you tell she was dead?

B I don't really know. The way she was lying, I suppose. I asked as well, of course, but I didn't get an answer. Maager didn't even look at me. I tried to make contact with him, but it was impossible.

V You didn't notice any injuries to the girl?

B No. It was just the way she was lying. And her face. Her eyes didn't seem to be properly closed, nor did her mouth. And she wasn't moving. Not at all.

V   And Arnold Maager?

B   He just sat there, stroking her hair and her cheeks. He
    seemed to be in another world, as I said. I called him
    by his name as well. 'Herr Maager,' I said. 'What's
    happened?'

V   Did you get an answer?

B   No. I didn't really know what to do. I just stood there
    for about ten or fifteen seconds or so. I asked again,
    and in the end he looked up. He looked at me very
    briefly, and there was something odd about his eyes –
    about his facial expression, in fact.

V   What exactly?

B   Something abnormal. When I was a lad I worked for a
    few summers in a mental hospital, and I thought I
    recognized that look. I thought about that right away.

V   What did you do?

B   I asked what was wrong with the girl, but he still
    didn't react. I bent down to take a closer look at her.
    I thought I'd take her pulse or something, but he
    shooed me away.

V   Shooed you away? How?

B   Brushed my hand away, sort of. Then he made a noise.

V   A noise?

B   Yes, a noise. It sounded, well, it sounded a bit like the
    mooing of a cow.

V   Are you saying that Maager mooed like a cow?

B   Yes. An inhuman noise in any case. More like the cry
    of an animal. I assumed he was in a state of shock,
    and that there was no point in trying to get any sense
    out of him.

V   I understand. Tell us what you did next.

B   I thought I needed to call the police and an
    ambulance. It would have been best, of course, if I
    could have stopped a car or contacted some other
    person who could help out, but it was the middle of
    the night and I couldn't see another soul. I didn't want
    to leave him there with the girl either, not without
    establishing what state she was in; but in the end I
    managed to take her pulse without him protesting.
    She didn't have one, as I'd suspected. She was dead.

V   Where did you take her pulse?

B   On her wrist. He didn't want me to come anywhere
    near her neck.

V   Did you recognize the girl as well?

B   No. I've heard since who she is, but I'm not
    acquainted with the family.

V   But in the end you went and got some help in any
    case, is that right?

B   Yes. There was nothing else I could do. I climbed back
    over the fence on to the road, went to the nearest
    house and rang the doorbell. I switched the car lights
    off as well – I'd left them on without thinking. It took

some time before anybody came to answer, but all the time I was waiting I kept my eye on Maager and the girl, and could see that they were still there, beside the railway line. It was no more than thirty or forty metres away. The woman who answered the door was Christina Deijkler, I know her slightly although I didn't know she lived in that very house. I explained the situation, and she could see for herself that it was exactly as I'd said. She went to phone the emergency services and I went back to wait: the police car turned up after about ten minutes – Helme and Van Steugen. The ambulance arrived shortly afterwards.

V   Thank you, herr Baarentz. You did exactly the right thing. I have just a few more questions. While you were trying to get through to Maager, did you get any idea of what had happened?

B   No.

V   He didn't give any indication at all? In words or gestures or in any other way?

B   No. He didn't express himself at all. Apart from that strange noise, that is.

V   And you didn't draw any conclusions?

B   No, not then. I heard today what it was all about. It's horrendous, but I had no idea about any of that at the time, in the middle of the night.

V   How did you find out about what had happened?

B Alexander, my boy. He'd picked up the gossip in the town – the news seems to have spread like wild fire, and I suppose that's understandable. Apparently Maager had had a relationship with the girl, that seems to have been common knowledge in the school. It's a scandal, of course. I don't really know what to say about it. They reckon he threw her down from the viaduct – is that true?

V It's too early to comment on the cause of death, but we don't exclude that possibility. Are you absolutely certain that you didn't see anybody else in the vicinity of the scene of the accident?

B Absolutely.

V No cars passing by, or that you'd seen shortly before you got there?

B No. I don't think I saw more than one single car after I'd dropped Otto Golnik off in Missenraade. And none at all anywhere near the viaduct, I'm sure of that.

V You seem to be an unusually observant person, herr Baarentz.

B I suppose I am. I'm a pretty precise sort of person – you have to be in my job. I suppose playing bridge helps as well: you have to be wide awake all the time.

V I take your point. Many thanks, herr Baarentz. You have been extremely useful to us.

B No problem. I've just done my duty, nothing more.

33

It was Thursday before the Wanted notice for Arnold Maager – 44 years old, 176 centimetres tall, slimly built and ash-grey-haired; possibly depressed, possibly confused, probably both – reached the public at large. By that time he had been missing for almost five days. He was last seen in the Sidonis Foundation care home just outside Lejnice, where he had been living for the last fifteen years, last Saturday – and it was probable that he was dressed in a white T-shirt, blue or brown cotton trousers, a light-coloured wind-cheater and Panther trainers.

That same day, at dawn, a search party comprising fourteen officers from the police forces in Lejnice, Wallburg and Emsbaden began to comb the immediate vicinity of the Sidonis home – an operation that was completed at about five in the afternoon without any clues having been found to throw light on what had happened to the missing mentally ill patient.

Simultaneously with the publication by the media of details of Maager's disappearance, the police also issued a renewed Wanted notice for his daughter, Mikaela Lijphart, this time country-wide. She had now been missing for eleven days, and anybody who had seen the girl at any time during that period – or who could provide any other information that could be of use to the investigation team – was urged to get in touch immediately with the Lejnice police. Or with their nearest police station.

The only person who responded to the latter request was the missing girl's mother, Sigrid Lijphart, and that was not in order to pass on any new information but – as usual – to ask why the hell they hadn't made any progress. Vrommel had no satisfactory answer to this question – as usual – and fru Lijphart threatened to report him to higher authorities if he and his colleagues failed to come up with something in the very near future. If for nothing else she would report them for negligence and a failure to fulfil a police officer's duty to citizens. Vrommel asked politely if she would like him to send her forms she could fill in in order to make a complaint – a B112-5GE with regard to negligence, and a B112-6C for a failure to fulfil their duty – but she declined on both scores.

Fru Lijphart asked no questions and lodged no complaints with regard to the disappearance of her former husband.

Constable Vegesack lived with his Marlene in one of the newly built blocks of flats in Friederstraat, only a stone's throw from the beach, and after a minimum of discussion – and an invitation from Vegesack – that is where their meeting was held. Discretion was essential, given the circumstances that had arisen: the police station was out of the question as a venue, and it would not be easy to hire a suitable alternative location at short notice.

Three rooms and a kitchen, Moreno noted as she was being welcomed by Vegesack. Large balcony with a splendid view of the sea and Gordon's Lighthouse. Not bad at all. She recalled that he'd told her that Marlene was an architect, and she wondered if she was also an interior designer. It looked very much like it, but she wasn't at home just now and so Moreno couldn't very well look any further into that. But the rooms and furniture seemed to have a well-thought-out colour scheme, the walls were not cluttered with kitsch – just a few high-quality reproductions: Tiegermann, Chagall and a few of Cézanne's self-portraits. Bookcases with quite a lot of books. Large green plants. A piano – she wondered if it was Vegesack or his girlfriend who played. Or perhaps both of them? Good, she thought. This gives me confidence in him.

But they weren't gathered here to pass judgement on style and homeliness. The grim expressions on the faces of Intendent Kohler and Inspector Baasteuwel, who were each installed in a renovated 1950s armchair, gave no room for doubt on that score. On the contrary.

'Fire away,' said Baasteuwel. 'What the hell is this all about?'

Vegesack went to fetch four beers, and Moreno sat down on the sofa.

'I smell a rat in this accursed business,' she said.

'Is its name Vrommel, by any chance?' wondered Kohler.

'The chief of police is bound to be in its vicinity in any case,' said Moreno. 'It's no doubt best to fill you in a bit. Would you like me to start in the present, or the past?'

'The past,' said Baasteuwel. 'For Christ's sake, when they picked out Kohler and me they told us it would be all over in two or three days. I was due to go on holiday today. But it's not the first time . . .'

'It probably won't be the last either,' said Kohler drily. 'Let's get a bit of flesh on the bones.'

Moreno glanced at Vegesack, but he gestured to her and encouraged her to take command. She took her notebook out of her bag.

'All right,' she began. 'Let's take things in chronological order. Sixteen years ago – almost to the day, in fact – something happened here in Lejnice that . . . well, I suppose you could say it left its mark. A teacher at the local school, Arnold Maager, had an affair with one of his pupils, a certain Winnie Maas. She became pregnant, and he killed her. That's the official version, at least. They say he threw her down from a railway viaduct – it's pretty high, she fell on to the rails down below and was killed. He was found sitting by the rails with the girl's body in his lap. In the middle of the night. He went out of his mind as a result, and he's been in a mental hospital ever since. The Sidonis care home, which isn't far from here. He was found guilty, although he never confessed because he wasn't of sound mind when the trial took place. Maager was married and had a little daughter when it happened; his wife distanced herself from him without further ado, and he hasn't seen her or his daughter since then. They moved away from Lejnice that same autumn. Anyway, that's the background. In outline. Any questions?'

She looked round the table.

'What a nice story,' said Baasteuwel, taking a swig of beer.

'Very,' said Moreno. 'But let's fast-forward to the present. When I came out to Lejnice, let's see – ' she worked it out in her head – 'twelve days ago, I met a young girl on the train who turned out to be Maager's daughter. We got talking. She'd just celebrated her eighteenth birthday, and was on her way to visit her father at the Sidonis care home for the first time. She hadn't seen him since she was two years old, and didn't even know he existed. Her mother had told her about him the previous day, and the girl was pretty nervous about meeting him.'

'No wonder,' said Kohler.

'Yes indeed. Anyway, a few days later her mum turned up here in Lejnice – Maager's ex-wife, that is – and announced that her daughter hadn't returned home. She'd gone missing.'

'Gone missing?' said Baasteuwel. 'What the hell . . . ?'

'Exactly,' said Moreno. 'We know she visited her dad at the home on Saturday, and spent the night at the youth hostel out at Missenraade: but nobody's seen her since Sunday. And now the strange goings-on begin.'

'Begin?' said Kohler. 'The strange goings-on *begin* now?'

Moreno shrugged.

'Well, *continue*, if you prefer. I'm only here in Lejnice on holiday, in fact, but I had a little job to sort out in the first few days. At the police station. Anyway, I'd met the girl on the train, and—'

'What's her name?' interrupted Baasteuwel.

'Mikaela. Mikaela Lijphart. As I said, I'd met her, and

now I bumped into her mother as well. She was very worried, for obvious reasons. Eventually Chief of Police Vrommel agreed to issue a Wanted notice – but don't let me hear anybody claiming that he prioritized it. The point, of course, was to ask if anybody had seen Mikaela last Sunday. Or later in the week. As far as we know only two people contacted the police as a result. One was a woman in Frigge who claimed to have seen the girl at the railway station up there, the other was a certain Vera Sauger – I spoke to her last night. It was after that conversation that Vegesack and I decided to arrange this meeting.'

'You don't say,' said Baasteuwel, leaning forward over the table. 'Go on.'

'Vrommel spoke to both the women, and according to him nothing significant emerged. Nevertheless, Vera Sauger told me last night that she'd been visited by Mikaela that Sunday, and they'd had quite a long talk. The girl was trying to make contact with anybody who'd been involved in one way or another in the happenings of 1983. Anybody who'd known her father or the dead girl Winnie Maas. We don't know why Mikaela wanted to do this, but it could be a result of something her dad told her when she visited him at the Sidonis home. That's mere speculation, of course; but she must surely have had some reason for starting to root around. Unless it was mere curiosity. In any case, she went to see Winnie's mother – I've spoken to her as well. But neither she nor Vera Sauger could be of much help to Mikaela – or so they say, at least. Fru Maas is more than a bit of a drunk, incidentally. We don't know if the girl met anybody else apart from these two.'

She paused briefly.

'I was under the impression that all this business was supposed to be linked with the case we're working on, somehow or other,' said Kohler.

Moreno cleared her throat.

'That's right. Vera Sauger gave Mikaela Lijphart two possible names. People she could contact if she wanted to pursue her queries further. And she gave the same names to Vrommel. One of them was Tim Van Rippe.'

'The gent buried in the sand,' said Kohler.

'Bloody hell!' said Baasteuwel.

Silence enveloped the table.

'This isn't the only complication,' said Moreno after Vegesack had nipped out into the kitchen to fetch four more beers. 'A week after Mikaela went to visit her father at the care home, he disappeared. Last Saturday afternoon, to be precise. Nobody knows where he is. Vegesack was there and spoke to him a few days earlier, but it was evidently impossible to get much out of him.'

'Not a word,' said Vegesack.

Baasteuwel ran his hands through his tousled hair and stared at Moreno; but it was Kohler who spoke.

'This Tim Van Rippe,' he said. 'Our body on the beach. What role does he play in this old story?'

Moreno turned over a page in her notebook to check on the details.

'According to Vera Sauger he knew the girl Winnie Maas pretty well. He might even have been in a relationship with her as well, before she jumped into bed with Arnold Maager. But that isn't so important. The important thing is that there is a clear connection here. Mikaela Lijphart was given his name, plus another one that I haven't had time to check up on yet, and it's very possible that she might have been to meet him on the Sunday. A week later he's found murdered and buried on the beach. It's an amazing coincidence that the body was discovered, of course – but then you'd have thought that the murderer would have been a bit more careful and dug a bit deeper down. Or what do you think?'

Kohler nodded.

'His head was very close to the surface, in fact. It would no doubt have been exposed sooner or later by the wind, or by the running around of holidaymakers.'

Baasteuwel stood up.

'And so all this business of what Vera Sauger said and did has been hushed up by the chief of police, has it? What the hell's going on? In addition to the fact that Vrommel's a berk. I need a smoke. Is out there okay?'

Vegesack nodded and Baasteuwel went out through the balcony door.

'Irrespective of what's behind it all,' said Moreno, 'it's obvious that Vrommel isn't playing the game. He doesn't want to root around in what happened sixteen years ago. He doesn't want anybody to find a link between the Maager case and the body on the beach. I don't know what, but it seems pretty clear that something wasn't what it seemed all those years ago. Correct me if I'm wrong.'

'Are there any more . . . irregularities?' Kohler wondered.

Moreno thought for a moment.

'There's bound to be,' she said. 'It's just that we don't know what they are. I spoke to the pathologist, the man who did the post-mortem on Winnie Maas, and I must say his reaction was astonishingly strong. He became terribly upset for some reason – as if I were somehow questioning his honour and credibility. Just because I wanted to put a few simple things to him. I didn't have a chance to ask him a single question before he boiled over.'

'It sounds like a damned conspiracy,' said Kohler. 'Or a

cover-up at the very least. Has anybody taken a look at the trial records? Is there anything dodgy there?'

'I haven't got round to it, I'm afraid,' said Moreno with a sigh. 'Don't forget I'm here on holiday.'

'Hmm,' said Kohler, with what could possibly have been interpreted as a melancholy smile.

Baasteuwel returned from his smoking break.

'Well, what do you think?' he asked, looking first at Moreno and then Vegesack. 'Personally, I've only had the time it takes to smoke one miserable little cigarette to think things over, and I have to say I just don't understand it . . . For those of you who don't know me, I should point out that this is very unusual.'

He pulled a face and flopped down into the armchair. Moreno hesitated for a few moments before responding.

'I think,' she said, hastily trying to keep her guard up and not say too much, 'I think that what really happened in 1983 wasn't quite as straightforward as they concluded then. And that Chief of Police Vrommel – and presumably others as well – had good reason to make sure that something was brushed under the carpet. I don't know what and I don't know why. I also think that there are people here in Lejnice who have known the truth but have kept quiet about it for sixteen years – and that Tim Van Rippe was one of them. And that somebody killed him to make sure that he didn't give the game away. Yes, in broad outline that's what I think.'

'Hmm,' muttered Baasteuwel. 'And how the hell could this somebody know that this girl was going to visit Tim Van Rippe that particular day?'

Moreno shook her head.

'I've no idea,' she admitted. 'But Mikaela stirred up quite a lot of things before she disappeared in a puff of smoke. She met both Winnie Maas's mother and this Vera Sauger. Perhaps several other people as well, but since nobody seems to be bothering to look into the matter, we don't yet know who. Vera gave me another name as well as Tim Van Rippe – one Claus Bitowski. I've rung his number several times this morning, but there's been no reply.'

'Are you suggesting . . . ?' said Baasteuwel, but hesitated for a moment. 'Are you suggesting that he's also buried on the beach somewhere? This Bitowski? Is that your hypothesis between the lines?'

Moreno hesitated and looked round the table.

'I don't have a hypothesis,' she said. 'But it wouldn't be all that difficult to check in any case. If he's alive it must surely be possible to get hold of him. Somehow or other.'

Baasteuwel nodded.

'Yes indeed,' he said. 'And what about Mikaela? What are we going to do about little fröken Lijphart? That's a harder nut to crack, I suspect. This damned Vrommel . . . What the hell's behind all this?'

Nobody seemed to have a good answer to that question, and silence reigned once more. Moreno thought she could almost see – or at any rate sense – the highly charged thoughts of each of them hovering like a cloud over the table. Good, she thought. It's good to have more brains at work in this connection. At last . . .

'Ah well,' said Baasteuwel in the end. 'I can see by the cheerful expressions on your faces that we can assume she's also lying there in the sand.'

'There's nothing to suggest that,' Moreno hurried to point out; but even as she said that she became aware that it had more to do with wishful thinking than anything else.

Kohler sighed.

'We'll have to arrange for the whole beach to be dug up,' he said. 'It should be quite straightforward. A few hundred men and a few months . . . Maybe we could get the army involved, they are usually keen on this kind of thing.'

'When there isn't a war on,' said Baasteuwel.

'I suggest we wait for a few days with that,' said Moreno. 'I mean, there are other angles of approach. How's the investigation into Tim Van Rippe going, for instance?'

Baasteuwel made a noise reminiscent of a lawn mower that failed to start. Or a Trabant.

'Sluggish,' he said. 'The Van Rippe investigation's proceeding sluggishly. But perhaps that's the intention.'

'Let's hear about it,' said Moreno optimistically.

Constable Vegesack, who had been sitting there and listening in silence for most of the time, decided to do the talking.

'No, not a lot has happened,' he said. 'The post-mortem is over and done with, we got the paperwork yesterday. It's not possible to be more precise about the time of death, it seems. He died at some point within a twenty-four-hour period – midday on Sunday the eleventh and Monday the twelfth at the same time. The cause of death is beyond dispute: a pointed instrument stabbed into the left eye that continued into the brain. No sign of any other injury, no sign of a struggle – no wounds or scratches, no scraps of skin and so on. But it's odd that somebody could just come up and stab him in the eye: it's possible that he was caught completely by surprise. Maybe he was lying asleep . . . Or sunbathing.'

He waited for comments from Kohler or Baasteuwel, but neither of them seemed to have anything to say. Vegesack took a mouthful of beer, and continued.

'We've spoken to several people who knew Van Rippe, but nobody had anything relevant to say. He'd planned to go away for a few days with a female friend of his – Damita Fuchsbein: she was the one who reported him missing, and she identified the body. The last person to see him alive, as far as we know at the moment at least, is a neighbour of his. He's called Eskil Pudecka, and he claims to have spoken to Van Rippe shortly after one o'clock on Sunday – that means of course that the twenty-four-hour period shrinks slightly, but maybe that doesn't matter much. We've also spoken to Van Rippe's mother and his brother, they are his closest relations, but they know as little as everybody else.'

'Hang on a minute,' said Baasteuwel. 'Who exactly has been talking to all these people? Kohler and I have spoken to four or five people at most, but who dealt with this girl-friend, for instance? And the relatives?'

Vegesack thought for a moment.

'I interrogated Damita Fuchsbein,' he said. 'You couldn't really say she was his girlfriend, by the way. Vrommel dealt with both his mother and his brother – the mother as recently as yesterday, I believe. She's been away.'

Baasteuwel slammed his fist down on the table.

'Bloody hell!' he snorted. 'Vrommel deals with the mother! Vrommel deals with the brother! Vrommel deals with every bastard who might have something to hide . . . For Christ's sake! He's running this show just as he wants to, the swine! Have you seen any transcripts from the inter-rogations he's conducted?'

Vegesack looked embarrassed.

'No . . .' he said. 'No, I don't think he's arranged for them to be typed out yet.'

'Have you seen anything?' said Baasteuwel, glaring at his colleague.

Kohler shook his head.

'Calm down now,' he urged. 'Don't get carried away again.'

Baasteuwel flung out his arms in frustration and sank back into his armchair. Moreno wondered if he often got carried away, and what might happen in that case. It seemed obvious that Kohler had some kind of point in any case, as Baasteuwel didn't bother to protest.

'We must look into this,' Kohler said. 'Obviously. But I suggest we do so with a modicum of discretion. Does anybody think we have anything to gain by putting Vrommel up against the wall straight away?'

Moreno thought about that. So did Vegesack and Baasteuwel: she could sense their minds working overtime. As far as she could judge neither of them would have anything at all against confronting Vrommel with a 500-watt lamp shining into his face and a whole arsenal of accusations.

She certainly didn't either, but that naturally didn't mean that Kohler's line was not to be preferred. Vrommel is presumably no thickie, even if he is a shit heap. Or a skunk. But it would be better to have a little patience and give themselves a chance of ascertaining a few facts first.

It wasn't at all clear what, but if there was anything

they ought to be familiar with by now it was a lack of clarity.

Baasteuwel put her thoughts into words.

'All right,' he said. 'We'll give the bastard a few days to stew. It might be fun to see how he acts in the circumstances, if nothing else.'

Vegesack nodded. Moreno and Kohler nodded.

'Let's do that, then,' said Kohler. 'But what now? Perhaps we ought to share out the workload a bit?'

'I agree,' said Baasteuwel. 'But what the hell should we do? All those who are on leave can go and buy themselves an ice cream if they'd prefer.'

34

That afternoon Moreno went to stay with Selma Perhovens. A promise was a promise, after all, and the
landlady at Dombrowski's had informed her firmly that
new guests were due to move into Moreno's room that
evening.

Perhovens hadn't sounded as if she'd regretted making
the offer when Moreno phoned her that morning. On the
contrary. We women must stick together, she said, and
the least we can do is to offer one another a bit of hospitality in times of need. Besides, they had quite a lot to talk
about, she thought.

Moreno thought so as well, and she had no hesitation
in taking over the box room. Box room and guest room.
The flat was in Zinderslaan, and was large, old and lived-
in: four rooms and a kitchen and high ceilings – far too big
for a rather small mother and her slightly built daughter,
but she had acquired it in connection with her divorce, so
why not?

The daughter was called Drusilla, was eleven going on twelve, and seemed to have about twice as much energy as her mother. Which was saying something. When Moreno crossed the threshold, Drusilla eyed her up and down, from top to toe.

'Is she going to stay here? Cool!'

Moreno gathered that she wasn't the first temporary guest in the box room. While a two-hour belt of rain drifted past, she devoted herself to playing cards, watching the television and reading comics together with Drusilla. Not one thing after the other, but all at the same time. Simply gaping at the telly was too boring, Drusilla thought. And the same applied to playing cards. You needed to have something to do as well.

Meanwhile Perhovens sat in her room, writing: there were two articles that needed to be written by half past four, she apologized for being a poor hostess, but what the hell . . .

She was afraid that she was also booked that evening, unfortunately, and at about five o'clock she took Drusilla with her and left Moreno to her own devices. They'd be back by about eleven, all being well.

Or thereabouts.

'You must stay for several days,' insisted Drusilla as they left. 'I shan't be going to visit my cousins until next week, my friend is in Ibiza, and Mum's so boring when all she does is work.'

'We'll see,' said Moreno.

When she was on her own she ran a bath. Luckily she had her mobile in the bathroom, for while she was lying there in the lime-blossom-scented foam, she had no fewer than three calls.

The first was from her best friend Clara Mietens, who had finally got back home and listened to her answering machine. She had been on a buying trip to Italy (Clara owned and ran a boutique in Kellnerstraat in central Maardam, selling clothing not produced by factories or sweat-shops), she'd met a man who wasn't worth bothering about, and had nothing at all against a few days cycling around Sorbinowo, as they had discussed earlier. Next week, Monday or Tuesday perhaps – she would need a bit of time to brief her stand-in. And to check and see if she really did still have a bike.

Moreno explained – without going into detail – that she was also tied up for a few days, and they agreed to get in touch again on Sunday.

Was the idle life by the seaside invigorating? Clara had asked.

Moreno assured her that it was, and hung up.

Then Inspector Baasteuwel rang. He reckoned the pair of them ought to have a meeting in order to discuss things. In view of the latest development, he and Kohler had booked into Kongershuus, and he was free that evening. So how about a bite to eat and a glass of wine? he wondered. And a bit of intelligent conversation about what the hell was going on in this godforsaken dump with that goddamned chief of police.

Moreno accepted without needing to give the proposal any further thought. Werders restaurant, eight o'clock.

Two minutes later Mikael Bau rang. He was also free that evening and really needed to talk to her, he claimed. To sort out this and that, no hard feelings, but surely they could have a bite to eat and a glass of wine, like civilized human beings?

She said that unfortunately she was tied up that evening, but that she'd have nothing against meeting him the next day, always assuming that she hadn't gone home by then. He accepted after a few seconds of reluctant silence. Then he wondered if she always behaved like this when she was having her period. Hiding herself away like a wounded lioness, telling all males to go to hell.

She laughed and said that he didn't need to worry about that. Her period was over, she was lying in lime-blossom-scented bubbles in a lion-footed bathtub and looking forward to new adventures.

He asked what the hell she meant by that, but she didn't know either and so they closed down the call having half agreed to meet the following day.

Inspector Baasteuwel had booked a table behind two dense artificial fig trees, and was sitting with a dark beer, waiting for her.

'Why did you become a cop?' he asked when they had completed their orders. 'I'm not an idiot, but I can't help asking that whenever I meet a new brother-in-misery. Or sister.'

Moreno had seven different answers prepared for whenever she was asked that question, and selected one of them.

'Because I thought I'd be good at it,' she said.

'Good answer,' said Baasteuwel. 'I can see that you're not an idiot either.'

She noticed that she liked the man. She had hardly been able to think along such lines during that morning's improvised meeting at Vegesack's place, but now she had no doubt that she was talking to a colleague she could trust. A man who could stand up for himself.

Slovenly and ill-mannered, to be sure – well, maybe not slovenly, but it was pretty obvious that he couldn't give a toss about convention. His facial stubble was no doubt four or five days old by now, and his grey-black, somewhat tousled hair had presumably not made acquaintance with a pair of scissors for at least six months. His eyes were deep and dark, and his crooked nose at least two sizes too big. His mouth was wide and his teeth irregular. He's as ugly as sin, Moreno thought. I like him.

But they were not sitting there in order to exchange compliments.

'Has anything more happened?' she asked. 'During the afternoon, I mean.'

'Yes indeed,' said Baasteuwel. 'Things might be starting to move at last. It's a bit awkward to do things without Vrommel noticing, of course, but we'll get round that. It's about time we had something to do as well – these first few days have been more like a wake than a murder investigation. But now we know why. Did you know that Vegesack calls him the Skunk, incidentally? He happened to let it slip.'

Moreno said that she had also heard that, and smiled.

'So far it's just a question of laying out hooks, I'm afraid,' Baasteuwel continued. 'No bites yet, but they'll come. Trust me: if Vrommel has any skeletons in his cupboard, you can bet your sweet life we'll dig them out. I've spoken to fru Van Rippe as well, only on the telephone mind you, and Kohler has had a chat with his brother. It didn't produce anything of interest, it seems. He's six years older and doesn't have much idea of what his younger brother got up to as a teenager. He'd already flown the nest when it happened in 1983.'

'What about Bitowski?' asked Moreno. 'The other name Mikaela got from Vera Sauger. Have you found him?'

Baasteuwel shook his head.

'I'm afraid not,' he said. 'Everybody's on holiday at this bloody time of year. According to what we've been told he's out in the archipelago with some of his mates, but we haven't been able to confirm that yet. A neighbour thinks he left on Sunday last week – that very same crucial Sunday, dammit . . . He's unmarried as well, so either he's out there hitting the bottle, or he's buried in the sand somewhere too. We'll be questioning a few more relatives and acquaintances tomorrow.'

'Have you any idea what sort of a person he is?' Moreno wondered. 'If he really did meet Mikaela Lijphart and had a talk to her, you'd have thought he'd have reacted in some way.'

'Not if he's sitting back in a deckchair drinking sun-warmed beer,' Baasteuwel suggested. 'Not if he's buried in the sand either, come to that . . .'

He popped a piece of meat into his mouth and chewed away thoughtfully. Moreno did the same, and waited.

'Anyway,' said Baasteuwel eventually, 'I've ordered

extracts from the court proceedings involving Maager. I should get them tomorrow. And a list of pupils who were attending the school at the time – I suppose I'll have to collect that myself, they don't have many staff around at this time of year.'

Moreno nodded. Efficient, she thought. He's not exactly sitting around twiddling his thumbs and ruminating. Not all the time, at least. For the first time during the weeks she'd spent in Lejnice she felt that she could safely leave things in somebody else's hands. That she didn't need to accept responsibility for everything, but knew that things would get done even so. It was a relief, no doubt about that.

Good, she thought. At last, somebody who has a clue about things.

That judgement was a bit hard on Constable Vegesack, she realized that; but you could say that Baasteuwel and Kohler were of a different calibre. A calibre that was probably necessary to elucidate these obscurities and half-truths. And what it was now clear was at the bottom of it all.

They'll solve this, she thought. I can wash my hands of it all.

'Oh my God, I nearly forgot!' said Baasteuwel as he swallowed a gulp of wine. 'Maager! He had a phone call last Saturday – the staff at the home eventually realized that, rang us and told us about it. Some stand-in or other took the call and went to fetch him. About twelve o'clock. Yes, the same day that he went missing. Last Saturday. What have you to say to that?'

Moreno thought for quite some time before responding.

'I'm not really surprised,' she said. 'I don't suppose they knew who the caller was?'

'No. A woman, that's all they knew. If she gave a name, they'd forgotten it. Who do you think it was?'

Moreno took another drink of wine while she thought about that.

'Sigrid Lijphart,' she said. 'His ex-wife. But I'm only saying that because he hardly seemed to know anybody at all.'

'Hmm,' muttered Baasteuwel, who evidently hadn't thought of that possibility. 'What might she have wanted, then?'

'To talk a few things over – it doesn't need to be any more remarkable than that. They were married for six years, haven't said a word to each other for sixteen, and they have a daughter together who has gone missing. There was no doubt all kinds of things to talk about.'

'Could be,' said Baasteuwel. 'But what might the telephone call – if it was her, in fact – have to do with his disappearance?'

Moreno shrugged.

'I've no idea. Maybe they agreed to meet. He finds it hard to say anything at the best of times, and it probably wasn't any easier on the telephone . . . Yes, she might well have arranged to meet him.'

Baasteuwel raised a sceptical eyebrow while he sat there in silence, apparently weighing up this suggestion. After five seconds, he lowered it. It needs trimming, Moreno noted.

'So why doesn't she mention this when she phones and pesters the police?' he wondered. 'She rings at least twice a day, according to Vegesack. She's a damned annoying woman – I've listened to her tirades myself.'

'I don't know,' said Moreno, shaking her head. 'I'm on holiday. Perhaps one should take into account the fact that her daughter has gone missing . . .'

'Yes, of course,' said Baasteuwel.

They finished their main course and ordered coffee. Baasteuwel lit a cigarette, placed his elbows on the table and leaned forward. Looked inscrutable for a moment, then suddenly broke into a smile.

'Vrommel,' he said. 'Would you like to know how I intend to tackle the problem concerning the chief of police?'

'Tell me,' said Moreno.

'Like this,' said Baasteuwel, and looked almost excited

at the prospect. 'As I can't very well punch him on the nose, and we can't go gadding about questioning people without him getting to know about it, I've turned to the press.'

'The press?' said Moreno.

'Yes, the local newspaper. Aaron Wicker, editor in chief of *Westerblatt*. They are deadly enemies, he and Vrommel, if I've interpreted the signs correctly. And he's old enough to know about the Maager case. He claims he wrote ten kilometres of columns on the subject. I'm going to meet him tomorrow evening – unfortunately he's away all day gathering material for some article or other . . . But then, as God is my witness, light will be cast on this whole murky business.'

'Excellent,' said Moreno. 'If you need any extra help, you might like to know that I happen to be staying with one of Wicker's reporter colleagues.'

Baasteuwel's jaw dropped for a moment.

'I've got to hand it to you, you know what you're doing. Do you spend all your holidays like this?'

'You should see me when I'm on duty,' said Moreno.

'I've been doing a bit of thinking as well,' Baasteuwel admitted when their coffee was served. 'I haven't only been faffing about and being a conscientious police officer.'

379

'You don't say,' said Moreno. 'And what have you been thinking about?'

'The murder. Of Van Rippe, that is. But I haven't got anywhere.'

'That happens to me sometimes as well,' admitted Moreno. 'Once a year or so. Let's hear it.'

Baasteuwel displayed his uneven teeth in a grin.

'You're a canny cop,' he said. 'Are you married?'

'What the hell has that got to do with it?' said Moreno.

Baasteuwel leaned forward over the table.

'I just don't want you making advances to me,' he said. 'I have a wife and four kids; I see it as my duty to humanity to spread my genes.'

Moreno burst out laughing and Baasteuwel bared his teeth again.

'But where were we?' he said. 'This poor Van Rippe – I can't help wondering about how he came to die. It's a damned unusual way of murdering people, sticking something in his eye, isn't it? It's difficult to get at an eye, I mean, unless he was lying down, asleep, of course. But why would he be lying asleep on the beach?'

'He could have been taken there,' said Moreno.

'Yes, I'm coming round to thinking that he must have been,' said Baasteuwel. 'Nobody sleeps on the beach at night, and it's an exceptionally cold-blooded murderer who goes and stabs to death somebody who's lying down and sunbathing. I gather you're not exactly on your own down on the beach during the day – even if my duties have prevented me from going down there to check. So he must have been moved there after the murder.'

Moreno thought about that.

'That can't be true,' she said.

'I know,' said Baasteuwel. 'But tell me why it can't be true.'

Moreno could see that she'd have nothing against working together with Baasteuwel on a daily basis as well. He seemed to be sharper than most, and he had a way of discussing things and playing with words that helped to move things forward. He was creative, in fact.

'The careless way he was buried,' she said. 'If somebody really had time to move the body from the place where it had been murdered, they ought also to have had time to dispose of it more efficiently. To dig it down deeper, at least. And why choose a place that's crawling with people every day? There must be hundreds of places where he'd never have been found. Up among the dunes, for instance. No, I think it must have happened in great haste, despite everything. The murderer was in a hurry. Dug the body down as quickly as possible, then got the hell out of there.'

'So not a lot in the way of premeditation, in other words?'

'Presumably not.'

'And it happened at that very spot?'

'Presumably.'

Baasteuwel lit another cigarette and sighed.

'Maybe we'll have to go along with Kohler's idea after all.'

'What was that?'

'Call in the army and dig up the whole bleeding beach.'

'Surely we've sorted the immediate vicinity already,' said Moreno. 'Have they found anything? The scene-of-crime gentlemen, I mean,'

'A shoe,' said Baasteuwel. 'The right size, could be Van Rippe's, but it's not certain. It was lying about ten metres away.'

'An excellent clue.'

'Brilliant. Vrommel has it on his desk, and is supposed to be studying it. I must remember to keep an eye on it and make sure he doesn't spirit it away. It ought to have been sent to the Pathology Laboratory, of course, but that hasn't happened. Ah well . . .'

He suddenly yawned, and Moreno had an immediate urge to follow suit.

'Make sure you do that, then,' she said, looking at the clock. 'Send off the shoe and keep an eye on Vrommel. Shall we ask for the bill? Or have you anything else to say?

You have to be at work tomorrow morning, if I'm not much mistaken.'

'Huh,' grunted Baasteuwel. 'You're right, of course. Not that I have anything against a hard day's work. It's sitting around and twiddling my thumbs that goes against the grain for me.'

Moreno recalled his initial question.

'So that's why you became a police officer, is it, if I might respond with a question? To avoid sitting around and twiddling your thumbs.'

Baasteuwel looked pensive for a moment.

'Not really,' he said. 'I became a police officer because I enjoy putting crooked bastards behind bars. I'll never catch up with all of them, of course – there's too many of 'em: but I feel a bit better every time I manage to nail another of the swine. My wife thinks I'm perverted.'

He smiled without showing his teeth.

'There are worse reasons for becoming a cop,' said Moreno.

'There certainly are,' said Baasteuwel. 'Anyway, I'll be in touch tomorrow. Assuming you'll still be around, that is?'

Moreno nodded.

'I'll be around until Saturday at least. I have an appointment with a young lady tomorrow.'

*

The young lady in question had gone to bed by the time she returned to Zinderslaan, but her mother was sitting in the kitchen, checking proofs.

'I feel like a gypsy,' Moreno said. 'Wandering around and changing my address several times a week.'

'Gypsies are nice people,' said Perhovens. 'Would you like some tea?'

Moreno said she would love some. It was turned half past eleven, but if they were going to exchange a few words and experiences, it could well be best to seize the opportunity while Drusilla was out of the way.

'Tim Van Rippe,' Perhovens said. 'We're going to reveal his name tomorrow. I hope you've nothing against that?'

'Not at all,' said Moreno. 'His next of kin know about it.'

'Good. I'd be quite interested in talking our way through this Maager business, in fact. I reckon it's about time I wrote something about that as well. If it turned out to be appropriate. A few little adjustments might be in order, perhaps? In the next week or so . . . What kind of tea would you like? I have sixty-two different sorts.'

'Strong,' said Moreno.

35

23 July 1999

The ridge of high pressure returned on Friday. The rain from the south-west had moved on, and it became rapidly warmer. As early as seven in the morning the big thermometer on the side of the Xerxes IT company building in Lejnice was showing 25 degrees in the shade, and it would get even hotter.

Detective Inspector Ewa Moreno was not one of those who got up to check the weather at seven o'clock that morning. Instead she was woken up at nine by Drusilla Perhovens, who immediately put her in the picture.

'The sky is as blue as flax flowers, and the sun's shining like hell.'

'Don't swear, Drusilla,' said her mother, who was standing in the doorway, brushing her hair.

'You've got to let yourself go now and then,' said Drusilla. 'You've taught me that.'

Then she turned to Moreno.

'You can come with me to the beach if you like,' she said. 'We'll be picking up a boy who's a friend of mine, so you won't need to entertain me all the time.'

Moreno thought about that for a couple of seconds, then accepted.

But as it turned out, merely lying around on the beach and making the most of the high pressure wasn't entirely without its problems. Drusilla kept her promise and spent most of the time with a young man by the name of Helmer – swimming, building sandcastles, swimming, playing football, swimming, eating ice cream, swimming and reading comics. Moreno rang the changes by first lying on her back, then on her stomach; but irrespective of her position she found it hard not to think about what was hiding away in this warm, soft sand less than a week ago.

And what might still be lying hidden there.

Perhaps I'm lying on a corpse, she thought as she shut her eyes to keep out the glare of the sun. Before long Drusilla and Helmer will come running up to tell me that they've dug up a head.

She had the feeling that it was beginning to be high time she put all this behind her. Time to leave Lejnice and life on the beach, and go back home to Maardam at last. The Mikaela Lijphart case wasn't her case any longer. Nor was the Arnold Maager case, nor the Tim Van Rippe case. They never had been her concern, strictly speaking; but now at least she had left them in competent hands: Kohler's and Baasteuwel's, and – if that weren't enough – those of the collective of local journalists: Selma Perhovens and, as far as she understood, Aaron Wicker. There was no reason why she should be involved any longer. None at all. She had done more than anybody could reasonably have asked; and if her aim was to return to work in August with anything like recharged batteries, it was high time that she allowed herself some real holiday. Cycling and camping in the wild Sorbinowo region, for instance. Warm evenings round the campfire with barbecued fish, good wine and existential conversation. Nocturnal swims in dark waters.

And if they really were considering digging up the whole of this beach, teeming with holidaymakers, that was something she had no great desire to be involved in. No desire at all.

Even so, needless to say that was precisely what she started dreaming about when she fell asleep. Hordes of sweaty soldiers, dressed in green, under the command of a bald senior officer (looking remarkably like Vrommel, in fact, but with a Hitler moustache rather than a thin conventional one), hacking away with pickaxes and spades and digging up corpse after corpse, which were piled up according to age and sex under the supervision of herself and Constable Vegesack. Baasteuwel was wandering round with a brush, removing the sand from their faces and bodies, and they appeared one by one before her horrified eyes. Mikaela Lijphart, Winnie Maas, Arnold Maager (whom she had only seen in a bad photograph but who nevertheless was more recognizable than any of the others for some incomprehensible reason), Sigrid Lijphart, Vera Sauger, Mikael Bau, Franz Lampe-Leermann . . . She had some difficulty in understanding how the last two were relevant in this context, but accepted it as an example of life's inherent lunacy. It wasn't until Drusilla came up hand in hand with Maud, Moreno's sister – not as she had turned out, but as she remembered her as a teenager – that she'd had enough of the show and woke up.

Her head was bursting. Never lie down and fall asleep in the sun! She remembered that as an instruction her mother – for whatever reason – had tried to ram into her brain when she was a child, and even if she didn't feel she'd derived all that much wisdom from that source, she felt she had to concede that today of all days her mother was right on that score at least. She struggled to her feet, and went for a swim.

★

'Baasteuwel, detective inspector,' said Baasteuwel.

Silence at the other end.

'Am I speaking to Dr deHaavelaar?'

'What do you want?'

'Just a few questions. I'm involved in the Van Rippe case – you've doubtless read about it in the newspapers. There seems to be a connection with another case from a few years ago – the murder of Winnie Maas. Can you remember that?'

'If I want to,' said deHaavelaar.

'I think you carried out the post-mortem, is that right?'

'I have nothing to add in that connection.'

'I'm only looking for some clarification.'

'No clarification is needed. Has the chief of police sanctioned this phone call? He's in charge of the investigation, isn't he?'

Baasteuwel paused before answering.

'May I ask why you are unwilling to talk about this?'

An irritated snort was audible at the other end of the line.

'I have more important things to be getting on with,' said deHaavelaar. 'I was pestered the other day by another police officer as well. A woman.'

'Inspector Moreno?'

'Yes. I ought to have reported her to Vrommel, but I erred on the side of mercy.'

'I see,' said Baasteuwel. 'But the fact is now that either you answer my questions over the telephone, or I shall send a police car round to collect you. It's up to you.'

Silence. Baasteuwel lit a cigarette and waited.

'What the hell is it you want to know?'

'Just a few details. I'm sitting here with the trial transcripts in front of me. The trial of Arnold Maager. And there's something about it that perplexes me.'

'Really.'

'You didn't appear to give evidence.'

'No.'

'Why not? You were the medicolegal officer after all.'

'It wasn't necessary. It's usual but not compulsory. It was an open-and-shut case, and I no doubt had other things to do.'

'But you signed the medical certificate? The one that was read out in the courtroom.'

'Yes, of course. What the hell are you getting at?'

'It says here that you examined the girl Winnie Maas – together with a pathologist by the name of Kornitz – and ascertained that she was pregnant. Is that right?'

'Of course.'

'But it says nothing about how advanced the pregnancy was.'

'It doesn't?' said deHaavelaar.

'No.'

'That's odd. It should have said. I don't recall exactly, but she wasn't all that far gone. Five or six weeks, perhaps.'

'Are you sure about that?'

'Absolutely.'

'So it wasn't in fact rather more advanced than that? Ten to twelve weeks or so?'

'Of course not,' protested deHaavelaar. 'What the devil are you insinuating?'

'Nothing,' said Baasteuwel. 'I just wanted to check because the information is missing.'

DeHaavelaar had no comment to make on that, and there were a few more seconds of silence.

'Was there anything else?'

'Not at the moment,' said Baasteuwel. 'Thank you for your help.'

'You're welcome,' said Dr. deHaavelaar, and hung up.

So there, Baasteuwel thought, eyeing the telephone with a grim smile. He's lying, the bastard.

Which he knew he could get away with, he then decided. There's not the slightest chance of putting him behind bars. Especially as Dr Kornitz has been dead for three years.

More interesting is to think about why he lied.

★

Moreno had not taken her mobile with her to the beach, but when she returned to the flat with Drusilla at about half past four, she found she had two messages.

The first was from Münster. He sounded unusually grave, and asked her to ring him back as soon as she had an opportunity.

She realized that she had yet again managed to erase Lampe-Leermann and the paedophile business from her mind (even if she recalled that the Scumbag had appeared fleetingly in her beach dream), and now that it cropped up again she could feel the noose tightening around her neck.

Oh hell, she thought. Don't let it be true.

She phoned back immediately, but there was no reply. Neither from the police station nor from Münster's home. She left a message on his answering machine, saying she'd tried to get hold of him.

That's the way it seems to be nowadays, she thought in resignation as she replaced the receiver. We live in a world of botched communications. The only thing we use the telephone for is to explain that we've tried to make contact but failed. A pretty depressing state of affairs.

She didn't need to respond to the other message. It was from her ex-boyfriend (lover? bloke? fiancé?) stating that he'd be expecting her at Werder's at eight o'clock.

The same restaurant as yesterday, she noted. And the same time.

But a different man. She thought it just as well that she was going home the next day. The staff will start to wonder. And draw a few less than complimentary conclusions, no doubt.

She decided to turn up in any case. But not to stay there for too long. She felt about as tired as Selma Perhovens looked when she came home at a few minutes past five.

'No burning of midnight oil tonight,' she said.

'No way,' said Moreno.

They had sat up talking until past two. Waded through the whole Maager–Lijphart business yet again. Spoken about relationships, men, work, books, the situation in the so-called former Yugoslavia, and what exactly it meant to be the first free woman in the history of the world.

Existential conversation, as stated before. Fruitful. But not another night, no thank you.

'Thank you for babysitting,' said Perhovens.

'She hasn't been a babysitter at all,' insisted Drusilla. 'Helmer and I have been looking after each other all day.'

'That's true,' said Moreno. 'Anyway, I'm going home tomorrow. I'll be dining out again tonight, by the way. You mustn't think that this is my normal habit.'

'Not a bad habit, though,' said Perhovens. 'What does my little sweetheart want to gobble for dinner tonight?'

'Fillet steak stuffed with gorgonzola, and baked pota-toes,' said the little sweetheart. 'We haven't had that for ages.'

'You'll get sausage and macaroni,' her mother informed her.

Just as she was about to leave the telephone rang again.

This time it was Baasteuwel.

'Nice to see you yesterday,' he said. 'Would you like a report?'

'Nice to see you, too,' said Moreno. 'I'd like a report very much.'

'I'm in a bit of a hurry,' said Baasteuwel. 'Only time for the most important things – okay?'

'Okay,' said Moreno.

'That doctor's lying.'

'DeHaavelaar?'

'Yes. Winnie Maas *was* pregnant when she died, but I wouldn't have thought Arnold Maager was the father.'

Moreno tried to digest the information and register what it meant.

'What the hell . . . ?' she said. 'Are you sure?'

'Not at all,' said Baasteuwel. 'I just have that feeling – but I'm shit hot when it comes to feelings. And he's come back.'

'Come back?'

'Yes.'

'Who?'

'Arnold Maager, of course. He came back to the Sidonis home this afternoon.'

Moreno was dumbstruck for a few seconds.

'Came back? You're saying he simply came back . . . ?'

'Yep.'

'How? Where has he been?'

'He hasn't said. He hasn't said anything at all, in fact. Just lies on his bed, staring at the wall, it seems. Whatever he's been up to, he's been without his medication for almost a week. Antidepressants, I assume. They're a bit worried about him.'

'How did he come back?'

'He simply came marching in, just like that. Vrommel's out there now, talking to him.'

'Vrommel? Wouldn't somebody else have been better?'

'We can't very well take all his bloody duties away from him without his suspecting something. Vegesack went with him to keep an eye on things, and as Maager's autistic now it probably doesn't matter much.'

Moreno thought for a moment.

'Let's hope not,' she said. 'I can't keep up with all this. Anything else?'

'Quite a bit,' said Baasteuwel. 'But I have to go to a

series of little interviews now. How long will you be around tomorrow?'

Moreno hesitated. She hadn't yet decided what time to leave. But surely there was no need to set off at daybreak come what may? And she needed to buy something for Selma Perhovens. And for Drusilla as well.

'There's a train at four o'clock. I'll probably take that.'

'Excellent,' said Baasteuwel. 'That means we can have lunch together.'

He hung up. Moreno remained standing with the telephone in her hand for a while. Well, well, well, she thought. So Maager wasn't the child's father? What does that mean?

Hard to say. But he must have thought that it was his in any case. Wasn't that the main thing?

Suddenly the questions started bubbling up inside her head again. The main thing for whom?

Winnie Maas, of course. Maybe somebody else as well?

After all, virgin births are rather unusual, just as Mikaela Lijphart had said on the train a couple of weeks ago . . .

Moreno stretched herself out on the bed and stared up at the ceiling.

What on earth had happened to Mikaela Lijphart?

What had Arnold Maager been doing while he was away, and why had Tim Van Rippe died?

There's a lot that isn't clear. A hell of a lot.

And how were things going with regard to the ensnaring of Chief of Police Vrommel? She'd forgotten to ask Baasteuwel about that.

Ah well, that could wait until tomorrow, she decided.

Every day has enough trouble of its own to cope with.

36

24 July 1999

Inspector Baasteuwel stood in the shadow of a warehouse, watching a seagull.

The seagull was watching him. Apart from that, nothing much was happening. The sun was shining. The sea was as calm as a millpond.

He checked his watch. It was no more than a quarter past ten, but he could swear that the temperature was already very close to the thirty mark. If it hadn't already passed it. So the high pressure was still dominant, and the sky was so cloud-free that looking at it almost gave him a headache. It struck him that this Saturday should have been the third day of his leave. Damn and blast. But that was life . . . He lit a cigarette, today's fourth. Or possibly fifth.

At last the ferry came gliding round the breakwater. It

looked half empty. Not to say completely empty. Needless to say there was no sensible reason why anybody should head for the mainland from the islands on a day like today. On the contrary. In the pens designated for passengers wanting to embark, people were packed as tightly as West-werdingen sardines, and the barrier had been lowered behind the last car that could be accommodated on the eleven o'clock departure ten minutes ago. Why on earth should anybody want to take a car with them into the archipelago?

Baasteuwel left the relatively cool shade behind the warehouse and walked towards the gate through which disembarking passengers would be siphoned out. He opened up his umbrella.

He regretted the umbrella business: it was his wife who had given it to him in an attack of grim feminist humour, but what the hell? Bitowski must have something to look for that could be easily identified, and a blue-and-yellow umbrella decorated with an advert for Nixon condoms was no doubt as good as anything.

Especially in weather like this. When he looked round, he couldn't see any other condom umbrellas pretending they were parasols.

So Claus Bitowski couldn't very well miss him.

★

And he didn't. One of the first passengers to disembark was a corpulent man of about thirty, perhaps slightly more. He was wearing sunglasses, and a back-to-front baseball cap. In one hand he was holding a dirty yellow sports bag made of PVC-coated fabric, in the other a half-empty bottle of beer. His T-shirt with the logo 'We are the Fuckin' Champs' was unable to keep his pot belly from hanging down over the top of his jeans.

'Are you that fucking cop?' he asked.

Baasteuwel closed the umbrella. His parents ought to have used Nixon, he thought.

'I am indeed. And I suppose you are Claus Bitowski?'

Bitowski nodded. Drank the rest of the beer and looked round for a rubbish bin. When he didn't find one, he flung the empty bottle into the water instead. Baasteuwel looked the other way.

'I've nothing to say,' said Bitowski.

'What do you mean by that?' asked Baasteuwel. 'I haven't asked you anything yet.'

'About Van Rippe. I know nothing.'

'We'll see about that,' said Baasteuwel. 'Good that you came in any case. Shall we find somewhere to sit down?'

Bitowski lit a cigarette.

'I haven't anything to say, no matter what we do.'

Great, Baasteuwel thought. A thirty-year-old baby. I'd better approach this pedagogically.

'How about Strandterrassen and a beer?' he suggested.

Bitowski took a deep drag and considered the offer.

'All right, then,' he said.

They crossed over Zuiderslaan and sat down at a table under a parasol. Baasteuwel beckoned to a waitress and ordered two beers.

'I take it you know that Tim Van Rippe has been murdered?' he said when the beers had been served.

'Bloody horrendous,' said Bitowski.

'You knew him?'

'Not nowadays. I suppose I used to.'

Baasteuwel took out a notebook and began writing.

'In 1983, for instance?'

'Eh?'

'In 1983. That's a year.'

'I know that. Yes, I knew Van Rippe when we were at school, and—'

'Did you know Winnie Maas as well?'

'Winnie? What the hell has that got to do with it?'

'Did you know her?' asked Baasteuwel again.

'Yes, but what the hell . . . ? Of course I knew Winnie a bit. I was at her funeral. We were at school together, and so—'

'The same class?'

'No, I was a year older. Why are you asking about this? I keep telling you I don't know anything.'

'We're investigating the murder of Van Rippe,' said Baas-teuwel. 'Surely you want us to catch whoever killed him?'

'Yes, but I know nothing.'

That's probably true, Baasteuwel thought. About most things.

'When did you go out to the islands?'

'Two weeks ago.'

'What day?'

Bitowski thought that over.

'Sunday, I think. Yes, we took the afternoon boat.'

'We?'

'Me and my mates.'

'I see,' said Baasteuwel. 'You and your mates. Were you visited by a young lady called Mikaela Lijphart before you set off?'

'Eh?' said Bitowski. 'Mikaela what?'

'Lijphart. Did you talk to her that Sunday?'

'Of course I bloody didn't,' said Bitowski. 'I've never even heard of her.'

'Did you know Tim Van Rippe well in your younger days?'

'Fairly well.'

'Did he have something going with Winnie Maas?'

Bitowski shrugged. His stomach wobbled.

'I think so. She had something going with lots of people.'

'When was she together with Van Rippe, do you re-member that?'

'No. How the hell could I?'

'Was it just before she died, for instance?'

'No, for Christ's sake,' said Bitowski. 'It was long before that. She screwed around quite a bit.'

'Screwed around?'

'Yes, she was that type.'

'Did you also have sex with Winnie Maas?'

Bitowski emptied his glass of beer and belched.

'I might have done.'

'Might have done? Did you have sex with her or not?'

Bitowski stared at his glass, and Baasteuwel waved to the waitress and ordered another glass.

'Once,' said Bitowski.

'When?' asked Baasteuwel. 'When she was in class nine?'

'No, before that. I was in class nine, she must have been in class eight.'

'And it was just once?'

'That I screwed her all ends up, yes.'

Baasteuwel contemplated his puffed-up face for a while.

'Are you sure that she wasn't together with Tim Van Rippe in May/June 1983?'

Bitowski was served with another beer, and took a swig.

'Sure and sure,' he said. 'She ought not to have been, at least. She gave me a blow job at the beginning of May.'

'Gave you a blow job?'

'Yes – for Christ's sake, it was a party, wasn't it? But I don't really remember.'

Baasteuwel repressed an urge to stab his Nixon umbrella in Claus Bitowski's pot belly.

Don't remember? he thought. Ten years from now you won't remember your name, never mind where your cock is.

'Can you give me the names of any other boys that Winnie might have had sex with? In the spring of '83, that is.'

'No,' said Bitowski. 'I don't think there was anybody special, and I didn't really know her all that well. I don't know anything about all this, as I've already told you.'

'Were you interrogated at all in connection with Winnie's death?' asked Baasteuwel.

'Interrogated? No, why should I have been interrogated? I don't understand why you're sitting here and interrogating me now, either.'

'So no police officer asked you any questions at all?'

'No.'

Baasteuwel suddenly felt that he had no more questions to ask either. Apart perhaps from asking Bitowski if he knew the name of the president of the USA. Or a town in France. Or how much was 11 times 8.

'That's all,' he said. 'Thank you for the beer.'

'Eh? What the hell . . . ?'

'A joke,' Baasteuwel explained.

Constable Vegesack was nervous.

It had nothing to do with going behind the back of Chief of Police Vrommel. Not at all. But it was hard to deceive other people. Unpleasant. Especially somebody like fru Van Rippe – her son had been murdered, and now he had to sit here and lie to her. It felt wrong and repugnant, even if what he was going to have to serve up to her was not a pack of outright lies.

It was more a case of keeping a straight face and not telling her the whole truth.

Pulling the wool over her eyes, as they say. But that was bad enough.

'I don't understand what's going on,' she'd said as she got into the police car. 'Why do you want to talk to me again? Has something new happened?'

'Not really,' Vegesack had replied. 'It's just that we need a bit more detailed information.'

'And because of that you need to drive me to Lejnice and back?'

'We thought that would be best.'

It was rather more than an hour's drive from Karpatz to Lejnice, but luckily she decided to keep quiet for most of the time. Vegesack stole a look at her as she sat in the passenger seat, squeezing a handkerchief in her lap. A sixty-year-old woman, over the hill, with a dead son. She blew her nose now and then. Perhaps she's got hay fever, he thought. Or perhaps it was her grief that was releasing itself in that way. These were difficult days for her, of course. Her son was going to be buried the following week: Thursday, if Vegersack remembered rightly. Cremation was not possible, for technical reasons connected to the investigation. It must be awful for her, that was the bottom line. As if her own life had come to an end, in a way.

Although he found it difficult to imagine what she was feeling, he was relieved that he didn't need to talk about it.

And uncomfortable at having to pull the wool over her eyes, as said before.

'Did you know Tim?' she asked when they'd gone about halfway.

Vegesack shook his head.

'No, he was a few years older than me. Besides, I've only been living in Lejnice since '93. I come from Linzhuisen.'

'I see,' said fru Van Rippe. 'No, he didn't have many friends, our Tim.'

'No?'

'No. He was a bit of a loner.'

Vegesack didn't know what to say to that, and she didn't enlarge on the subject. She sighed and put on a pair of glasses instead.

'It's nice weather,' she said, as if she'd only just noticed that.

'Yes,' said Vegesack. 'Warm and sunny.'

Not much more was said during the rest of the journey. They arrived in Lejnice at five minutes to one and he parked in Zeestraat outside the *Westerblatt* office.

She looked at him in surprise.

'The newspaper? What have we come here for?'

Vegesack cleared his throat.

'It's full up in the police station, so we've borrowed a room from them, that's all.'

He couldn't make up his mind if she believed him or not.

Moreno bought a bottle of port for Selma Perhovens, as a thank-you for her hospitality, but she was a bit worried when it came to finding a suitable present for Drusilla. In the end she plumped for a book for so-called young adults that had won several prizes, and a box of chocolates: she had noticed that Drusilla had a rather full bookcase in her room, and she shouldn't have any trouble in forcing down the chocolates.

Both mother and daughter seemed pleased with their presents, and Moreno left the Perhovens' home after various exchanges of mutual admiration and promises to keep in touch. She deposited her suitcase at the railway station, had a final sunbathing session on the beach, and at two o'clock – as arranged – she met Inspector Baasteuwel at Darms' for lunch.

'Things are warming up,' said Baasteuwel when their salad had been served, 'but there's some way to go before we catch up with the weather.'

'Do you mean you're not going to be able to serve me up with the solution?' said Moreno.

'I'm afraid so,' said Baasteuwel. 'We've not quite sorted everything out yet. God only knows how it all hangs together, in fact.'

Moreno waited.

'And God only knows what's happened to Mikaela Lijphart. We haven't had a single response to the Wanted notice – not even the usual loonies who always ring to say that they've seen the devil and his auntie. It all seems a bit dodgy – but we've checked up and made sure that Vrommel isn't hushing something up.'

'What about Maager?' said Moreno. 'Have you asked

Sigrid Lijphart about that telephone call to the Sidonis home?'

'Yes, of course. She swears blind it wasn't her. She hasn't spoken to him for sixteen years, she claims, and has no intention of doing so for the next sixteen either. A warm-hearted lady, no doubt about that. But I suppose she has her reasons.'

'Perhaps she's lying.'

'Could be,' said Baasteuwel. 'I haven't spoken to her myself, it was Kohler who took care of that. Anyway, Maager is lying in his bed, staring at the same stain on the wallpaper. When he has his eyes open, that is – they had to shovel all kinds of stuff into him in order to help him sleep. But Winnie Maas is a bit more interesting – would you like to hear?'

'I'm all ears,' said Moreno.

Baasteuwel drank half a glass of mineral water and steered his fork round two laps of his salad before responding.

'She wasn't exactly God's little angel.'

'So I've gathered,' said Moreno.

'Hardly anybody wants to admit that they knew her, in fact. Everybody I've spoken to goes into their shell as soon as I start asking questions about her. They simply don't want to talk about her. They all say that they knew who she was, but nobody has owned up to being a friend of hers. So her role is becoming pretty clear. A young and shameless *femme fatale*, to over-dramatize it a bit. This damned Bitowski fellow admitted that he'd been in bed with her once – but God only knows how many others were. And she was only sixteen when she died. And nobody seems to doubt that it really was Maager who pushed her over the edge of the viaduct. Nobody at all.'

Moreno thought for a moment.

'So even if he wasn't the father of the child, everybody thought it was him?'

'It seems so. The important thing was that he thought he'd made her pregnant. Not that it was necessarily the truth. She intended to exploit the situation somehow or other, and he put a stop to that. Well, it couldn't get much more straightforward than that.'

'What about Vrommel? And that doctor?'

Baasteuwel sighed.

'God only knows. Even if deHaavelaar really did withhold information, it wouldn't necessarily be all that important.'

'Yes it would,' protested Moreno. 'He must have had a reason for doing so. And Vrommel must have had a reason for keeping quiet about Vera Sauger. It's simple logic.'

'Hmm,' muttered Baasteuwel. 'I know. Damn and blast. All I said was that things were beginning to warm up. We'll sort this mess out eventually, if for no other reason than the fact that I'm determined to teach this chief of police a lesson he won't forget. He has something on his conscience, and so help me God, I'm going to make him face up to it as well. I promise to keep you informed about the date of the execution. And everything else, of course – if you're interested.'

Moreno nodded.

'I'm most concerned about that girl,' she said. 'I don't want anything to have happened to Mikaela Lijphart, but I'm afraid that . . . well, you know.'

'Yes,' said Baasteuwel. 'Of course I know. We've seen it all before, you and I. But it doesn't do any harm to be an optimist until the opposite is proved to be the case, that's the principle I usually observe. We're going to turn our attention to the mother today. Van Rippe's mother, that is. With the assistance of Wicker, the editor of the local paper.' He looked at the clock. 'They should be sitting in the editorial office right now. It could produce results – Wicker knows this dump inside out. Anyway, that's the situation in broad outline.'

'And Vrommel doesn't suspect anything?'

Baasteuwel displayed his teeth.

'Not yet. He just wonders why Kohler and I haven't gone home.'

'And how have you explained that away?'

'That we like Lejnice, and have crap marriages,' said

Baasteuwel, with a new grin. 'He believes it, the silly bugger. He's never been married, and seems to think that's a blessing.'

Moreno had no comment to make on that.

'Time we started eating,' she said instead.

37

Intendent Kohler introduced himself and invited fru Van Rippe to sit down.

'I assume you recognize herr Wicker, the editor of *Westerblatt*?'

Fru Van Rippe sat down and looked in surprise at first one, then the other of them.

'Yes, of course,' she said. 'But where's the chief of police? I thought he was in charge of this case?'

'He's a bit busy at the moment,' said Kohler. 'There's an awful lot to do, as I'm sure you realize. I've been called in from Wallburg to assist with the investigation into the murder of your son.'

'Would you like some coffee and a sandwich?' asked Wicker.

For a moment Vegesack thought that fru Van Rippe would stand up and refuse to cooperate. She gritted her teeth and stared down at the ground.

'Yes please,' she said in the end. 'But I don't understand why I'm here.'

'We're just doing our best to throw some light on this tragic incident,' said Kohler. 'The more information we have to assist us, the greater the chance we have of succeeding. In finding the murderer. We have a few questions we'd like to put to you, in order to build up a more comprehensive background picture of your son.'

Wicker poured some coffee and produced a plate of sandwiches from Doovers tea shop, which was next door to the newspaper office.

'I'm sitting in on this because I have quite a bit of local knowledge,' he explained. 'Help yourself, fru Van Rippe.'

She took a ham sandwich and examined it suspiciously.

'I'd like to be back home by four.'

'No problem,' said Kohler. 'Constable Vegesack will drive you home as soon as we've finished. Now, can you tell us a little about your life?'

'My life?'

Fru Van Rippe stared at Kohler as if she hadn't understood the question. As if she'd never had a life.

'Yes please. In general terms.'

'What . . . What do you want to know? I've lived here in Lejnice since I was a child, but moved to Karpatz when I met Walter, my new husband. About ten years ago. I don't understand what you are looking for.'

'Just a bit of background, that's all,' said Kohler again. 'I think you have another son, besides Tim – is that right? A bit older, I gather.'

'Yes.'

She hesitated. Took a bite of her sandwich and chewed slowly, then washed it down with a sip of coffee. Kohler waited.

'Yes, Jakob,' she resumed. 'I have him as well. He's six years older than Tim. I had him early. I was only nineteen, but that's the way it goes. But you know all this already, I'm sure. Wicker here at least—'

'Of course,' said Kohler, interrupting her. 'You married Henrik Van Rippe that same year, we know that as well. So you were very young. How long were you married?'

Her expression became more strained. She's going to refuse to cooperate soon, Vegesack thought.

'He left me in 1975,' she said, her voice more shrill now. 'Jakob was fifteen, Tim nine.'

'Left you?' said Kohler.

'For another woman, yes. That's not something anybody needs to root around in.'

Kohler nodded.

'Forgive me. Of course not. What was Tim like as a child?'

'Why are you asking that?'

'Please help us by answering the question, fru Van

Rippe. I see that you haven't taken your new husband's surname.'

'We're not actually married. I thought about reverting to my maiden name, but I'd become used to Van Rippe.'

'I see. And what was he like as a boy, Tim?'

She shrugged.

'He was quite shy and retiring.'

'Really?'

'But he was nice. Tim was never any trouble, he always did what he needed to do, and liked to keep himself to himself. Jakob was different.'

'In what way?'

'He was more of an extrovert. He always had friends coming to visit him. Tim preferred to do things on his own.'

Vegesack glanced at his watch. What the hell are they going on about? he wondered. If they continued like this he would have to drive like the very devil if he were going to get fru Van Rippe back in Karpatz by four o'clock. He'd been given strict orders by Kohler to keep quiet during the interview, and only speak if he were spoken to. It seemed the same applied to Wicker, who was sucking his biro and looking sleepy.

'You met your current husband in 1988,' said Kohler. 'Is that right?'

Fru Van Rippe nodded.

'Walter Krummnagel?'

No wonder she didn't want to take his name, Vegesack thought.

'Yes.'

'And you moved to Karpatz the same year?'

'Yes.'

'Did you live alone between – ' Kohler put on his glasses and consulted his notebook – '1975 and 1988?'

Fru Van Rippe's face became strained again.

'Yes.'

'So you didn't have any other relationship during that time?'

'No.'

'Really? An attractive woman like you?'

No answer. Vegesack wasn't sure whether or not she blushed, but he thought so. Kohler made a short pause.

'Why?'

'What do you mean?'

'Why did you live alone?'

'Because I didn't want a man.'

'But surely you must have had a little fling? It sounds hard going to live alone for such a long time. I mean, your children were quite grown up, and—'

'I chose to have it that way,' said fru Van Rippe, interrupting him. 'One has the right to live any way one chooses.'

Kohler took off his glasses and put them away in his breast pocket. Nodded almost imperceptibly at Wicker.

'Well,' said Kohler, leaning a little bit closer towards her. 'I think you're lying, fru Van Rippe.'

She grasped the arms of her chair. She was obviously thinking about standing up, but after a few seconds she sank back.

'Lying? Why would I lie?'

She stared at Kohler, who, however, lowered his gaze and was contemplating his coffee cup. Clever, Vegesack thought. There followed five seconds of silence.

Then Wicker took over.

'Fru Van Rippe,' he said, slowly folding his arms. 'Isn't the fact of the matter that you had an affair with a certain person here in Lejnice . . . At the beginning of the eighties, if I'm not much mistaken – eighty-two or eighty-three, or thereabouts?'

'No, no . . . Who would that have been?'

Her voice wasn't quite steady. She let go of the armrests.

'Who would that have been?' said Wicker, feigning surprise. 'You know that better than anybody else, fru Van Rippe. I don't think it's something to be ashamed of . . . I don't understand why you are sitting there denying it. We're all human, after all.'

'I don't know what you're talking about,' said fru Van Rippe, and suddenly her voice was no more than a whisper.

A few more seconds passed.

'I'm talking about Vrommel,' said Wicker, leaning back in his chair. 'Chief of Police Victor Vrommel.'

Edita Van Rippe didn't answer. Instead she leaned slowly forward over the table and put her arms over her head.

Kohler loosened his tie and went to the toilet.

Moreno thought about Baasteuwel's comment as she was waiting for her train.

Never being married is a blessing? According to Vrommel?

It didn't feel especially uplifting. If not getting hitched meant you became like the chief of police in Lejnice, she'd better find herself a man in the twinkling of an eye, that was obvious.

Perhaps she should take up Mikael Bau's discreet offer of a meeting in August, for instance? Yesterday's dinner had been more or less problem-free, she had to admit. Irrespective of his bad sides, he didn't seem to harbour grudges. Whether they were linked to a broken-down Trabant or a detective inspector addicted to work. She had to grant him that.

So maybe we could start all over again in August? she thought.

She made up her mind to postpone a decision until then. An invigorating cycling holiday would surely help her to make discerning judgements, and just now she had more than enough to think about.

Instead, she made a different decision.

She telephoned Münster.

Unfortunately he replied. She'd hoped he wouldn't.

'Well?' she asked, noticing that she was holding her breath.

'I'm afraid Lampe-Leermann was right,' said Münster.

Neither of them uttered a word for a good ten seconds after that.

'Are you still there?'

'Yes,' said Moreno. 'I'm still here. So you know who it is?'

'We have a name,' said Münster. 'I have no intention of telling anybody what it is until we're one hundred per cent certain. Not even you.'

'Good,' said Moreno. 'I feel ill, but keep that to yourself, for God's sake.'

'This isn't pleasant,' said Münster.

Silence again.

'How are you coping?' Moreno asked.

'Hmm,' said Münster, clearing his throat. 'I didn't really know what to do. In the end I got in touch with *the Chief Inspector*. Van Veeteren, that is.'

Moreno thought for a moment.

'I think that's what I'd have done as well,' she said. 'If I'd thought of it, that is. So you confronted this journalist together, did you?'

'We certainly did,' said Münster. 'He started by laughing it off, but soon changed his tune. VV scared him so much that he ended up by paying for the beers. I wouldn't have been able to manage it on my own.'

'And he came up with a name, did he?'

'He certainly did,' said Münster.

'And he's not bluffing?'

'It doesn't seem so.'

'I see.'

'The only thing is that we haven't confronted him yet. He's on leave, and we thought we'd wait until he got back. I thought that would be best, and so did *the Chief Inspector.*'

Moreno tried to recall which of her colleagues, apart from herself, were taking their holidays in July – but she stopped almost immediately.

I don't want to know, she thought. Not until I have to.

'Anyway, that's how things stand,' said Münster. 'I just thought you ought to know.'

'Okay,' said Moreno. 'Bye for now.'

'TTFN,' said Münster.

★

This time she had chosen to travel on the express, but she soon discovered that there were just as few passengers as when she'd travelled in the other direction, and sat down in a window seat.

But of course, there was no pressing reason to leave the coast on a roasting hot Saturday like today. Two weeks, she thought. Exactly two weeks of my holiday have gone, and now I'm heading back home again.

Not exactly rested and refreshed. Not a lazy fortnight by the sea. What the hell had she been doing? What was certain was that it hadn't turned out as she'd expected in advance. She had told her boyfriend (bloke? lover? stallion?) to go to hell, she'd played the amateur sleuth day and night, and she hadn't achieved a thing. Not a damned thing.

She didn't know what had happened to the weeping girl on the train.

She didn't know who had killed Winnie Maas.

She didn't know who had killed Tim Van Rippe.

And there was a paedophile in the Maardam police station.

Great, Moreno thought. A top-notch outcome, no question about it.

422

FIVE

38

22 July 1983

When he had passed the school again a breeze blew up from the sea, and he stopped once more.

He couldn't be sure if what had made him pause was the breeze, or the illuminated information board with the school's name and a map with the functions of each of the buildings pedagogically listed. But he stood there, staring at the board, and something moved inside him. A sort of diffuse feeling of security, perhaps. His place of work. As empty as a desert on a summer's night at half past one in the morning. But still?

He flopped down on a stone bench outside one of the long walls of the gymnasium. Elbows on his knees, his head in his hands.

What am I going to do? he thought. What the hell is going to happen now? Why am I sitting here? Bugger, bugger, bugger . . .

He noticed that a jumble of words was buzzing around inside his head. Not thoughts. Not action plans. Just a meaningless mish-mash of questions and desperate cries that seemed to be hovering over an abyss that he was not allowed to look down into, not at any price; that he didn't dare to look down into – a swirl of words that only served to keep everything else at a distance. At a distance and out of sight. That's all there was to it. It struck him that he was going out of his mind.

Home? he thought. Home to Mikaela? Why? Why have I stopped here? Why don't I rush up to the viaduct and look her in the eye? Who? Who do I mean? Winnie? Or Sigrid? I've lost everything in any case. I shall never come back here . . . Not to Mikaela, not to Sigrid, not to the school. I've lost. Just now I've lost everything . . . At this very moment I'm losing everything on this damned bench outside this damned gymnasium. I knew it, I've known it ever since that damned evening, why didn't I do anything about it, what shall I do now when everything's too late? Damn and blast! It's too late. Damn and blast! Everything's too late now . . .

He stood up. Keep quiet! he said to his thoughts. Shut up! He took a deep breath and tried to concentrate one last time. Last time? he thought. What do I mean, one last time?

He started walking to the viaduct again. Is she still

there? Are *they* there? Did Sigrid go rushing *there*? Was that where she went? It must be nearly half an hour ago.

He increased his pace. Crossed over Birkenerstraat level with the cemetery and turned into Emserweg. And it was then, just as he came round the corner at Dorff's book-shop and stationery store and into Dorfflenerstraat that he saw her.

She passed the illuminated entrance to the sports field on the other side of the street, walking quite fast. Ener-getic and resolute steps. Sigrid, his wife. She didn't see him, and he repressed an impulse to shout out her name. Instead he stopped under the bookshop's awning and remained standing there until she was out of sight. She's been there, he thought. She's been up there and met Winnie.

He hurried across Dorfflenerstraat, continued past the sports field and came down to the railway line. Once he had skirted the brewery the viaduct came into view.

But in the distance. He still couldn't see if there was anybody standing up there. Standing and waiting for him? He slowed down. What the hell could he say? Or do? What did she expect of him? She had ruined his life. She'd crushed him by telling the facts to his wife some – he looked at his watch – thirty-five minutes ago. It was no more than that. Just over half an hour since the telephone call. What the hell did she want of him now?

Pregnant? She was pregnant, with his child. He remembered what she'd said that night. 'Come on, Sir . . . come, come, come, I'm on the pill!'

Sir, she'd said. At the height of the act, while he was screwing her, she had actually used that word.

The pill? Like hell she'd been on the pill.

He started walking along the long, curving road and stupidly enough wondered if she wanted to go to bed with him again. That was a disgusting thought which must surely say something about the kind of man he was. Deep down. And that it was probably quite justified for him to be going mad. I'm a filthy swine, he thought. Swine, swine, swine! – he could almost hear Sigrid yelling those words. Have sex with Winnie Maas? Again? Let her ride him forwards and backwards and plunge his cock into her until she gasped in ecstasy, let her give him head while he stroked her stiff little clitoris until she screamed . . . What the hell was he fantasizing about? His brain was racing like a car in too low a gear. What's happening to my head? he thought. In any case, she's not there.

She wasn't there.

There was nobody up there on the viaduct. Not a soul, not even that little devil Winnie Maas, and nobody else either. He paused and looked around. To both the north and the south. He had quite a good view from where he was standing. He could see the whole town – the streets, the squares, the two churches, the beach and the harbour with its breakwaters and concrete foundations and protected entrance. The little wooded area beyond the football pitches. Frieder's Pier and Gordon's Lighthouse furthest to the south . . . Everything enveloped by the grey darkness of the summer night.

He looked down at the area below. Scanned the railway line from the distant station to where he was. There was something lying down there. Right next to the right-hand track, diagonally below where he was standing. It wasn't quite so dark there, and a street light projected its dirty yellow beam over the street and the railway line at that point.

There was something lying there. Something white and slightly blue and a bit skin-coloured . . .

It was a second or two before he realized what it was.

It took another second before he realized who it was.

39

Constable Vegesack made the sign of the cross, and went in.

Chief of Police Vrommel was lying on the floor in front of his desk, doing leg-raises.

'Just a moment,' he said.

Vegesack sat down on the visitor's chair and watched his boss. The raises were a bit on the strenuous side, it seemed, as Vrommel was groaning like a stranded walrus, and his shiny bald pate glowed like a red traffic light. When he had finished he remained lying there for a while, recovering. Then he got up and sat down at his desk.

'So you're going on leave tomorrow, are you?'

Vegesack nodded.

'Tomorrow, yes.'

'The weather's not up to much.'

'No,' said Vegesack.

'It was better last week.'

'Yes.'

Vrommel opened a desk drawer, produced a paper tissue and wiped his brow and the top of his head.

'This Van Rippe case. It's time to make a summary of where we've got to.'

'Are we going to close it down?' Vegesack asked.

'Not close it down, no,' said Vrommel. 'One doesn't close down murder investigations just like that. But I'm going to sum it up. It's been hard going – I don't think we've got anywhere at all, have we?'

'No.'

'I think we'll have to scale it down. We've been using extra resources for three weeks now. It'll be normal routines from now on.'

'I see,' said Vegesack.

'So we need a summary. A sort of report on what we've achieved so far. I thought we'd have a little press conference tomorrow morning. We need to report to our superiors as well. Those girl guides from Wallburg haven't been a lot of use.'

'Not a lot.'

Vrommel cleared his throat.

'So, if you type out this summary, you can leave it on my desk before you go home. You have the whole day to devote to it.'

Vegesack nodded.

'Don't make it too long-winded. Just the facts. Brevity is the soul of wit.'

Vegesack started to get up.

'Was there anything else?'

'If there had been, I'd have said,' said Vrommel. 'So, on my desk. Have a good holiday, and keep fit.'

'Thank you,' said Vegesack, and left the room.

Ewa Moreno woke up and looked at the clock.

Ten to twelve.

It dawned on her that she was in her own bed, and despite everything had slept no more than nine hours. She tried to feel if there was any muscle in her body that wasn't aching, but couldn't find any.

I feel ninety, she thought. And this was supposed to be useful . . . ?

She had gone to bed shortly before three. She'd got home dead on two o'clock, but had enough sense to take a hot bath before creeping between the sheets. If she hadn't done that, she probably wouldn't have been able to move at all now. The last lap of the cycling holiday with Clara Mietens had comprised seventy-five kilometres into a headwind, and the last thirty in rain. They'd expected to set off rather earlier than they actually did, so that they would have a pleasant east wind at their backs and would glide into Maardam with the setting sun in their faces. Well, that was the plan.

An east wind? Moreno thought as she sat up gingerly on the edge of the bed. Had there ever been an easterly wind in Maardam? When they said their mutual goodbyes down at Zwille at a quarter to two, Clara had promised faithfully that if ever she had the strength to get out of bed again, the first thing she would do would be to attach a very heavy weight to her accursed bike (with six gears, two of which worked), throw it into the Langgraacht canal, and sing a hymn.

But it had been quite a good holiday (apart from the last lap, that is). Eight gilt-edged days, brimful of camping life, swimming excursions, conversations, cycle rides (but never in the rain or with a headwind), and total relaxation in the picturesque Sorbinowo region. Clara's red tent had been newly bought and easy to handle. And the weather had been splendid. Until yesterday.

She went to the bathroom and had a shower. After ten minutes her body began to feel as if it were hers again. And as that happened, her thoughts began to branch out in another direction.

That was inevitable, of course. It was time to re-enter the real world. High time.

She put on her dressing gown and started by going

through her mail. Bills, adverts, four picture postcards and a wage slip. Very interesting.

Then she listened to the messages on her telephone answering machine. After considerable thought, she had decided to leave her mobile at home while she undertook the Sorbinowo Tour: so there ought to be quite a few messages waiting for her attention.

And so there were. All kinds of things. A couple of cheerful greetings from Mikael Bau, for instance, and a message from her mother explaining that they (her father as well, presumably, always assuming that nothing hair-raisingly horrific had happened while she'd been away) were on the point of setting off for the airport to catch their flight to Florida, and that they wouldn't be back until the end of August. In case she tried to contact them and wondered why there was no response.

Eleven messages in all, explained the cool female voice on the tape.

But nothing from Baasteuwel.

Nothing from Vegesack or Kohler. Nothing from Münster.

Not even anything from Selma Perhovens.

Ah well, Moreno thought as she went out to buy something for breakfast. One should never overestimate one's importance.

★

It was half past six in the evening when she finally got hold of Inspector Baasteuwel.

'Oh,' he said. 'Are you back?'

'I got home yesterday. I thought you said you'd be in touch?'

'I tried, but I don't like leaving empty messages on an answering machine.'

'Really? Well?'

Baasteuwel paused.

'We've shelved it.'

'Shelved it?'

'Yes. That was the best thing to do. We came to that conclusion, Kohler and I. I'm on leave now.'

Moreno's mind was swamped by a tsunami of absurd incomprehension.

'What the hell are you talking about?' she said. 'What about Vrommel? You said it was just a matter of time.'

She could hear Baasteuwel lighting a cigarette.

'Now listen here,' he said. 'You have to trust me. It wasn't possible to pin down that bastard as we'd hoped. We were in total agreement, Kohler and I, that we should stop digging into it any further. Vegesack as well. There was nothing else to take up, and no reason to take things any further. Not as things turned out.'

'Not as things turned out?' said Moreno. 'What do you mean? I don't understand what you're saying.'

'Maybe not,' said Baasteuwel. 'But that's how things turned out in any case. You would agree with me if you had all the details in front of you.'

'Details? What details?'

'Rather a lot of them, in fact. I can assure you that this is the best solution. It's just the way it turned out – that's how it is in a lot of cases, as you ought to know.'

Thoughts were piling up inside Moreno's head, and she pinched herself on the arm several times to check that she really was awake before continuing.

'You swore blind that you were going to put Vrommel behind bars,' she reminded him angrily. 'An innocent girl has disappeared and a man has been murdered. You became a police officer in order to get the chance of putting guilty swine behind bars, and now . . .'

'It wasn't possible on this occasion.'

'And Van Rippe?'

'The case is in the chief of police's hands. Kohler and I were called in merely to help out with the early stages of the investigation, don't forget that. We've left it now.'

Moreno removed the receiver from her ear and regarded it with suspicion for a few seconds.

'Is it really Inspector Baasteuwel of the Wallburg police who I'm talking to?' she asked eventually.

Baasteuwel laughed.

'I am indeed that who,' he said. 'But I think I can detect

a trace of impatience in the inspector's voice. It sounds almost as if she's wondering about various things.'

'Too right I am,' said Moreno. 'You've hit the nail on the head, dammit. I don't understand what language you're speaking. You are abandoning a murder and a missing girl, and going on leave. On which side is your brain haemorrhage?'

'Right in the middle,' said Baasteuwel cheerily. 'I agree that I might well sound a bit off course now that my holiday is beginning to take root. But if you really do want to find out a bit more about what's been happening in Lejnice, I suppose I might be able to get a grip and accede to your request.'

'It's your duty, dammit,' said Moreno. 'Where and when?'

'Tomorrow?'

'The sooner, the better.'

Baasteuwel seemed to be thinking it over.

'Somewhere in Maardam, perhaps? So that you're on home ground.'

'Sounds good,' said Moreno.

'Gamla Vlissingen – is it still there?'

'It certainly is.'

'Okay,' said Baasteuwel. 'Tomorrow at seven o'clock, will that be okay? I'll book a table.'

'That will be excellent,' said Moreno.

She hung up and stared out of the window, which was just beginning to be splattered with a new downpour of rain coming in from the west.

I don't understand this, she thought. I haven't a bloody clue what's going on.

40

The Vlissingen restaurant was just as full as usual. She was slightly late, and passed by the solitary girl in the corner without reacting. It was only when she had walked around and investigated the whole of the premises – and established with some irritation that Inspector Baasteuwel didn't seem to be there – that she realized who it was.

And even then it was some time before her brain was able to interpret what her sight had told her. She shut her eyes tightly in order to reinstate reality, then walked over to the table. The girl began to stand up, then changed her mind and sat down again. Then she gave a tentative smile. Very tentative.

'Mikaela?' said Moreno. 'Mikaela Lijphart? Is it really you?'

'Yes,' said the girl, with a nervous laugh. Moreno could see that her lower lip was trembling.

439

'Inspector Baas . . . ?' Moreno began, but at the same moment the penny dropped and it dawned on her that no, Inspector Baasteuwel would not be coming to the Vlissingen restaurant this evening. This was how he had planned it. This was what lay behind the inconsistencies of the previous evening's telephone call.

Good Lord, she thought, surely I ought to have caught on? Then she produced the biggest smile she was capable of and encouraged the girl to stand up so that she could give her a big hug.

'I . . . I'm so glad to see you,' she said.

'Me too,' Mikaela managed to say in return. 'It was him . . . Inspector Baasteuwel . . . who said you would no doubt want to meet me. He said I should wait here for you. And he gave me some money so that I could treat you to a meal as well.'

If it hadn't been for the girl's anxious voice, Moreno could have burst out laughing. But Mikaela felt anything but at ease, that was very obvious. They sat down. Moreno put a hand on her arm.

'You're worried.'

'Yes. It's so horrible. I can't sleep at night.'

'You realize . . . I expect you realize that I want to know what happened?'

'Yes . . .' Mikaela looked down at the table. 'I know I have to tell you everything. I'm so grateful that you were so kind to me on the train, and I know that you've been working very hard ever since as well.'

Moreno tried to produce another encouraging smile, but could feel that it had difficulty in establishing itself.

'It wasn't all that much of an effort,' she said. 'Shall we order so that we can eat while we're talking, perhaps?'

It took some time to place the orders. Moreno wondered if she had ever been in a situation like this before. She didn't think so. Her feelings told her this was the case, although it was of course anything but clear what the precise situation was. She had spent days, nights, weeks, trying to understand what could have happened to this girl who had disappeared without trace, and now she was suddenly sitting face to face with her at a restaurant table. Without so much as a second's warning. That damned Baasteuwel, she thought. No, she'd never experienced anything like this before.

And Mikaela wasn't well. She looked pale and out of sorts. It seemed pointless starting to talk to her about banalities – the weather and the wind, and if she'd been to the cinema lately – totally pointless.

'Let's hear it, then, Mikaela,' she said instead. 'You've got to do what you've got to do. I think you said that the last time we met.'

'No, it was you who said that,' said Mikaela. 'Where shall I start?'

'At the beginning, of course. From when we said good-bye outside the station at Lejnice.'

Mikaela raised her gaze and looked Moreno in the eye for a few seconds. Then she took a deep breath and launched into her account.

'Well, at first everything went just as I'd expected it would, in fact,' she began as she slowly clasped her hands on the table in front of her – as if it were an accomplishment she had just learned and was still finding it a bit difficult to achieve, Moreno thought.

'I went to that home and met my father. It was . . . it was so odd, so horrific to enter a room and see a complete stranger who was in fact my dad. I'd thought about it and tried to imagine it, of course, but even so it felt much stranger than I could ever have believed. He was so small and alien and so . . . ill. I thought he looked like a bird. This is my bird daddy, I thought. But nevertheless I knew that it was him the moment I clapped eyes on him, it was somehow so obvious, I can't explain it.'

Her voice was a little steadier now, Moreno noticed, once she'd got going.

'Go on,' she said.

'You know . . . the background?'

Moreno nodded.

'I didn't tell you everything I knew on the train; I think I was a bit ashamed. My dad had an affair with a schoolgirl who was only sixteen – when I was two. It happened, and there's nothing I can do to change it. The girl died, and he was found guilty of having killed her. But it's wrong. That's not what happened. He told me that day that it wasn't him who pushed Winnie Maas down on to the railway line. It took him two hours to tell me. He gave me a letter he'd written, and it said the same thing. He was with the girl, but he didn't kill her . . . He was ashamed something awful when he tried to talk to me about it, but I forced him to do it. He's not strong, my dad: he's like a bird. A sick bird. I feel so sorry for him . . .'

She paused, and looked enquiringly at Moreno, who encouraged her to continue.

'I was crying when I left. I went to the youth hostel, but it was completely full and I very nearly didn't get a bed – but it turned out okay in the end. I didn't really know what to do next, but I believed my dad when he said that he was innocent of the girl's death and so after I'd thought things over for a while, I decided to try to trace the girl's mother – if she was still in Lejnice – and tell her what I'd discovered. And maybe ask her a few questions as well. And that's what I did, without any real problems. I met her on the Sunday – she wasn't very nice: a bit of a drunk, I think. She even showed me a revolver she kept in order to defend herself – goodness only knows what she needed to defend herself against . . . I'm quite sure she didn't believe me when I said my dad had been wrongly convicted. She called him a disgusting creep and a murderer and plenty more besides, and claimed that he had ruined her life. Obviously I felt sorry for her as well: it must be awful if your child dies in such a horrible way . . .'

The meal was served, but Mikaela didn't seem to want to stop, now that she was under way.

'As I sat there in fru Maas's disgusting flat, I started thinking seriously about what had really happened when her daughter died – all my dad told me is that it wasn't him who killed her – and it occurred to me that maybe I ought to try to talk to some more local people about it all, seeing as I was at the scene, after all. I regret ever having such an idea – my God, how I regret that . . .'

'Did it ever occur to you that the girl might have jumped off the viaduct rather than being pushed?' Moreno wondered.

Mikaela shook her head.

'I thought about that, but my dad didn't think she had, and nor did fru Maas when I spoke to her.'

'I see. Anyway, what did you do?'

'I got a couple of names from fru Maas. People who had known her daughter, she claimed – I don't really know why she gave me them. Most of the time she sat there

going on about how I was the despicable child of a murderer, and how I ought to be ashamed of showing myself
in public, and lots more along those lines.'

'I can imagine,' said Moreno. 'I've also met her.'

'Have you really?'

Mikaela looked guilty for a moment – as if she were
worried about having caused any trouble. Moreno urged
her to continue.

'Anyway,' she said, 'I went to a woman called Vera
Something . . .'

'Sauger?'

'Yes, that's it. Vera Sauger. She had known Winnie
Maas quite well, and had my dad as a teacher, it seems. I
told her I believed that my dad was innocent, and then . . .
well, then she sort of shut up. Withdrew into her shell.
I had the impression . . . No, I don't really know.'

'Go on,' said Moreno.

'I had the impression that she'd known that was the
case all along. That he was not guilty. No, I don't mean
that she actually knew, just that I had that impression at
the time, when I was at her house. Do you follow me?'

Moreno said that she did.

'Well, this Vera Sauger gave me a couple of new names,
people I ought to talk to. There was one whose name I've
forgotten, and the other was Tim Van Rippe. God, but I
wish I'd never been given those names . . .'

'I understand,' said Moreno. She was actually beginning to understand. At last. 'How did that go?' she asked.

Mikaela took another deep breath. Picked up her knife and fork, but then laid them down again on the table.

'It was so awful,' she said. 'So horrendously awful, I'll never be able to forget it . . . Never, never ever. I've dreamt about it every single night since it happened. Several times every night, as soon as I fall asleep . . . All the time, non-stop, it seems like.'

For a moment it looked as if the girl was going to burst into tears, but she gritted her teeth and continued instead.

'I phoned him. Tim Van Rippe, that is. I told him who I was and asked if he had time for a little chat. He sounded a bit odd, but I didn't think so much about that . . . He said he was busy until that evening, and we agreed to meet at a certain spot on the beach at nine o'clock.'

'Nine o'clock in the evening?'

'Yes. On the beach. I asked if he couldn't make it a bit earlier, but he said he couldn't. So I went along with nine o'clock. I checked the train times and there was one at ten to eleven, so I'd be able to get home anyway. Then I tried to get in touch with that other person . . . Ah yes, Bitowski his name was: but no luck. So I spent all the afternoon lying on the beach. It was lovely weather.'

With a stab of self-reproach Moreno recalled that she had also spent the same afternoon on the same beach. A few kilometres further north, but still . . . It was that first Sunday, she was a bit hungover, on holiday and happy.

'That evening I sat there waiting for him from about half past eight onwards. In the place we'd agreed on, quite close to that pier, whatever it's called. Frieder's Pier, I think. There weren't many people on the beach, but it wasn't dark yet. He came at about ten to nine, and we started walking slowly along the beach, northwards. I did the talking and he just listened. After a while we sat down – I thought it was unnecessary to walk, and my rucksack was quite heavy. I took it off and there was something wrong with it. One of the metal rods that make it more stable had started to come loose and was poking out from the pleat that was supposed to keep it in place. I took it out altogether in order to try and put it back in properly – or just throw it away, I didn't really know which . . . By that time I'd almost finished talking, but I hadn't said anything about my dad being innocent. I said so now, and that's when it happened.'

She bit her lip. Moreno waited.

'I said: "I know my dad didn't kill Winnie Maas." Those were my exact words. He stood up while I was messing around with my rucksack. And when I looked up at him I suddenly realized what had really happened. It all came to me as quick as lightning. He was the one who did it. It was Tim Van Rippe who murdered Winnie Maas. I knew it in a flash, and he must have realized that I knew. I've thought about it a thousand times since then, and that's how it must have sounded in his ears when I said that it wasn't my dad who was guilty. He thought I was accusing him of having done it . . . And I could see that he intended to do the same to me. He took a step towards me and raised his arms and I could see in his face that he intended to kill me as well. He intended to kill me right there on the beach . . .'

Now she crumbled at last. She had started talking faster and faster towards the end, and Moreno wasn't caught off guard. She hurried round the table and put her arm round Mikaela's shaking shoulders. She moved a chair up close and hugged her tightly. She could see in the corner of her eye how a young couple at the next table were looking at them with concern.

'I'm sorry,' said Mikaela when the worst was over. 'I just can't cope with talking about it.'

'I can understand that,' said Moreno. 'But it's good that you're doing so in any case. Many people say that's the best way of coming to terms with horrific experiences. By experiencing them again.'

'I know,' said Mikaela. 'Go and sit down on your own chair again. I haven't finished yet.'

She smiled bravely, and Moreno returned to her chair.

'I go in for fencing, have I told you about that?'

'No,' said Moreno. 'I don't think you have.'

'Both épée and foil. I'm quite good at it, though I say so myself. So when he attacked me I stabbed him in the eye with the metal rod.'

'What?' said Moreno. 'With the metal rod?'

'Yes, the pin that was supposed to stabilize the ruck-sack. It was about this long.'

She demonstrated with her hands. Moreno gulped.

'About thirty to forty centimetres. Made of metal. I was holding it in my hand, and it was a pure reflex reaction. I didn't think at all. I just stuck my arm out and stabbed him right in the eye. He fell – fell on top of me, in fact: it wasn't intentional, it was a purely automatic reaction, but I killed Tim Van Rippe out there on the beach, and it didn't even take one single second.'

Her voice was trembling, but it held. Moreno could feel that she was getting goose pimples on her lower arms.

'The rest was panic, sheer panic. I realized straight away that he was dead. It wasn't all that dark. People were passing by about twenty or thirty metres away from us, but nobody noticed anything amiss. If anybody looked in our direction they presumably thought that we were a courting couple larking about and having fun. So I dug him down. I suppose it must have taken an hour or so, but it was getting darker all the time, and soon there was nobody else around at all. He lost his shoes when I dragged him into the hole, and I threw them away. I took his wallet and his watch as well, I don't know why . . . I threw them away later. When I'd finished, I left.'

'When you'd finished, you left.' Moreno echoed her words. 'For God's sake, Mikaela, you must have been scared to death.'

'Yes,' said Mikaela. 'I was. I was so frightened I didn't know what I was doing. It was as if I'd become somebody else . . . I walked and walked all night.'

'Walked?'

'Yes, all night. Northwards. At seven in the morning I came to a greasy spoon cafe in Langhuijs, where I got a lift in a lorry up to Frigge. I had breakfast and slept in a park for a few hours. All the time, I was dreaming over and over again about how I stabbed Tim Van Rippe in the eye. And how I buried him. When I woke up the first thing I thought was that I should go to the police. But I didn't dare. Instead, I withdrew all the money I had left in my bank account – just over a thousand, in fact – and bought a rail ticket to Copenhagen. I also nicked another thirty from Van Rippe's wallet before I threw it away.'

'To Copenhagen? Why there?'

Had anybody checked with the banks? Moreno wondered. Evidently not. Careless. It shouldn't have been difficult to track down the withdrawal.

'I don't really know,' said Mikaela. 'I'd been there on a school trip. I liked the place. And I had to run away to somewhere, didn't I?'

Moreno didn't answer.

'I mean, I'd killed him. Murdered him and buried him. It was obvious I had to hide away.'

Moreno nodded and tried to look neutrally benevolent.

'So then what did you do? Took the train to Copenhagen, presumably?'

'Yes. The night train. I arrived the next morning and booked myself into a hotel called the Excelsior. Behind the railway station. A pretty seedy-looking district, but it was the first hotel I came across. Then I wandered around the city or lay in my room until I felt I was going mad. So I rang my mother. I don't know how many days had passed by then, and I'd hardly had anything to eat from start to finish. I told my mother I was still alive, but I wouldn't be for much longer if she didn't collect my father – my real father – and come to see me. I suppose you could say I threatened her, but it was true. I felt absolutely awful. Anyway, they turned up eventually.'

'Your mum and dad came to your hotel in Copenhagen?'

'Yes. I don't know what day it was when they arrived. But it must have been more than a week after I'd killed Van Rippe on the beach. And I killed him again and again every

451

night, as soon as I managed to fall asleep . . . I suppose I was out of my mind for several of those days. But when my parents arrived, things became a bit better. And I made them talk to each other. We were together for four or five days, but my dad wasn't feeling at all well without his medicine and . . . well, in the end we drove back. Mum phoned the police in Lejnice every day to ask about how the investigation was proceeding, so that nobody would suspect that the three of us were together. We agreed that we'd continue to say nothing about it, my mum and I. Dad never really understood exactly what had happened, apart from discovering that we knew he wasn't guilty of the murder of Winnie Maas. It was difficult to talk to him – and then Baasteuwel gave us that horrific piece of news: I feel so heartbroken whenever I think about it. It's so unfair that—'

'Hang on a minute,' said Moreno. 'I'm not quite with you. Where does Inspector Baasteuwel fit into the picture?'

Mikaela blew her nose into her table napkin and continued.

'We came back from Copenhagen,' she said. 'We dropped my dad off not far from the home, then Mum and I drove to Aarlach. We stayed for a few days in Aunt Vanja's house – she wasn't at home, but Mum has the keys to her flat. We discussed what we were going to do – with regard to my stepfather, for instance: should we tell Helmut the facts of what had happened, or not? In the end we agreed that we wouldn't say a word about anything at all, not to anybody. It just wasn't possible. And so we came home, it was a Monday evening, and the next morning the bell rang – and it was that Baasteuwel standing there. Helmut wasn't at home, thank goodness, because within an hour Baasteuwel had squeezed the whole story out of us. And then he told us the worst thing of all.'

'The worst thing of all?'

'Yes. That he'd spoken to my dad at the Sidonis home, while Mum and I were in Aarlach. I don't know how he managed to squeeze the information out of my dad – but then, he got my story out of us so I assume he's pretty good at that kind of thing.'

'He's well known for it,' said Moreno. 'What was it that your dad told him?'

Mikaela clenched her teeth and tried to blink away the tears that flooded into her eyes.

'That he thought it was my mum who had killed Winnie Maas. That was why he said nothing. In order to protect us.'

She fell silent. Moreno suddenly felt a burning sensation behind her eyelids, and she took a swig of mineral water to balance it out. Is that possible? she asked herself.

But she could see immediately that it was.

Not just possible. It was logical, and it all fitted together.

'But of course, it all drove him round the bend,' said Mikaela. 'He really did go mad. But he's always thought it was my mum who did it. All the time. She was the one who received the telephone call from Winnie that night . . . And found out about what had happened. She got furious, and went storming out into the night. And then when my dad found Winnie lying dead by the railway line, he thought . . . Well, you can understand the situation, can't you?'

'Yes,' said Moreno. 'I understand.'

And Van Rippe was protected by the chief of police, she thought. Who had an affair with his mother.

Selma Perhovens had explained that on the telephone during the afternoon. And that the investigation, as far as she could understand it, was no longer being conducted especially intensively.

For certain reasons.

What certain reasons? she had asked: but Perhovens knew no more than that.

Now, however, everything was clear. Crystal clear. The equation had worked out at last. Baasteuwel's equation.

The Skunk was going to get away with it.

But Mikaela was also going to get away with it.

And Winnie Maas's murderer had received his punishment.

Moreno noticed that she was clasping her hands so

tightly that they almost hurt, and she had her mouth half open. She closed it, and tried to relax.

Bloody hell! she thought. Have the gods finished their games now? Yes, it seemed like it, and the final result seemed to be a sort of draw, you could say. At least, that's how Van Veeteren would have put it, she was sure of that . . . A Solomonic draw.

'I intend to get my dad back on his feet,' said Mikaela, breaking Moreno's train of thought. 'I'll have a jolly good try, anyway.'

'Good,' said Moreno. 'That's certainly the right thing to do. But make sure you get back on your feet yourself first. It's difficult to carry such a lot of this kind of stuff inside you – you ought to get some help, somehow or other.'

Mikaela's response came as a surprise.

'That's already organized,' she said. 'I'm going to see a vicar here in Maardam once a week. He's a brother of Inspector Baasteuwel's.'

Moreno stared at the girl.

'Are you telling me that there's a vicar here in Maardam with the name Baasteuwel, with all its links with the devil?'

Mikaela shook her head and managed a faint smile.

'He's changed his name. He evidently didn't think it was appropriate for his job, so he changed it to Friedmann. That's much more suitable.'

'You can say that again,' said Moreno. 'Hmm. Shall we

ask them to warm up our food in the microwave? I think it's gone cold.'

Mikaela looked at her plate and smiled a little more broadly.

'Oh dear,' she said. 'I'd forgotten I was hungry.'

Mikaela was collected by her mother and stepfather outside Vlissingen, as they had arranged. Moreno suspected that Helmut had been brought along as a sort of safety measure – so that Moreno wouldn't take it into her head to ask Mikaela's mother any awkward questions. It wouldn't have surprised her.

For there was at least one unanswered question.

The one about where exactly Sigrid Lijphart had been that night.

Had she been up on the viaduct or not? Had she seen the girl's body lying on the railway line before her husband did?

And hence had she known that the murderer must have been somebody else? Somebody she had protected by keeping silent for so long.

And had she possibly . . . well, could she possibly have known all along what Arnold had believed?

Yes, Moreno thought. That question still needs to be answered. That one above all others.

When all the implications slowly dawned on her, she started to feel sick.

She would eventually be able to create a situation in which she could speak this suspicion out loud, but of course there was no reason to do it in Mikaela's presence. No reason at all – the girl had travelled far enough into the heart of darkness as it was.

'Let's meet again some other time,' she said instead. 'Then it'll be my turn to treat you.'

After they had left Moreno went for a long walk to think over the whole business, and by the time she got home it was twenty minutes past eleven. She hesitated for a moment, then phoned Inspector Baasteuwel.

'Congratulations,' she said. 'I mean it.'

'Thank you,' said Baasteuwel. 'I mean it.'

'A Solomonic solution. Was it you who persuaded the girl to keep quiet, or was it her mother?'

'Hmm,' said Baasteuwel. 'Mostly Mikaela herself, in fact. Why?'

'I'm not certain it's right.'

'Nor am I,' agreed Baasteuwel after a pause. 'But when I'd squeezed it all out of them, I explained that I was no longer involved in the case, and that I had only called in on them out of pure curiosity. I left the choice in their hands, and promised to help out if things became too difficult and she wanted to go public with it.'

'Help out?' wondered Moreno. 'How would you do that?'

'I've no idea,' said Baasteuwel. 'Cometh the hour, cometh the thought. But I reckon it would be pretty stupid to start talking, given her position. For Christ's sake, she's ensured justice all round. Well done! The murderer's dead, RIP. We can take Vrommel some other time.'

'I suppose there's no doubt that it really was Van Rippe?'

'No doubt at all. His mother banished any doubts there might have been on that score. She knew her son, and she was having it off with Vrommel at the time, and . . . Well, he made sure things turned out as they did. He'd had some kind of hold over that doctor for quite some time, it seems, but we didn't poke our noses into that. Anyway, of course it was that bloody Tim Van Rippe who killed Winnie Maas, but that doesn't mean it would be absolutely straightforward for the girl to plead that she killed him in self-defence. There's a crystal-clear revenge motive, and she's kept quiet about it for rather too long.'

'And why was Van Rippe forced to kill Winnie Maas?'

'There's forced and forced,' said Baasteuwel. 'Necessity can always be argued about, but it's quite obvious that he was responsible for her pregnancy. And that he very definitely – and successfully – tried to put the blame on Arnold Maager. It's remarkable that he was actually present that evening when Winnie seduced her teacher. If you were to ask me to speculate, I'd say that he was involved in the plot and that they'd worked out in advance that they'd make Maager appear to be the father. You can say what you like about Winnie Maas, but she wasn't much of a bright spark. But this is only speculation, of course.'

'So what really happened that evening up on the viaduct?'

'Van Rippe shoved her over the edge, I'd bet my life on it. But the question is to what extent it was planned . . . Why she phoned and who thought up the idea that she should do so. One possible set-up is that the girl no longer wanted to go through with the plan, and when Van Rippe caught on to that he arranged things the way they turned out. He was bloody lucky, of course. He can hardly have reckoned with Maager going out of his mind and not saying anything at all. But in any case, there's surely no reason to go on rooting around in it any more. Do you have any other comments?'

'Just one question,' said Moreno. 'Was it necessary to bring up this business of Maager believing it was his wife who was the murderer? Bringing it up with Mikaela, I mean.'

'Yes,' said Baasteuwel. 'I reckon I'm on pretty firm

ground there. I think he needs a few plus points, that poor bloke. He's only a shadow of a man, for God's sake. But protecting his family is surely a noble thing to do. Young girls like noble actions. I must admit that I also thought it was the wife who'd done it. But only for a few days. Maager thought so for sixteen years.'

'And she allowed him to think that?'

Five seconds passed before Baasteuwel answered. She could hear him inhaling deeply on his cigarette.

'Ah,' he said. 'So you've noticed that as well.'

Moreno thought for a while instead of responding. She felt she needed a little time in order to consider what Baasteuwel had said. No doubt there would be opportunities to come back to the subject, but she didn't have any more vital points to raise.

'Nice to have met you,' she said eventually. 'Is your brother the vicar as crafty as you are?'

'He's the clever one of the family,' said Baasteuwel. 'With a heart as big as hell. For a vicar, that is. You don't need to worry about that aspect of things.'

'Excellent,' said Moreno. 'Then I don't have any more questions. Good night, Inspector.'

'Ditto,' said Baasteuwel. 'May the angels sing you to sleep.'

41

7 August 1999

Inspector Moreno had never set foot in The Society's premises in Weivers steeg – or Styckargränd, as it was known locally – but she was not entirely ignorant about the place. It was generally known that it was *the Chief Inspector's* favourite haunt – or at least that he used to sit there and play chess and drink beer several times a week. That was his habit when he was in charge of the Maardam CID, and there was no reason to believe that he had abandoned this custom since he had changed his profession and become an antiquarian bookseller three years ago.

She hadn't seen Van Veeteren for over six months – not since that tragic business concerning his son – and it was with mixed feelings that she walked down the stairs leading from ground level to The Society. In normal circumstances it would have been interesting to meet him, to find out if there were any truth in the rumour that he

461

was writing a book, for instance: but the reason why they were meeting this mild August evening was sufficient to keep at bay all forms of expectation and enthusiasm. Sufficient to keep such things light years away.

The room was large and whitewashed, she noted once she had got used to the semi-darkness that was normal down there. The ceiling was low, and several dark beams and pillars, and oddly shaped nooks and crannies, made it difficult to get an idea of how big it really was, and how many customers it held. Most of the tables were screened off, and diners sat in little booths – each of them, as far as she could see, fitted with a dark-coloured, heavy pine table and benches fixed to the floor. The bar was directly in front of the entrance, and looked like all other bars anywhere in the world. A notice chalked on a slate announced that today's special was rosemary-lamb and fried potatoes.

She caught sight of Münster's head and raised hand in one of the booths at the very back, and made her way there. Van Veeteren stood up and greeted her, then they all sat down. Moreno thought he looked younger than when she'd last seen him. More lively and vivacious: his tall, well-built body seemed to emit an aura of energy – an aura she remembered from several years ago, but which had been absent during the years before he finally resigned. She was sure he'd passed his sixtieth birthday, but if she hadn't known that she would have guessed he was about fifty-five to fifty-seven.

When you're a police officer you grow older more quickly than if you're not, she thought. That was hardly an original observation.

'Nice to see you again, Inspector,' said Van Veeteren. 'But sad that it has to be in these circumstances.'

Moreno nodded.

'How did he do it?' she asked.

'Rope,' said Münster.

'I see, rope,' said Moreno.

'Yes, he hanged himself. One might ask why he didn't use his service pistol, but perhaps there was some kind of inbuilt respect, or a mental barrier . . . Anyway, it's a horrific story, obviously.'

'Did he leave a message?'

'No. Nothing. But we know why he did it, of course. That is, *we* know. We three plus that blasted journalist. But he's not likely to say anything. Don't you think?'

He looked at Van Veeteren, who was messing around with his ungainly cigarette machine.

'Most probably not,' said *the Chief Inspector*, looking at first one, then the other of his former colleagues for several seconds. 'It might have been better if he'd scribbled a line or two, but it's easy to say that. I mean, he had an ex-wife and a daughter to take into consideration. I'm not suggesting he should have come out with the real reason, but if you don't leave any kind of message behind, you leave the field wide open for speculation. I don't suppose any of us thinks that it would be a good thing if all the shit were to hit the fan? Bearing in mind his daughter, for instance.'

'Nobody,' said Münster, having first waited for eye contact with Moreno. 'Certainly not me, that's for sure.'

He produced a brown envelope and placed it on the table between them.

'You might like to take a look at the pictorial evidence before we burn it.'

But he didn't touch the envelope. Nor did Van Veeteren. Moreno hesitated for a moment, then opened it and took out a photograph. Obviously an enlargement: black and white, about 20x30 centimetres. It wasn't difficult to see what it depicted.

A cafe table. On the pavement, night or evening: the photographer must have used a flash, the background was pitch black. Only two people were in focus, but there was something white, blurred, in the bottom right-hand corner – possibly a shoe or a part of a trouser leg belonging to somebody else. On the table – apparently made of rattan, with a glass top – were two glasses: one with a straw and a miniature paper parasol, the other an almost empty beer glass. Nothing more, not on the half of the table depicted in the photograph at least.

Two chairs. Sitting on one of them Detective Intendent deBries. Leaning back and wearing a short-sleeved shirt, and light-coloured shorts. Suntanned. On the other chair a girl of South Asian appearance. Young. Dark-haired. Aged about ten or twelve.

She was looking straight at the camera, her eyes wide open. Her lipstick and make-up couldn't conceal the fact that she was young. The white man had his arm round her slender shoulders, and was looking at her from the side. There was a trace of a smile on his lips. She was wearing a very short, light-coloured dress with a flower pattern. Her right hand was resting on Intendent deBries's left thigh. Quite high up. His legs were slightly apart, his shorts loose-fitting, and her hand disappeared into the darkness. It was not possible to misinterpret the picture.

'Thailand?' Moreno asked.

Münster nodded.

'Phuket, this last January. He's been there once before as well.'

Moreno thought, and recalled that it was true.

'The photographer?'

'A freelance journalist. Who evidently recognized him. Used a special lens, and deBries apparently didn't notice a thing. But then, he was a bit preoccupied . . .'

'How old is his daughter?' Moreno asked, putting the photograph back into the envelope.

465

Van Veeteren cleared his throat.

'Twelve. About the same age as she is,' he said, gesturing in the direction of the envelope.

'They haven't been in contact,' said Münster. 'I've spoken to Maria, his ex-wife. She reckons that since they separated he's gone downhill – to be honest, she didn't seem all that surprised. But she knows nothing at all about this.'

Downhill? Moreno thought. You could say that again. She was having difficulty in sorting out her own emotions. That had been the case ever since Münster had phoned that morning. On the one hand, disgust at what deBries had been up to; but on the other, dismay at the fact that he was dead. That he had taken the consequences so extremely quickly. After only a few hours, by all accounts. Münster had spoken to him on Friday afternoon, and he'd done it that evening, or that night at the latest. A good friend had found him the next morning: the door hadn't been locked. No room for doubt. Nor for explanations or excuses.

But then, what was there to say? Moreno thought. Make excuses? How?

'How did you find out?' she asked, because Münster hadn't told her.

'That friend phoned me. DeBries had written my number on a scrap of paper on the kitchen table.'

Van Veeteren lit a cigarette. They sat in silence for a while.

'I thought it must be him,' Moreno admitted. 'If it had to be somebody. He seemed to be the only possibility, as it were. Do the others know about this? The fact that he's dead, I mean?'

Münster shook his head.

'No. Not as far as we know, that is. We thought that we'd first . . .'

He was searching for words.

'That we'd consolidate our silence,' said *the Chief Inspector*. 'If you don't have anything against that. The simplest line to take is that you are just as devastated as everybody else. That you don't say a damned word, and don't circulate this photo around your colleagues. But perhaps you see things differently? From a woman's perspective, perhaps?'

Moreno thought for a few seconds. She didn't need any longer.

'For the moment I'm prepared to put the man's and the woman's perspective on the shelf,' she said. 'There seem to be general human considerations which are much more important.'

'I agree absolutely,' said Van Veeteren. 'I just need to check that we all agree that I should take charge of this, okay?'

Moreno exchanged looks with Münster and nodded. Van Veeteren took the envelope, folded it in two and put it in his inside pocket. Checked his watch.

'Might I have the honour of treating two old colleagues to a glass?' he then asked. 'My chess match isn't due to start for another hour yet.'

Moreno left The Society at about nine o'clock together with Münster. He offered to drive her home, but she declined and decided to walk instead. It was still quite warm, and there were lots of people in the streets and the pavement cafes. She chose a longer route, via Langgraacht and Kellnerstraat. Over Keymerplejn and Windemeerstraat. She passed by *the Chief Inspector*'s antiquarian bookshop, and noted that they were closed for the summer, until the twenty-second.

As she was walking through the town she tried to think about Intendent deBries: but it hadn't become any easier to conjure up some sort of retroactive image of him after the conversation with Münster and Van Veeteren. More difficult, in fact. But even so, there was one question she couldn't avoid. Would she always remember him as *the child-molester*? Was this destined to be his epitaph? Would she ever be able to see any other sides of his character?

She hadn't known him all that long, but she had

respected him as a colleague. As they say. As a competent and efficient police officer. Surely she had? Did that sort of judgement really have to be tainted by this other business? Would the passage of time ever be able to make it possible to plead extenuating circumstances to counterbalance the condemnation she was feeling just now? She didn't know.

And what about Arnold Maager? it suddenly struck her. She had never met him, only seen a photograph of him. What did she feel when she tried to conjure up an image of him?

It was the same as with deBries, she concluded. Difficult to feel any kind of sympathy or understanding. One might feel sorry for them – Maager's punishment was out of all proportion to his crime: but these men, both deBries and Maager, should surely have understood that there was a cause-and-effect chain? That what they did would sooner or later have consequences.

Always. Somehow or other.

Or am I judging them too harshly? she wondered. Is this just the bitchiness inside me that I'm trying to elevate into some kind of morality?

What the hell! she allowed herself to mutter. There was no doubt a big difference between the sixteen-year-old in Lejnice and the eleven-year-old (or however old the girl actually was) in Phuket; but even so, she could understand those who maintained that male sexuality was the devil's contribution to the Universal Plan. But that's life.

As far as deBries was concerned, she was grateful that she wasn't the only one in possession of all the details. Good that Münster knew all about it as well – no doubt there would be an opportunity to discuss matters further with him, once it became clear what the fall-out was. Perhaps also with *the Chief Inspector*.

But then she remembered something Reinhart had once said.

A human being is an animal with a very dirty soul – but an amazing ability to wash it.

As she passed the Keymer church the clock struck a quarter to ten. She registered that she had one whole day left of her leave. Great.

On Monday, it was back to routine. Great.